I0733939

M6

The Royals

Millennium Series

Staci Morrison

For my father, Jack Robinson, who always made sure we girls knew the love of the Father, on Earth as in Heaven. We miss you, but we know one day we will be together again. This one, Dad, this one is for you.

Table of Contents

Enter the Millennium

Welcome back! The reader will recall that years in the text are indicated with ME, Millennial Era, instead of BC or AD. Thus, 999 ME is 999 years into the Millennium.

Character names use a Hebrew construction, whereby 'ben' means child of, so Josiah ben Eamonn means Josiah son of Eamonn.

So, what is the Millennium, and when will it occur?

It is a prophetic time, the next great age. Our world today will not continue ad infinitum. At some point in the future, the Lord will appear in the Heavens and call His church to Himself. This global cataclysmic event is called the Rapture and sets off a series of events that will usher in the Tribulation, seven years of wars, famine, earthquakes, fire, and pestilence; hell on Earth. But in the end, the evil forces are defeated. The Lord returns to rule, ushering in the Millennium, one thousand years of paradise, a return to what was lost in Eden.

Series Notes

As the series progresses, we move deeper into the tale, often going on the "other side of the door". And while each book could technically be read as a stand alone, I do not suggest it. The breadth and depth of the story is fleshed out in vivid detail by reading the series in order. I am not big on recapping, but I do my best to anchor each part where appropriate. Sometimes I leave those things to the reader, as I think it adds some little tidbits to discover.

M6-The Royals is something special, and if you have made it this far, you are in for a treat. There are a few places, especially in the beginning where we jump in the timelines, but that was how the story unfolded as I was writing it, and I believe it reveals the mysteries in a greater and compelling way.

I am honored and humbled to have you back. From the bottom of my heart, thank you. Take my hand; I am going to tell you an amazing tale.

You know my reproach, my shame and disgrace. All my
adversaries are before you.

—Psalm 69:19

Glossary

Characters*

Alaina ben Thomas – Supermodel and covert computer hacker, born December 12, 971 ME. Best friends with Filippo ben Vincente, her photographer and former roommate, and Himari Nakamura, her neighbor. She is one of the first members of The Resistance. Significant other Beau Landry. Code name Miss Pink.

Angelica ben Omri – Former Alanthia Supreme Court Justice, the exiled Witch of Endor, born August 9, 932 ME. Goes into exile after battling her nemesis Esmeralda ben Claude.

Astrid ben Agnor – Pilgrim girl turned Duchess, born April 28, 980 ME to Agnor ben Randall and Emaline ben Gregory. Davianna ben David's best friend. Significant other Peter ben Korah. Nicknames Red and Tridi.

Beau Landry – Noble Army Veteran and heir to the Lenox fortune, born July 11, 968 ME to Jorge and Sarah Landry. A charming Cajun, and the youngest of six children. Best friends with Ian ben Kole. Significant other Alaina ben Thomas.

Davianna ben David – Pilgrim girl turned Princess, born May 27, 980 ME to David ben Jesse and Zanah ben Joseph. She receives a mysterious artifact from the Last Age that sparks a global manhunt. Astrid ben Agnor's best friend. Significant other Josiah ben Eamonn. Nicknames Davi, Minx, Sparrow, and Fireball.

Esmeralda ben Claude – The White Woman, born in Rephidim, Pennsylvania, January 10, 975 ME to Claude and Julianna. She is a seer whose special abilities make her a target for the forces of evil. Significant other Thaddeus ben Todd. Nickname Vixen. Codename Curly.

Filippo ben Vincente – Painter, Photographer, Italian, born November 17, 963 ME. He is best friends with Alaina ben Thomas and goes undercover in mafia boss, Marco ben Massimo's house. Significant other Himari Nakamura. Codename Leonardo.

Genevieve ben Willard – Peter and Josiah's former nanny, and honorary grandmother to the members of The Resistance. Also known as Auntie G., her codename is G.

Himari Nakamura – Japanese/Alanthian computer genius, Professor, Elite hacker, born June 30, 965 ME. An Alcatraz 5 member, a group of teenagers who discover a Last Age computer lab. Friends with Lavinia, Kayah, and Alaina. Significant other Filippo ben Vincente. Her codename is Sunflower.

Ian ben Kole – Noble Army Veteran, Charity Worker, born January 18, 969 ME to Kole and Salome. At eighteen, he encounters the Lord and is filled with the Holy Spirit, which turns his hair white. He lives an itinerant life before settling at the Center for Street Kids of Alanthia. Best friends with Beau Landry, brother of James ben Kole, his significant other is Lady Joanna ben Luke.

James ben Kole – Co-owner of Pepperwood Horse Ranch and World Champion Equestrian, born September 4, 965 ME to Kole and Salome. He earns distinction in the Noble Army and becomes a solid presence in Peter's life. Childhood sweethearts with his wife, Persa ben Yereq. Nickname Jay.

Joanna ben Luke – Humanitarian, born August 31, 967 ME to Lord Luke ben Simon and Lady Elizabeth ben George, the Earl and Countess of Stockton. After her parent's house arrest, she starts the Street Kids of Alanthia. Significant other Ian ben Kole. Nicknamed Lady J, Princess Workaholic, Princess W.

Josiah ben Eamonn – Prince of Alanthia, born June 8, 969 ME to Prince Eamonn ben Adam and Princess Marguerite ben Alfonso. The rightful heir to the Alanthian throne, who goes into exile in 985 ME after his father is murdered. Serves in the Iron King's Army, a trained surgeon, alias Einar ben Yane. Significant other Davianna ben David. Codename Doc.

Kayah ben Samuel – Badass, born August/September 964 ME, she is left at an orphanage. Founder of the Alcatraz 5, she is the only one who goes to prison. Released when the technology laws are repealed, she aligns with Sir Preston ben Worley and becomes a covert agent. A woman of many faces, her significant other is Reuben ben Judah.

Korah ben Adam – King of Alanthia, born November 16, 943 ME to Prince Adam ben Simon and Princess Mary ben Abraham. He seizes the throne after murdering his brother, Eamonn. Married to Princess Alexa ben Seamus (deceased) and father of Peter.

Lavinia ben Anthony – Genius, born October 16, 964 ME to Anthony and Violet. She is a member of the Alcatraz 5, but her involvement never becomes public. Founder of The Resistance with Prince Peter. The proprietress of Peccioli, mother of Richard, and friends with Kayah, Himari, and Esmeralda. Significant other Mack ben Robert. Nickname Valentine. Codename Ms. Euler.

Mack ben Robert – Leader of The Resistance, former Royal Guard, born October 14, 960 ME in Virginia. Army veteran and sheriff, he becomes Peter's Head of Security before settling at Peccioli to become a vintner. Friends with Thaddeus. Codename Bobby.

Persa ben Yereq - Co-owner of Pepperwood Horse Ranch and World Champion Equestrian, born December 12, 965 ME. She is capture by Marduk and forced to give birth to Rapha, the nephilim, before escaping in the closing hours of the Alanthian Civil War. She befriends Peter and provides a haven for him. Significant other James ben Kole. Nickname Fey.

Peter ben Korah – Playboy, Revolutionary, Prince of Alanthia, born January 6, 987 ME to Prince Korah ben Adam and Princess Alexa ben Seamus. The presumed heir to the Alanthian throne, leader and founder of the Resistance. Significant other Astrid ben Agnor. Codename Falcon.

Preston ben Worley – Lawyer, Knight of the Realm, born September 9, 909 ME. Memorable for his bushy eyebrows and moustache, he was Prince Adam's closest advisor and mentor to Kayah. He lives and practices law in New York.

Reuben ben Judah – Mossad Agent, born in the Golden Kingdom October 9, 965 ME. Served with Josiah in the army where he was wounded, avenging the deaths of his family. He is assigned to follow Davianna and Astrid across Europe and meets his significant other, Kayah ben Samuel.

Thaddeus ben Todd – Director of the FBI, lawyer, born February 2, 960 ME. He is a former basketball star who loses his family in a terrorists attack and seeks refuge in Rephidim where he meets a young girls who changes everything. Friends with Mack ben Robert. Significant other Esmeralda ben Claude. Codename T.

*Check out their portraits at Alanthia.com/characters

Places

Alanthia – One of ten Millennial Kingdoms, occupying the North American continent.

Bunker – A fallout shelter built in the Last Age where The Resistance wages war against Korah's government. Located in the basement of Genevieve ben Willard's home on the outskirts of the New City.

Gilead - Ancient seat of Alanthian power, the Palace of the Princes, referred to as the Castle.

New City – Capitol of Alanthia, built on the ruins of San Francisco.

Peccioli – Mack and Lavinia's vineyard in Redding, California, approximately 3 hours north of the New City.

Pepperwood – James and Persa's horse ranch in Redding, California, approximately 3 hours north of the New City.

Thyatira – An isolated region in rural Pennsylvania that contains the village of Rephidim, Bezetha, and the ruins of Endor.

Part 1 - Winter Roses

December 30, 999 ME

Winter Roses - New City - Korah and Davianna

King Korah ben Adam paced his bed chamber, feeling electrified, intoxicated by a seductive power surging through his body. The catalyst was ironic, a maid, a girl—again.

"Bring her," he commanded, the sound of his voice reverberating off the walls. Its rich timbre honed by hundreds of rousing speeches, delivered to adoring crowds. He could light up a room with that voice. He charmed, he persuaded, but most of all, King Korah controlled.

The valet hesitated, then met the King's eyes and said, "My Esteemed, thou shouldst rest."

Korah chuckled at the man's ignorance. He no longer required sleep, and pushing his body past its physical boundaries unleashed a power he had never known. "Do as I say, McSwilley."

The valet cleared his throat, shifting from foot to foot. "I am Barton, my Esteemed. McSwilley retired years ago."

Korah stared at the man. He was right, but they all looked like McSwilley to him. "Yes, of course, Barton. I desire a stroll in the gardens."

Barton hesitated.

"Send Davianna ben David to me," Korah said impatiently.

"As you wish, my Esteemed." Barton backed out of the room.

Korah stared at the open door, anticipation building into a mixture of hunger and need. Each time they brought her, he feasted upon her life energy, taking it into himself. The sublime transference revitalized and resurrected him. That girl fed something in him, lost for decades.

He had been dead and never realized it.

Today marked the fifth day since her arrival, and he sensed the last threads of her resistance breaking. He would have her and the artifact under his control—soon.

Davianna appeared like a welcoming ghost, ephemeral in the pale light, as if she were not quite flesh and bone, a mythical presence of colossal importance. She curtsied on unsteady feet, catching herself against the door frame as her balance gave way. "My Esteemed, you wished to see me?"

"Come, let us walk in the gardens," he coaxed, taking his cloak, and ushering her outside.

The cold jolted her, reviving her just enough. Trembling in the frigid wind, she did not protest when he draped an arm around her. As they strolled, Korah relaxed, basking in the indescribable sweetness of holding a tender young woman. She felt small at his side, but not fragile or frail. A gymnast's body lay beneath her shapeless black tunic. Sudden heat spread in his loins, unexpected in its intensity. Desire, also lost for decades, pulsed from his core as an idea was born.

"Davianna," he pitched his voice low like warm honey, "are you cold, child?"

"Yes, and I'm tired. Please let me sleep."

He gave her a patronizing smile. "Perhaps after our walk."

She rubbed her eyes and stifled a yawn. "As you wish, my Esteemed."

Drawing her hand around his waist, he steered her toward the edge of the gardens. Her floral shampoo evoked a long-forgotten memory. Pressing his lips to the crown of her head, he whispered, "There are winter roses. Would you like to see them?"

"My mother loves roses." Her head lolled, and she blinked at him. "Is she here?"

"No, your mother is home, just as you are. This is your home now, Davianna."

She tried to pull away.

He tightened his grip and snarled, "Say it! Say you will not leave."

"I can't." She pushed at his chest, struggling to break free.

"Stop!" he shouted, tightening his grip.

He felt like a wanderer lost in the desert, near death, with Davianna ben David, his oasis. The abrupt change, from barren wasteland to cool Eden, disoriented him, exposed his need, made him vulnerable, which in turn, made him dangerous.

She grew still. "You are hurting me," she said in a voice barely above a whisper, almost lost in the wind.

"Then quit fighting me," he rasped, digging his fingers into her shoulders.

She turned her face away.

He changed tactics, loosening his grip and making a tsking noise. "It is dangerous for a young girl alone. All manner of evil lies in wait beyond those walls, as you well know, since you have been running for almost a year. I know how tired you are. I have simply given you shelter and protected you from those who would do you harm. Davianna, I have kept you safe."

Her shoulders drooped, and she made a faint whimpering sound.

He hugged her, holding her upright. "We are friends, you and me. It has been so long since I have had a friend, Davianna," he said in a cracked whisper.

She sniffed, nodding her head, resting her cheek on his chest.

"It has been so long since I have had anyone by my side. You cannot imagine the life I have lived." Tears pooled in his eyes; shocking, life giving—real.

She looked up at him, compassion written across her pretty little face.

"I find that I become anxious about you, your future, your safety. I need…" He faltered and shook his head, trying to clear it. "I only want to take care of you."

"You do?" she asked dreamily.

"I am your servant, madam," he said, giving her a deep, formal bow. But breaking their hug, shattered the moment. The sudden emotional storm abated. The rain stopped falling as his tears dried up, blasted in the heat of his hellfire soul. He kept his head bowed, hiding the abrupt change.

She did not see.

No one ever saw.

"All right," she said.

Korah raised his head. There were tear tracks down his cheeks. Like dried riverbeds in the desert, they indicated life had been there once.

"Take me to see the winter roses. Perhaps it will be warmer in the greenhouse."

He flashed a genuine smile, showing her the charming dimple on his left cheek. Removing his cloak, he wrapped it around her shoulders. "I shall command the nurseryman to hybridize a rose in your honor. We shall use your extraordinary eyes as inspiration." He tilted her chin up and stared into their rich brown depths. "How lovely they are. I find that I am lost in them."

"Don't be lost, my Esteemed." Her voice was gentle, almost childlike in its innocence. "There is still love in your heart. I can see it." She placed her hand on his chest. "I can feel it."

His breath caught as her words echoed in his hollow soul. "You are the first since my wife died. I am a wicked man, Davianna."

She tilted her head, studying him. "But you were not always, were you?"

Korah scoffed, "I was born wicked, given the name of a rebel by a vicious bitch of a mother who made sure I knew my destiny from the time I was in swaddling."

Davianna rested a hand on her forehead. "My mother is not very nice, either, if I am perfectly honest."

Korah threw back his head and laughed. "Honesty? What a rare quality." Quirking a gold and silver eyebrow, he asked, "Shall I kill her for you?"

Thinking it was a joke, she played along. Tapping the side of her cheek, she considered. "Hmm. She was hateful to my father, and I doubt she even loves me."

"Is that so?"

Davianna threw up her hands in exasperation, his long cloak pooling at her elbows. "She abandoned me in Greece, in a pilgrim camp, with no money. What kind of mother does that?"

"Oh, I know." Korah grew very still. His eyes seemed to transform, the pupils elongating like those of a reptile.

She stepped back as the serpent entered the garden and stalked Eve.

Korah smiled at the flash of terror in her eyes. "Shall I tell you, little girl? Would you like to know… how I became who I am?"

February 4, 1000 ME

London Summit

"Good evening, I am Ebenezer ben James, reporting live from London," the aging reporter said into the camera, employing his signature perfectly modulated delivery. For twelve years, Alanthians received their evening news from Ebenezer ben James. They knew him. They trusted him. And three weeks ago, he had been unceremoniously fired.

Ebenezer launched his career with Prince Josiah ben Eamonn's suicide story, and in the end, it brought him down. The executives at News 1 set him up. The last night he occupied the anchor's chair, they humiliated him in front of the world, and thirty minutes after the broadcast aired, they terminated him.

Officially, they deemed his departure a retirement, but they held no tributes to his celebrated long career, gave him no public send off, and allowed him no forum to regain his credibility. That night, leaving his office, he walked a gauntlet of shame past his staring and snickering colleagues. Once the finest investigative journalist in the world, he realized he had grown lazy, content to read the news instead of uncovering it. Alone in his palatial house in Saxony Hills, two-thirds into a bottle of Scotch, he realized a newsman's heart still beat in his chest.

News 3 called the week after he was sacked and offered him a 10 o'clock news magazine, pitched as a glitzy news program, sure to be a hit. His agent, Murray, was over the moon. Murray claimed they had not approached him before because they knew he would turn them down, but now that he was available, he was the perfect choice.

Ebenezer sent his agent into an apoplectic fit when he declined their offer. However, he did not turn them down outright. He countered, but not for the anchor's chair, like everyone expected, he wanted the title of Senior Investigative Journalist, a return to his roots, a chance to redeem himself, and repair his reputation.

Two weeks after leaving News 1, he walked through the doors of his new job with a burning determination. He needed to wipe out the opening line on his online biography that currently read, 'Disgraced journalist, best known for popularizing the story that

Prince Josiah ben Eamonn threw himself from the Golden Gate Bridge, committing suicide.'

Standing in the London fog, with the faint echoes of fighting still going on in the distance, he simmered over the fact that the conniving bitch Sondra ben Pearson had scooped him again by releasing an explosive series of video tapes that exposed King Korah ben Adam for the monster he was. However, Ebenezer planned to dig up some dirt of his own. Korah fed him that bogus suicide story, and the resurrected Prince buried him. From where he stood, those damn royals ruined his life. So had those assholes at News 1. He was going to regain his reputation, and they were all going to pay.

Today, Ebenezer took the first step.

"Behind me," he gestured, "is the Golden Kingdom Embassy in London. Located among some of the highest priced real estate on the planet, the Ruling Princes, and official delegations from eight of the world's ten kingdoms have converged for an emergency Summit.

"Inside those white marble walls, the fates of every man, woman, and child are being discussed and debated. The Summit, organized and arranged by Prince Yehonathan ben Hezekiah of the Golden Kingdom, was initially greeted with tepid interest, with most of the Ruling Princes planning to send delegates in their stead. Earlier this week, speculation abounded whether Europe's Prince Edward ben George, who lives in Kensington Palace across the green, would attend."

The camera panned to the heavily guarded seat of European power.

Feeling a thrill to be back in the game, Ebenezer delivered the next segment with suitable characteristic gravity. "In the last twenty-four hours, everything on the global stage has changed, and the Ruling Princes began arriving this morning. The Summit's purpose is twofold, to discuss the strategies needed to curtail the riots spreading across the globe, and to debate whether to remove King Korah ben Adam from the Alanthian throne and replace him with his nephew, Prince Josiah ben Eamonn.

"Here in London, officials report the riots have left seventy-five dead, hundreds wounded, and an estimated thirty million shekels worth of property damage. The violence has spread to every major city in the world, and by all accounts, it caught the Ruling Princes by surprise, which led this reporter to ask, what is behind this global unrest? I spoke to one young man today who had this to say."

"Right, yeah, you got to ask?" The black-clad youth glared into the camera; the lower half of his face disguised with a red scarf. "It's about oppression, man, and those (bleeping) royals keeping us down. They take all the bloomin' money, living in their fancy palaces, and don't do nuffin' for us. We out 'ere dyin' in the streets, starvin' on the farms, and they got nah clue." He turned and pumped his fist to the similarly attired, scruffy men behind him. "No peace, no peace!"

The chant was taken up by the youth's companions, the camera focusing on a handsome boy about sixteen with bright blue eyes who snarled, "Down with the bloody royals!"

The broadcast returned to Ebenezer, who stood stalwart and serious, an Embassy patrol moving in the background. "This sentiment echoes through the ranks of the protestors and inside neighborhood pubs. Those who have taken to the streets wonder if their plight is being discussed behind these walls," Ebenezer motioned behind him, "or if something more sinister is going on?"

The camera cut away and a brief montage of still framed pictures, taken from News 1's report on King Korah, flashed across the screen. "It is clear by these pictures what the public perceived as benevolent was, in actuality, malevolent." The pictures stopped and the live feed returned. Ebenezer looked repulsed. "If these sorts of atrocities have been going on in the New City Palace, we wonder what else is going on in the halls of power, specifically in Cairo."

He paused, letting his statement sink in. "Egypt is the only kingdom not in attendance. They deigned to send a delegation, declaring their unwavering support of King Korah and the alliance forged by the January 10th marriage of Princess Keyseelough to the Alanthian ruler. But we, here at News 3, can report that while publicly Egypt is supporting Korah, there is chaos behind closed doors."

Pause, one, two, three.

"Our sources confirm, the bride departed Alanthia on her wedding night and has not been seen in public since." The screen flashed a picture of an unconscious, bandaged woman being wheeled across the tarmac on a stretcher. "A ground control worker took this photograph at Korah International Airport in the pre-dawn hours of January 11th. We have confirmed it is indeed a picture of Princess Keyseelough just hours after her wedding ceremony."

A vile photograph of a woman's slashed body flashed across the screen, one of the video stills quickly replaced by the beautiful face of the Egyptian Princess. "The public has a right to know. What happened to the Princess on her wedding night, and why are officials in the New City and Cairo covering it up?

"Even after it became clear Prince Josiah's death was an elaborate hoax perpetrated against all Alanthians, including this reporter, the Ruling Princes have hedged their position, refusing to support the change in Alanthian leadership. They have done so despite increased pressure from the Golden Kingdom and Prince Yehonathan, who has rallied behind the recently resurrected Prince Josiah. Their motivation and reluctance might just come down to money."

Ebenezer paused, letting that sink in before continuing, "After the Geneva Summit last summer, technology flooded the global market, and with it, tax revenues. Lifting the ban on Alanthian exports temporarily placated the public, who have called for a repeal of the archaic restrictions for more than a decade. My inside sources claim the Ruling Princes are reluctant to entertain Prince Josiah's petition out of fear a change in leadership might disrupt the flow of goods and hinder their newfound wealth and popularity at home.

"What they have seemingly failed to understand is that a cell phone," Ebenezer reached in his jacket pocket and produced a slick new device, "will not relieve the pervasive drought, disease, and the threat of global famine as crop after crop fails. To the royals in their ivory castles, all was well.

"For fifteen years, the Ruling Princes turned a blind eye to the evil going on in the New City and aligned themselves with King Korah ben Adam. Doubtless, they regret that decision tonight." Ebenezer suppressed a smile as he went for the jugular. "With the release of a series of shocking tapes, documents, and photographs cataloging King Korah's treacherous reign, the public must wonder why the Ruling Princes have supported a man involved in ritual murder, witchcraft, bribery, and corruption? The people of the world look out their windows and see their streets running with blood and wonder how this summit can produce any solutions if the Ruling Princes cannot control one of their own.

"But one thing is clear tonight. The instability of the Alanthia government is fueling the fires of global chaos. Will this Summit correct the course, or are we headed down a path to destruction?"

Ebenezer smiled, assuming the expression of a benevolent uncle, ready to deliver the scoop of the day. "On a final note, News 3 can confirm, inside those gilded halls, a new royal is taking center stage. Our exclusive source has confirmed, exiled Prince Josiah ben Eamonn married accused technology thief Davianna ben David in a secret ceremony three weeks ago."

A photograph, taken with a high-powered zoom lens, flashed on screen, depicting a young woman taking a miniature dachshund for a walk in the gardens behind the Embassy.

"Making her first public appearance since her arrest and clandestine nuptials, the newly minted Alanthian royal is scheduled to attend the opening reception and social gatherings. We have no official confirmation whether she will attend the formal negotiations and meetings."

Another picture came up on the screen, this one showing Davianna speaking to one of her hulking guards. She looked about twelve years old.

Ebenezer raised a speculative brow into the camera. "In London, global leaders will get their first glimpse of the young woman whose notoriety dominated headlines for months." He paused and looked suitably compassionate. "Davianna ben David is diving headfirst into royal life in the midst of a firestorm. We are all left to wonder, will she survive?"

Unlikely Roommates - London - Astrid and Kayah

Astrid sat in the Golden Kingdom Embassy apartment, eyeing Kayah ben Samuel, the recently dubbed "Angel of Kensington Park," and wondering what she might say to the woman. After making a quick introduction, Peter kissed Astrid's cheek and departed with Reuben in tow, heading downstairs to greet the arriving Ruling Princes. At Josiah's request, Peter would participate in the Summit. They knew his popularity, charm, and intelligence would be indispensable in the upcoming negotiations. It would be petulant to complain, but his absence left Astrid at loose ends with her new roommate.

A knock at the door offered a reprieve from the uncomfortable silence. The embassy employee assigned to their floor flashed her a disingenuous smile. The beige livery he wore hung loose on his slight frame, and his beady black eyes were rimmed with pronounced dark circles. He popped his head up every time she left her room, reminding her of a suspicious meerkat. Despite his assertions that he was stationed to see to their needs, Astrid knew his true purpose was to act as chastity guard, keeping her out of Peter's bed. She loathed him.

"A delivery, madam," he intoned.

Astrid stepped aside and three embassy employees ushered past her, carrying boxes and packages from London's most exclusive retail shops. She rolled her eyes in exasperation. "More clothing for me?"

The meerkat answered, "This delivery is addressed to Miss Kayah ben Samuel."

Perched on the edge of the sofa, Kayah raised a speculative eyebrow and pointed to her bedroom. "Take them in there, please."

Astrid closed the door behind the efficient staff, shaking her head. "The Wonder Servant strikes again."

"Jarrod?"

Astrid shrugged. "Sure, who else? He has been on a shopping spree. I suppose he is ecstatic to have someone other than Peter to dress." She gave a pointed look at Kayah's gray tunic, tattered after her treacherous ride across London. "He has impeccable taste, though a bit conservative," she said, gesturing to her sable brown cashmere sweater and silk trousers.

Kayah lifted her pointed chin and said, "Well, at least you are dressed like a girl… this time."

Astrid creased her eyebrows. "What?"

In the broad, flat New City accent, Kayah murmured, "Do you boys know how to get to the Two Towers?" Kayah swept past her, then added in a conspiratorial whisper, "There is a Mossad agent watching you. Quit breaking cover."

Astrid's jaw dropped.

"I suppose I should thank you," Kayah called from the bedroom, holding up a sage silk blouse with approval. "If not for that little comment in Bologna, I might not have ever met Reuben."

Astrid shook herself out of her stupor. "That was you?"

"Obviously." Kayah rolled her eyes, conveying how stupid she found that question.

"I thought you were an assassin," Astrid said bluntly.

Kayah shrugged, turning to the mirror, studying a cream wool overcoat. "I am." Then pointing a finger, she added, "Or better stated, I was. As of yesterday, I am pardoned. So, I am turning over a new leaf. Haven't you read the news? I am an angel."

Astrid blew out a slow breath and fingered the stiletto in her right pocket.

Kayah caught the move and snorted, "I am not going to kill you, girl. Saving your ass got me pardoned." She smiled sweetly. "I'm harmless."

"Said the spider to the fly," Astrid countered.

"From what I hear, you are no fly, not anymore. You stabbed that swine, Orian ben Drachmas, right here in London last autumn." She gestured to Astrid's pocket. "Did you use that blade?"

"Perhaps," Astrid said, meeting Kayah's challenge head on. "But how do you know it was me? No one saw what happened in that alley."

Kayah dropped the red cotton sweater and turned; incredulity written across her face. "Sparrow stabbed the Greek Captain? Please."

Astrid lowered her lashes, regarding Kayah with cat blue eyes. "Do not underestimate Davianna ben David."

Astrid's tone and the fierce calculating look surprised Kayah, who paused in the act of pulling out a pair of snakeskin Benito pumps. "Oh?"

"You do so at your own peril."

Kayah snorted scornfully. "I'll keep that in mind."

Astrid bristled. "We've taken on far scarier enemies than you."

Kayah rolled her eyes, her patience with Astrid and this conversation reaching an end. "I am not your enemy. As a matter of fact, Josiah has asked me to step in as Davianna's Royal Guard." That garnered Kayah her second shocked expression of the day from the overconfident little chit. "I suppose that means when I go through the gates of the Palace, they won't throw me out or try to arrest me. That will be a welcome change."

February 12, 1000 ME

Royal Restoration and Proclamation

Ten days after the emergency London Summit concluded, Prince Yehonathan ben Hezekiah stepped onto the balcony of the Golden Kingdom Palace in Tel Aviv to address the world. His remarks were broadcast live, and the proclamation reprinted in every news publication across the globe.

But there was one in the crowd with more of a personal stake than most. She had come in hopes of hearing that their long quest had succeeded. Moving among the crowd, dressed in her Gune Black, Astrid ben Agnor held her breath and waited.

"By Royal Decree, the sovereign, benevolent, and eternal King, who rules His Creation with an Iron Scepter, declares that the Alanthian government formed under Prince Korah ben Adam ben Mary is deemed illegitimate and ordered to disband by sunset fourteen days hence. Any official who refuses to comply will face immediate and swift judgment, up to and including, forfeiture of their lives and property."

Astrid closed her eyes and breathed a long sigh of relief.

"The Most High decrees that from this day forward, my servant, the honorable and upright Prince Josiah ben Eamonn ben Marguerite is exalted to his rightful position as Ruling Prince of Alanthia, his coronation to occur at the King's Palace on the 28th of February in the one thousandth Millennial year of our Lord."

Tears coursed down Astrid's face as her heart both soared and broke. She longed to be with them, to share this moment, but she knew she could not. Rising on her tiptoes, she struggled to see around the crowd, trying to catch a glimpse of Josiah, Davianna, and Peter, but none of them appeared on the balcony with Prince Yehonathan.

"Prince Josiah ben Eamonn ascends the throne with the blessing and authority bestowed upon him by Yeshua, who grants him all power, authority, and properties that are his due, to rule the Kingdom of Alanthia and bring the rebellious nation back to order. For if my people, who are called by my name, will humble themselves and pray and seek my face and turn from their wicked ways, I will hear from Heaven and will forgive their sins and restore their land, declares the Most High, King of Kings, and Lord of Lords."

Astrid turned to leave, believing the proclamation was finished. She arrested her steps as Prince Yehonathan continued.

"It is further announced that Prince Josiah ben Eamonn will formally wed Miss Davianna ben David, chosen by the Iron King among all the maidens of the world to be his bride, for her chastity, bravery, and faithful service. Together, they have honored the Lord and fulfilled the purpose for which they were created. The marriage ceremony will precede the coronation."

"Oh, Davi," she whispered quietly, closing her eyes and covering her face.

"The Ruling Princes' Counsel urges all faithful people of Earth to pray for the Kingdom of Alanthia, Prince Josiah ben Eamonn, and his new bride.

"Lift up all peoples of the Earth who have taken to the streets, that they might put aside their violence and hatred, and restore the harmony and peace of our glorious age. To the rebels, the disenfranchised, and the lost, seek the face of the Lord, put aside your unbelief and anger, lay down your weapons, and repent! For the Lord is long suffering and full of mercy, but His patience wanes, and it is a fearful thing to fall into the hands of the Living God."

The crowd of foreign journalists exchanged dubious looks as the faithful fell to their knees in prayer. Astrid slipped away, sobbing, as she ran back to her hotel room, alone.

February 15, 1000 ME

Portrait Gallery - Gilead - Peter and Astrid

Three days after the Royal Proclamation, everything in Astrid ben Agnor's life changed. Her morning began in Tel Aviv in the arms of Yeshua and ended in the New City in the arms of her new husband, the Prince. In between, she flew with an angel, prevented Peter from committing patricide, encountered her dead doppelgänger mother-in-law, and escaped a marauding mob intent on killing them.

At 2am, she rolled over in her marital bed, searching for her bridegroom, only to discover Peter's side empty. Fatigue caused her insides to flutter, a queer feeling that only abated with adequate sleep. A low fire cast the room in a faint orange glow, and she snuggled under the thick down comforter, seeking warmth. Listening for Peter, she expected to hear him in the lavatory, but nothing save the groan of the old house and a pop of embers broke the silence. She closed her eyes and waited, feeling perfectly entitled to stay in bed.

They were at Gilead, the Alanthian Palace of the Princes. A gust of wind howled outside the magnificent stone walls, vibrating the thick glass windows in their ancient frames. Like lonely ghosts, cold drafts swept through the old chamber, chilling everything in their wake and causing the fire to dance. The castle was enormous, ancient, and stalwart, but lacked any modern conveniences. Surrounded by brown velvet hangings embroidered with gold, she felt like a time traveler. Yet, Peter was born here, and the Castle bore witness to the rapid transformation Alanthia underwent in the last two decades.

She raised up on her elbow, searching the shadows. Collapsing with a groan into the pillows, she did not think she could make her body move from the feather mattress. "Peter," she called, "are you here?"

Silence.

With an exasperated sigh, she threw off the thick blankets. "I am going to kill you for making me get up."

A woolen rug kept the chill from her bare feet, its muted colors ancient and fine. Spanning the entire room, it covered the old stone tile, and Astrid was grateful for it. Goosebumps broke out over her skin as she scampered naked across the room. Donning the beautiful nightgown and robe she wore to her bridal chamber, the soft silk slid over her body in a perfect fit, as if it had been made for her. She shivered, rubbed her arms vigorously, and poked at the fire, mindful of the embers. Killing time, she hoped Peter would return.

When he did not, she resigned herself to roaming the halls, searching for her erstwhile groom. Jarrod had sent up a tray, so she gobbled a piece of cheese and a handful of grapes before setting out on a 2:00 am excursion. Peeking outside, she found the hallway spooky and dark, so she returned to the chamber for a candle.

"Peter?" she called softly.

The old place sang a night carol of creaks and groans. Whistles and echoes accompanied the keening wind. No servants stirred at this hour, and she had no idea where they posted the guards. Retracing her steps to the Great Hall, she began to search.

She found him twenty minutes later, standing in a portrait gallery in the far east wing. He stood stock still, an old-fashioned torch burning in his hand. The flames cast him in ghoulish hues of black and gold. He did not sense her presence, lost in deep contemplation. She cleared her throat, leery of startling him. Life with Davianna taught her to be wary of sneaking up on people.

He turned in surprise, his face a macabre mask, a caricature of himself. She approached on silent feet, her heart pounding, sensing something had gone terribly wrong. Without a word, she moved to his side, took his arm, and followed his gaze to the portrait.

Korah and Eamonn stood side by side, dressed in formal court attire, dark and light, shadow and sun. Their resemblance to Peter and Josiah unnerved her.

"He killed him," Peter murmured, biting his bottom lip, "his brother."

Astrid rested her head on his shoulder, offering him her silent strength.

"And I nearly killed him tonight, my father. I would have if you had not stopped me." He blew out a shaky breath, full of self-loathing. "I am no better than he."

"Nonsense." She pulled his arm, directing the torch light down the gallery. "I know what he did to you, to her," she pointed to the portrait of Princess Alexa, "and to them." The haunting image of Josiah's parent's, Margaret and Eamonn on their wedding day came into sharp focus.

Peter studied the picture of his aunt and uncle, resplendent in their royal wedding clothes. Princess Margaret died less than a year after giving birth to Josiah. An accident, they all believed, but Korah confessed to Eamonn's corpse he had been the culprit, the murderer. He and Josiah overheard it that day, so long ago, hiding in the secret passageway. Peter never told a soul, not even his mother, out of fear that if he did, his father would kill her too. In the end, it had not mattered.

Astrid made a rueful laugh and said, "I am glad Davianna does not look like Princess Margaret. That would be bizarre, like the four of us were recreating the last generation."

Peter looked at her, his eyes lidded with heavy strain, as he snorted in derision. "Like we were trying to make things right, to amend the history Korah destroyed on his murderous rampage, killing them all?"

"I expect he is answering for his crimes now. Your mother saw to that, and if she did not, that mob screaming for his blood certainly did." Astrid gripped his arm. "However, he did not die by your hand."

He looked down at his feet and nodded, sedate. They took a few steps down the hall and the torch light illuminated another portrait.

"Who are they?" Astrid asked, staring at the imposing couple.

"My grandparents, Adam and Mary." Peter narrowed his eyes, studying the portrait. His face clouded. "I think he called me father again, tonight, when I was beating him."

Astrid flinched, both at his tone, and at the memory of Korah's unconscious body, a bloody mass at Peter's feet. She refused to cower in the face of his trauma, refused to give Korah anymore power over them. So, she adopted an awestruck tone and teased him about his grandparents. "Well, they are quite formidable, and I can see some resemblance, but you are much better looking." Moving the torch closer, she laughed, "Check out the broken veins in his nose. He was a drinker, and she looks like she might just whip your ass."

The corner of Peter's mouth lifted. "He died before I was born. I have vague memories of her, but I do believe you are correct on both counts."

"Look at her eyes." Astrid shuddered. "Korah has those same eyes, like they would kill you, just as easy as look at you."

"I am quite familiar with that," he said, studying the portrait of his grandparents.

Astrid took his hand and gave it a squeeze of support.

"I think she was the only person he ever feared. He never speaks of her. Mother told me once they doted on Eamonn and despised Korah, but she never said why. Grandmother Mary died when I was three or four. That was when we left Gilead and moved to the New City Palace. Korah refused to live under the same roof as his mother. They hated each other."

Astrid thought of her complicated relationship with her step-father Frank, who turned out not to be the villain she imagined. "That will twist up a person."

Peter raised a golden eyebrow at her. "Beware then, Red, because I am as twisted as they come."

"I know," she rose on her tiptoes and kissed his cheek, "but the difference is you took the terrible things that happened to you and channeled them into something bigger than yourself. You did not let them turn you into a monster, not like he did."

Peter moved away from her and extinguished the torch. Astrid's meager candle became the sole light in the dark portrait gallery. When he turned, his face was lost in deep shadow. "I almost did."

He sounded so broken, her heart hurt. She reached out, beckoning him to her side, searching for something to say that might bring him peace. Sudden inspiration struck; she knew what he needed. "Peter, will you take me to Pepperwood to meet Persa and James? Show me the place where you did not live in darkness. Take me to your family, not these ghosts. I want to meet the people who love you."

"Pepperwood…" He always breathed the name like a prayer. "Oh, Love, that is an amazing idea."

News From Home - Alanthian Embassy, Golden City - Josiah

"My Esteemed," the Embassy steward entered the room with a bow, "your correspondence. Shall I put them on your desk?"

Josiah nodded his assent and placed the delicate china coffee cup on the table between him and Davianna.

It arrived every morning—the box. Since the proclamation recognizing him as the Ruling Prince of Alanthia, official documents, correspondence, and intelligence briefings arrived promptly at 8:00 am.

Davianna sighed. Often it took him all day to work through the contents. While they were in London meeting with global leaders, he worked eighteen hours a day. His surgical residency prepared him for such a schedule, but it exhausted her. The stress of entering royal life, watching every word, and guarding her facial expressions took every ounce of energy she could muster. Thrust onto the world stage, the thought of doing something embarrassing petrified her. Eventually she would screw up, so she went through her days never knowing if her big *faux pas* lurked around the corner. There was a distinct possibility she already committed one and did not even know it. However, she did not cower, and she did not hide. She would not leave Josiah to face this alone, so she remained by his side each night until he finished. Yesterday, he ordered a small couch moved into the study. She settled in with a book while he worked and was abashed when she fell asleep.

"The box." She stared at it with baleful resignation. "I think I will grow to hate that thing."

"Perhaps." He bent over and kissed her cheek. "After the coronation, you shall receive your own."

Her head fell back in the chair, and she closed her eyes. "Every day?"

Josiah chuckled and moved to his desk. "Except Sundays."

He cracked the wax seal, pulling the blue ribbon an Embassy employee replaced every day. Overnight, they gathered the missives, and the senior staff sorted them in order of importance. This morning the top document was sealed with the Alanthian royal crest, which indicated the correspondence was from Peter.

He read the message twice. After a lifetime of anger and years spent plotting his revenge, Josiah never imagined he would feel… nothing.

Korah was dead.

It was over.

He dropped the paper and gazed at his young bride, who suffered so terribly at the hands of that villain. Everyone had suffered. He should be elated, shouting to the heavens, relieved to the pit of his soul, but the only faint emotion he could summon was relief.

"Davianna?" His voice sounded strange to his own ears.

She looked up, alert, cradling her coffee cup. "What is it?"

"This is a message from Peter. Korah is dead."

She blinked rapidly, then turned away, a convulsive sob caught in her chest.

He came around the desk and knelt in front of her, taking the trembling cup. "It is okay, now. He cannot hurt you ever again."

Davianna covered her face and swallowed thickly. "How?"

"He does not say, though I am sure we will receive some sort of briefing."

She nodded.

Josiah pulled her hands into his and held her gaze. "He sends other news," he said with a smile. "They were handfast last evening."

"Peter and Astrid? She changed her mind?"

"Apparently she did." Josiah rose and pulled her into his arms. "They are in the New City."

"What?" Davianna drew back in confusion. "They were both just here. How did they get back to Alanthia?"

Josiah chuckled. "You know my cousin. He is full of surprises. I expect there is quite a tale behind it." He lifted her chin, his whiskey-colored eyes warm and soft. "What do you say, Princess, shall I give the word and have arrangements made for a double wedding, or would you prefer that day all to yourself?"

Davianna blinked in surprise, still reeling at the news, while Josiah maneuvered and adjusted. She marveled at his uncanny ability to assess facts and make quick decisions. He was always three steps ahead of everyone around him, though he did not always show it. She suspected he learned to do that in the army or the operating room. Trusting his instincts, she whispered, "I think a double wedding is a brilliant idea. We started this together. We will go into the next chapter the same way."

Josiah leaned in for a kiss. Just before their lips touched, he murmured, "The difference being, we begin this chapter without Korah."

Davianna closed her eyes, hiding a sudden flash of pain.

The Last Debt - New York - Kayah

Kayah craned her head around the taxi driver, agitated by the snarl of New York traffic. The fighting that rocked the major cities abated three days ago, but with the Alanthian government in upheaval, municipal cleanup stalled. Burned-out vehicles and wreckage littered the streets, making the ride from the airport, which should have taken forty-five minutes, stretch into two hours.

She was late for the most important appointment of her life and ready to explode. "Go around. Drive on the sidewalk if you have to."

"*Canna* do," the Scottish taxi driver protested. "There is naught *tae dae* bit *hauld* yer horses. 'Tis the only way *intae* the borough, through 'ere."

Kayah sighed with exasperation.

Ten minutes, and less than a quarter of a mile traveled, she passed a wad of cash through the window and said, "Here, take the fare. I will walk."

"Is no safe, lassie." He gestured at the still smoldering shops and shattered plate glass. "They're *nae* fightin' 'n looting right now, but it could begin again. Ye *dinnae* want *tae git* caught *oot* in it."

Kayah hid a secret smile, thinking after her wild ride in London, this was nothing. Adjusting her dark sunglasses, she shrugged on her coat, and pulled the hood over her hair. "I can take care of myself. Thank you."

She exited the vehicle and took to the streets. The smell of burnt automobiles assailed her, unfamiliar and acrid. New York had a black eye, but he was a brute of a city, a blue-collar brawler, and wore the destruction like a badge of honor. Shopkeepers swept up glass, and construction workers boarded up windows and rehung doors. Assorted garbage and debris were piled up at the curb, and a hot dog vendor served a lengthy line of customers. The incessant sound of beeping horns filled the air, as New Yorkers went about their business, though with a deeper level of suspicion than before.

Kayah always felt at home in New York, and she was on her way to meet the man who first brought her here. The time had come to settle their debts, to conclude their relationship with a final transaction. The thought gave her a vague sense of melancholy since Sir Preston ben Worley played an integral part of her life since their first meeting thirteen years ago. He had the making of her, at least the woman she was before Reuben, so it seemed fitting that their last meeting would be a demarcation line. He would sever their bond and reveal the origins of her first bond, the broken one. By the end of the day, she would know the answer to the question that haunted her from the moment she became self-aware, 'Who am I?'

Standing on a precipice, she had a choice, ignore the past and proceed, or find out. Part of her did not want to know, content with the woman she had become. She had a new life before her. Restored to full citizenship, pardoned, with the favor of the Ruling Prince, she could move forward with her faithful, beloved fiancé by her side. She was free to live without the taint of prison, without blood on her hands, or the ever-present specter of arrest looming. She was going to be a wife and secretly entertained the thought that one day she might become a mother. One thing was certain, she was adopting a cat. She had friends who loved her and enough money that she never had to work again, if she chose. She did not have to know. She had never even tried to find out.

However, given the temptation, it was too enticing not to know, and she knew the mystery would continue to haunt her. Aged as he was, Sir Preston would not live forever, and she could not take the chance that something might befall him before he fulfilled his last promise to her. 'Help restore Prince Josiah ben Eamonn to the Alanthian throne, and I will tell you who your parents were.' His use of the past tense in that sentence suggested they were dead, which gave her the assurance she needed. That became the deciding factor. She could learn the truth then proceed with her life, unimpeded by the past.

Kayah ben Samuel was thirty-five-years-old and everything to this point in her life set her feet on this path. Walking down the battered streets of New York, she went toward the past and the future, an old life and a new one, her destiny.

It almost got her killed.

Screeching tires interrupted her reverie. She jumped out of the way as a black car careened to a halt on the sidewalk in front of her. The driver leapt from the vehicle, gesturing frantically.

"Get in!" Filippo ben Vincente shouted.

When she did not move, just stood there looking at him like he was a lunatic, he raced around the car, took her arm, and hissed, "They've put a hit out on you. We've got to go."

February 16, 1000 ME

Retraction - Alanthian Embassy - Josiah

"My Esteemed, I am sorry to interrupt your meeting," the Embassy steward said, bowing to Prince Josiah and the Alanthian Ambassador. "We have just received an urgent communique from the New City Field Office of the FBI." He handed the sealed envelope to Josiah, his entire body trembling.

Josiah broke the seal and read, "After completing an exhaustive search of the New City Palace, we are able to confirm that the body of King Korah ben Adam was not among the wreckage or ruin. Witnesses report seeing a wounded man, matching the King's general description, near the Palace stables shortly after the mob breached the walls. A subsequent inventory revealed the King's personal horse and tack are missing. It appears that he survived, and he has escaped."

Part 2 - Homecoming

February 15, 1000 ME

Homecoming - Pepperwood - Peter and Persa

Nestled among the Redwoods on the outskirts of Redding, California, the Pepperwood Horse Ranch had a full house. Hidden from the pockets of unrest still rocking the New City and fresh out of two weeks at Mill House Beach, James, Persa, Ian, Joanna, Beau, and Alaina were in residence when a helicopter touched down in the upper pasture. Peter and Astrid received a jubilant welcome, surrounded by warm hugs and handshakes.

After the hubbub died down, Persa drew Peter aside for a private word. "We have been so worried about you," she whispered and puckered for a kiss.

Peter obliged with a smile and swept her up in a hug. "I have my own news, Pers," he whispered. "Astrid and I were handfast last evening."

She arched her back to see if he was teasing but read the excited glint in his emerald eyes and knew he was not. Tears bathed her lashes, and she breathed, "Truly?"

"Yes." Peter rested his forehead against hers, inhaling her familiar scent that always reminded him of fresh grass and saddle soap, precious. "I love her."

Persa began to weep.

Peter held her and walked into the kitchen. Joanna and Ian left, giving the pair a moment of privacy. They stood together in the cozy kitchen while she cried.

"Oh, I'm sorry," she sobbed into his neck. "I'm happy for you, lad. I truly am. It's the hormones, the baby."

Peter laughed through the sting of his own tears and buried his face in her strawberry blonde hair. "I was worried about you, too. After that conference call…" His breathing became labored as he squeezed her tight. "What that bastard did to you."

A damn broke inside Persa.

The terror of the last twenty-four hours swamped her, surreal until that moment, held at bay, too terrible to process. But in Peter's arms, Persa let it flow over her as he held on. "It came here… yesterday…" A horrid screech tore from her throat.

The guests in the living room exchanged looks and went outside.

"It killed James," Persa wailed. "He was dead, Peter."

Peter held on, whispering urgently, "James is not dead. He is right outside."

She gasped, close to hyperventilating as her eyes grew wild and panicked. "He was, for over an hour. That vicious devil's spawn, Rapha, killed him." She buried her face in the side of his neck and wept. "I wanted to die, too. But we are having a baby. Jay always wanted a baby, but the one I had killed him."

Peter moved to a kitchen chair and sat with her cradled on his lap. He brushed away her tears and pulled a stray tendril out of her mouth. "Shh, it is all right now. Everything is okay."

She closed her eyes and nodded, not trusting herself to speak.

"What happened, Pers? Shall I get James?"

"I'm here," James said, moving inside. Neither noticed him standing in the doorway.

Peter's voice was hoarse as he quipped, "Well, unless you are the most substantial ghost I have ever seen, you seem to be alive." He cleared his throat, shaken and unaccountably angry. "So, how about you tell me what happened?"

"Marduk's bastard son came here and tried to kill Persa." He looked away. "We both died in the battle. I got a second chance."

Peter's head fell backward. A wave of dizziness made the room spin. "Bloody hell."

The three of them sat in silence. The enormity of James' loss blanketed the kitchen like a shroud.

"Thank God you are alive." Peter's face contorted, looking at the man who was both friend and father figure; stalwart, brave, and true—James ben Kole. Since he was fourteen years old, James had been his role model and mentor; shelter from the horrors of Korah's house.

James walked behind him and wrapped his arms around his shoulders, hugging them both. "I could say the same about you."

As abruptly as the tempest began, Persa squelched it, surrounded by the arms of the men she loved. She lost too many years to that devil and his machinations to let it ruin Peter's homecoming. James was alive. Rapha was dead. Peter was safe. She palmed the tears running down her cheeks and smiled up at James. "Jay, Peter and Astrid got married last night."

James released his hug and stood up. "Is that right?"

Persa answered for him. "Yes, it is, and that calls for a celebration."

Peter scrubbed his hands over his face, regathering his wits. "You do not have to do that."

She wiggled off his lap and stood in front of him with her hands on her tiny hips. "I will not take no for an answer."

Peter shared a private grin with James and said, "When has anyone ever been able to tell you no, Pers?"

She looked between them and blew out an exasperated breath. "Don't the two of you be starting in on me now."

And just like that, harmony returned to Pepperwood.

Are You Ready? - Pepperwood - Astrid and James

Midafternoon, Astrid leaned against one of the paddock fences, watching the remarkable white horse, Lightning, graze. James joined her with a nod of greeting. They stood in silence, simply watching the horses.

Astrid tilted her head, studying him. Silver streaked his dark auburn hair at the ears; sun lines creased his eyes. The hands resting on the fence were leathery and tough, but the nails were clean. He lacked the lively wit his brother Ian possessed, but he had a quiet strength and dignity Astrid had rarely observed in anyone. Since their arrival, he had been taking her measure. She sensed he was trying to determine if she was good enough for Peter and had not yet made up his mind.

"Do you like horses?" he asked, the soft hint of an Irish burr making itself known in the way he said you. His speaking voice was quiet. He did not say much, but when he did, everyone stopped to listen.

She ran her tongue over her front teeth, then decided to be honest. "Not really."

The corner of his mouth twitched. "Peter does."

"Yes, he does." Astrid folded her hands on the fence and rested her chin, watching Lightning break into a trot.

"He's quite a horseman, a true natural."

"I saw him ride on the beach when we were in Tel Aviv."

"You left him in Tel Aviv." James looked at her with uncompromising brown eyes.

Astrid inhaled deeply. "I did," she said, offering no further explanation. She already had this conversation with Persa while the men played horseshoes.

"Persa left me once. There was more to it than met the eye," James said, staring out over the pasture. "But I guess you know that, after the conference call."

Astrid paused, pushing a cuticle back on her thumbnail. The horror of the call and the aftermath were fresh in her mind. "Yes. Peter told me."

James nodded, looking grim. "After what we have all endured, I'm not one to stand in judgment. I expect you've also had a hard time."

Astrid pulled her long red hair over her shoulder and stroked the curls in contemplation. "Mr. ben Kole, one year ago yesterday, my friend Davianna showed me a device a stranger gave her outside our camp. Since then, I've lost my mother and my stepfather, been on the run as an international fugitive with a king's ransom on my head. I have traveled across the world and back, twice. I was captured and tortured, bombed by jihadists, attacked by a fallen angel, faced Satan, and fell at the feet of Yeshua." Her eyes narrowed, then she smiled. "And amid all that, I met, fell in love, and married Prince Peter ben Korah." She flicked her hair back over her shoulder and said, "How's your year been?"

A crooked smile lifted the corner of his mouth, and his eyes took on a charming sparkle she had not previously seen. "A bit like yours."

"Your year has been like mine?" Astrid choked off a hollow laugh and cast him a sidelong look. "Peter wanted y'all to be safe here. It was important to him. He wanted y'all protected."

"We've wanted to do the same for him. Though, in the end, we've done a poor job of it."

"He is not an easy man to protect." Astrid bit her thumbnail, feeling pensive.

"Given who he is, you are right." He paused and seemed to select his words with care. "Even with Prince Josiah on the throne, it will be dangerous. Peter has powerful enemies, and as his wife, you will be right in the line of fire. Are you ready for that, lass?"

Bravado, the sort that carried her through every calamity and situation, died on her lips. Her shoulders slumped as she confessed, "I don't have a choice, do I?"

"I suppose you don't." He met her eyes. "But remember this, if it gets bad, bring him home."

She swallowed hard and murmured, "That's why we're here."

James ben Kole smiled, a genuine smile that lit his eyes and displayed both rows of straight white teeth. "Smart girl."

Astrid turned pink under the compliment. It was not flattery. The future Duchess needed to learn the difference, quick. Life in the royal court depended on it.

Take Charge - Pepperwood

"I sent a message to Josiah last night, regarding events at the Palace and our marriage." Peter draped an arm around Astrid's shoulders. His emerald eyes shone with affection, and he carried a peace about him. "He just sent the reply. Our union has been blessed and sanctioned by the Iron King. There will be a formal announcement tomorrow."

"Truly?" Astrid's voice caught.

"Yes," he confirmed, resting his forehead against hers. "Josiah and Davianna asked if we would like to have a double wedding."

She paused two heartbeats, then nodded.

Alaina wiped a tear and said, "That is marvelous."

Peter looked up, an enigmatic expression on his face. "Miss Pink, thank you."

"Absolutely, Falcon. We made it."

"We did indeed." Peter turned, meeting everyone's eyes. "I would like to invite each of you to the celebration that will take place in the Golden City on February 28th."

A general round of congratulatory hugs and handshakes followed the exciting news.

Persa clapped her hands, drawing everyone's attention. "We will still celebrate tonight. Ian, go down to the cellar and bring up a case of wine. Then pull my Grandmother's crystal down from the china cabinet. Beau, Alaina, for the last two weeks, we have been hearing about this famous gumbo you two make. I think it is time you show us how it's done. Joanna, you and Astrid figure out how to squeeze all ten of us into the dining room and set a nice table. Peter, move the furniture around in the living room to make a dance floor. James, run into town. I am sure we need supplies."

Astrid looked around, amused. No one else batted an eye at the 4'10" Commander-in-Chief. It was her role as lady of the house, but Astrid surmised Persa took charge no matter the circumstances, and Peter's meek acquiescence charmed her. He dropped his typical 'Princes don't do that' schtick and set about moving furniture. Here at Pepperwood, he was just Peter, and she loved it. Taking a mental note, James' words rang true. When things got crazy, she would bring him home.

"Pardon me, your Grace." Lady Joanna ben Luke curtsied. "I believe you and I have table setting duty."

"Your Grace?" Astrid raised an eyebrow.

"Indeed, it is the proper address for a Duchess."

Astrid pressed two fingers against her left temple and closed her eyes. This was coming, whether she liked it or not. She squared her shoulders, let out a deep sigh, and met Joanna's kind brown eyes. "I suppose it is."

"Well then, your Grace, shall we lay the table?"

Astrid raised her chin, looking like she was prepared to go into battle. "I am afraid I know nothing about this."

Joanna's excellent blunt cut hair swung to the side as she tilted her head, an ironic and resigned expression crossing her features. "I might be of assistance in that regard." She nodded, her voice becoming wistful. "If I may be so bold to speak plainly. There are protocols, rules, and standards of deportment and etiquette they will expect you to know and adhere to. Failure to do so will embarrass yourself and your husband. It will make you an object of ridicule and scorn. Society is not kind, your Grace. However, I am intimately acquainted with these customs and would be willing to assist you as you enter, what must seem, a foreign and daunting society." She curtsied and kept her head bowed, waiting for Astrid's reply.

Astrid's eyes widened, and her stomach plummeted. Heretofore, the prospect of royal life had been Davianna's concern. She never intended to become part of the royal court. Until yesterday, she had flatly refused to marry Peter, and this had been one of the primary reasons. She was not an aristocrat, and everyone knew it. The full weight of what the future held curtsied right in front of her. "Um, ma'am. I don't quite know what to say, but I suspect it is apparent that I could use all the help I can get."

Joanna looked up, a smile glimmering in her eyes, her hands folded demurely. "I am honored by your condescension, your Grace. Shall we begin?"

Astrid nodded, resolute. "Yes, ma'am."

Joanna gave her a sidelong look. "I am the daughter of an Earl; thus my proper address is Lady Joanna. Here at Pepperwood, I am simply Joanna, but were we at court, you would outrank all but your husband, Prince Josiah, and Princess Davianna. To them, you curtsy. The rest of us curtsy or bow to you."

"Oh, my heavens, I thought avoiding the Princess title would get me out of this." Astrid paled.

"Quite the contrary," Joanna said, not unkindly. "As a royal Duchess, you outrank all one hundred thirty Alanthian peers."

Peter chose that moment to pop his head into the dining room, flushed from moving furniture. "Are you all right, Red? You are not getting a headache, are you? You look pale."

She spun on her heel to face him, then composed her features, flared her nose, and curtsied low. "Perfectly fine, my Esteemed."

He threw back his head and barked with laughter. "Oh, I will have fun with that. Thanks, Lady Joanna!"

Joanna whispered, "You would not necessarily address him as my Esteemed. Prince will suffice in public, though he outranks you."

"Well, that was stupid."

"Not necessarily," Joanna began. "You did well, opting for the lesser title, which will be viewed by the nobility as proper. Whether you realized it or not, that was a shrewd decision on your part."

"Why?" Astrid asked, arranging the cutlery in a pattern that matched the one Joanna laid.

"You could have negotiated the title of Princess, but there is greater precedent for a woman in your position to be a Royal Duchess rather than a Princess."

"But Peter's mother was a Princess." Astrid said, recalling the ethereal image of her mother-in-law.

"Yes, but Korah was the son of the Ruling Prince, not the grandson, as Peter is. It is all a bit complicated, given our recent history, but trust me, it will be viewed favorably at court."

"Court," Astrid mumbled and felt a shiver of panic slither down her spine.

Dinner With Friends - Pepperwood

As promised, Alaina and Beau delivered a New Orleans inspired feast that evening. Over dinner, Peter regaled the table with their adventure in the Big Easy, along with a comical recitation of the sheer numbers of body doubles that crowded the French Quarter.

Alaina giggled. "Himari was monitoring the police scans the entire time y'all were there. Half the city was running around naked."

"It is Mardi Gras, *chèr*," Beau said, raising his glass. "Next year, I'll take you."

She slapped his arm playfully. "I'm not running around the streets of New Orleans naked."

"Who said anything about the streets?" Beau waggled an eyebrow at her.

"Astrid and I will assuredly go back. She promised to disguise me again. I found that particular aspect of our adventure appealing." Peter winked at her.

She gave him a knowing smile as some of the heaviness melted away. The relaxed atmosphere felt familiar, the conversation friendly, the banter light. They would not always be at court. He hated State Dinners and receiving lines. If they could throw on disguises and be normal once in a while, things would be okay.

With dinner over, the fruit of the Peccioli vineyard flowed, and the dinner party took on a merry atmosphere. "To Mack ben Robert," Ian held up his glass in a toast, "for a superb Cabernet Sauvignon."

Peter caught a strained look that passed between Persa and James at the mention of Mack. Obviously, whatever occurred between them remained unresolved.

Alaina leaned her head on Beau's shoulder. "I know Mack is ready to get home. Himari spoke to him yesterday; they are staying in Rephidim a few more days."

Ian's eyebrows narrowed. "Mack's in Rephidim? So, he's with Esmeralda and Thaddeus?"

In the chaos of the uprising and Korah's final purge, members of The Resistance went into hiding. For security reasons, only Mack, Alaina, and Himari knew where everyone hid. But the need for secrecy was over, so Alaina nodded. "Yes. Mack said Esmeralda's mother convinced her to reschedule the wedding they canceled."

Ian rolled his eyes. "They canceled it because the bride and the groom nearly died." He blew out a long breath. "I am glad to hear they are going ahead with the ceremony. I hate to miss it since I was supposed to be a groomsman last time."

Beau took a sip of his wine, enjoying the excellent vintage. He rarely drank, but for this celebratory occasion he made an exception. "I am not the groom's favorite person, but *Grandpere* did ask me to pay a visit to the place. He has an interest in acquiring Arachnid Weaving."

Ian brightened. "That is the most amazing mill on Earth. Mark my words, those tunics Jarrod sent with our stuff were made from Arachnid cloth."

"Jarrod sent y'all clothes, too?" Astrid laughed, then tilted her head, curious. "What tunics?"

"Oh, *chèr*, they are the coolest thing you have ever seen. I seemed to disappear while I was wearing it. I thought I was going crazy." Beau shrugged. "Go get yours, Whitey, and tell us if that is Arachnid cloth. If it is, I have got to visit this place."

"I want to see those tunics." Astrid leaned forward; her face alight.

Joanna, attuned to the strain emanating from their hosts, rose and began gathering plates. "I'll help you clear."

James and Persa were not keen to relive any part of yesterday, including the clothes James was wearing when he died, so they excused themselves into the kitchen. The rest of the party retired to the living room, transformed into a makeshift nightclub, complete with speakers and Peter's ever-ready pink iPod.

Ian bounded down the steps, holding the lightweight garments. He gave the tunic to Astrid and the pants to Beau. "You can tell it's Arachnid cloth, not only by the weight, but look at the weave. That herringbone pattern is distinctive, I tell you." He traced his finger over the fine silky cloth. "Look, you can stretch it, and it snaps back."

Astrid looked up, slightly dazed. "It does not hold a stain or wear out. It won't hold a scent, even if you sit directly in front of a smoking campfire. The fabric seems to adapt to surrounding colors, which gives the illusion of invisibility."

The corner of Peter's mouth lifted. "That's the same material you and Davianna wear, is it not?"

Astrid nodded. "Exactly. I wonder if Jarrod got it from the Gune like we did."

"Gune?" Ian's forehead wrinkled in speculation. "She would not happen to have been a tall, bossy Serbian, would she?"

Joanna stuck her head around the corner from the kitchen. "She was outrageous."

"Jelena." Astrid covered her mouth in wonder.

Ian laughed. "Esmeralda does the most amazing imitation of her, spot on."

"This Esmeralda person, she knows the Gune?" Astrid asked, dumbfounded by the coincidence.

"Oh, yes, as do I, though not as well as Esmeralda. Jelena has been visiting her since she was a little girl."

Astrid turned to Peter and took him by the arm. "And is Esmeralda a member of The Resistance?"

Peter nodded. "She and her husband both are. Mack calls her a seer."

Persa walked into the living room and sat down quietly, interested in the conversation, remembering the unusual woman from her visit to Pepperwood the year before.

"She's more than a seer. She's a witch fighter, a spiritual warrior." All eyes turned to Beau, and he shrugged. "I've been in battle with her."

Ian met Beau's eyes, solemn and serious. "I have, too. She took on the Witch of Endor and won."

"She took on Mademoiselle Charlotte and won," Beau said. "I was planning to enlist her help when we go back down to the bayou."

Persa perched on the edge of the couch, folding her hands in her lap. "I think she may have encountered Marduk."

"Why do you say that, Fey?" James asked as he joined the group.

Persa turned to her husband; her brow knitted in thought. "I'm not sure, Jay, but something happened when she and Thaddeus were leaving. I sensed something was wrong, so I rode up to see if they were okay. She was terrified, and I swear she had another streak of white in her hair. I recognized her fear but couldn't identify the source at the time. What does she see, Ian?"

"Hang on." Peter pulled a signal jamming device from his bag and nodded to Alaina.

Alaina opened her laptop, disconnecting all communications. "Turn your phones off."

"We don't have any phones, Alaina. You threw them out the window," Joanna lamented.

Alaina looked up, chagrined. "Sorry." Then nodded at Peter. "I scanned the place this morning. There aren't any bugs. We should be clear."

Ian took Joanna by the waist. They put their heads together, silently seeking the Iron King's protection. Ian opened his eyes and said, "Esmeralda sees behind the veil. When the power of Yeshua is on her, she can read auras and see supernatural beings. She has visions, and she's seen the two of you," he said to Peter and Astrid, "particularly you, my Esteemed."

Ian turned to Persa and continued, "I was with her a month or so after she visited Pepperwood. She was not at liberty to say all that she encountered but told me a few things before hell broke loose in Thyatira." He pointed to his hair. "You did not imagine she got a new white streak while she was here. She did, and that is a mark of spiritual battle." He directed a question to Beau. "She came out of the fight she had at your place with another, right?"

Beau shook his head. "I can't say for certain, but you might be right."

"After the Battle of Thyatira, her hair was almost completely white. Right before they attacked us, she pointed to the hedge of protection surrounding Rephidim and said a similar one covers Pepperwood."

"A hedge? She saw it?" Persa's voice cracked.

Ian nodded. "She said it was beautiful, and it encompassed the property."

"I thought it was just figurative." Persa bolted from the sofa. "That is why I was afraid to leave! Marduk stalks the perimeter, doesn't he?"

The room grew still.

"He might, Persa," Ian conceded.

She closed her eyes, balling her hands into fists. James slipped an arm around her shoulders, pulling her close.

"Well, he left me alone while I was here." Peter's voice was low and deadly. "I never understood why I was safe at Pepperwood."

"She saw him, and she fought him," James growled, looking at Ian, "here, on my land?"

"I do not know, Brother, but it would not surprise me."

Peter met James' eyes. "Mack fought him for years in the Palace. It could not stand to be around him."

James pursed his lips. "Well then, we need to talk to that little seer, don't we? And as much as I hate to say it, I'll need to have a word with that son of a bitch."

"Mack or Marduk, James?" Peter narrowed his eyes.

"Mack," James grumbled. "We killed Marduk's evil bastard son yesterday, but it won't be finished until I send that monster permanently to Hell. If Mack ben Robert can tell us anything that might be useful, I'll kiss his ass and make up."

Persa cut a sidelong glance at her husband. "I don't think that will be necessary, Jay. I suspect you will find Mack ben Robert extremely accommodating."

Peter looked between them. "What the bloody hell happened between you three?"

"Nothing I cannot handle, Peter." Persa rose from her perch on the sofa. "Do make the necessary arrangements to fly us all to this Rephidim. It will be an ideal stop on our way to the Golden City." She swept a look around the room. Her voice shook slightly, but she squared her shoulders. "This was intended to be a celebration, and it has become entirely too serious. Someone pour me half a glass of wine, which I am allotted." She rested a protective hand over her little pooch. "I have a groom to dance with."

And with that, the party began. Lady Joanna stepped forward to offer the first toast. Though informal, protocol demanded that as the ranking peer, she begin. "At the formal wedding in two weeks, there will be much pomp and circumstance. Tonight, we are simply a group of friends celebrating a young couple beginning their lives together, just as Ian and I did a month and a half ago," she smiled beatifically at her groom, "and Beau and Alaina did two weeks ago. May we all aspire to achieve a lifelong happy marriage like James and Persa."

A chorus of agreement echoed among the guests.

"To Peter and Astrid, may the light of the Savior shine in your lives. May your days be filled with laughter and smiles. May you hold tight, steadfast, and true to the gift of each other. Congratulations."

They raised their glasses and drank.

James stepped forward, and everyone quieted. "The first time I met you, you ran off with my wife."

Everyone laughed, and Astrid turned sparkling eyes on Peter.

Peter shrugged a shoulder and countered, "I was seven, James."

Persa gazed up at James, teasing. "Are you still jealous?"

James leaned down and whispered words from that night, long ago. "If I did not know, Persa ben Yereq, that I have your heart, I would be jealous of the wind that caresses your skin."

Persa closed her eyes and rested her cheek against his chest, smiling. "Oh, that is a good line, cowboy."

James patted her back affectionately and continued, "Afterward, when you came to live with us, I discovered what a fine young man you were." James pressed his lips together and swallowed. "Our lives have been infinitely blessed because you have been a part of us. We love you like our own. We always have."

He paused, looking between the newlyweds. "You are starting a new chapter with a lovely bride. And for the first time in decades, the ominous shadow hanging over Alanthia does not seem invincible. I suspect that is due in large part to your hard work. Persa and I stand in awe of you, for what you have overcome, and the man you have grown into. We are so proud of you." He raised his glass. "Congratulations."

Peter handed Persa his glass of wine and embraced James, touched beyond speaking, beyond words. He leaned down and kissed Persa.

Alaina stepped forward, her beautiful aquamarine eyes shimmering. "The Prince and the model, we were the two most unlikely revolutionaries." She looked down, wiping a tear. "But we became friends. I know what you've been through, and how hard you worked to see us to this day."

Peter pressed his lips into a grim line, nodding. Alaina had been by his side in the darkest hours of his drug addiction. "I would not have made it without your skills and your friendship."

"Thank you," Alaina said, turning to Astrid. "I watched his face the first time he saw you on camera. I have known Peter for many years, and I have never seen him look at anyone the way he looks at you. You are the answer to my prayers for him." Alaina turned pink. "May you be blessed and happy."

"That is so sweet. Thank you," Astrid said, wiping a tear and looking helplessly down at the black smudge of mascara on her finger.

"Here you go, *chèr*." Beau passed her a tissue.

Peter took the floor. "Astrid, one of the first personal things I shared with you was about my family at Pepperwood."

Astrid smiled, remembering the ambulance and how his face lit up when he told her about Jay and Fey.

"I pray we will build a life like the one I lived here. It will not be the escape we dreamed of, nor will it be devoid of danger, intrigue, and politics." He crossed the room and took her hands. "Given who I am, the responsibilities I carry, and the duty to which I am bound, we could not run away. However, I shall put no one else above you. I will love you with all my heart, my body, and my soul."

They kissed and everyone raised their glasses.

Astrid felt her face flush, realizing it was her turn. In the privacy of Gilead, she pledged her life and her love, but in the presence of strangers she grew uncharacteristically shy. "I am not good at this."

"You do not have to say anything," he whispered.

She stared down at his hands, battered from the beating he

delivered to his father last night. She rubbed the minor cut on his wrist, where they sealed their vows and said, "I love you, Peter, for who you are, all the parts." She kissed a cut on his left thumb. "This part."

Outlining his crooked pinky finger, broken while he was being tortured, she said, "This part."

Her face flushed as she traced her nail over his gold and diamond watch, a symbol of his wealth and status. "This part."

Then she looked up and smoothed an expressive golden eyebrow that could raise in sardonic amusement or scowl in anger. Cupping his cheeks with both hands, she adored him. "This part."

Then she tapped his temple, indicating his intelligence, quick wit, his mind. "This part."

Laying her palm over his heart, her eyes shimmered with love. "And this part. I take them all." She held his gaze. "I take the whole man, Prince."

Peter brushed her lips and whispered, "I think you left out one part, Duchess."

Astrid laughed, "I did indeed."

They celebrated into the evening.

In the end, Beau, Alaina, Ian, and Joanna boarded the helicopter and Peter flew them back to the Lenox Mansion before he and Astrid returned to Gilead. Joanna was ecstatic to be back, so was the butler who had charge of sixty displaced kids who fled the Center during the fighting and took refuge in their patrons' fortified compound. She and Ian needed to resettle the kids and plan the operations for all three Centers while they were gone.

For Beau, his grandfather was growing anxious. He planned to make a side trip while they were in New York to see the old man and soothe his growing concerns that Beau had lapsed into another black period. Cut off from his family in Louisiana, Beau also needed to debrief his father. If Mademoiselle Charlotte and her wicked son made a move on the Landrys while he was gone, they needed to be ready.

Alaina received the upsetting news from Himari that her house had been ransacked by Korah's men during the purge. She wanted to take an inventory and felt guilty that Himari had borne all the computer work for The Resistance for weeks. She sensed Himari was at a breaking point and wanted to give her some relief.

Much needed to be accomplished before departing for the Golden City, but no one complained. Their hard-fought victory was decades in the making, and it was sweet.

February 16, 1000 ME

Treasure Hunting - Gilead - Peter and Astrid

Astrid's mother, Emaline, used to say her daughter came out of the womb curious and had a high need to touch everything. It was true. And while most people primarily used their sense of sight, Astrid explored the world through touch. She would run a finger over a chair railing as she walked by or lay a hand on her companion's forearm as she spoke. Specifically with Peter and Davianna, she touched them often, stroking Davianna's hair or caressing Peter's hand. Astrid loved peeking into drawers, closets, chests, and cabinets, not being nosy *per se*, just interested in what might be in there. Gilead offered a bonanza of possibilities, so over breakfast she announced she wanted to go exploring.

Peter glanced up from his plate of eggs. "Where?"

"Here."

"Okay, any particular reason?"

She shrugged. "I think the mob tore the Palace apart. Even if Josiah refurbishes it, I don't want to live there. I don't expect you will either. I thought perhaps we might live here."

Peter's fork paused halfway to his mouth. It never occurred to him that she would want to live in this old place. "You want to live here?"

She scanned the enormous dining hall. "It has a certain gothic appeal, don't you think?"

He raised an eyebrow at her. "There is no electricity."

"Actually, that is not true. According to Edison," she said, referring to Gilead's ancient butler, "your mother commissioned a project that began wiring the upper family wing. They did not finish, and with the Castle serving as a museum these last years, the staff chose not to use it, but he assures me it is there." She bit her thumbnail and narrowed her blue cat eyes. "Let's check it out. Then we will decide, okay?"

"As you wish, Duchess." Peter flashed her a grin.

She made a jaunty little shake of her shoulders and raised her chin. "I do wish, Prince."

Peter rolled his eyes and laughed. "That was very kind of Lady Joanna to offer her services in court. She will be a great asset to you and Davianna. I promise, it is not nearly as difficult as it may appear. When in doubt, do what my mother always taught me, 'Smile, nod, and keep your mouth shut.'"

Astrid gave it a shot.

Peter chuckled and offered his arm. "See, there is nothing to it. Now, shall I ring for the steward? He is the resident historian and will be able to guide us toward whatever sort of hidden treasures this freezing heap of stones might hold."

"Perhaps later. I would like to start on our own. Shall we begin in the stables?" She flashed him a secret smile. "I believe that is one of the more important elements of any residence we choose, is it not?"

He leaned around to see her expression, to ascertain if she was teasing him, and saw she spoke in earnest. "You are correct."

She squeezed his arm. "What you said last evening, about us creating a life like you lived at Pepperwood, I realize for you that will include horses. I saw you ride when we were in Tel Aviv." She bowed her head, remembering how beautiful he looked on the horse. With the Mediterranean Sea serving as a backdrop, the vision of him was seared in her mind, tinged with heartbreak, love, and longing. She had wanted to break cover and run to him with her arms stretched wide, but she had not.

He frowned, remembering Tel Aviv, too. "You were watching me, were you not? I thought I was going mad, but I kept feeling you nearby."

"I came every day," she whispered. "I just could not stay away. But until I saw you riding, I could not fathom why you stayed in the Palace with your father and Marduk stalking the halls. It was the horses, wasn't it?" She felt a jolt of surprise course through his body. "I know you better than you realize."

Peter regarded her with raised brows. "That is a novel experience."

"Get used to it," she replied, adopting a tone of droll boredom he often employed.

"I plan to," he said, kissing her cheek. "But yes, the horses were part of why I stayed."

"And the other part?" she prompted.

"Ah, a host of other complicated reasons."

"Obviously. What is it you and Alaina say? Treason is dangerous business?"

"It is indeed, and more of a business than you would imagine. Running a revolution takes a tremendous amount of capital."

She paused, looking around at the enormous wealth on display at Gilead. She had not given a thought to how he financed a revolution and was suddenly curious. "How did you do it?"

He gave her a pained grimace.

"Ha!" Astrid chuckled. "Is that one of those 'royals don't talk about it' subjects?"

The corner of his mouth lifted. "Yes, I suppose it is."

"Well, I did not marry you for your money, but if you do not want to discuss it—"

"No, it is not that. It is just," he paused, taking her hand, "it is just odd. But you are correct, we are married, so you have a right to know where we stand financially."

She wrinkled her nose. "We are not broke, are we?"

"Heavens no," he laughed.

Astrid gestured around the grounds of Gilead and said, "I didn't think you were, but it is all a matter of perspective, isn't it?"

"Yes, I suppose it is." He pointed up at the Castle. "Taxes pay for the estates, the upkeep, and the salaries of those who work for us. They do not wholly support the noble families, the royal family being no exception. The founders of the Alanthian constitution framed it that way. They studied history and decided that for men to be able to retain their titles, they had to be innovative enough to earn their own livings, the rationale being that they would not excessively levy taxes, adopt regulations or laws that inhibited business, or become out of touch and isolated. Some noble families were great at it, others were not. There have been many heiresses who married into the nobility over the centuries."

"So, you married me for my money," Astrid deadpanned.

Peter laughed, "I would not be opposed to having those intriguing boots of yours."

Astrid shook her head. "Do you know they stopped working when I left you?"

Peter looked up at the sky and said, "Thank you."

Astrid gave his arm a playful punch.

They walked through the western garden, on their way to the stables. "So, how did you finance The Resistance?"

"My grandfather, on my mother's side, was well to do. His estate makes up the bulk of my personal portfolio, but Korah managed and monitored those, providing me a paltry monthly allowance."

"Poor Prince d'Or," Astrid teased.

"Yeah," Peter said with a pretend pout. "He barely gave me enough money to cover my wardrobe, let alone finance a revolution, and that was absolutely by design. However, my mother expected that I might need funds independent of what Korah could control, so several months before she died, she made arrangements through her godfather. Korah never knew, and Sir Preston ben Worley kept them in trust for me until I turned nineteen." Peter touched her back, guiding her down a set of worn stone steps. "Do you remember him, the ancient barrister we met in New York?"

"The inspiration for those giant eyebrows I made for Josiah?" Astrid smirked.

Peter nodded. "Yes, the same. He is the one who gave me her letter when we were in New York." They moved onto the lawn with the stables in sight. "Jarrod came to me from Sir Preston's household. He worked for him for decades before becoming my valet. Mack, too, took the position as my head of security at Sir Preston's urging."

"So, Sir Preston looked out for you after your mother died." Astrid squeezed his hand. "That's nice."

"It is. When I see him again, I will thank him. I would have when we met in New York, but I did not know."

"So, your mother's money financed the revolution? That is beyond ironic."

"Well, she certainly provided the seed money, but it was not nearly enough. You have not met her, but Mack's wife, Lavinia, is a genius. She and I conceived The Resistance at her kitchen table, and she calculated down to the shekel how much we would need. I remember thinking it was an enormous amount of money."

He shrugged and said offhand, "It just grew. Everything we tried worked. At first, we traded in secrets, but then Himari, Lavinia, and Alaina started writing code and building programs.

We sold those, and that is when the real money started. We did it through shell companies, trusts, and charities, all completely hidden. It is disjointed and scattered across a hundred companies, for obvious reasons, but it grew into a sizable enterprise.

"Had I tried to leave, I would have tipped my hand. The last thing I needed was Korah looking closer at me. So, I let him assume I was who he thought I was, a stupid playboy, capable of nothing more than cutting ribbons." He smiled sadly. "He never saw past the face."

"It was his loss." Astrid shook her head at the folly of the wicked King.

The Royal Gilead stables sat empty. However, the smells of manure, hay, and feed made Peter inhale to the bottom of his lungs. "I have vague memories of being here as a child." He traced a loving hand along the polished wood in the fourth stall. "My pony, Mr. Buzzy, stabled here."

"You had a pony at three? I think I was eating mud pies at three."

He grinned. "Had they allowed me to get dirty, I likely would have, too. However, I rode as soon as I could walk. Our family has always been avid horsemen, though my mother never cared for them, a lot like you."

"I think I can learn. They are just so big. Cats and dogs have always been more my style."

As if conjured by her words, an old barn cat peered around the corner, checking out the intruders in his domain.

Peter took no notice and gestured down the rows of gleaming and polished empty stalls. "We kept the purebreds here. The work horses are in the rear of the property, near the barns. They structured Gilead in the old way, with a small village and working farms. There are several hundred thousand acres still in production, and they grow most of the fresh food served at the Palace here."

"Several hundred thousand?" she asked. "How large is Gilead?"

He looked up at the ceiling, trying to pull that fact out of his brain. His tutor had taught him the specifics of all the royal estates. "If I recall, it is somewhere in the neighborhood of fifty by fifty."

"Miles?" she asked, trying to comprehend.

"Well, it is not feet, Love."

"Brat."

"Duchess," he said with a smile.

"Do you think Josiah and Davianna will settle here?"

He shrugged. "He might. There is a solidity to this place that I am certain will appeal to him."

"You are probably right," she said.

"But do not think Gilead is our only option." He reached out and touched a long red curl. "I inherited two estates through my maternal grandfather, one on the coast, about an hour north of Pepperwood, and another in New Jersey." He cleared his throat, uncomfortable. "I have, uh… not been to Capernaum, the New Jersey estate, since she died. Perhaps we will visit on our way to Rephidim. It is an hour or so outside of New York City, and only about twenty miles from Thyatira Woods."

Astrid wrapped an arm around his waist. "Is it large enough to accommodate our party?"

Peter suppressed a grin. "Yes."

"Don't look at me that way. I am just asking. It could be a lodge, for all I know."

"I think there are a few of those, as I recall." Peter shook his head. "But Capernaum served as the manor house for the Easton Barony."

Astrid nodded, the matter settling in her mind. "Well then, everyone could stay there while we could pick up Sir Mack and the rest of the team. I suspect our presence in Rephidim will be disruptive, and I doubt they have much in the way of accommodations, so it would save them trouble."

Peter beamed. "See, you are already beginning to think like a royal. It embarrasses people if you show up unannounced. Even if you try to assure them you do not need special treatment, they insist. Though, if we employ some of your ingenious disguises, we might be able to attend the wedding."

Her eyes brightened. "Then we could just blend in, even have a little fun. We could pretend to be friends of the bride and groom from New York."

"Capital idea, Duchess."

They wandered arm in arm down the long stable. Astrid pulled away, intent to investigate the closed doors. An immense tack room held all manner of halters, bridles, reins, stirrups, and saddles. Astrid relished the tactile pleasure of touching the oiled and conditioned accouterments. "Since I married a horseman, you must begin my education in all things equestrian. I confess, I am sorely lacking." The corner of her mouth lifted in remembrance. "You should have seen the expression on James' face when I told him I did not like horses."

Peter turned, a teasing glint in his eyes. "It is a wonder he did not boot you off the ranch."

"I think he considered it. He watched me all day, taking my measure."

"That is his way." He paused and walked over to an oddly constructed saddle. "There are many facets to James. This, for instance, is a surcingle, a specially designed saddle for vaulting. Have you ever seen it done?"

"I have seen gymnastics vaulting. Davianna says that was her specialty."

"I can see Fireball flying through the air, but no, horse vaulting is different." He looked around, scanning the tack room, then began flipping through a variety of horse blankets and pads. "They put one of these on the back of a horse and saddle it with the surcingle, then upwards of three or four athletes perform a routine to music on the back of a cantering horse. It is wicked difficult, even the most basic moves are hard to master, and James and Persa won a world championship. I saw their performance. They were amazing."

"Do you vault?" Astrid looked up at him through her auburn lashes.

"Me? No. Though the summer I lived with them when I was fourteen, they taught me a couple moves. I busted my ass about a thousand times just standing on the back of the horse. I can ride, but vaulting is not just riding, or lifting, or even acrobatics. To be great, you have to perform, to charm the crowd, and you have to choreograph all the stunts to music. Now, think about the man you met yesterday. Can you imagine him doing that?"

Astrid giggled, "No!"

"My point, exactly. There is more to him than meets the eye. He is the great grandson of the Duke of Sierra, though not from the line of inheritance. I believe his uncle is a baron, though I cannot remember which one. His mother is also some sort of minor nobility through her stepfather, who may have been a landed knight. I have met her once or twice at charity functions, though she does not know I spent time at Pepperwood. I suspect she would be insufferable otherwise. She is a social climber." Peter apologized with a pained smile. "You will become well acquainted with her type soon enough."

"How does she not know about your time at Pepperwood?" Astrid asked, not wishing to contemplate facing a room full of people who traced their lineages back ten generations.

"It was part of my pre-employment negotiations with James. No one was ever to know I was there. Though, towards the end I started going to Rivergate for Sunday dinners with Persa's father."

"Pre-employment?" Astrid chuckled and poked him in the arm. "You worked at Pepperwood?"

He drew himself up. "I did, as a stableboy. He paid me forty-five shekels a week, in addition to my room and board." He poked her back. "Do not think I lounged around that entire summer. James worked me from sunup to sundown."

Astrid draped her arms over his shoulders, her eyes dancing. "Well, that makes me happy."

He rested his forehead against hers. "Why?"

"Because it means that for at least a summer," she said softly, "we lived in the same world. It concerns me that our backgrounds are so different."

Peter brushed her lips with a soft kiss. "They will not always be. As time passes, and we grow old, we will be each other's past, and where we came from will not matter."

"Do you truly believe what came before does not matter? Will we be able to leave it behind, or will the specter of the past always return to haunt us?" She closed her eyes, hoping.

"I think it is our choice, but it is one we have made every day since we met, is it not?" He lifted her chin, staring into her cat-blue eyes. "Every day you showed me how. You put the past in the past and moved forward." He brushed his lips against her ear, whispering, "Would you have fallen in love with me, if you dwelled on what happened in the Palace? Would I have fallen in love with you, if I had? How easy would it have been to just give up and become drug addicts? That was our choice, when you get down to it. Strip away all the layers, and we have both made a choice, the heroin, or Peter and Astrid."

She ran her fingers through his thick blond hair and pulled his mouth to hers for a passionate kiss. Heat exploded between them. Their choice became obvious.

"Well," Astrid panted, as she raised up on her elbow, "that was fun."

"Dirty Duchess." Peter stretched his arms over his head, a tangle of horse blankets bunched around his body.

Astrid cut him a look. "Do not let Lady Joanna hear you call me that."

"Oh, we shall scandalize everyone by regularly kissing in public," Peter declared. "My Grandmother Mary would roll over in her grave." He caressed her hip with his long finger. "I will say, that was one thing my father did for the better. He dropped court language in the Palace and relaxed the dress code, along with most of the archaic protocols. We can only hope that Josiah will not reinstate them, but if he does, he can expect that we shall be absent at court more than we are present."

Astrid looked pained as she wiggled into her trousers. "I will have a word with Davianna. I am certain she can persuade him otherwise."

Peter buttoned his shirt and sat up, setting himself to rights. "I expect Josiah will have enough obstacles to overcome without unduly complicating matters."

"Yes, and there is the minor matter of Satan and his army we have conveniently chosen to avoid discussing." Astrid rolled her eyes.

Peter pursed his lips. "That makes the discussion of table manners a bit banal, does it not?"

"Exactly," Astrid inhaled, "yet they faced him down, again." She studied the closet door in the tack room, lost in thought. "The Davianna I met a year and a half ago jumped at her own shadow."

"The woman I left in Tel Aviv did not fear much," Peter answered, following her line of sight.

His eyes narrowed, distracted by a distant memory. Rolling to his feet, he moved across the tack room and opened the closet door. Two rows of uniforms hung inside along with knee-high boots, helmets, and mallets, organized and ready. He sucked in a breath and stumbled backward.

"What is it?" Astrid moved behind him, feeling like Sleeping Beauty discovering a spinning wheel.

"Polo equipment," he said in a cracked whisper.

Her eyes narrowed as she took a step forward. Polo had been outlawed in Alanthia most of her life. She touched a dark blue silk jersey. A royal insignia had been embroidered on two of the uniform sleeves, HRH EbA and HRH KbA. She looked over her shoulder and asked, "Are these Eamonn and Korah's?"

Peter pursed his lips and nodded. "I think that is why he killed him. I think it started over a polo match."

Part 3 - The Genesis

February 07, 943 ME

High Equestrian Week - New City, Alanthia

It grew over the millennia, the love of equestrian sports. Sans automobiles and technology, man reconnected with their ancient companion, the horse. As generations passed, equestrian sports rose from obscurity to dominate Alanthian and Millennial society. Agrarian culture lent itself to celebrating their favorite pastime at the end of the harvest, before spring planting began. Every winter, the twenty Alanthian Earls sponsored events where top equestrian athletes competed for their chance to represent the earldoms at High Equestrian Week. The Ruling Prince sponsored the yearly festivities that became affectionately known as the Hewies. The first week in February, high drama and competition gripped the entire kingdom. Top athletes, animals, and teams competed for trophies, prize money, and the right to represent Alanthia in the global games held each April.

Ladies flocked to the quadrille, dressage, and vaulting competitions. Gentlemen frequented the hunt, the steeplechase, and the endurance events. Farmers and rowdy young men loved the rodeo, especially the bull and bronc riding. A crowd favorite, and by far, the most popular were the races. The great track constructed on the outskirts of the New City hosted throngs of spectators who poured in to watch the thundering horses and tiny jockeys race for glory. High-stakes gambling was outlawed, however, event coordinators permitted small wagers at the track betting windows. Larger bets took place below the bleachers, in gentlemen's clubs, and in the back rooms of bars. Officials turned a blind eye and supplemented their income with a yearly 'bonus' from their cut.

The aristocrats loved polo.

Unlike other sports, where competitors sourced from the earldoms, the ten Alanthian Dukes and the Ruling Prince took charge of polo. They competed for the most talented players and stacked their teams without regard to origin or even nationality. The best players were wealthy, spoiled, and adored. They became the superstars of the Hewies.

Polo, the sport of Princes, became a microcosm of the corruption creeping into the hearts of the men who ruled the ten kingdoms. Alanthian Ruling Prince Adam ben Simon was not above the fray, becoming a fanatic who spared no expense or enticement to lure the best players to his team. Through his machinations, Ignacio ben Alejandro arrived at Gilead to play for the royal team. It was a mistake Prince Adam regretted for the rest of his natural life.

At the 943 Hewies, the beautiful Argentine, Ignacio ben Alejandro, was the undisputed king of the pitch. He was also a legendary flirt, cad, and womanizer. He possessed the morals of a stray dog, though his manners were impeccable in public. His private life was another story. Like any handsome superstar, he had his choice of women, from gorgeous well-bred socialites to groupies and party girls. It was not unusual for Ignacio to find a naked woman in his bed, sometimes more than one. However, inside Ignacio's chest beat the heart of a competitor. So, while he never threw a naked woman out of his bed, he preferred a challenge and loved the chase.

He accepted Prince Adam's invitation with a dual purpose in mind, to play polo and to discover if he could capture the most elusive prize in the kingdom. Ignacio set out to melt the heart of the legendary Ice Princess, Mary ben Abraham.

When he met the twenty-eight-year-old, raven-haired beauty, he realized the Princess would be the biggest challenge of his life, and Ignacio set out to conquer her.

February 14, 943 ME

It Did Begin With Polo - Gilead - Adam and Mary

"What art thou doing in here?" Mary spat, swinging around from her dressing table and pulling her robe tight. "Get out."

Adam glared at her from the door, then moved into her chamber, and slammed the heavy oak door with a decisive bang. "I will be here if I choose to be, Wife."

She stiffened at his tone and the title, took in his disheveled blond hair and untucked shirt, and snarled, "Thou art drunk."

"Any man who finds himself married to you is entitled to be drunk," he said, his deep voice dripping with scorn.

"I do not countenance drunkenness, nor dost the Iron King. Depart from me, Adam." She dismissed him with an imperious jut of her chin and turned her back on him. From her dressing room mirror, she watched his face go crimson with rage.

"Does the Iron King countenance adultery?" Adam took three steps forward and spun her around, accusing her through gritted teeth, "I saw you."

Mary narrowed her hazel eyes, translucent and pale with indignation. "Thou art raving mad. There hast been nothing to see."

Her dark hair was down for bed, flowing around her creamy shoulders. She was indeed one of the greatest beauties of the age. Adam seized a handful of her ebony hair and jerked her head back. "I did not see this?" He covered her mouth with a bruising kiss, shoving his tongue down her throat, dominating her.

Her hair pulled at the roots, the pain making her arch into him. She shoved against his chest, trying to push him away. His teeth scored her lips, fouled with whiskey and too many cigarettes. She scratched his face and shouted, "Get off me!"

"You did not say that to him, did you?" He grabbed her around the waist and ground his hips against hers. "You did not tell him to stop, like you do me, your husband."

Mary narrowed her eyes, brimming with hatred. "Do not touch me, Adam. We had a deal. I did my duty. I gave thee Eamonn. Thou hast thy son. Go take thy pleasure with thy whores."

Adam's lip lifted in scorn. "That's just it, Mary. It was your deal." He backed her up three steps. "I never agreed to it. I never agreed not to touch you." He pressed into her again, his desire evident. "Nevertheless, whether it existed or not, you have broken the deal."

She cast about, looking for an escape, fear entering her heart. "Nothing happened."

"Liar!" he shouted as his eyes bore into hers, red from drink, green with jealousy. He pushed the gown off her shoulders, revealing her filmy negligee that offered a tantalizing peek at what she withheld from him. "Did Ignacio ben Alejandro melt the Ice Princess when he touched you?" He cupped her breast and squeezed. "Did he, Mary?"

She slapped him.

In a drunken, jealous rage, he backhanded her with all his might. Her head snapped back, and she stumbled. Blood from her nose flew in an arc across the chamber and splattered across the golden coverlet. The back of her knees met the bed, and she landed with her legs spread wide, her gown bunched around her thighs.

Adam fell on top of her. "You bitch. You flaunt yourself in front of me day and night. You marry me for my kingdom, then withhold your body. You flay me alive with your vicious tongue, then spread your legs for some Argentine polo player?" He raised his hips and opened his fly. "I am your husband. This is my right. I am the Prince."

She kicked at him, crying, twisting away, fighting him, but he was stronger than she and held her down. "Don't!" she screamed. "Damn thy soul to hell, Adam. Don't!"

He did.

Without an ounce of tenderness or love, amidst violence, blood, and tears, Korah ben Adam was conceived.

December 30, 999 ME

A Bad Call - New City Palace - Korah and Davianna

After their walk in the winter garden, Korah brought Davianna to his favorite place on the royal estate, the stables. "Do you remember the night we met? I told you I was a polo player?" Korah asked Davianna as he fed a carrot to a beautiful chestnut mare.

Davianna nodded, transfixed by the horse's dark eyelashes, which seemed impossibly long and extravagant. "Why is her mane cut short?"

"She is a polo pony." Korah leaned his head against the long nose and scratched under the horse's ear with affection.

Why a polo pony had her mane docked confused Davianna, but almost everything confused her at this point, so she did not question him. "Are you going to ride her? Are you going to show me how you used to play polo, my Esteemed?"

He rotated his right shoulder as if testing it. "I have not played polo in many years. I outlawed it when I became King, though I kept the ponies."

The warmth of the stable enveloped her, and she teetered into him, giddy with laughter. "That is silly. You need to ride that horse. It does not matter if you got hurt once. Look, I can still do gymnastics." She took off down the aisle of the stable and executed a round-off back handspring combination. Losing her balance, she over rotated and landed on her rump in the dust. She shook herself and smiled like a drunk. "Oops." Then she fell to the ground, laughing. But it felt so nice down there, cool and covered in sweet soft hay. She fell instantly asleep.

"It was a bad call, Brother. No doubt." Eamonn said from behind him.

Korah whirled, but instead of finding the ghost of his dead brother, he saw a scene played out in a stable, miles from here, decades past.

"I was fouled. You know it. I know it. Everyone watching knew it," his eighteen-year-old self protested.

Eamonn, twenty-one, turned a jaded eye to his brother. "I am sorry."

Korah threw his helmet across the dressing room. "He looked at her, didn't he? The umpire took his clue from Mother before he made that call."

Eamonn moistened his lips and swallowed. He spent a lifetime having conversations like this one. "I am not certain."

"You know he did. Any chance she gets to knock me down, she takes it." He sagged in defeat. "I am almost done at the RMA, Eamonn. I cannot come back here. I cannot live under their roof again. Just being back for the Hewies has almost killed me."

"Dramatic and over-exaggerating the facts, as always." Princess Mary swept into the room. "Thou art simply a poor loser, Korah. There was no foul, other than the one in thy mind. Thou art paranoid and thinkest everyone is out to get thee, imagining things that do not exist."

His mother's apparition turned and stared straight into the eyes of present-day Korah. Her face morphed into a hideous mask, cruel and taunting, her shrill voice sending chills up his spine. "Just as thou art imagining me right now. Thou art pathetic, still." The ghost of his mother faded into the body of Davianna ben David.

Korah erupted.

Stalking over to the prostrate form, he set Davianna on her feet and punched her in the stomach with all the impotent fury raging in his soul.

February 15, 1000 ME

Fast Car - New York - Kayah and Filippo

"What the hell do you mean there is a hit out on me, and where in the hell have you been?" Kayah demanded as she jumped into the passenger's side of the shiny black sports car.

"Is good to see you, too." Filippo did not spare her a glance, twisting around to navigate reverse. With a squeal of tires and burning rubber, they shot away in the opposite direction of her destination.

Two pistols lay in the open console, an assault rifle wedged between her seat and the floorboard. A quick glance over her shoulder showed a cache of other weaponry in the rear. Even without the weapons, his warning and the set of his shadowed jaw conveyed the seriousness of the situation.

"That is the most unimaginative hat I have ever seen you wear."

Filippo lowered his dark eyelashes and shook his head, the black baseball hat pulled low on his forehead. He grunted and fixed his attention on the snarled traffic. Energy pulsed off him. Alert to every movement, his eyes darted like a hunted beast.

"So, who is trying to kill me?" Kayah took up the surveillance, watching for anomalies, scanning the faces on the sidewalk, looking for danger.

"Is a long story." He drove up on the sidewalk, scattering pedestrians who screamed and made rude gestures as they flew past. "I get you out of New York. Then we talk."

Kayah fought off a wave of crushing disappointment and suppressed a wild urge to jump out of the car to continue down the path she set for herself. This was supposed to be over. Today was supposed to end this. Running, hiding, fighting… she had done it her whole life. With a few simple words, Filippo pulled her back into that world. She squeezed the bridge of her nose and closed her eyes, weary and tired.

"You keep a watch. It's a ten million shekel bounty on your head."

Kayah sucked in her breath at the extraordinary figure. "Ten million?"

"Since the Angel, they issued the hit right after."

"The jihadists?"

"They would like everyone to think so, but no," Filippo replied cryptically.

"What is that supposed to mean?" Kayah demanded.

"It is an old ploy." Filippo shook his head, resigned. "The mafia, they disguise their violence."

Kayah narrowed her eyes. "Like at Facetec?"

Filippo pressed his lips into a thin line and said, "It was a hit, mafia war."

"It was not Massimo's men, for the insurance money?" Kayah gripped her knees and stared out the window.

"I thought so, at first." Filippo skirted a stalled vehicle and shot like a rocket over the bridge, away from the island, away from New York. "It was not."

"What are you telling me? Are you saying the mafia has put a hit out on me? Why? I steer clear of them. I always have." Kayah threw up her palms, the picture of innocence.

"No, you have not." Filippo cut her a sidelong glance. "You have been embedded with them since the beginning. You just did not know."

"That is bullshit," Kayah exploded. "I have never taken up with them, ever."

"Kayah," Filippo's voice was very low, "I am pretty sure Sir Preston ben Worley is the head of the mafia in Alanthia and has been for decades."

Part 4 - Sacrifices

April 7, 963 ME

Outward Appearances - New York - Korah and Eamonn

In the drawing room at Merea, the Duke of Philadelphia's estate, nineteen-year-old Prince Korah ben Adam raised a glass of champagne and turned to his brother. "To your future bride. At least she does not look like a troll," he said with a sardonic lift of his eyebrow. "Then again, Mother would not saddle you with an ugly wife."

"I am certain Lady Alexa will be just as beautiful," Eamonn replied, with placating, practiced ease.

"One can only hope," Korah replied with bored resignation. "I suppose I will find out soon enough." He was to be introduced to his betrothed during the wedding festivities for his brother. "If she is not, I am thankful she is not out of the schoolroom yet. I have two years before I am shackled to her. Yours, on the other hand, is ripe for the picking. The Italians produce fine wine and beautiful women, do they not?"

"She is beautiful," Eamonn said, watching the ebony-haired Marguerite smile at the scads of admirers seeking her attention. "Then again, so was Mother."

Korah turned an incredulous eye to his brother. Eamonn rarely spoke a harsh word about their mother.

Eamonn took a sip of wine and said, "I am not blind to the realities of their marriage, nor her faults. Half the reason Father drinks is because she is so nasty to him." Eamonn nodded toward

Adam, who lounged in a grand chair, well into his cups. His best friend and loyal supporter, Sir Preston ben Worley, leaned in, the two sharing a quiet joke.

"She is nasty to everyone but you," Korah observed. He often thought that he and his father should have bonded over Princess Mary's mutual disdain, but they had not. It always seemed to Korah that his father blamed him for his wife's hatred, though he kept that opinion to himself, lest they accuse him of being paranoid again.

Eamonn glanced at their mother. She stood ramrod straight, dripping with jewels and disdain, her faithful ladies by her side. They observed their surroundings as if detecting a foul stench in the air, the source of which seemed to be his future father-in-law, Alfonso ben Leosi, the Duke of Milan. The Duke chose that moment to raise his glass of red wine and wink with extravagant roguishness at Mary. She scowled, which made Alfonso laugh. The corner of Eamonn's mouth lifted as he murmured, "Milan does not seem daunted by her."

"He is wearing red. She disapproves of red," Korah said dryly. "Who disapproves of an entire primary color?"

Eamonn hid a smile behind his glass. "Our mother."

"I shall wear red to her funeral," Korah muttered.

Eamonn made a quick roll of his eyes and quipped, "She would haunt you forever if you did."

May 5, 963 ME

New York vs. New City - New York - Korah and Alexa

It was supposed to be a friendly exhibition, part of the endless wedding festivities. In the end, it turned out to be anything but. From the moment the Duke of Philadelphia's team took to the pitch, Korah realized they were in trouble. On ponies fast as lightning, they outran the royal mounts by two lengths in every race. He and Eamonn were the most skilled players, yet Philadelphia's superior horses beat them repeatedly.

As Captain of the Royal Squad, Korah seethed. The one place he won, the one place he dominated, and the one place he took total command was the polo pitch. Today, it all fell apart, and there was not a thing he could do about it. Outwardly, he appeared the affable and dashing Prince Korah—he had to.

He was being watched.

So, he joked with the other team, smiling in exaggerated humor. He made the spectators laugh, and got his ass kicked in front of his new fiancée, his peers, and the global delegation who traveled to New York for the wedding.

He fooled everyone… except his mother.

At the end of the final chukka, he dismounted and handed his pony over to the groom. Doffing his helmet and tucking it under his arm, he extended his hand in hearty congratulations to the victors.

The sun seemed to follow him wherever he stepped, his golden-haired beauty setting him apart from his darker companions. The Prince moved with long-limbed, effortless grace, always ready with a charming smile or an outrageous flirtation. He flattered and smirked. He drank and rogued. Korah spent lavishly and wagered outrageous sums in private clubs and card tables. Dressed in the highest fashion, he dictated style standards and trends each season. When he graced a drawing room or ball, the hostesses delighted in their social triumph. Prince Korah ben Adam was, quite simply, the darling of high society.

And for sixteen-year-old Lady Alexa ben Seamus, he was hers.

Her betrothal had been a *coup d'état*, for she was only a Baron's daughter. However, her father possessed vast reservoirs of the oldest form of power—money. Seamus ben Kearney was an inventor and corporate tycoon who controlled enormous wealth and influence in the northeast portion of the kingdom. As his only child, Lady Alexa ben Seamus was the sole heiress to one of the biggest fortunes in Alanthia, which she felt entitled her to the most eligible bachelor. And what Lady Alexa wanted, Lady Alexa got.

Her godfather, Sir Preston ben Worley, made it happen. Largely regarded as the second most powerful man in the kingdom, he was Prince Adam's closest friend and confidante. His influence could not be overstated, especially as the Prince's penchant for drink manifested, but they did not think she knew that.

Lady Alexa began her campaign after seeing Prince Korah at a regatta when she was twelve. He cut a dashing figure aboard his sloop, racing his boat to solo victory. Standing on the deck, with the cup raised above his head and a gorgeous smile across his face, a gust of wind ruffled his blond hair, molding his loose white trousers to his long, lean body. He was absolute perfection, embodying everything she ever dreamed of: handsome, rich, charismatic… royal. He carried himself with confidence, was not awkward or self-conscious like most boys his age. That day at the yacht club, he shone as bright as the sun, and watching him from beneath her sunbonnet, Alexa wanted him.

Now she had him, or at least she would as soon as she came of age. Sitting in the stands, flanked by her father, her future in-laws, Sir Preston, and the entire Italian delegation, she narrowed her blue eyes, devouring Korah in greedy relish. However, she controlled her features and sat with her hands folded in her lap, presenting herself as a sweet, demure young maiden instead of what she was, a calculating, pampered, spoiled brat.

Princess Mary looked between Korah and Alexa, understanding how well suited they were. Both of them were playing a role, and they were both rotten to the core.

December 30, 999 ME

Does Anyone Love You? - New City Palace - Korah and Davianna

For Davianna ben David, there was no air, no life-giving oxygen to fill her lungs. After Korah's gut punch, her body froze, bent over in shock, unable to function. She grabbed her stomach, hollow and spasming, feeling like a cannonball hit her.

'In through your nose, out through your mouth, that's it. Nice and easy.' Josiah's words that night in the park came to her mind. She tried to do what he told her, struggling not to throw up. Gasping and sputtering, spittle leaked from her mouth, dangling like spider silk filament to the ground. She choked and swallowed, then took a massive gulp of life-giving air, but she did not straighten, did not dare look up at him. She simply concentrated on her next breath and tried to stay alive.

"You were asleep. I told you not to sleep," Korah growled.

Clutching her belly, she rocked, unsteady and panicked. She had to find the words, or he would hit her again. "I'm sorry."

"You should be. It is your fault. If you do what I say, I will not hurt you."

She nodded, bent over and gasping. "You're right."

He lifted her chin, glaring into her watering eyes. "Where is it, Davianna? Where is the treasure you carry? Are you going to give it to me, or will you make me hurt you again?"

She fell to her knees, putting her forehead on the top of his shoes. "My Esteemed, if I still had it, I would give it to you. I do not have it any longer. It was taken from me in London, by the Gune."

He gave her credit. She stuck to her story. She was lying, of course, but he felt a grudging admiration for her fortitude. "Would you give it to me if you had it?"

"I would. I would give you anything. Please, do not hurt me anymore."

"Anything?" Korah moistened his lips and looked down at her.

"Whatever you wish," she pleaded.

The corner of his mouth lifted in a diabolic smile. "Gratifying to hear, my lovely."

He reached down and set her on her feet. She swayed in his arms, so he picked her up like a groom carrying his bride over the threshold. "Come, you need rest. Tomorrow evening, you will attend the gala as my special guest."

Her head lolled because she had no strength. The gut punch, coupled with his relentless interrogation and days without sleeping, jumbled her mind. Resting her cheek in the crook of his neck, she sighed, inhaling the pleasant scents of bergamot and pipe tobacco. "You smell nice, warm."

A potent emotion ran up his spine, like a fast-burning fuse, foreign and powerful. He shuddered.

An odd comfort stole over her because her daddy used to carry her like this. She smiled up at him and mumbled as if she was in a dream, "I have nothing to wear to a gala, my Esteemed."

"'Tis no matter. I am the King and can provide everything that you need." He nuzzled the lovely crop of thick hair tickling his chin and murmured, "I will take care of you, and I will not leave you like the rest of them have. I won't abandon you, Davianna."

She laid a trembling hand on his cheek, studying his face. "Does anyone love you, my Esteemed? You are so beautiful, but you are so broken."

He froze mid-step, then answered her honestly. "My wife did. When she died, that is when I broke."

Standing alone on the lush green lawn between the stables and the Palace, Korah held on as Davianna ben David wept—for him.

From the Moment I Saw You - New City Palace - Korah

"I despised you from the moment I saw you," Korah said to the drugged girl lying in his dead wife's bed. He walked to Alexa's dressing table and uncorked her perfume. The smell evoked her presence more than the unconscious look-alike. "Stupid girl, you should have never insisted we marry. We were ill matched from the start."

He caught his reflection in her mirror and said, "All you could see was this face, wasn't it?" He smoothed the haggard lines under his eyes, no longer the perfect Adonis Lady Alexa ben Seamus had coveted above all others. "I should have burned it off. I should have run into the flames and disfigured myself. Would you have let me go then, Alexa?"

Korah laughed at her folly. "But looks can be deceiving, can they not? I was not the Prince Charming you imagined, was I?" He strolled idly over to the bed and pulled back the blankets, revealing the drugged and naked figure. "You wanted me. I made you want me." He skimmed the tip of his finger over her budding breast, coaxing the nipple.

The woman shifted under his hand, making a helpless sound, but the drugs kept her paralyzed in darkness.

He chuckled in evil remembrance. "My virgin whore, oh how you played the role." He lowered his mouth to her breast and teased it with his tongue. "You would do anything I told you, wouldn't you?"

He dribbled warm oil over her body and began to touch, driving her to the brink. Then, just as he had always done, he withdrew and laughed all the way out the door.

May 6, 963 ME

Horses of Legend - New York - Korah

The morning before the wedding of His Royal Highness Prince Eamonn ben Adam to Lady Marguerite ben Alfonso, Korah sought refuge in the stables, desperate to get a closer look at the Duke of Philadelphia's extraordinary ponies.

Still burning over his humiliating loss, he bristled under the taunts from his peers after the match. It was intolerable. Yet, he smiled to their faces while he imagined beating them to death with his mallet.

"*Guten morgen*, my Esteemed," called one of the grooms. "Ist early to be about. Shall I saddle a mount for ye?"

"Perhaps later. I have come to look at the ponies. You are familiar with these beasts?"

"Aye, that I am." The groom doffed his hat and bowed. "I am Lars, at your service, my Esteemed."

"In what stable were they bred?" Korah asked, eyeing a handsome chestnut.

"The New York Polo club. We've been breeding them for nigh on three years now. They have the same sire." Lars swept his hand down the line. "He is a wicked beastie, but fast as lightning, with good legs and lungs. Too damn smart for his own good, if ye don't mind me saying."

"You stud him?" Korah studied the ponies, noticing they bore similar features.

"Only for our club." A grin broke across the old man's face. "Polo is a competitive sport, aye?"

Black anger roiled in Korah's gut. "This stud, from where did he hail?" Reasoning if he could not get the sire, he would go to the farm that bred him.

"I think straight out of the pit of hell, if you are asking me. He nearly killed two of my grooms, and it is an unlucky mare who is put with him. I dislike doing it. He is Lucifer, in a horse."

Korah lifted an eyebrow and remarked with sardonic humor. "It is a little early for ghost stories."

"El Diablo is no ghost, perhaps a demon. Some say he came out of the fires of Endor. I am inclined to believe it."

"Endor? You may as well say he is from Camelot. The place is a myth, a legend."

Lars shrugged a shoulder. "We hear rumors. They are back."

Korah dismissed him with a snort. "Spin your yarn to some other poor chap. Saddle the bay." He pointed to an eighteen-hand stallion and strode off to await the mount.

He paused at the stable door and said over his shoulder, "I find you have piqued my curiosity. El Diablo sounds like an interesting fellow."

Summer to Winter 963 ME

Correspondence - Prince Adam and Sir Preston

June 16, 963 ME
My dear Esteemed Prince Adam,

May you live long and your rule be prosperous. I trust your return journey to the New City is proceeding with health and safety. I am certain you are finding the people of our kingdom as receptive as we hoped. It is good for you to visit the villages along the way.

I write today with news from Capernaum. Apparently, Prince Korah cut his visit with Lady Alexa short. While Easton assures me the couple appeared to get on splendidly, reading between the lines, I do not believe this to be the case, particularly since Prince Korah departed in the middle of the night, unaccompanied by his retinue and security detail. Being acquainted with his mercurial nature, I expect we will find him at some bawdy house or gambling hall. Rest assured, I will handle the situation with tact and see that he is restored to the fold with as much expedience and discretion as possible.

Your faithful and obedient servant,
Sir Preston ben Worley

August 30, 963 ME
Dear Friend,

It was with great distress that I read your previous correspondence, but I fully expect in the lapse of time between my receipt of it and this day, the situation rectified itself. As you can imagine, Mary is furious.

I, myself, am more concerned. I do not have to tell you how desperate our financial circumstances have become. The dowry and settlement Princess Margaret brought will sustain us, but given our current rate of expenditure, it is imperative we secure Lady Alexa's dowry no later than planned. As such, Korah must be found and brought to heel.

I would have sought a richer heiress for Eamonn, so we did not find ourselves in such circumstances, but Mary would not hear of another. She has been bride shopping for Eamonn since he was born and determined Margaret (which is how she now refers to herself out of respect for her new home) would make an ideal wife for our son. All the persuading I could bring to bear would not change her mind. I must say, traveling with them, she seems to have been right. The newlyweds dote on each other, and in that, I take comfort. I pray Eamonn will enjoy a long and happy marriage, for his mother and I certainly have not.

These are perhaps the maudlin ramblings of a tired monarch, writing injudicious words after too many glasses of claret, my friend. I am weary from the months of travel and look forward to the familiar sight of home, where we will arrive next week. We hope our prodigal son will already be in residence.

Your faithful sovereign,
Adam

December 6, 963 ME
My dear Esteemed Prince Adam,

May your life be long and your reign prosperous. Please express my deepest condolences to Prince Eamonn and Princess Margaret. I was saddened and distressed to hear the news of the Princess' miscarriage but harken to the fact that she is young and healthy. I am certain, before long, all the bells in the kingdom will ring, celebrating the birth of a healthy child.

As per your instructions, I have hired several investigators to ascertain the whereabouts of Prince Korah. Of my volition, I engaged firms in London, Athens, Moscow, the Golden City, Cairo, Rio de Janeiro, Beijing, Calcutta, and Baghdad. Thus, there is not a place on earth where we are not searching, and I feel confident we will soon locate him.

Having lost my own daughter, I empathize with the strain you and Mary find yourselves under. Were it foul play or ransom, I think we would know by now, which leads us to the logical conclusion that he has simply run away, and if that is the case, we will find him.

I am in full agreement with you. We have kept his disappearance private. Neither Easton nor Lady Alexa are aware he has left. To cover his absence, I have dictated several letters to my clerk and posted them to Lady Alexa in the Prince's name. I felt it prudent, given the circumstances of his departure, and did so to quell any lingering uncertainties my goddaughter might harbor. She can be a bit high-strung, and with the delicacy of the situation, I thought a few well-worded lines to play on her girlish emotions would do no harm. I beg your forgiveness if this is impertinent and will cease immediately at your word. It is my only desire to serve your interests and that of the kingdom.

I remain your faithful and obedient servant,
Sir Preston ben Worley

December 30, 999 ME

Sacrifices for the Kingdom - New City Palace - Korah and Davianna

"Duck your head," Korah said as he and Davianna passed under a low branch, riding double on his favorite gelding. "I used to ride in this forest often, and you have inspired me to do so again, my dear."

Davianna brushed a dried leaf out of her hair and looked around the misty woods. "It's spooky."

He chuckled. "Perhaps that is why it has always appealed to me, but I think it reminds me of somewhere else."

"It certainly could not have been a pleasant place." She drew closer to him, absurdly seeking protection from the dormant woods in the arms of a monster.

"It was both horrible and wonderful," he murmured. "Did you encounter any such place on your travels?"

"I think there are many in the world, are there not, my Esteemed?" Dark shapes moved between the trees, darting across her line of sight. She rubbed her eyes, trying to clear her vision, trying to keep her wits about her. After the gut punch, he had let her sleep, but a single hour was not enough.

"Such as?" he prompted.

"Greece, I think."

"Greece." Korah made a disgusted sound in the back of his throat. "Antiochus was a fool who destroyed his own kingdom and never learned to wield the weapon they gave him." He leaned his head around to see her face and said, "You must admit, Alanthia has prospered under my rule, while Greece disintegrated under his."

"I would much rather be in Alanthia than in Greece, my Esteemed."

He smiled, satisfied by her answer. "It was all I truly wanted to do, free the people, give them technology, and restore this kingdom to its former glory. Do you think I accomplished that?"

She recognized his tone of voice; they were on dangerous ground here. After five days, she knew the sorts of things he wanted to hear, but as she thought about his question, she found she could answer in truth. "I saw many lands in my travels, but none so great as Alanthia. You have indeed brought us from the dark ages into the light. The New City is a marvel to behold. Astrid was so excited when we got here."

Korah pressed a kiss to the top of her head. "It is gratifying to hear you say so. You cannot know how it lifts my heart to understand that the sacrifices," he muttered, "were not in vain."

"Like polo? You sacrificed polo so you could rule. You stopped riding in these woods because you were running the kingdom." She closed her eyes and relaxed with the movement of the horse. He was not tense. She was safe for the moment.

"I sacrificed more than polo, my dear."

"I think it was worth it," she whispered, nodding off.

"Was it?" he growled.

Her eyes flew open, alert to the sudden danger. She swallowed painfully, her throat dry and scratchy. "Is there water?"

As she hoped, the segue distracted him. "Water is a fascinating thing, Davianna. I made an extensive study of its properties in my youth. I once stumbled upon a waterfall in an enchanted forest, though my words always fail to capture the magic. There are far grander or more impressive waterfalls in the kingdom, but it was like nothing I have ever seen, bordered by live oaks as tall as the redwoods, the pool below turquoise and clear. I was weary from traveling and filled my canteen. It was the coolest, sweetest water I ever tasted, and when I drank it, I could see."

"You could see what?"

He gave a rueful shake of his head. "I cannot describe it."

Davianna moistened her cracked lips, thirsty like she had always been in Greece. She hated that feeling. "Can you take me there? I would like to drink such water."

"It is a long journey." He sighed and handed her a canteen from the saddlebag. "This is not Rephidim water but help yourself."

Tiny rivulets ran out of the side of her mouth as she gulped the tinny tasting liquid. She smoothed the excess over her chapped lips and gave him back the bottle. "What is Rephidim, my Esteemed?"

"A hamlet," he said, his face becoming a mask of cynicism, "where they grow little girls like you."

She looked up at his face, leery of his expression.

"I should bear that in mind. Angelica found out the hard way."

Davianna drew her brows down in confusion and ventured, "Who is Angelica, my Esteemed?"

He narrowed his eyes; they grew dark and cold. "The horrible part."

Davianna bit her quivering bottom lip and bravely asked, "Then who was the wonderful part?"

Korah sucked in his breath and turned away. "I do not speak her name."

"Princess Alexa, your wife?"

He scoffed, his voice full of mocking irony. "No."

"So, she is not the one." Davianna had paid attention to everything Korah said over the last five days, knowing her life depended on it. And in the strange, fragmented way her mind was working, she seized upon several bits of information and put them together. The answer became obvious. "You had another wife, didn't you, one you loved, who loved you back?"

He lifted a golden and silver brow in surprise and wary speculation. Making a sweeping gesture with his hand, he encompassed the vast forest and the lands beyond. "Eamonn was not the only one who sacrificed for this kingdom, my dear."

June 16, 963 ME

Intrepid Explorer - Upstate New York - Korah

It started out as a rebellion, a lark, a way to thumb his nose at his parents and reject the royal straight jacket they planned to stuff him in. The girl was intolerable. Korah doubted if he searched the globe, he would not find a worse match for him than Lady Alexa ben Seamus.

He hated her, absolutely hated her.

Spoiled and indulged, she looked at him as if he were her possession, a toy. She simpered and pouted when she did not get her every desire, which changed with the direction of the wind. Her thoughts seemed to be confined to gossip or whatever new bauble she fancied, and if the conversation strayed to any subject of consequence, she grew bored and petulant. On the rare occasions she joined him and Easton in discussions of taxes, land management, or policy, Korah discovered Alexa did not have a single original thought in her head.

At sixteen, she fancied herself a flirt and employed a squeaky little girl's voice she must have thought winsome; it made him want to strangle her. She dressed in flounces, ribbons, and lace, and to his discerning eye, she looked like an over decorated birthday cake. Worst of all, she despised horses, hated them. She made a mewling face when he came to breakfast after his morning ride, then fanned her hand in front of her nose and declared he smelled like a barn. He would have hated her for that alone, but there was so much more.

Yet, he smiled and charmed. Prince Korah played the role.

He did it because she was rich, and that was the sole reason for the match. He was not a fool. When the dunning letters began to arrive from his tailor and his club, he dismissed them as oversights, but months later, the bills remained unpaid. When he confronted his father, Adam erupted in a drunken rage, threw an ink pot at his head, and ordered him out of his study. That was when Korah realized something had gone terribly wrong in the financial management of their personal estates.

Taxes provided for the upkeep of their residences, travel, security, and entertainment costs for official functions. However, the remainder of their expenditures were drawn out of the royals' personal estates, and they were in trouble. He understood rescuing the family from financial ruin was his duty but balked at marrying the abhorrent little beast.

So, he left.

In the weeks since the humiliating loss to New York, his thoughts often turned to the mysterious stallion El Diablo, so when he left Capernaum, he decided to see the beast for himself. Espionage and sabotage were not unheard of in polo, so they would never allow a rival, Prince or not, to walk blithely in and check out their secret weapon. So, he bribed a feed delivery driver, changed his clothes, dirtied his face, donned a large-brimmed hat, and drove through the gates.

El Diablo turned out to be more than a horse. He was a phenomenon. Eighteen hands tall, black as onyx without a single white or auburn hair on his coat, he was the undisputed leader of the stable. Korah watched him canter around his paddock, awestruck by the most beautiful animal he ever saw.

For a blinding instant, he wanted to jump on his magnificent back and ride away. They would never be caught. There was not a horse alive who could catch El Diablo, Korah was certain. But cold reason crept in. He was a Prince, not a horse thief, though for this animal, he might make an exception. The futility of it all made his heart sink. The Duke of Philadelphia's New York team would dominate polo for decades if they capitalized on El Diablo's bloodline, which they were.

As Korah stood at the paddock fence, his future stretched before him in depressing gloom. He was to become a perennial loser at the one thing he loved. They would crush him on the pitch and in the Castle. Forced to marry that detestable girl, they would suck every ounce of happiness out of his life, while his mother looked on with disapproval, and his father disappeared into a bottle. They would force him to endure it all while watching his brother, giddy with happiness, in love with his new bride.

Korah turned to leave the New York Polo club, a defeated man.

"Hey, buddy, here's your tip." The head groomsman pressed two shekels into his hand. "Have a good day."

Korah looked at the bills in openmouthed astonishment. Standing there in workingman's clothes and old boots, a world of possibility was born. If he could make money, he could disappear into the masses, just check out and enjoy his freedom, at least for a little while.

He would ultimately have to return to the Castle. He knew that. They always found him eventually, and he was not delusional. Resigned to the inevitable, he would still have to marry that girl, but not for two years. Why not enjoy himself while he still could? He managed to steal away before going off to the RMA, and at nineteen, he was a hell of a lot better prepared than when he was ten.

Far from being dour, Korah imagined embarking on a glorious quest and cast himself as the tragic hero, fleeing dragons, in search of a mythical destination and a golden horse, the finest in the land. If he succeeded, then at least one part of his future would not be so wretched. He would still have polo.

He folded the two shekels, put them in his pocket, and vowed never to spend them because they represented freedom.

That day, he began a journey all Millennial Earth would later rue because those two shekels set Prince Korah ben Adam on the path to Endor.

December 30, 999 ME

Pizza in the Palace - New City Palace - Korah and Davianna

"Are you hungry?" Korah asked as he and Davianna cleared the woods and cantered back to the stables.

"Starving," she said, brightening at the prospect of food.

After their ride, Korah felt indulgent and light-hearted. "What do you desire? I shall order the kitchen to make anything you wish."

Davianna chuckled, low and throaty. She tilted her head back and smiled. "When we were in Italy, I had a pizza. It was the most amazing thing I have ever eaten. Not like the pizza we have here. This was different. Neapolitan… oh, I dream of it sometimes." She kissed her fingers in a burst of sunshine, pure Italian. "*Magnifico*, just sauce, cheese, and basil.

"Margherita," he said with a quirk of his eyebrow, "she craved it, too. As I recall. she had the chef try to recreate it. I think in the end, he might have come close. Shall we ask the kitchen to try again?"

Davianna had no idea who he was talking about and did not dare distract him from pizza, so she nodded. Her stomach growled in anticipation.

He rested the flat of his hand around her belly, concave with hunger, young and perfect. "I am the King, so I can give you more than pizza, my lovely. I can give you the world. Would you like that?"

His hand hit a ticklish spot, and she giggled. "I would settle for pizza at the moment, my Esteemed."

He collapsed behind her, laughing. "You are so much like her. She never cared a damn thing about money, or power, or what I wanted to give her."

"Did she like pizza?" Davianna asked with a one-track mind.

Korah wrapped his arms around her and howled. "No. They did not have pizza in Endor, my dear."

She smiled up at him. She liked him when he was like this. "Hmm, well we have pizza in the Palace, don't we, my Esteemed?"

He kissed her cheek, still laughing. "We do, indeed."

July 4, 963 ME

Independence Hall - Philadelphia - Korah

No one recognized Prince Korah. He grew out his hair and his beard, modulated his accent and coarsened his speech, then disappeared into the rank and file of the kingdom. All his life he lived apart from them, above them, removed. In the months of his travels, he got to know them. He discovered what was important to them and realized that while their lives were devoid of money, luxury, and servants, they were happy. Rain fell, crops grew, and harvests were plentiful. Taxes were light, perhaps too light in his opinion. The local baronies and municipal governments functioned well, and by and large, Alanthians prospered.

In Philadelphia, Korah took up with a band of technology renegades and watched in wonder as they showed him a few pieces of ancient technology they coaxed into partial function. Philadelphia became a beehive of technology advocates. Young men, disillusioned with farm life, flocked to the meeting halls and pubs to exchange ideas, dream, and argue. Most of all, they planned.

His group, and a few others, staged a rally, choosing as their backdrop the ancient ruins of Independence Hall. Korah blended with the crowd and listened with avid interest as they delivered impassioned speeches about the unjust restrictions on technology. They railed against oppression and predicted the dire consequences of stifled creativity and passion. The men claimed to represent the hidden desires of an entire generation, who envisioned a future where Alanthians recaptured the glories of the past, where men would once again travel by car and by plane. They extolled the virtues of computing and painted this future world in fantastic, brilliant colors.

Korah paid particular attention to the method of their persuasion, attuned to their cadence, the rise and fall of their voices. Their choice of words intrigued him, and he saw the brilliance of employing repetitive themes and phrases. The crowd seized upon the slogans and shouted back. He dissected their speeches and determined what made a rousing or a dull one. He watched the crowd grow, felt their cheers. Korah saw their faces come alive as they dreamed of a better tomorrow.

As he studied them, their fiery words reverberated in his mind. They impacted him, revealing he was in bondage, as much as they were. He discovered an affinity with these young men and realized he agreed with them. A world of rediscovery awaited. Alanthia's magnificent future could be achieved if they worked hard enough and fought for change. The vision, drive, and resources were here. They must simply seize the moment.

Fireworks exploded at the end of the speeches. Standing outside Independence Hall, marveling at the dazzling sky show, history repeated itself. A radical revolution was born.

December 30, 999 ME

Behold the Future - New City Palace - Korah and Davianna

Korah ordered the kitchen staff to prepare Davianna's pizza for lunch, then called across the foyer to Davianna. "Come, I want to show you something."

Davianna stared up at the ceiling of the vast entryway, entranced by the sky blue and white dome the skilled craftsmen created. The ornate plasterwork was studded with tiny lights that shimmered like stars in the gray afternoon. When she realized Korah was speaking to her, she smiled and said, "Yes, of course, my Esteemed," though she did not have the foggiest notion of what he suggested.

As they walked down the hall, domestic servants stopped their duties and demurred with bows and curtsies. Davianna noticed Korah called them each by name, spoke an encouraging word, or complimented them. He was the most incongruent, paradoxical man she ever encountered. Currently, he had a spring in his step, like a boy headed to the playground.

"Where are we going?" she asked as they turned down an unfamiliar hall.

"You will see." He grinned as two huge double doors came into view. He paused just outside. "When I was a young man, I envisioned a future for Alanthia. Let me show you what I dreamed." He punched in a security code and a lock released on the imposing doors.

Davianna's breath caught as she saw the chamber beyond. He took her elbow and ushered her inside. "This is the data center for the Palace." He nodded as a dozen workers sprang to their feet. "From here, we monitor not only the security on the grounds, but the entire kingdom."

They walked between two rows of long tables and workstations; huge banks of monitors covered the walls. "And it is not just security, but weather patterns, health threats and diseases, both human and livestock. We can direct resources, avert disasters, and respond rapidly anywhere in the kingdom. Before this advancement, it might take months to even receive reports, now we have the information we need almost instantly."

They moved through another set of doors, into what appeared to be a gallery, a museum of technology. Crystalline lights illuminated glass cases with screens mounted above each exhibit.

Their first stop was transportation. Model cars, motorcycles, planes, trains, and boats of various sizes sat on blue velvet. The motion activated video began a documentary detailing the rise of Alanthian manufacturing, the revolution of transportation, and the benefits it delivered to the kingdom.

Davianna turned dreamy eyes to Korah and said, "The first car ride I took was in the New City. I liked it better than the plane."

He raised an eyebrow at her and remarked sardonically, "The plane from London?"

She became wary, but there was no reason to lie. "Indeed."

He nodded with acceptance, but instead of interrogation he surprised her by moving on to the next display—communications. Davianna controlled her expression but could not stop the rush of blood to her face. Inside the case, inches from where they stood, lay a perfect replica of the Black Key. Her heart hammered, and it took every bit of self-control she possessed not to touch her left pocket.

The video began, detailing the rise of computing and the life-saving aspects of rapid communications. She stood on shaking limbs, glued to the screen. Afraid to breathe, afraid to look at him, she braced for the next blow, the next assault.

It did not come.

He did not say a word, he simply put a gentle hand on the small of her back and showed her his museum. From heavy manufacturing to public utilities, to advances in medicine and agriculture, Korah showed Davianna the amazing achievements of Alanthian technology.

At the end of the tour, he paused, lost in thought.

She looked around the room, impacted by the gallery. "It is extraordinary, everything you have accomplished."

He met her eyes, his strangely vulnerable, imploring. "I did not do it alone, Davianna. Citizens of the kingdom, just like you, gave their time, their talent, their treasure." He gestured with his hand. "They made the sacrifices. I became the facilitator."

She blinked up at him.

He was asking, not demanding or browbeating; he simply showed her what he had done.

Staring into his hazel eyes, she whispered, "I wish I had something to give you."

His brow lifted in speculation, but for once, there was no lurking violence behind his eyes, only the infinite patience of a man who soared to the heights of success. When he smiled, she saw he was conceding, at least, for the moment.

Korah took her elbow and eased her back through the doors, into the operations room. "The staff here can manage and report on everything across the kingdom if they must. Most work is done off site, but we have state-of-the-art equipment in the Palace in case of emergencies."

He paused and addressed the man who appeared to be in charge. "Have you diagnosed the system anomalies I read about in this morning's report?"

The head data engineer bowed, "We are working on that, my Esteemed. We are experiencing intermittent power disruptions that drain the system. We have been unable to determine the cause, but rest assured, we will discover the source and root it out."

Korah raised an eyebrow, his amiable demeanor gone in an instant. "See that you do. We have a large contingent of guests arriving tomorrow."

"Yes, my Esteemed, we will be ready." A faint sheen of sweat shone on the engineer's forehead. "Security is our number one priority."

Korah's mouth pressed in a flat line. They departed without a word. Strolling toward the dining hall, his dark mood evaporated. "I showed you that because I wanted you to see that perhaps I am not the wicked King you imagined. I have done some good, Davianna."

October 22, 963 ME

Weary Traveler - Thyatira Woods - Korah

Korah's horse threw a shoe, which forced him to travel on foot, not a terrible choice considering the terrain. He navigated the densest forest he ever encountered, isolated and removed from all traces of civilization. After months of searching, he feared his noble quest amounted to nothing. Mythical Endor was just that, a myth.

There were rumors, to be sure. They swirled in bars and local equestrian events. Any animal that showed extraordinary promise was marketed as having Endorite blood. He suspected this had always been the case, especially in this part of the kingdom where Endor was rumored to have existed.

Yesterday he had a breakthrough when he stumbled upon a quaint village in the heart of this forsaken woods. However, when he made a casual inquiry about Endor, the locals grew suspicious, and all conversation stopped. They remained polite, but the twenty or so hulking men who came to the pub to bid him farewell made it clear he was not welcome to stay. Korah obliged and left Rephidim without spending a night, but he judged by their reaction he was close.

It was the water, he swore it was, something magical lived in that water. He took a sip from his canteen and a path opened, the woods came alive, and Korah could see. His breath caught, and he suppressed the urge to run toward his destination. He made it. He was here.

Then, so was she.

She burst out of the dense forest, riding a magnificent white horse. Blocking his path and standing in the stirrups, she aimed a weapon straight at his heart. A gentle wind blew the long blonde hair away from her face as she stared down the barrel of a pistol. "If you want to live another moment, you will turn your horse around and leave."

She spoke with a heavy German accent that suggested English was her second language. His eyes widened, the Endorites were rumored to be German speakers. "*Fraulein*, I mean you no harm. I have traveled for months, searching the kingdom to find you."

"Say all Rephidimite spies." She scanned the thick woods, wary of attack.

"I am no spy." He dropped the horse's reins, doffed his hat, and bowed with polished ease. Throwing caution out the door, he went for it. "I am Prince Korah ben Adam, and I would like to buy a horse."

As he hoped, that got her attention. She narrowed her blue-green eyes, studying him, but did not lower her weapon. She rode a fabulous white mare, but the incredible animal did not eclipse her stunning beauty.

"The Mistress will know if you are lying, and if you are, you will die." She cocked her weapon, mocking his claim. "Do you still wish to proceed, Prince?"

No one mocked Korah. He resented her tone and did not appreciate having a weapon trained on him. "The Mistress?" He adopted a relaxed, indolent posture, but inside his heart thumped.

"She rules Endor." She tilted her chin up, full of arrogant pride. "Many have sought our destruction. They do not win."

His face shone with innocence and threw his palms wide, showing her his open hands. "I am a potential customer."

She gestured with her weapon at his lame horse. "You have money?"

"Am I being robbed?" he asked, royal disdain oozing from his pores.

"If you come to buy a horse, you will have money in those saddlebags." She shrugged and aimed the gun between his eyes. "If you come to spy, you will have none. Then I will shoot you, and I do not miss, Prince."

"Well, you are a hell of a welcoming committee." Korah rolled his eyes and went to his saddlebags. Living as frugally as he had, most of his escape cash remained in his saddlebag. "Gold or cash? I have more cash, it is lighter, makes less noise." He shook a hefty bag of gold in demonstration.

"If you are the Prince, where are your guards? Where is your retinue?" She sat down in the saddle and uncocked the pistol, though she did not stow the weapon.

He raised a cynical brow at her, money always talked. "I have gone rogue, in search of you."

She scoffed, deep and throaty. "Perhaps you are the Prince."

Adopting an exaggerated royal cadence, he asked, "Why do you say that?"

"Because no one from Thyatira would dare face the Mistress if they were lying. They know." She looked at him like a cat with a field mouse. "Do you?"

"She is the proprietor of the famed stables of Endor?"

"Even the Mistress does not command the horses of Endor." She patted the neck of her magnificent animal and whispered in its ear, "*Habe ich recht, Fräulein Blitz?*"

The horse tossed its head in agreement, stamping a hoof.

Korah observed the pair, decided he was no longer in imminent danger of being shot, and quipped, "All right, I believe this is the part where I say, take me to your leader."

The Black Mansion–Endor

They bred more than beautiful horses in Endor. At fifteen Korah discovered the kingdom's maidens were at his beck and call. In the years since, he became a connoisseur of women and horseflesh.

Endor was heaven.

The Mistress was stunning, even as jaded as he was, she took his breath away. She descended the curving stairway of her opulent manor house, dressed in red from head to toe. His mother would hate this woman on sight, though Korah held no such prejudices. Blonde hair cascaded down her back, stopping just below her tiny waist. She filed her nails into sharp talons and painted them crimson. She held a black lacquered cigarette holder, the red tip glowing in the dark hallway, pearling gray smoke behind her as she swayed her hips, walking toward him—a vision.

"Well, well, well look what the cat dragged in." She eyed him with amused glee. Without a word, simply a flick of her hand, his gorgeous escort and the manor's servants departed.

Her haughty arrogance exuded power. He recognized it. He had perfected it.

She took a long drag off the cigarette and exhaled in leisurely contemplation. "I am Angelica ben Omri, Mistress of Endor. I have been expecting you, Korah ben Adam. Do come in."

December 30, 999 ME

Caffeine Makes Everything Clearer - Korah & Davianna

They both agreed that while the chef made a valiant attempt, pizza in Italy was superior. But the kitchen staff got one thing right, espresso. From the first shot, Davianna felt power surge through her body, sweeping the misty haze away. Invited to drink her fill, she did. After her third shot, she spun around from the side table, her pupils dilated, making her eyes black and shining.

"This stuff is amazing," she declared. "Rephidim water? Whatever. Espresso is a revelation. I feel so much better. I am not sleepy at all. What do you want to do, my Esteemed? Let's run!"

"Run?" Korah laughed, a true easy laugh, without the mocking humor that usually accompanied the sound. "I am fifty-six years old, Davianna ben David, and I am the King. I do not run." Laughter punctuated his words. "I pay others to do it for me."

She put her hand over her heart, grinning. "How does that work?" The absurdity caught her just right, and she laughed, "Can you see Barton running?"

He imagined the sight of his dignified valet running, incongruent and absurd. "No, I cannot," he chuckled.

Then she made a mistake.

With a jaunty point of her finger, she said, "You should make Reginald run. He is mean as a snake."

Korah froze, and all humor left his face. He threw back his chair and stalked across the room, squeezing her arm in a python's grip. "Reginald is doing his job, my dear. Do you know what would happen to you if he did not?"

Davianna tried to make herself very small. She brought a protective arm over her belly and asked meekly, "No, my Esteemed, I do not."

His face transformed, becoming a mask of pain. "They will come. They will take you, and they will kill you. They have done it before." His voice faltered and his eyes looked past her. "It will not matter what I say or do. It will not matter what I want."

He closed his eyes and pulled her into his arms and squeezed. "If my father decided…" his words died as she felt tremors running through his body, his breathing shallow and rapid.

"It's all right," she murmured, letting him hold her.

"Oh, how I hated him. He was a weak coward who let that bastard and my mother run the kingdom because he was too drunk to do it."

He released her and walked to the window, staring out at the mid-afternoon sky, growing cold and gray after a moment of sunshine. "Do you know what he did? He squandered our money, gambling. He bet the horses and lost everything. Then he climbed in a bottle and never came out.

"Not that I blame him for drinking. They married him to my mother, after all. But he never stood up to her, never told her to shut the fuck up. He just took another shot and disappeared."

"I'm sorry," Davianna said, keeping her distance. She could not see his face, could not tell if he was the nice king or the mean one but suspected she might be seeing the true Korah for the first time.

"They were never that way to Eamonn, only me."

Silence filled the room. Davianna was scarcely able to breathe, fearing what might come next.

He wiped his nose and cleared his throat. "Why am I telling you this?"

"Because, my Esteemed, you are human, and we are friends, even if you are kind of scary sometimes." Davianna's voice grew fainter as her courage floundered.

He looked over his shoulder. "I have a right to be scary."

"I do not think I would have understood that a year ago, but I do now." She moistened her lips, staring at the set of his shoulders. He stood proud and broken at the same time. "Can I tell you something?"

Korah turned, intrigued by her tone of voice. "You may."

"I stabbed a man when we were in London. He tried to grab Astrid, and I drove my knife into his chest. I watched his eyes when I did it; it shocked him. He was a swine who hunted us for months. I suspect he played a role in killing my friends in Greece, Portia and poor George, Mrs. Gingle and her toddler, Nico… Astrid's parents. He killed them all, and I wanted to kill him. I have never lost a moment's sleep over it. I would do it again."

Something rose inside her, and she strode across the room, brimming with fury. "You told me that if I stayed with you, Astrid would be safe. Do I have your word?"

"You saw your friend Astrid leave yesterday. She is safe. You will stay? You will let me take care of you?" He reached out and traced her jaw with his finger, using a delicate touch.

Davianna grabbed his wrist and squeezed. "You are lying to me," she hissed through bared teeth.

He stretched his neck forward, coming nose-to-nose with her. "So are you. You still have it, don't you?" He seized her upper arms and gave her a neck snapping shake.

"Stop!" she shouted, clawing at his hands.

"Little Davianna wants to play, do you? You want to step into the ring with me?" he snarled. "Come, my dear, I think it is past time we end this charade."

She tried to jerk away, but the snap of a blade drew her up short.

Staring straight into her eyes, he held the knife to her neck. "Do not fight me, or I will slit your throat where you stand."

Then he spun her around and licked the side of her face. "If we are keeping score, I have racked up far more kills than you have, little girl."

He moved with her to the door. "Let's pay Eamonn a visit, shall we?"

Part 5 - Bonds & Bondage

A Word of Advice - Endor - Korah

Korah emerged from his meeting with Angelica ben Omri, amused. The woman was utterly insane, and from experience, those types were best avoided. He traveled to Endor to purchase a horse, not dive down some rabbit hole with a lunatic. However, she held sway in this little hamlet, and he recognized power when he saw it.

"I see that you are still alive." His blonde escort came alongside as he descended the black stone steps of the manor house.

He flashed her a cocky grin. "Apparently, I was telling the truth."

"*Ist* good to know." A satisfied smile hovered in the corner of her mouth. "She would be displeased with me if I brought her a spy. You would be dead, and that would have been a waste." Her German accent rendered w's into v's, which Korah found charming.

"A waste? I suppose that would depend on who you asked."

She frowned in mock condemnation. "Oh, you are a scoundrel? Many papas in the kingdom wish for your demise? Are you a despoiler of innocent girls?"

"They are not so innocent anymore." He winked.

She laughed, a sound of easy humor, musical. "At least you admit you are a reprobate. I would not have believed you otherwise."

He swept his hands over his body, presenting himself for her inspection. "What is to say those women did not seduce me?" Holding his arms open, his lecherous grin invited her to do the same.

She tried not to smile, giving him an appraising sweep of her blonde eyelashes, but she could not hide that she liked what she saw. "May I give to you a word of advice?"

"By all means. I am a stranger in a strange land," he said as they strolled companionably down the cobblestone street toward the outer row of stables.

"Do not sleep with the Mistress whilst you are here." She gave him a rueful frown. "She kills her male lovers. Like a black widow spider, she mates with them, then they die."

Korah lifted a golden eyebrow. "Her male lovers?"

"I think she prefers the females. They tend to live longer."

Heat rushed to Korah's loins. "And are you one of her lovers?"

She grimaced and furrowed her brow. "No. I am a Horse-woman of Endor. Even the Mistress does not touch one such as I. We were here before she came. We will be here after she leaves. This is Endor."

"According to the monologue that woman just delivered, every inhabitant of this place does exactly what she tells them to do." Korah's face registered his skepticism over such a claim. He knew the nature of rulers. "No one, not even the Iron King, exercises the level of control Angelica ben Omri claims."

"For most, she does." His escort nodded a greeting to a group of residents as they strolled past. "She does, do not doubt. But for the ones such as I, we are perhaps a bit more pragmatic. We are the horse people, Guardians of the Blood."

He furrowed his brow, but before he could ask her to elaborate, they reached the first row of stables.

Her face shone with pleasure, and she asked, "Do you like horses, Prince, or are you simply here for the legend?"

"Both," he breathed, almost speechless at the sight of the most gorgeous animals he ever beheld.

"Honesty again, such a rare quality." She took his elbow. "Come, meet the horses of Endor."

Korah blinked, dumbstruck. "What is your name?"

"They say to give a name is to give away a part of your soul. I do not yet know if you are worthy of my name. Perhaps you will earn the right to know it."

With those words, she turned and opened the gate.

For the second time that day, Korah ben Adam entered a world with a woman who would change his life—forever.

October 31, 963 ME

1 in 4 - Endor - Korah

"*Guten morgen*, Prince."

"Good morning, darling," Korah replied, leaning against the door of Heilig's stall, the three-year-old stallion he wished to purchase.

"*Ist* not my name. Try again." She shot him her toothy smile, a teasing gleam in her eyes.

Twelve days after arriving in Endor, the game was still afoot. He could have discovered her name from one of the villagers. He might have asked Angelica, who jumped at any opportunity to demonstrate her power. But he did not. He found he rather enjoyed their little contest and set about convincing her to share it with him. Thus far, he had been unsuccessful, though not for lack of trying.

He thought once she saw his manner with the horses, she would tell him. She had not. He expertly worked with the horses and rode like the wind on every mount she presented him, demonstrating his prowess and skill. Yet still, she withheld what he wanted to know. He worked with her, side-by-side, in the stable every day. She thanked him and left for her own tiny house, four doors down from the one he rented. He brought her breakfast and lunch. She would not go to dinner with him. He flirted, teased, and made her laugh. Still, she kept her secret.

Last night, Korah tried a different tactic, showing up on her front porch with flowers. She accepted them, then shut the door in his face. She refused to sell him the stallion, even after he offered her all the money he had, quadruple the value of the beast. It became the biggest challenge of his life, to earn a stallion for his stable's bloodline and a name from a girl.

"Will you ride with me, Sally?" Korah took down a saddle pad and draped it over his arm. She did not react to the ridiculous name. She was no more a Sally than he.

"Princes ride the day away. I have work to do here."

Her tone brought him up short. "What is wrong?"

She pursed her lips and gave a faint motion with her head toward Heilig. "Nothing. Go ride."

Korah noticed the stiff set of her spine and asked again, "What is wrong?"

This time she looked away, holding herself rigid. "You should leave. I will sell you Heilig, but you should go now."

"Why?" he asked. Her angst transmitted across the stable, forming an icy stone of dread in the pit of his stomach.

"Endor is no place for a Prince, especially today."

He replaced the saddle pad on the neat stack. "What is different about today?"

"*Vergiss esm,*" she said, waving him away.

He needed no German to understand he was being dismissed. He had a lifetime of experience. But she did it without a cruel twist to her mouth, without judgment. This was different. "I do not think so." He walked toward her. "Not until you tell me."

She looked at him from beneath her luxurious golden eyelashes, her expression weary and troubled. "Until I tell you what? My name?"

"Among other things," he countered, not breaking stride.

Her shoulders drooped in resignation. "*Ist* merely a game to you."

"Perhaps," he conceded, standing in front of her. "But it is not to you, and I would know why."

She touched her collar bone, holding the flat of her palm over it. "Because they will fight tonight. You need to go. Do not involve yourself any longer here. *Ist* not safe."

"Who will fight tonight?" he growled, not going anywhere.

The look she gave conveyed that she thought he was dense. "The Mistress, she will ride against Rephidim tonight."

He had noticed an increased tension among the residents as he made his way to the stable. Now he understood the source. "What is this feud?" he asked, though he had his suspicions.

She shrugged and turned away. "You should ask her. She is clear on the subject. I am not."

"Tell me," he coaxed, his voice pitched low with a hint of a challenge.

"Spies and lovers are not the only people she kills." She pointed to a graveyard beyond the boundary of the town. "That ground is full of my family and those who have tried to go against her, Prince. I wish not to join them, but if you keep bringing me flowers, you will soon be laying them on my grave."

"She would kill you because I brought you flowers?" Korah

asked, incredulous. He understood Angelica's volatile nature but could not believe she would commit murder over a bouquet.

"She has killed for less." With those words, she strode out of the stables.

He froze for an instant, then followed her, enjoying the view despite the gravity of the conversation. She moved with effortless grace. He appreciated the curve of her forearm, lean muscle and tendon, over sun bronzed skin. It was strong, yet there was nothing masculine about it, an odd thing to admire in a woman, but he knew the power that rested in her arms. They aimed a weapon at him, controlled thousand-pound stallions, and hefted heavy bags of feed. He wanted her to wrap those lovely limbs around his neck. He wanted her.

"She is not my lover, if that is what you believe," Korah said, coming up behind her. He did not touch her yet stood close enough that his breath brushed her skin.

She gave a faint snort. "That matters little."

"Then *you* should leave. If she is as dangerous as you say, you should go." He did not add that he would take her and her horses. She would not even tell him her name, let alone run away with him.

"Many have tried. Many have not been so fortunate to do it on their own, and those who succeeded?" She bowed her head. "Their horses die."

Korah looked at the blond Friesian cantering around its paddock, tossing its flowing mane and extravagant tail. The stallion was gorgeous and proud, like her. Korah surmised, as a dressage horse at the Hewies, he would be a champion. Here, he was just an Endorite horse, one of a hundred in his class. The thought of the horse's death sickened him. "That is ridiculous," he protested. "Only the Iron King has that power."

"The Mistress, she has tapped into something old, and it is not light." She turned her head, measuring her words, glancing at him sidelong. "She is intent on raising darkness. I do not question. I just try to stay alive and keep my horses from the dust."

"What can I do?" Gooseflesh pebbled his arm, and he had a sudden eerie feeling they were being watched.

"You can leave and never speak of this place. She will probably let me live."

"Probably?" Korah asked, feeling a bubble of dark fury.

"It might not be politically expedient for her to kill me," she said morbidly, staring off into the distance. "I am the last of my line, and it is said that when the Guardians of the Blood are gone, judgment will befall Endor. There are only four of us left. So, you see, I have a twenty-five percent chance that she will not murder me in my bed."

He stepped in front of her, beholding her beautiful face, her shimmering blonde hair, her sun-kissed perfection. She enchanted him, beguiled, and challenged him. She made him laugh. Some days, he forgot who he was, forgot the outside world, forgot his dismal future. "I would know the name of the woman I bargain with Jezebel for." He did not touch her. He did not move. But from the moment they saw each other, it was going to come to this; they were inevitable.

"She will probably then kill us both," she whispered.

"I do not believe she is stupid. You are a Guardian, and I am two heartbeats away from the throne. We are far more valuable to her alive than dead."

Her indifference melted as she looked at him, heat and passion burning in her eyes. It sparked between them, wild and dangerous. "There will be more than just the Mistress who would seek my death," she ran a delicate finger over his jaw, "for simply touching you."

Blood rushed from his head to the center of his being. He desired her beyond anything in heaven or earth. "Then you and I must outsmart them."

"Said the moth to the flame?" She moistened her lips and moved within a hair's breadth of his body. "You should go, Prince, while you can, for I cannot."

He made a low masculine moan of pleasure. Without ever touching her, without even knowing her name, Korah ben Adam knew in that moment that his soul had found its mate. "Your name," he gasped, "tell me."

She brought her lips just above his, a whisper before a kiss. "I am Sussanna."

And as she predicted, she did indeed give him a piece of her soul in the telling. He seized it like a starving man. But he did not know, when it was all over, that tiny part of her would be all that remained of his own soul.

December 30, 999 ME

The Last Vestige - New City Palace - Korah, Davianna, & Josiah

Davianna pushed her body into Korah's, trying to lessen the pressure of the knife at her throat. The noises she made sounded like a woman in bed, and it set him aflame. Her frenzied terror when he opened the passage door to the dungeons nearly sent him over the edge. The perfume of blood, the power of sulfur, the intoxicating lust of domination consumed him.

Korah heard the chains rattle and the echo of Eamonn's cry in the darkness. "Oh, let the games begin," he taunted and watched the ghost of his brother's face grow pale as he presented the girl.

Davianna clung to his forearm, desperate to break free from the glimmering blade.

"Shall I kill her?" Korah snarled, feeling power course through his veins.

"You wicked bastard, let her go," the Prince bellowed and lunged against his chains.

"What fun is there in that?" He raised a cruel eyebrow and grinned. "It is justice, retribution for what you did."

"I have never wronged you, and there is no justice in murdering an innocent girl, Uncle," Josiah snarled, his chest heaving.

Uncle, the title crashed through his brain. He had been seeing Eamonn, but his brother was dead. It was his son, chained and staring daggers into his heart. Regaining a bit of his equilibrium, Korah smiled. "Perhaps I will kill her for the pleasure of feeling her blood run over my hand. You know the intoxicating power of a cut. Don't you, Doctor?" He ran the blade feather-light over the girl's body. "You are a man such as I, one to cut, burn, and bleed."

"I am a healer. You are a butcher. We are nothing alike."

"Ah, so you claim, but even butchers have talent." He threw Davianna against the cell with a sudden crash. By reflex, she caught herself before her head smashed into the cold steel. He pounced on her, pressing her face between the bars. "She is pretty, isn't she? It would be a shame to cut her up."

Davianna sobbed, blind with terror, her eyes fixed on the stone wall.

"Don't," Josiah snarled, his voice cracked with fear and anger.

"Give me the key, Davianna," he whispered in her ear, smelling her terror.

Her body convulsed against his. "I don't have it. It was taken from me in London, by a Gune."

"You are still lying to me!" Korah screamed, outraged by the stubborn temerity of the girl. He snapped a handcuff around her wrist, binding her to the cell bars. "I see I will have to employ further persuasion."

Then he left her, backed away, and disappeared down the dark passageway, his footsteps steady and ominous in the silence.

"Davianna?" Josiah panted.

Her head lolled, and her knees gave way. She jerked in pain as the manacle bit into her wrist, and she pushed herself back up with a faint, mewling cry. "He's going to kill us."

"No." Josiah's hoarse voice denied what they both knew to be true.

A sinister whirring noise came out of the depths of the passageway, a high-pitched song of destruction. Korah moved into the light, swinging a polo mallet with a horseshoe nailed to the end. "You wanted to see me play polo, Davianna?" he jeered.

She shrunk away. "No, not like that, please?"

"Please?" he mocked in a high-pitched imitation of her, then hissed like a viper. "What will you give me?"

She tossed her head, refusing to look at him and his chosen instrument of torture.

The metal of the key in the cell door sounded like hell being unleashed.

Korah did not say another word. He simply struck. Chained as he was, Josiah could do nothing but absorb the blow. The weapon hit him full force in the right thigh.

"Open your eyes, or I will kill him!" Korah demanded.

With a great intake of breath, Davianna forced herself to obey.

"What will you give me, Davianna?" He smiled and struck again.

Josiah gagged as the mallet found purchase in his gut.

Davianna covered a scream with her hand. Tears blinded her. "What do you want that I can give?"

"You bargain for his life?" he laughed. "It is a powerful motivator, is it not?" He wielded the mallet again, striking Josiah in the ribs.

"Damn you to hell," Josiah managed through a gasp.

Korah aimed a warning finger at him. "If you speak another word, she will die. This is between me and her."

Josiah closed his eyes against the fury and prayed for the strength to die in silence.

Davianna brought a trembling fist to her mouth. "I know what you want, and it is not the key."

"Oh, is that so?" Korah swung the mallet in a deliberate slow arc, like a hypnotist's watch.

Her body convulsed with each shallow breath, and she turned to the bloody, beaten, and chained figure of Prince Josiah ben Eamon, knowing if she did not do this, he would die. "I will give you what you want, someone to love, someone to hold. I will give you back what was broken." Her face ticked with fear, and she swallowed a sob. "I love you."

Korah knew she did not, knew she was lying, but there remained within him a tiny vestige of the man who once bargained with the devil for the life of another. She did so with more courage and valor than he had. His desire to touch her spirit trumped the bloodlust. His brother's son would die tomorrow, anyway.

He moved out of the cell and dropped the mallet to the stone floor. It clattered with a hollow, unearthly sound. Then Korah took Davianna's face in his hands and claimed her with the devil's own kiss.

Josiah could do nothing to stop him.

Nightmares - New City Palace - Davianna

Davianna dreamed she was back in Geneva, running through a market where German-speaking vendors called for her to stop and buy their wares. She and Astrid were running from the Dark Prince, but Davianna kept trying to tell Astrid that they should not be afraid that he needed their help.

But Astrid would not listen and kept pulling her further away. "We have to get out of here, Davianna! Do not be a fool. It's a trick."

"No! He needs me," Davianna cried and wrenched her hand away, leaving Astrid in the dark.

She ran through the dark alleys of Calais, calling out for him.

"Don't die," she sobbed and turned the corner, finding herself in an evil place, rotten and putrid. She could not see him, but she could hear him calling out. However, she knew if she spoke, the monster would find her.

"I am here," he choked.

She stumbled and fell on a floor slick with blood. Sticky and sickening, it covered her, and she cried out. Gentle hands lifted her off the ground, a soothing cloth wiped her brow. A man murmured reassurance, speaking German. "All is well, little girl."

She turned to thank him and watched in horror as his beautiful face morphed into a beast.

She came awake with a startled cry.

Korah sat at her bedside, wiping her tears with a warm cloth, murmuring German to her. She could not move. She was so tired, so afraid.

"I heard you call out. You were having an unpleasant dream." He looked down at her like an indulgent father. "They can seem so real, can they not?"

"A bad dream?" She clutched her head. "No, it was real."

"What was real? We ate pizza, then you took a nap. Here, let me help you sit up." He fluffed the pillows behind her. "I am worried about you. You are not resting as you should."

"Just pizza?" Davianna asked and began to panic. "No, the Doctor… downstairs…"

Korah shook his head in reproving concern. "There is no one downstairs. That must have been a terrible dream."

Davianna breathed into her hands, controlling the sobs that threatened to burst forth. He did not like it when she cried.

"Come, it is best if you move around a little to shake off the nightmare. Let me take care of everything. I know exactly what you need." He smiled and offered his hand.

"It was only a dream?" she murmured and accepted his hand. "Yes."

As he helped her sit up, she could not fathom why her wrist hurt so badly, but it did not matter. The nice king was here, and everything was going to be all right.

December 5, 963 ME

Bonds - Endor - Korah and Sussanna

When Korah negotiated with Angelica, there had been a cost, and he willingly paid it; Sussanna's life for Korah's favor. However, he threw in a caveat Angelica had not expected—wedding vows.

Jealousy ate a hole in her gut as she presided over the marriage ceremony of Korah ben Adam, Prince of Alanthia, to Sussanna ben Ross, Guardian of the Blood of the horses of Endor. However, as she spoke the words, Angelica consoled herself. She controlled them both now.

The ceremony she performed was utterly pagan but contained enough trappings of a traditional one that it failed to raise eyebrows or elicit questions. Angelica wrapped herself and her brand of religion in light. She employed the right buzzwords, struck the correct emotional chords, quoted their holy book, and twisted its meaning. She let them believe they were walking in genuine faith, but by shining a light in their faces, she blinded them. Along the path, she seduced and persuaded by degrees, until they could no longer distinguish between the two because when the counterfeit holds hands with the genuine long enough, even the righteous can be deceived. It was a ruse, and it always worked.

The incantations, spells, and potions she produced confirmed this ceremony was the beginning of everything. One day, Prince Korah ben Adam would rule Alanthia. The Book of Power foretold the truth, and it was never wrong. Angelica planned to be at his side.

In the weeks he had known her, Korah had never seen Sussanna ben Ross nervous. She was the most self-confident person he ever met, yet she trembled at the altar. The halo of daisies in her hair betrayed her, and he watched the little petals vibrate as she stood beside him. Throughout the celebration, the quivering flowers caught his eye. Outwardly, she was a beaming, radiant bride. Below the surface, she was terrified. He did not know if it was him or their marriage that frightened her, but he determined she would never know a moment's fear from him.

"Sussanna, I believe the time has come for us to retire," he said, taking her hand. For the first time that day, she let her terror shine in her eyes, and it cut him.

"Prince," she breathed and cupped his face, "it is not too late. I will saddle Heilig. You can still escape." Her voice cracked on the last word. "If you take me to your bed, if you marry me with your body, she will own you." She looked around, beginning to panic, and sobbed quietly, "I love you. I love you. I do not want you to do this."

"Shh, it's okay." He pulled her into his arms and whispered, "I will take care of everything."

The crowd gave an uproarious cheer. They, too, knew it was time for the wedding couple to depart. Korah raised his head and smiled, his roguish dimple showing on his cheek. Then he swept his bride off her feet and carried her to their house. As he walked across the square, her long white gown trailed to the ground. The fabric was ancient and fine; its luminescent fire refracted in the sunlight. Her cousin ran ahead of him to open the door.

Korah never broke stride. He never faltered.

As the door closed, he kissed his bride, smelling the daisies in her hair, feeling the tender velvet of her lips. Then he set her on her feet and looked deep into her blue-green eyes. "I will not give up on us before we even begin. Never say to me again that I must leave you."

She blinked back tears and took his hands.

"No one has ever seen me as you do. No one," he cleared a lump in his throat, "has ever even tried to love me, Sussanna."

"But will you die for my love? Could you not carry it in your heart and know that I will always think of you?" She brought their clasped hands to her lips and whispered, "The Mistress will demand everything. Your family will never let us be married."

"They cannot stop us. It is done," he declared. "And I know how to handle a woman like Angelica. She will get nothing except what I give her."

He stood before her, proud, exquisite, and royal. She wanted him above all others, loved him beyond what she could understand or explain, and had since the day they met. "The Mistress, she will take more. I know."

"What I feel for you is worth any price, Sussanna. Let me love you. Let me prove to you that I am worth it, that we are worth it."

"As if our love was the pearl of great price?" she asked with a smile, falling, and there was nothing she could do to stop it.

"My pearl." He kissed her hand where she wore a plain gold band. "What is that in German?"

Sussanna flashed the first genuine smile she had given him all day. "*Meine Perle.*"

He chuckled, "Oh, it's one of those."

"Yes, it is. Like *Prinz*, sounds the same in German and in English. Perhaps it is an omen, a blessing from the Iron King that you should come to this place to be *meine mann*, my husband."

"Will you let me?" he asked with a note of desperation. He did not touch her, knowing if she denied him, he would shatter. "Will you let me make you my wife?"

"Yes," she breathed. He was her destiny, and as she moved into his embrace, she knew she would keep him as long as he and the world would let her.

It was not a royal bedchamber. There were no silks on the mattress, no rich tapestries on the walls, no sumptuous tray laden with delicacies. It was a plain room with a sturdy wooden framed bed and an old chest of drawers that weighed about eight hundred pounds, one her parents bought three decades before. The sheer curtains were drawn, decorated with hand stitched daisies, like those she wore on her head. Beyond the window lay a paddock where a blonde mare and her foal kept company. The walls of the bedroom were painted a creamy white. The wood planked floor, grown dark with age, creaked under their feet. On the bed lay a fine, old quilt, turned down in invitation, showing soft, clean sheets.

He closed the door and beheld his bride. Faint afternoon sun sneaked through the curtains, haloing her in light. Her abundant blonde hair curled around her shoulders and down her back.

Sussanna smiled at him. "I was conceived and born in that bed, and there, you shall make me a wife."

"And you shall make me a husband, and our marriage will be born there." His voice cracked with the tenderness of the moment.

They stared at each other as an undercurrent of nervousness blanketed the room. Korah felt unaccountably afraid. He had taken his pleasure with a dozen older society women who fancied a young Prince in their beds. But faced with his wife, he faltered, suffering a full-blown case of stage fright. After weeks of impassioned embraces leading up to the wedding, they stood across from one another like eighth graders at a school dance.

Her laughter broke the tension as she asked, "Do you know what to do?"

He joined her in giddy laughter and nodded like a simpleton. "I do. We start by taking our clothes off."

She flushed and turned her back to him, saying over her shoulder, "Will you unbutton me?"

His hands trembled over the tiny buttons. Korah, who learned control of his emotions by the back of his mother's hand, could not exert the will he needed to still his fumbling fingers. When he was halfway down the row, he breathed a shaky sigh and rested his forehead on her back. "Who designed this dress? Why would anyone put a hundred tiny buttons on it?"

"It is the Guardian's gown, designed to see if the groom will be patient with his bride."

"That is an evil notion," he said, pressing his lips to her silky skin. "It is abominable cruelty."

Sussanna laughed, "The buttons have had to be replaced many times."

"Oh, it is a challenge then?" He straightened up, and with surprising dexterity, freed her down to the last button.

She turned, an enigmatic expression on her face. "You did well, Husband." Then she lowered the gown off her shoulders and stood before him in pale cream lace.

She was so lovely. It took his breath away, long lean limbs, full breasts, soft curves, with a delicate mole by her belly button.

"Now, we disrobe you," she said, unknotting the cravat at his throat. She unbuttoned his waist coat, took his jacket, and draped it over a rocking chair in the corner, over her dress. He unbuttoned his shirt and sat on the edge of the bed to remove his boots.

She smiled when he rose. "You are perfectly made. It is how I imagined Adam."

He swallowed and said, "Well, they do say I look like my father, but if it is all the same to you, I would prefer to leave that subject for another day."

"Not that Adam. You are silly." She caressed his face and moved close, heat building in her belly. "You are also beautiful. I think now, we touch."

Korah smoothed her skin, touching her with reverence, as he would a priceless vase.

They explored each other's bodies, feeling the lines, the smooth planes, until the last garment lay in a heap, and they trembled with desire. He laid her down gently, tracing his fingers down her belly to cup her rich golden curls, dewy and warm. He throbbed with need but did not rush, did not ravish her. With exquisite tenderness, he teased her into squirming, panting desperation, only then did he mount her.

"Sussanna," he pressed slowly, carefully, cradling her precious face, "may this be the only pain I ever inflict upon you, my love." He felt the barrier break, heard her sharp intake of breath, and stilled. His arms shook, his body screamed for him to move, but he did not. He held her, buried deep within, and waited.

Her breathing quieted, and she opened her eyes. The setting sun burnished him in gold, and he was the most beautiful man she ever saw. She could feel his restraint, saw what it cost him, and gave him a gift. She spoke his name. "Korah."

Then she stretched her arms above her head, arched her back and rejoiced as he made her his wife—binding them, forever.

December 30, 999 ME

Music Room - New City Palace - Korah and Davianna

As they finished dinner, Korah stared across the table, watching Davianna ben David, thinking how lovely she was. He let her wear her own clothes to dinner because he noticed she was less agitated in them. He wanted her easy and relaxed. She promised to stay; he would not give her a reason to run. "Come, I want to show you something."

"All right." She rose, taking his offered hand, moving like a sleepwalker.

They meandered down the darkened corridors, strolling in silence. He touched the small of her back and asked, "Do you like music, Davianna?"

She gave him a dreamy smile and said wistfully, "Do you want to come listen to some music with me?"

He furrowed his brow, confused.

"It was the first thing Astrid said to me, back at the camp." She made a breathless laugh, hollow and rueful. "I went with her. So, I suppose the answer is yes, I like music, my Esteemed."

"Good." He pushed open a door across from his bedchamber. They were in his personal apartment.

Davianna smiled and looked around. "Your music room?"

"Aye. I put it in shortly after becoming the Ruling Prince. It is where," he crossed the floor and opened a large drawer, "I keep my treasures." He pulled out a silver device and waved it between his fingers. "I have perhaps the largest collection of these in the world. Did you know that? Long before we repealed the technology laws, people brought these to me."

A spike of adrenaline went down her spine. She stood still with her mouth slightly agape. "I did not know that, my Esteemed."

"Indeed. And do you know what I did with them?"

"No," she said in a tiny voice, taking a step backward, suddenly very afraid.

"I played music." He smiled, but his sarcasm was witty, not wicked.

She laughed but tried to smother it with her hand. Relaxing a degree, she wagged a finger at him. "That could be dangerous."

"Pff*tt," he snorted. "Music is not dangerous, Davianna ben David. Come here, I will even let you pick the first song."

As she walked toward him, he watched the play of emotions flicker across her face. Unnerved, she tried to hide her terror. She was unsuccessful. Suddenly, it did not matter. The device, he was certain she still carried, became secondary, enjoying an evening with a pretty girl held far greater appeal. "What sort of music do you prefer, blues, rock, dance? Please tell me you do not like country. I cannot abide it."

"I like gospel music."

"I don't."

She gave him a wry look. "Not surprising."

"You are a brave little chit, aren't you?"

She shrugged, but there was an edge to his voice that warned her not to bait him. "I do not know the titles of ancient music. You pick the first song."

"It does not matter." He held the silver device out to her. "There is a list of genres. Just pick one." It was a command. He wanted to see what she knew.

She snatched it from him, irritated. "Fine. Show me how it works."

Coming alongside her, he guided her finger over the selections. "Be careful what you select, my dear. They say music calms the savage beast. If that is true, the opposite is as well."

"I'll keep that in mind," she said, giving him a hard stare.

He chuckled, always appreciating a sarcastic wit.

"This one." She made her selection and handed the device back to him. "Play it."

Korah quirked an eyebrow at her. "There are over one thousand songs on this device, and you pick *Mmmbop*?"

She crossed her arms over her chest and tapped her toe. She actually tapped her toe at him, feisty little thing. "Yes. You said I could pick. I've heard it before. Astrid and I liked it. That's the first song."

"Your choice. I warn you though, I get the next one." He plugged the device in and pressed play. The smile that lit up her face was worth the ridiculous music.

She began to spin, to dance, laughing at his expression. "You are too serious." Backing up with a shimmy, she sang.

As he listened to the words, sung by this unlikely ray of sunshine in his life, he smiled in genuine affection. He crossed his ankles and leaned against the wall, watching her dance, light in an evil world. She was younger than Sussanna had been when they met. Not that she was like Sussanna, but the spirit… that was the same, an indomitable force that refused to let darkness overcome her. And at that moment, he no longer wished to break her.

"You are making me dance alone," she called. Then, Davianna ben David held out her hand.

He took it like a drowning man, going under for the last time.

On and on, they danced, laughing, teasing. She picked lively music; his choices were darker.

At 3am, exhaustion overcame him. Neither had slept more than a few hours for almost a week. He was tired, soul deep, bone tired. "Last song, my dear, and it is my choice." And he knew what he would play. The open chords rang over the speaker, haunting—desperate.

He held out his arms, and she came to him. He felt her body press against his, smelled her floral shampoo. She was smaller than Sussanna, who had been tall and lithe. But he realized he had not held a woman in his arms like this… since Alexa, who danced with him in this chamber the night before she died. He had not taken a lover since. Davianna ben David lit a fire he thought he buried with his wives.

"I will make you my Queen, little girl, and I will love you with all my heart," he whispered a kiss into her ear. "You have given me another chance, and I will give you everything. Say yes."

She blinked up at him, confused. "Your Queen?"

"Indeed."

She swayed in his arms, quiet. When she looked up, the desolation in her eyes cut him to the quick. "I like this song."

He bowed his head to hers. "It is indeed a wicked game, my dear." But he smiled to himself because Korah ben Adam was a master of the game.

Part 6 - Heartbreak

January 1, 1000 ME

Faithful Servants - New City Palace - Korah

Just before midnight on New Year's Eve, Korah went to retrieve Davianna so they could make their grand entrance into the royal gala. At first, he was annoyed to find Reginald not standing guard, but the spattered blood on the door of Davianna's room sent a wave of terror rushing up his spine. He burst inside, fearing the worst, bracing himself to find her murdered.

The room was empty.

He stormed into the hall, ready to tear the Palace apart with his bare hands. Following a smear of blood, he discovered the dead bodies of Reginald, his head of security, and another guard. His cry of fear and outrage brought a contingent of Royal Guards running.

"Find her and bring her to me!" he ordered. In a moment of clarity, he realized the woman he encountered outside of Alexa's room must have been in on the plot. He grabbed a radio out of the Guard's hand, describing the woman. "Find them both!"

He stormed upstairs, angrier than he had been in a very long time. She had run. She left him. Dammit to hell—everything—he was going to give her everything, and she threw it in his face. Bitch!

Alone in his study, his temper exploded. Tearing his shirt, fine pearl buttons flew across the floor, making small pinging noises in the silence. Anguish, not felt in half a lifetime, swamped him, and he cried out in pain. Falling to his knees, he buried his face in his hands and wept.

Unaware of how long he stayed there, when he came back to himself, he realized he was alone in the dark. Staggering to his feet, he stumbled toward the light switch, flipping it on and off in vain. "Why in the hell is there no electricity in this room?"

He opened the door to scream at the servants but found the corridor deserted. "What is happening?" he mumbled. Then yelled down the hall, "Find her!"

Feeling his way through the room, he walked toward the windows. Outside, lines of cars waited to leave the grounds, headed toward a city that lay in darkness. He backed away, his brain awash in confusion and pain, disoriented by the pitch black of the room.

Light… he needed light.

Carefully moving around the familiar study, he found the fireplace and lit a match, gratified to see the servants had laid the hearth. Going to the sideboard, he poured a glass of brandy and downed it in a single gulp, letting the spirits burn his throat and warm his belly. His head throbbed, and he closed his eyes against the pounding. He poured another drink and collapsed into a chair, staring into the flames.

He wondered if the woman he had seen outside Alexa's room tonight had been real or a figment of his imagination. She looked and sounded like his mother, and in the aftermath of Davianna's disappearance, he believed the woman might have been involved, but now he was not sure.

For days he had seen them, the ghosts of his mother, his father, his brother, even Alexa. They haunted the Palace rooms, playing out scenes from the past, ignoring him, as if it were he who was invisible. Several times this week, his father passed him in the hall without speaking a word. However, the man was always drunk, incapable of coherent speech, so that was not odd.

But one ghost had not come, the only one he truly wanted to see. As the years passed, he found it difficult to remember her face, which caused him untold anguish. Sussanna should have portraits covering his walls, decorating his desk. He would have given anything to hear her voice, to see her face, to touch her.

The power he felt coursing through his body these last few days deserted him. His glorious plans lay in tatters. He was humiliated, disgraced, and utterly annihilated.

At length, Korah looked up. Another ghost stood in his study.

"My Esteemed? Come, let me be helping you to your chambers."

"McSwilley, she is gone," he lamented.

"I know. Come now, laddie. You must rest." The aged valet hobbled across the room and offered his hand.

Korah stared at it, perplexed. Ghosts never touched him. He reached out tentatively and found it substantial. He looked up in shock. "What are you doing here?"

His faithful servant smiled with compassion and helped him to his feet. "Barton called me. He said you were having a wee rough patch and asked me to come." McSwilley squeezed Korah's shoulder in reassurance. "We have been through these tough times before, haven't we, laddie?"

Korah closed his eyes and nodded, overwhelmed by the kindness of his long-serving valet. Compliant as a child, the King allowed McSwilley to lead him to his chambers. McSwilley undressed him, clucking like a mother hen over the self-inflicted wounds on Korah's back, remnants of a ritual designed to appease Marduk. The valet ordered a bath with soothing herbs, then dressed Korah's injuries. With the care of a loving parent, McSwilley put the exhausted and broken man to bed. Taking a chair beside him, he watched over Korah while he slept, as he had many nights in the past.

At 4:12 am, Korah rolled over and saw McSwilley. His mind still swirled with confusion, but he spoke from his heart. "You know I never got over losing Sussanna, and I never stopped loving her. But I think perhaps she was right. She knew it was going to cost more than I ever bargained for. It turned me into a monster. I am sorry, McSwilley. I am so sorry."

When Korah woke two days later, McSwilley was gone because they were still searching for his son, Stephen, and his wife needed him.

April 30, 964 ME

Sins of the Fathers - Gilead - Adam and Preston

Prince Adam ben Simon left his study at Gilead to greet his visitor. "Preston, it is a pleasure to see you, my friend."

Preston bowed and said, "My Esteemed, it is good to see you as well."

The friends shared a rueful smile, and Adam was grateful Preston did not ask after his health. He knew he looked like hell. If he ever caught a glimpse of himself in the mirror, he saw the truth. Stress furrowed deep lines between his brows, tobacco carved a road map of broken blood vessels across his cheeks, and the redness of his nose conveyed the damage the alcohol was wreaking in his body. However, Preston did not chastise him, did not preach. He simply smiled and gave his forearm a reassuring pat.

Mary bore down on them like a malevolent spirit in clicking heels and billowing green silk. Adam hoped to have a private word with Preston before giving an audience to the virago, but it was not to be. Her cold hazel eyes narrowed as she regarded them, as if they were excrement on the sole of her shoe. Pernicious disapproval etched lines across her once lovely face. She was fanatical about covering her white hair, but her colorist failed to recreate the rich sable her hair had once been, rendering it a severe dark brown that failed to lend even a hint of softness to her face. But that was Mary.

Adam felt Preston stiffen as she neared. Everyone did that.

"My Esteemed Princess, it is an honor to see you again."

"Court language whence thou addresses me, Sir Preston ben Worley," Mary scolded.

"My most humble apologies, my Esteemed Princess," Sir Preston bowed and murmured to the ground. When he straightened, he met her cold eyes. "Thy beauty always maketh me forget myself."

"Impudent flatterer," she said, but the blossom of color in her pale cheeks revealed her pleasure in his words. "Thou doest not fool me. Come, we shall taketh tea, if thou canst remember who I am and extend proper respect."

Adam let out a long sigh of irritation.

"I am thy humble servant, my Esteemed Princess," Preston said smoothly, accustomed to Mary and her shrewish tongue.

Sweeping from the hall in a swirl of silk, she led the way.

Preston cast a conspiratorial eye at Adam and said under his breath, "She is always so charming."

"Mary is a good mother to Eamonn," Adam replied, a pat answer he used for two decades, an underhanded compliment because everyone knew she was not a good mother to Korah.

They entered the Green Drawing Room, where Mary took afternoon tea and received guests. Refurbished during her pregnancy with Korah, Adam granted her an unlimited budget to outfit the room as she wished, poor compensation, but a gesture, nevertheless. A hand knotted rug covered the wooden floor, done in beautiful swirls of sea mist green, pale yellow, terra cotta, and russet. Fragile chandeliers of blown glass cascaded from the ceiling, crafted into ethereal leaves that blossomed into perfect tulips of Paris green. A master plasterer embellished the ceiling and moldings with delicate flowering vines. Elegant cherry wood furniture filled the room, with the settees and chairs upholstered in sea-foam silk and velvet. White roses and daisies sat in the jade vases that had been a gift from the Prince of Asia upon the birth of their second son. Arched windows provided warm filtered sunlight in perfect harmony with the butter-colored walls. Mary created a beautiful, welcoming room in stark contrast with her waspish personality. Adam always experienced a sense of melancholy in this room because he never managed to reach the elusive softness that lay dormant in his wife's soul.

They observed the protocols of high tea, making small talk about the weather on Preston's journey from New York. After an acceptable interval of time, Mary turned to Preston and said, "The Prince and I require an update on the situation."

Adam rolled his eyes. Mary always referred to Korah's disappearance as 'the situation'. She never uttered his name, nor did she seem unduly disturbed by the prospect that their son might be dead. Sometimes, Adam surmised she hoped he was. Her abhorrence of him manifested from the moment he was born. She would not look upon him, let alone hold or nurse him. The midwife took him away and a series of wet nurses, nannies, and governesses raised him.

Adam bore responsibility for that, and to his shame, had done little to rectify his son's plight. However, after that wretched night of his conception, he could scarcely look upon Korah without re-membering his shame. He did not despise his son, he simply failed to muster the energy to show much interest in him.

Mary discouraged contact between Eamonn and Korah, as if Korah might contaminate her beloved firstborn. Despite her efforts, Eamonn often crept across the Castle to play with his baby brother. He endured more than one spanking and dressing down for defying her, but Eamonn inherited Mary's stubbornness and appointed himself Korah's protector and advocate.

Korah had not taken Eamonn's departure to the RMA well, rebelling in every way imaginable. And three years later, when Korah left for school and found his own friends and interests, the bond between the brothers slackened. The single passion they shared was polo. They were well matched on the pitch, with Korah outshining Eamonn in that single area of their lives. Adam had a hell of a time explaining Korah's absence at this year's Hewies, floating the story that Korah was abroad, sowing a few wild oats before marrying Lady Alexa.

The marriage would be advantageous politically as well as financially. Chief Seamus was held in high esteem by many in the Council of Representatives, who regarded him as one of their own. Preston assured Adam that beneath the spoiled veneer, Lady Alexa possessed a kind heart and a sweet spirit. Preston claimed that, given time, she would grow into an extraordinary woman. Adam hoped he was right. But more than anything, he needed the boy to be found, and the dowry deposited into their accounts. The grave expression on Preston's face did not bode well, and Adam sorely wished for a drink.

"I regret to report, thus far, we have been unsuccessful in locating thy son." Preston aimed the statement at Mary, stressing the word son as if to remind her who they were discussing.

Mary did not flinch. "My son is on holiday with his lovely bride." The look she gave Preston suggested if he wanted to spar with her, she would cut him to pieces, which may or may not have been true since Preston was a talented barrister.

"Spare us the linguistic gymnastics, Mary!" Adam barked. "You knowest well, he is referring to Korah."

She shot him a look of abject loathing, then continued addressing Preston as if he had not even spoken. "As far as thy failure to rectify the situation, it surprises me not. He has been astray for eleven months, so I shall direct the inquiries henceforth. Thou art relieved of thy responsibility, Sir Preston." She looked between the two men, dismissal in her expression and tone.

Adam cleared his throat and glared at her. "I bid thee good day, madam. It is always a pleasure."

"Egad, no wonder you drink." Preston accepted a glass of claret and settled into a leather recliner in Adam's study.

"She has her reasons," Adam replied, using another pat answer he repeated for two decades.

"I do not have to tell you, there are not ample funds for her to undertake a parallel investigation. You are strained as it is."

Adam's heavy sigh rippled the claret in his glass. "She does not know."

Preston raised his ample eyebrows in shock. "You kept that from her?"

"Can you imagine my life in this house, with that woman, if she knew I gambled away the royal fortune?" Adam drained his glass. "You may as well bring me a loaded pistol, because I am telling you, I would blow my fucking head off rather than face that."

"Good god, man, don't even say something like that," Preston exclaimed, reading the truth in Adam's face.

"You have got to find him," Adam urged, pouring another glass, as knives of stress stabbed him in the gut.

Preston grimaced. "We have torn the world apart and found no trace of him. He has simply vanished."

Adam slumped in his chair. "We might never find him, and if we don't, what then?"

"I may have a solution." Preston gave him a sly look. "But it is a deal with the devil."

"If it saves me from the devil in the Green Drawing Room, I am listening."

Preston set his glass on the side table and regarded Adam shrewdly. "Last year, at Eamonn and Margaret's wedding, I had an interesting exchange with Milan."

Adam raised a golden eyebrow, curious. The Duke amused him. He liked the ancient Italian; the man had panache. "Go on."

"It seems the old codger has set himself up quite nicely in Italy and is currently making a fortune."

"Good heavens, we should have negotiated a better dowry."

Preston gave him a pointed look. "We investigated his finances, given what we knew at the time, the dowry was extremely generous."

"But…" Adam prompted.

"There were perhaps certain accounts that escaped our scrutiny."

Adam took a healthy swig and said, "Do tell."

Preston glanced around the empty room, lowered his voice, and said, "There are two powerful families in his duchy, the Martinellis and the Giovannis. They are, how shall I put this politely, enterprising, in the Italian sense of the word?"

"Mafia?" Adam provided. "Bloody hell, are you telling me that my son's lovely bride is a mafia princess?" He threw back his head and howled with laughter. "Mary will have a litter of puppies right on that damn green rug, if you are correct."

Preston grinned and held up his palm. "No, I would not characterize her as such. Milan is not directly involved, so Princess Margaret is as ignorant to his activities as is the rest of the world. The only reason I know is because he approached me with an offer."

"What sort of offer?" Adam asked, still smirking at the thought of Mary having puppies.

"Milan takes a tax, so to speak, on the transactions the two families engage in. In exchange, every year he arbitrates a parlay between them, where they settle disputes, come to agreements, and avoid killing each other. It's good business."

"If you don't count murder, drugs, prostitution, corruption, extortion, or the fact that the Iron King might wipe the entire duchy off the face of the Earth." Adam pressed his lips in a cynical line. "Indeed, good business."

"Well, there is that aspect to consider," Preston conceded.

Adam let out a long breath. He stared at the imposing portrait of his grandfather, who seemed to look down on the proceedings with a disapproving eye. "What was Milan's proposal?"

"The Giovannis want to expand into Alanthia, just them."

"And in exchange?" Adam asked.

"We take the tax directly into the Royals' personal estates."

Adam dropped his head in his hands. "Blood money."

"As dirty as it gets," Preston confirmed.

A groan escaped Adam as he contemplated the first viable solution they had come up with since Korah's disappearance. Mary would never have to know he had lost almost everything. At length, he said, "I suppose we already have crime, don't we, Preston?"

"We do indeed, my Esteemed," Preston replied. "I see it every day in my practice."

They sat in silence for a time. At the bottom of the bottle, Adam turned to Preston and said, "Tell Milan we require ten million in advance. You administer it. I know nothing, and when we find Korah, we end it."

Preston nodded.

And for the second time in his life, Prince Adam ben Simon brought great shame to the royal house of Alanthia.

Sausage - Endor - Korah and Sussanna

"Good morning, Pearle," Korah murmured as he leaned over to kiss his bride.

Sussanna opened a sleepy eye and growled, "Why are you so cheerful, always in the morning?"

"Because I am married to the most beautiful girl in the world." Korah rubbed his nose against hers. "How are you feeling?"

"I do not know yet. I just woke up. Why do you ask me questions and expect for me to talk?" She rolled over in a grunt, hiding under a heap of covers.

He chuckled. "I made breakfast."

"I do not know if I am going to throw up. Go!" she growled.

"Toast and eggs," he coaxed in a sing-song voice.

"Gahhh!"

Korah tickled her foot as he left, which she quickly withdrew, grunting at him again.

He sat at their tiny kitchen table, sipping coffee. It would only take her a few moments, but she needed to rise on her own. She was not actually mad. Sussanna just did not like to talk when she first woke up. He found it adorable and delighted in pestering her every morning. But he had always been an early riser, enjoying the dawn. So, he took over the morning chores, and they fell into a routine. He made the coffee, fed the horses, then he woke her up.

She stepped into the kitchen with purpose. Sun shining through the living room window backlit her, and Korah could see the outline of her body through her white night dress. Her hair was tousled and matted, sticking up in the back of her head. She scowled at him, sleepy and fierce, then a toothy white smile illuminated her face. She was the loveliest thing he ever beheld.

"I am not sick this morning. I am hungry." She raised her hands in praise. The gown lifted and tightened across her belly, a little shy of five months pregnant.

"Toast and eggs," he said, gesturing to the counter.

"I want sausage, too." She padded into the kitchen and poured a cup of coffee.

"You vant sausage?" he teased, mimicking her accent. "You have not been able to abide the smell of meat for months."

She turned, completely unapologetic. "Today, I want sausage. You go get for me?" She strolled over and sat in his lap, stroking his hair. "Please?"

"Well," he said, giving her a lecherous smile, "when you ask like that…"

"Oh, Prince," she whispered very low and seductive, "you know I love it when you get me sausage."

"I've got a sausage for you." He wiggled her in his lap.

She bounced in delight. "You bring me breakfast meat, and I promise I will take excellent care of your sausage. But I am hungry for the first time in four months, and I am going to eat."

"I am going to eat you." He nuzzled her neck.

"You have a one-track mind. I am hungry." She jumped off his lap, flashing him a grin. "I will take you up on your offer later."

He went after her, trapping her body between his arms and pressing her against the counter. "I will get your sausage, because I love you."

"Korah, you make me so happy." She smiled.

The baby kicked, and his eyes flew open. "Was that?"

Sussanna beamed with secret maternal pride. "You felt it?"

"I did," he said, awestruck as he fell to his knees and pressed his face against her belly. "Hi there, little one. It's me… your pappa. I love you."

July 11, 964 ME

Birthday Girl - Endor - Korah and Sussanna

"So, today I am officially married to an older woman." Korah woke Sussanna with a kiss and a bouquet of fresh daisies.

Sussanna buried her head under the pillow.

He opened the drapes, letting in bright sunlight which filtered through the lace, casting flowered shadows across the floor. "That makes you a cradle robber."

"We are the same age. Go away."

"No, today you are twenty-one." He smiled at her. She was covered up, hiding from the day. "I am still twenty."

"You will not live to twenty-one if you do not get out of here."

He laughed, "Pearle, you are so mean in the morning."

"I am not mean. Go!" Sussanna threw back the covers and glared at him.

It was his favorite part of the day, and hers too if the truth be told. But if he asked her that question, she would vehemently deny it. He sat at the kitchen table among the birthday presents, waiting for her. If they had been at Gilead, he would see that she had a roomful of them. Instead, there were only three, and one of them was not much, though he hoped she would like it.

Sussanna peeked around the corner, saw the presents, and gave him a bottom lip pout. "I am sorry, Prince. I was very mean this morning and look at you. You bring me flowers and presents." She sniffed back a sob. "I am sorry."

"Pearle," he soothed and pulled her into his arms. "There is no need for tears. Don't cry. It is your birthday."

"I am terrible. What a mean wife that you have." She buried her face in his chest.

"No, my father has a mean wife." He raised her chin and smiled into her eyes. They swam with tears, the color of the Caribbean. "You are adorable."

She hung her head. "I am a cow."

"You are not," he breathed. "You are a mom, or you will be in nine weeks."

She looked up at him through her blonde lashes, placated. The tears stopped as the promise of their new baby brought a smile to her face. "He will be so lucky to have you as his pappa."

"Yes, she will," Korah countered. "But she will be even luckier to have you as her mamma."

"I wish mine was here." Sussanna closed her eyes and leaned her head on his shoulder. "She would have been so happy. She would have loved you, Prince."

Korah kissed the top of her head but did not comment, knowing his history with mothers was not great. Her parents had died two years ago in an influenza outbreak that swept through Endor. Sussanna never said, but it occurred soon after Angelica arrived. Horses and people perished at an alarming rate before the pestilence subsided.

Korah and Sussanna lived in Endor, but he isolated them from Angelica's little wars and intrigues. He stayed out of the Black Mansion. He knew one day she would call in his debt, but it was not today.

"Come on, birthday girl, you have presents." He pulled out a chair for her and poured her a cup of coffee.

She tilted her head back and puckered for a kiss. "You spoil me."

Korah kissed her and said, "If you think three paltry presents are spoiling, I would love to show you what actual spoiling looks like."

"I like three presents, thank you," she declared in a stubborn, imperious tone.

Korah settled in beside her, resting his chin in his hand. "I hope you will. Open the little one first."

Sussanna flashed him a smile and tore into the pretty blue paper. She gasped when she opened the box. Nestled inside were a pair of pearl earrings. She covered her mouth, unable to speak.

"Do you like them?"

The vulnerability in his face brought her to tears the second time that morning. She threw her arms out to him. "Oh, Prince, they are the most beautiful things I have ever seen."

He sat back from her tearful hug, brimming with satisfaction. He wiped his brow in exaggerated relief. "Okay, good. If those fell flat, the other present was a bust. Open the second small box."

Inside lay a silver chain and pearl pendant necklace with one small diamond. "It is beautiful!" She swept her hair over her shoulder and presented her neck. "Here, put it on me."

The delicate clasp was a little tricky, but he managed.

She pushed herself out of her chair and went to the mirror in the hallway to put the earrings on, then returned to model for him.

"Pearls for my Pearle," he said, smiling. "One day, I will buy you the most exquisite, gaudy triple strand of pearls, but until then, these are a promissory note."

She waved him away. "The horses do not appreciate a triple strand of pearls. This I can wear every day, and no one will think, 'What has happened to Sussanna? She has gone crazy, wearing jewels in the stable.' You know that is what they would say."

Korah raised his brows. "I think Heilig would appreciate a triple strand of pearls."

Sussanna agreed with a laugh. "He is very regal, which is why you like him."

"There is nothing wrong with that," he said, affecting an exaggerated upper-class cadence.

Leaning in, she kissed his cheek and said with great affection, "Prince."

He gestured to the remaining box, feeling his face flush. "Now, this is a dual present, sort of for you and the baby."

Sensing his insecurity, she quipped, "I am sure I will like it, and even if I do not, I love my first two presents. This could be horse apples, and it would still be a wonderful birthday."

Korah laughed. "I have not boxed up horse manure for your birthday. Can you imagine?"

Sussanna had a hard time catching her breath as peals of laughter overtook them. "I would love it," she teased, "because it was from you."

He closed his eyes and smiled. "You are indeed a pearl of great price."

"Of course, I am. Now, I will open my not horse apple present." She had to stand to open the large box, then exclaimed in delight. "You did not! Where did you find her?"

Korah lifted the rocking horse out of the box. It had a fresh coat of paint, a newly refurbished horsehair mane and tail, with eyes of painted flowers. "Up in the loft about a month ago, buried beneath some junk."

"She was mine when I was a baby girl." Sussanna swallowed and sniffed. "My pappa made her for me on my second or third birthday. I thought she was gone."

He thumbed away a tear sliding down her cheek. "Our daughter will ride that rocking horse, and you will tell her stories about her grandpa."

"Korah," she said, overwhelmed.

He closed his eyes, glowing with love. She said his name so beautifully, beginning with a lyrical soft "k", rolling the "r" just so, and ending with an 'ah' instead of 'uh'. No one said it that way.

No one after her, ever would.

March 5, 968 ME

Not as Funny the Second Time - Gilead - Korah and Alexa

Princess Alexa ben Seamus rolled over the morning of her twenty-first birthday to find her husband sitting in a chair, watching her. She startled awake, instantly wary of finding him in her bedroom.

"Happy birthday," Korah said in a droll tone that could mean he was bored, or he was about to do something cruel.

"Thank you." She stiffened and sat up, holding the blankets to her chest. She wore a gown, but the blankets felt like another layer of protection.

He gestured with his head. "I brought you a present."

Alexa's heart began to pound, unable to read his mood. A package sat on her coffee table, wrapped in gold foil, and topped with an extravagant white bow, her favorite colors at the moment. Half her wardrobe this season was gold and cream.

"Go ahead, open it." He sat back in his chair and crossed his arms over his chest, daring her.

"Korah," she growled.

"It's just a little something, darling." His smile did not meet his eyes.

Alexa knew he would taunt her until she opened it. She flung back the blankets and stalked over to the coffee table. When she lifted the lid, she recoiled in disgust. "Oh, that is nasty!"

"I put a lot of thought into that. You don't like it?" He pretended to be hurt.

"It's horse poop!" Alexa's chin quivered. "Who gives their wife horse manure on her twenty-first birthday?"

"Apparently, I do." He raised his chin and regarded her through lidded eyes. "She would have loved it. She would have thought it was funny. I am sure you will go buy yourself something nice."

He rose without another word and left.

September 10, 964 ME

What Will You Give Me? - Endor - Korah

Two days… Sussanna labored for two days, and still there was no baby.

On the evening of the second day, she grew feverish, her strength ebbing with every wracking, futile contraction. She was not progressing, and it became apparent she and the baby were both dying. Korah paced the room completely beside himself. He wanted to kill the incompetent midwife. He wanted to howl at the moon.

This was part of the curse Angelica brought to Endor. He had heard the rumors that no babies had been born alive since she arrived but thought since he and Sussanna did not participate in Angelica's little coven they would be spared. Obviously, he had made a terrible miscalculation. And as the hours dragged on and life leeched out of his wife, he began to reason that if Angelica had brought the curse, perhaps she could counter it.

"Pearle," he murmured in Susanna's ear, "I will be right back. Hold on, baby. I love you."

He left their little house with tears streaming down his face.

Korah and Angelica had struck a bargain. If and when their exile in Endor ended, they would align and help each other in the outside world. Until then, Angelica agreed to leave Korah and Sussanna alone. He knew if he sought her now, she would bleed him dry, demand more, but he no longer had the luxury to care. He did not knock or announce himself. He stepped into the dark mansion and cried, "Mistress!"

To date, he had only ever called her Angelica.

In her study, with the Book of Power open on the dais, and a swirling black potion on the table, she looked up from her incantations and grinned. In a rustle of red silk, she left to capture her quarry. "I have been expecting you, Korah."

His fists clenched at his sides, and he held himself ramrod straight. "Sussanna and the baby are in trouble. Is there anything you can do?"

She smiled, evil incarnate. "Of course, but what will you give me in return?"

"What is the cost?" He did not mince words. Time was not his friend. He had perhaps waited too long as it was.

"Follow me." Angelica left him.

He watched her go, watched her disappear into her library, and smelled the stench coming through the door. Bile rose in his throat. He wanted to run, but he knew if he did not walk through that door, his wife and child would die.

Angelica waited, the ritual already prepared. Painting his face, a skeletal white and black, she gave him some text to read, then handed him a ceremonial knife and bade him cut his wrist. Dripping his own blood into the black potion, she brought the vessel to his lips and ordered him to drink. He did so, without emotion, without regard for the consequences.

He did it to save their lives.

When he returned home, he found his wife sitting up, her color restored, nursing their perfect newborn baby daughter.

They named her Hope.

March 28, 977 ME

Tamar - Gilead - Alexa

Princess Alexa ben Seamus was thirty years old, had been married since she was eighteen, and to her utter frustration and secret shame, she was still a virgin. Not that her husband did not regularly visit her bed, he did, to torture her. He kissed her, touched her, caressed her body, and drove her wild with passion. He brought her to her knees, begging, doing anything he wanted, anything he asked, everything he demanded. Then he would leave her, time after time, after time.

She burned for him, wanted him, feared and hated him. Sometimes, when he touched her, he forgot. On those rare magical occasions, they enjoyed each other's bodies, kissing tenderly, just touching. She loved him. But he never lost control, and he never made love to her.

Her mother-in-law kept track of her monthly cycles through the laundress. Each month she would drop a subtle, biting comment about barrenness. It was unendurable, and twelve years was long enough.

She found inspiration in an unlikely place, a small miniature of a long ago Alanthian Princess. The painting captured something that intrigued Alexa, there was a sparkle in the girl's eyes, and she, too, was a redhead, so that may have played a part. Intending to discover who the girl had been, Alexa dug around in the Castle's archives until she discovered her name and a diary. The diary saved her sanity and provided the inspiration she needed to remedy her predicament.

The young Princess had been betrothed to the Prince since she was five years old, in a contract negotiated with her father, the Baron of Toronto, and the Duke of Quebec. The marriage was meant to soothe growing tensions between the New City and the Canadian territories, and the wedding was celebrated with great fanfare. However, Princess Tamar soon discovered her new bridegroom may have gone along with the wedding, but he had no intention of actually having a marriage.

Alexa knew that feeling all too well.

As the years passed, Tamar despaired she would never have a child. Barren and disgraced, she feared for her future and that of Alanthia since her husband's corrupt nephew was next in line for the throne. Not content to sit back and do nothing, Tamar hatched a plan.

She followed her husband on a hunting trip to the wilds of Calgary. Knowing his penchant for drinking and whores, she disguised herself as a prostitute and went to her husband's bed. When he did not have the funds to pay her, she demanded his royal ring as surety, telling him she would wait downstairs for his servants to deliver her fees, but when the servant sought her out, Tamar was gone. Three months later, when her husband discovered she was with child, he ordered her exiled. But she produced his ring, which saved her life and the kingdom.

Alexa marveled at the daring plan, and for three years she waited. She had been married to Korah long enough to learn his habits. She could predict what would make him angry, understood when to placate him, and when to steer clear. She knew what he liked in bed and how to touch him. And she also knew when he would be most vulnerable. A pattern emerged over the years. She suspected certain dates held significance for him and *her*. She cursed the woman's very existence. Korah and Alexa might have stood a chance if *she* had never come along.

However, she was not the only ghost who haunted her husband. The specter of his father played a bigger role than Korah would have ever admitted. Prince Adam had been gone for seven years, but liver failure was a brutal death, and the ravages of the disease shook the entire household. The violence of his passing impacted them all, consequently Korah rarely drank. He might sip a glass of wine with dinner guests, have an occasional brandy with a cigar, but for the most part, he abstained.

But he made an exception every year on March 28th. There were other dates: July 11th, September 10th, October 22nd, and December 5th. However, the big one fell in March, and even she knew what happened that day.

Alexa had finally stopped denying her part in it. No good came from deceiving herself. She had been selfish, indulged, and spoiled, but also sheltered and naïve. For two years, she believed Korah had written her love letters, and through those impassioned words, she had created a fantasy man, a beautiful golden hero, and she wanted him. He was hers, and she was going to have him, no matter what.

She simply did not know how damaged he was, nor could she have imagined what Prince Adam and Sir Preston were going to do. She thought they would simply have his first marriage annulled—they had not. It took years for her to ferret out the full story, and while she had not committed the deed, she certainly bore some responsibility for what happened. So, she stayed and tried to love him because she played a part in making him who he had become. Alexa was not innocent.

She was also not a martyr, and she wanted a child. Korah owed her that much. Her fortune saved the royal family. He had a duty to the kingdom, to her, and ultimately, to himself. He needed someone other than his dead wife to love, and Alexa hoped a baby might give him back something he lost.

The timing had to be right, she could not regulate her cycle to coincide with his dark days. One year, she was fertile on July 11th, but he went out of town, and she missed her chance. She calculated the various dates and planned forward. In January, she knew she had an open window this March 28th. If he left, she would find him. He was taking her virginity and getting her pregnant, even if she had to tie him to the bed to do it.

They kept separate quarters, which was not unusual in royal households, though Eamonn and Margaret had not. Their adjoined rooms proved to be a blessing and a curse. For years she thought his control would break, that he would come to her bed and make love to her at last. She hoped proximity would entice him more readily than if he had to tramp across the Castle to join her. The strategy backfired, making it easy for him to slip in and out. No one knew what he did to her. The Virgin Whore, he called her, taunting her with that moniker.

Tonight, she planned to drop the virgin part of that title once and for all. But as the evening wore on, she feared for the first time in a decade he was going to remain sober. He did not drink at dinner. He did not drink in his study. When he returned from his evening ride without alcohol on his breath, she despaired all was lost.

Then, she heard him weeping.

He never cried, not that she knew.

She tiptoed into the sitting room between their bedrooms and listened. He was mourning, crying out for *her*. Alexa turned away, unable to bear it, but then she heard him say, "Pearle! Oh Pearle, what I would not give to see you, to touch you, to lie down, and love you."

Alexa closed her eyes and made the decision. She crept into her room, put on the white gown and a wig. She checked her reflection and went to her husband, disguised as his first wife.

When the Pain is too Great - Gilead - Korah

Alcohol was not strong enough to take away Korah's pain. It also made him feel like his father, which was almost worse. This year on the anniversary, he tried something different—mushroom tea.

Angelica procured it for him because she knew how he suffered. At first, he felt nothing, so he brewed another cup, which proved to be a mistake.

When the drug began coursing through his system, he felt a mild euphoria, peace. It was not oblivion, not like the alcohol. This felt pleasant, reminiscent of Rephidim water. He smiled and looked out at the vivid sunset, which shifted and changed, and seemed to pulse with energy.

He liked this. It was nice.

Several hours later, sitting alone in the dark, the sadness hit him, so he brewed another cup. While he waited for the effects to kick in, he did what he feared most, he felt. The drug lowered his defenses, and he cried out in grief, longing for Sussanna with such intensity he thought he must surely die from the pain.

Since her death, Korah had become a shell, a man without emotions, like a store mannequin, beautiful, stylish, and hollow. He cared for nothing and no one. But he donned a facade, played a role, and smiled through official functions, but there was no life in him. He never truly laughed. The best he could manage was an occasional cutting wit. Everyone thought he was who he had always been, amiable Prince Korah. He was not. That man was dead, though his body did not know it.

With the hallucinogen coursing through his veins, Sussanna appeared in his doorway. He wanted to fall on his knees and weep. She looked so lovely in the misty shadows. "Pearle," he called out to her in anguish and opened his arms.

"Shh," she whispered and kissed the side of his neck, the way she always had, the way he loved.

It set him aflame.

He did not care if this was a hallucination, she felt wonderful. "My darling, my darling, Pearle," he cried. "How I have missed you. How I love you." He began to weep as she held him.

"Shh," she soothed again. Then with the graceful elegance that made him cry out, she extended a hand, and took him to bed.

It was beautiful, like it had always been between the two of them. She knew exactly how to touch him, how to set him on fire, it was intoxicating. When he pushed into her body and felt the barrier break, he wept. It seemed so real, so poignant, she even made the same sound. He held above her and waited, waited for the pain to pass, just as he had done all those years before.

Then she smiled and said his name.

He froze.

It was wrong.

It was all wrong.

His eyes focused, the vision shifted, and the face below his body was not his Pearle, it was the treacherous bitch, in a blonde wig.

"You!" he snarled, outraged beyond anything he ever felt. But he was inside her, and his body did not care what his mind screamed. He pounded into her. "You fucking bitch." He repeated the words like a mantra and took her without mercy, without tenderness, without love. He hurt her.

When it was over, he collapsed atop his wife, but not the wife he intended to make love to. Weeping in frustration, anger, and confusion, he looked down on her through his bitter tears and vowed, "One day, I will kill you for this."

In a bed of deception, heartbreak, and betrayal, Prince Peter ben Korah was conceived.

January 6, 978 ME

Like Mother, Like Son - Gilead - Korah

Korah could not leave, he wanted to, but that would run counter to the carefully crafted persona he had built. Before Alexa's deception, he was hollow. Afterward, he became an active volcano, full of molten lava and rage. But he learned to hide his emotions as a child, mastering the art of the mask. He could smile and hold a pleasant dinner conversation while imagining driving a fork into someone's eye socket.

So when the news came that Alexa had gone into labor, he pretended to be concerned and excited, concealing his genuine hope that the misbegotten child would strangle on its umbilical cord and the treacherous whore would hemorrhage to death.

Claiming he needed to burn off some nervous energy, he left the house and went out for a ride. In the fading afternoon light, he tried not to remember another child, another birth. He never let himself think of his baby, ever. Sussanna came to mind often, he allowed her memory, but not his daughter's because he could not bear the pain, it was simply too great. So, he locked her away in his heart, put her memory in a box, and sealed it.

But as he entered the wooded riding trail, her little spirit came with a key and unlocked the box. She did not speak. She had never spoken. Hope was too little, too precious, but he saw her smile. Memories of her washed over him and swept him away.

He felt the reverence of holding her for the first time. She was born beautiful, rare like that. Her little head fit in the palm of his hand. She had been blonde, and her hair stood up in the back just like Sussanna's did in the morning. Her skin was so delicate and smooth, softer than anything he ever touched. She had perfect little hands with pink fingernails. He marveled at them, having never considered how wondrous a baby's hands were until Hope.

She had lived two hundred days. They had been a family for two hundred days.

He dismounted, unable to keep his seat when he could not breathe. Sitting in the dirt, he let the memory of Hope have him. He felt her, smelled her, kissed her silky belly, and heard her laugh. It annihilated him, and he fell over, writhing on the ground in agony.

Hope would have been thirteen now. Perhaps she would have loved horses, like he and Sussanna. He had no doubt she would have been feisty. Willful, even as an infant, she had a personality all her own. She could give him a look, so reminiscent of the expression he saw in the mirror, it made Sussanna howl with laughter. This prompted Hope to do it again, and again. Bored cynicism on a baby's face was the funniest thing they had ever seen, and baby Hope perfected it.

Korah sat in the dust, exhausted with remembrance. But by opening the memory box of Hope, he saw not only his daughter, he found his wife, the mother of his child. She glowed like an angel, her breasts, heavy and full. He tasted them, feeling the primal, elemental pleasure of suckling her while they made love. Her warm sweet milk nurtured him in a way he could never describe, like finding a home he never knew existed. They often fell asleep with the baby nursing between them. He encircled them with his arms, holding them tight, shielding his family with his body. Closing his eyes, he smiled, refusing to let the pain crash in. He held it at bay for just a moment and absorbed their love; he remembered.

After a time, he carefully and reverently wrapped their memories in a box of shiny blue paper and put it away.

When he got back to the house, he learned he had a son. His heart rejoiced. He could hate a son. His mother had shown him how.

Part 7- A Moment in Time

December 5, 979 ME

For Better or For Worse - Gilead - Korah and Alexa

Alexa should never have picked a fight with Korah on one of his dark days. She knew better. However, the announcement he made over dinner clouded her judgment, and after they retired, she stormed into his bedchamber. "What do you mean we are not moving to the New City Palace? Everything is prepared, and the date is set. Two weeks, we are supposed to move in two weeks! We are all going! The entire royal family is relocating. You cannot simply announce that we are not."

When he turned, she saw the monster had him.

"Okay, fine. We will talk about this tomorrow."

"Oh, no. I think we will settle this tonight." Then he moved in that peculiar way, like a snake had control of his body. His eyes turned black.

"No," she cried and attempted to run.

But he was quick, pouncing on her in an instant. He grabbed her hair and jerked. Her legs flew out from under her, and he dragged her across the room. "No, Alexa, you won't get off that easily. Not this time," he snarled. "You don't get to come into my chambers, scream at me, then run away."

He threw her onto the bed. "Moreover, you do not get to tell me where we will live." He crawled after her like a stalking lion, his blond hair wild, fanning around his face like a mane.

She pushed back on her heels, trying to escape. He never did this, never let her in his bed. He never cracked. The rigid self-control that governed his every thought, every word, every outward action, shattered before her eyes, and it terrified her.

"You want to live in the new Palace because your money restored it?" He smiled with wicked delight. "You have been planning this for months, haven't you? Everything is picked out. The nursery is decorated, and you have a new room with electricity?"

He mocked her, a cruel imitation of the way she spoke to their baby. "Did you have your widdle heart set on your shiny new house? Is mean ole bad Kowah denying you what you want? Does it make you want to cwy?"

His pupils elongated and turned into dragon's eyes. His voice grew dark and dangerous. "Does it?"

She stared at him, afraid to move, afraid to blink. He was like a rattlesnake, three inches from her face. "You are frightening me."

He smiled with such diabolic satisfaction that her blood ran cold. "Good," he cooed like a lover. "Take off your clothes, Alexa."

She went rigid. He had not come to her bed since she tricked him. "No, not like this. Not when you are so angry at me."

He threw back his head and laughed. "You stupid woman, I am always this angry at you."

"Will you never forgive me, ever?"

Korah jumped on her, pinning her to the bed. "You set in motion a chain of events that killed my wife and baby daughter so you could have me, like I was a gown you wanted. And for fifteen years, you have never admitted what you did. You have never once apologized or expressed a scintilla of regret for the decisions you made." He shuddered, and the dragon disappeared but it left him open, and Alexa glimpsed the true depths of Korah's pain. "Then on the anniversary of their deaths and your treachery, you… you… impersonated my wife, came to my bed, and raped me."

Alexa gasped, unable to speak, unable to defend herself.

His entire body convulsed, as his voice cracked like lightning. "And tonight, you storm in here, on what would have been our sixteenth wedding anniversary, and demand to know why I no longer want to live under the same roof with my vicious bitch of a mother? And when I react, you have the temerity to say I scare you, then with your next breath demand that I forgive you? What gives you the right to demand anything of me, after what you have done, after what all of you have done?"

"Get out!" He flung himself off of her and covered his face. "Get out of here before I kill you."

He did not have to ask her twice.

January 6, 980 ME

I Cannot Take it Back - Gilead - Korah and Alexa

"Good god, Alexa, it is not yet dawn. What are you doing in here? Go away." Korah rolled over, dismissing her.

They were alone at Gilead now. The family was gone, and the silence between them had grown oppressive.

"I keep thinking about what you said to me last month. I have started to come in here at least a hundred times." She sniffed and her chin trembled.

"Make it a hundred and one. Get the hell out," he demanded through sleep-thickened vocal cords.

"You were right," she whispered. "I was wrong. I should have told your father and Sir Preston that I would not have you, but I was selfish, willful, and spoiled. I did not know what they were going to do. I swear I did not. But the fact remains, I played a role, and I never asked for your forgiveness. I never told you I was sorry." Her breathing became labored, but she had to get it out. "I just kept trying to love you, so you would see it, and I would not have to speak the words."

He rolled over and looked at her with his signature bored, cynical expression. "Are you done?"

She shook her head and backhanded the tears away. "You called what I did the night Peter was conceived, rape." A huge convulsive sob rocked her body. "I am sorry. I am so sorry."

Alexa covered her eyes, crying. "You don't look at him. You never look at him. He is so beautiful. He is two today, and you have never held him. Korah." She could barely continue, sobbing into her hands. "Let Peter love you. Let me love you."

She almost recoiled when he touched her, so accustomed to cruelty at his hands. For as long as she lived, she thanked the Iron King she did not pull away because for the first time in her marriage, her husband took her in his arms and held her with tenderness.

He brushed her hair out of her eyes, looking at her, so tired and weary. "I'll try, Alexa. I will try."

Alone for the First Time - Gilead - Korah and Peter

Free from the daily censure of his mother, his father ten years in the grave, and his brother ruling from the New City Palace forty-three miles away, Alexa's words struck a chord in Korah's heart.

Fifteen years post-Endor, he took his first tentative steps, trying to live again.

He started with his son.

There was no doubt about the boy's parentage. Peter was Korah's miniature. When he walked in the nursery for the first time, the little boy turned from his blocks. Surprise registered on his face but was quickly replaced by Korah's signature expression, bored cynicism. "Father."

Korah pinched the bridge of his nose and closed his eyes. He had made another one. "Good morning, Peter. I understand it is your birthday."

The little boy got to his feet and executed a bow. "I two today."

Korah nodded. "I am two, today."

Peter quirked a blond eyebrow, another identical expression, and said, "You not two, today," he pointed to his little chest, "I two today."

Feisty. Korah took a deep breath and asked, "Are blocks your favorite toys?"

Peter's eyes lit up, and he shook his head. Then he toddled over to his toy chest, retrieved two wooden horses, and offered one to his father. "Want play horsey wiff me?"

Korah fought the well of tears that sprang to his eyes. This was so dangerous. If he loved this boy, he opened himself up to that devastating pain again, but if he did not, he may as well jump off a bridge. "I'll try, Son. I will try."

February 3, 980 ME

Ice Melt at the Hewies - New City - Alexa

The Second Royal Family of Alanthia made all the papers the week of the Hewies. Alanthians got their first look at Prince d'Or and fell in love with him. The little tyke was rarely out of his father's arms, and dressed in identical attire, the duo charmed the kingdom. Newspaper sketch artists went into overdrive, capturing the Second Family at every event. Columnists wrote extensively about their wardrobe, the reception, and the balls they attended, noting that neither the Prince nor the Princess ever danced with anyone else. The gossips wondered how they failed to notice what a stunning couple Korah and Alexa made.

But one image captured the kingdom's hearts and dominated the front page of countless newspapers and magazines. It depicted Prince Peter riding on his father's shoulders, smiling down at Alexa, as she gave Korah a good luck kiss on the polo pitch.

It was priceless.

Alexa took Peter from his father and settled into the royal box to watch the match with her mother-in-law, eleven-year-old Prince Josiah, and several honored guests. Mary cast an eye at Alexa, and Alexa prepared herself for a dressing down over her vulgar display of public affection.

"He kissed you back," Mary said, her face impassive.

"Yes, Princess, he did." Alexa kept her voice level.

"That is good." She coughed into her handkerchief. "Whatever you are doing, Alexa, keep doing it."

Alexa gaped at her austere mother-in-law. In all the years she had known her, Mary never addressed Alexa informally, used common speech, or uttered a word that might be interpreted as kind regarding Korah.

Peter wiggled off her lap and held up his arms to his grandmother. "Nanna, hold me."

Mary drew herself up. Alexa started to pull Peter back, when Mary did the second shocking thing of the day. She smiled and lifted Peter into her lap.

The sketch artists went berserk. Prince d'Or melted the Ice Princess, at last.

The Second Family left the Hewies with a polo trophy and a new pony, Mr. Buzzy.

March 30, 980 ME

Fishing - Gilead - Korah

Still finding their way under the fragility of a truce, neither mentioned the timing of a solo fishing trip Korah took the last week of March. He had intended to be gone a full week but returned to Gilead mid-afternoon on the fourth day.

He discovered Peter and Alexa napping, snuggled in Alexa's bed with an assortment of toys scattered over the bedroom floor. Peter was sucking his left thumb, his little cheeks pink with sleep, and Alexa curled around him.

Korah took off his coat and boots and climbed into bed beside them. When he lifted his arm and held them tight, Peter stirred. He pulled his thumb out of his mouth with a pop, tilted his head, and said, "Love you, Daddy."

Very quietly, Korah whispered into Peter's golden mop of hair, "I love you, too, Son."

Alexa did not stir, but a single tear fell on her pillow.

All was well at Gilead.

Korah went to Alexa's chambers that night. He stood in the doorway and asked a question he had never asked before. "May I come in?"

Alexa sat up, feeling her heart begin to pound. "Yes."

He nodded and shut the door to the sitting room that joined their bedrooms, but he did not move closer. He clasped his hands behind his back, standing rigid with an almost military bearing. "You asked for my forgiveness for your role in what happened in Endor. I never gave you an answer."

He moistened his lips and swallowed. "What you did not ask, what you did not say, was that I," he faltered, "I have never asked for your forgiveness, either. I punished you every day of our marriage. You just kept showing up, you kept trying, and I hated you for it. What you did the night Peter was conceived does not hold a candle to what I have done to you a hundred times before."

She froze, barely able to breathe, listening.

"I forgive you, Alexa." His breath caught, and he said in a rush, "Will you forgive me?"

She looked across the room. He was more handsome today than when she first laid eyes on him at the Regatta when she was twelve years old. He could be cruel, cutting, and volatile. But there was this side to him, the one she tried to reach, the Korah she loved. "I forgave you every time you walked out the door. That is how I could keep trying."

A faint smile lurked in the corner of his mouth, not sarcastic, not cruel. She had never seen that expression on his face. "Princess," his voice sounded like a lover's caress, "will you come to bed with me? I've had the Master's Chamber made up for us."

She matched his smile and said, "I would like to change."

He bowed. "As you wish, madam."

On his way out the door, he flashed her a grin, his adorable dimple showing, such a rare gift. "Don't wait too long."

Korah and Alexa had been married for almost fifteen years, and this was their wedding night. Their original wedding night had been a disaster and set the tone for the hell they had both lived in, until now. Alexa scrambled out of bed, considering whether or not to call her maid, but she was too nervous and knew if she did the servants would gossip.

After a quick bath and a dab of her favorite perfume, she contemplated what to wear. She ruled out white, they both knew she was no innocent. Holding up a red gown, she smiled at the jab at his mother, but she looked terrible in red and did not want to bring her mother-in-law into their bedchamber. After considering and discarding a half dozen gowns, she settled on a bronze peignoir, which had been part of her wedding trousseau, packed away in tissue, never worn. It flattered her skin tone and shimmered in the candlelight. Her fuller breasts spilled over the top, and it was tighter around her waist and in the rear than it had been when she was eighteen. A woman's body reflected in the mirror, not a girl's, and certainly not the little brat who had chosen it. Alexa left her bedchamber to meet the man who was her husband, not the fantasy or the shell she created.

Korah paced, as nervous as he could ever remember being, so far out on a limb he was shaking. What he was so sure of while he was fishing, now seemed an incredible folly. If he made love to

Alexa, he opened himself up. However, he took the risk with his son, and that decision bolstered his courage to try with his wife. The little boy was an absolute delight, and by holding back, he hurt only himself.

The time had come for him to live again.

She just needed to hurry before he lost his nerve.

Then she was there, wearing a stunning gown, with her deep red hair falling loose around her shoulders, her blue cat eyes shy. But as he looked at her, he realized with a jolt that she was perfect for him. He knew her body, knew what made her crazy with pleasure, knew what she smelled like, tasted like. He knew how to touch her, what he did not know was how to love her, but he was going to try.

"You are beautiful, come." Korah held out his arms.

The silk gown rustled as she moved, it hugged her curves. And in a second realization, he saw that her body had changed. It was full and ripe. Her breasts were luscious, spilling over a tease of lace, her hips rounded, curvy. His doubts disappeared.

It began with a kiss.

"Make love to me," he whispered.

He let her take his clothes off. His body throbbed with desire, but he allowed her to set the tone. He had always been in command of their encounters, and in an act of supreme sacrifice, he surrendered to her care.

She outlined his body with her hands, caressing him, molding him. Then she pulled her gown over her head and stood before him naked.

He smiled and laid back on the bed, their eyes never parting. "You are magnificent."

"So are you." She ran her tongue along the length of his shaft, and he arched his hips with a groan. She smiled with feline satisfaction. "I love when you make that sound."

"Oh, I will keep that in mind," he said breathlessly. "I think you have a few of my favorites."

She moved over him, hovering on her hands and knees. "I do?"

"Mmm-hmm." He ran a gentle finger around the tip of her nipple, bringing it to a peak. "Let me taste you." She made the sound he liked. "That one."

She did it again, rubbing her golden dewy curls over his shaft.

"Alexa," her name strangled in his throat, "put me inside you, please."

She trembled. Until now, this was familiar ground, love play done a hundred times. Her hand fumbled, uncertain. "How? Korah, show me how. Show me how to love you."

"Like this." He moved into position, pulsing with desire. A wellspring of emotion, unfelt for so long welled up, and he could barely contain himself. "Gentle, be careful. I do not want to hurt you."

Her breath caught at the unfamiliar invasion. It hurt, burned. She made a small gasp of pain.

"It's okay. Take your time." Those words cost him just about every ounce of his control. Then, like he belonged there, her body adjusted, and he slid home. He made a noise she liked, and Korah and Alexa learned to love each other.

April 15, 980 ME

Ring of Truth - New City Palace - Josiah

"It's my birfday," Peter declared to the gathered family in the New City Palace's blue drawing room.

"It is not," Josiah protested. "It is Grandmother Mary's birthday."

Peter bulled up at Josiah, "My daddy gave me pwesent, so it's my birfday. See!" Peter made a little fist and showed Josiah a small gold ring with a miniature crest. "It says Pwince Door, and it pwecious gold, like me."

"Let me see." Josiah took his hand, examined the very handsome ring, and felt a stab of jealousy. "Royals are not supposed to have nicknames, Prince d'Or."

Peter pulled his hand back, his little chin quivering. "Not nice, Dosiah."

"It's true. Go ask Grandmother Mary. She will tell you." Josiah gloated, anticipating the dressing down the little brat was going to get.

Peter's shoulders fell just a fraction. "I will." He turned on sturdy legs and toddled across the drawing room.

Genevieve ben Williard, Josiah's former nanny, had stayed at Gilead to take care of Peter when Mary, Eamonn, and Josiah relocated to the New City Palace. She overheard the conversation and gave eleven-year-old Josiah a squeeze on his trapezius muscle. Josiah flinched and tried to get away. She clamped down tighter. "Peter was right. That was not nice, Josiah."

He looked up at her sulky but defiant. "It is true."

"Perhaps it is, but the sentiment behind what you just did was nasty." Her voice was low, the conversation between them alone. "You saw your cousin had something that you did not and decided to hurt him over it. Jealousy is not an attractive quality."

Genevieve pointed to Korah. "That name, that nickname, is a sign of affection between them. It is a way for his father to express love to his son." She softened her tone and her expression. "Josiah, it is easy for your father to show affection and love to you, but that is not the case for everyone. That ring and that name are important to them."

Across the room, Princess Mary rebuffed little Peter. He looked down at the ring he had been so proud of a moment before and began to cry.

"You will be the Ruling Prince one day, Josiah. I want you to remember this moment."

Genevieve moved across the drawing room and gathered the crying little boy in her arms. Josiah watched as she carried him out, shamed to the pit of his soul.

July 1, 980 ME

A Ball in Gilead - Gilead - Korah and Alexa

Alexa loved fashion, she always had, since she was six and declared that all the dresses in her closet that did not 'twirl' were not acceptable. She began her marriage with a wardrobe that took three wagons to transport from Capernaum to Gilead. Fifteen years later, her tastes were refined, her demands for dozens of gowns a season economized, and while she still appreciated a well-made garment, an elegant hat, or a fine pair of shoes, she no longer needed them.

Korah had subtly and ruthlessly mocked her in the early years, humming the Happy Birthday song under his breath if she wore anything he found particularly overdone or extravagant. He dressed in austere elegance, favoring black as the staple color in his wardrobe. She asked him about it in the second year of their marriage. He shot her an ominous glare and told her it was the color of mourning. She never mentioned it again.

The year Peter was born, she did not go into society. So, instead of having an entire wardrobe commissioned for her post-pregnancy figure, she instructed the dressmakers to take several of her older gowns, remove the flounces, ribbons, and excessive lace and re-structure them. The simple lines and unembellished garments grew to be her favorite. She ceased being the spoiled girl who arrived at Gilead. She was a mother, a thirty-three-year-old woman, who no longer needed to attract the attention of every man in the room to provoke her husband to jealousy. It had never worked anyway.

Thus, it had been three seasons since she summoned the dress-makers with their bolts of silks, samples of buttons, fashion plates and dolls, much to the consternation of the tailors who relied on hefty purchases from the Princess to bolster their bottom lines. In May, Korah shocked her with a declaration that he planned to host a ball at the height of the Summer Season.

Alexa had nothing to wear.

The delicate and tenuous relationship they were building seemed so precious and fragile, she was loath to do anything that might evoke memories of the old Alexa. So, she decided that noth-ing would signify her transformation more than refusing to go into a tizzy over a ball gown. She gave a cursory look at a dozen she already owned, several of which had never been worn, pulled out three that might suit, tried them on, and had her lady's maid let out the bodices. Two and a half years post-baby, her figure had changed, but so had she.

The ball marked the first social event they hosted as husband and wife. They had fun planning it. He favored understated ele-gance; she gravitated toward whimsical charm. They bantered and teased. He picked the most austere designs, simply to get a rise out of her. She countered with extravagant, outlandish suggestions, such as turning Gilead into Versailles and demanding everyone wear powdered wigs and bustles. He suggested a sultan's tent was far more seductive and ferried her off to their bedchamber, where she played harem girl to his menacing sheik.

Physically, they bonded like never before and enjoyed new freedom with each other. She discovered she was a sensual woman, he was a virile man, and they made up for lost time.

The change in Korah began gradually. He could still be brooding, but he was no longer morose. He adored Peter and took him to the stables every morning. At the Hewies in February, Korah bought Peter a pony, Mr. Buzzy, a three-year-old classic American Shetland, with four white stockings and a white muzzle. His coat, mane, and generous tail were red. He had fine lines and a docile temper. Mr. Buzzy quickly became Prince d'Or's pride and joy.

Korah often forwent his morning ride to spend time in the paddock, holding a lead line, teaching his son to properly sit and ride a horse. Sometimes, Korah hefted Peter in front of him, and they rode through the trails. When they were out of sight of the watchful eyes of Alexa, who still did not love horses, Korah spurred his horse into a fast canter, much to his son's ecstatic delight.

Every morning in 980 ME, Korah and Peter spent time with each other and the horses.

The morning of the ball, a frenetic energy enveloped the house. Like a general preparing for battle, Alexa fielded questions, made last minute adjustments, and dealt with no fewer than six minor crises. At it since dawn, she felt frazzled, on edge, and under tremendous self-inflicted pressure to make everything perfect.

Korah appeared in the doorway of Alexa's study, and she experienced a flash of irritation at his relaxed demeanor. He observed her with that bored, cynical expression, still dressed in his riding clothes. They had two hundred thirty-eight guests arriving in less than five hours. "What? Do you need something?"

The corner of his lip twitched. "I do."

Alexa craned her head forward and gave him a big-eyed stare, silently conveying he needed to spit it out. There were still a dozen pressing matters yet to be dealt with.

"My mother would remark that you have worked yourself into a tizzy."

Alexa bristled. "Your mother is half the reason I am in a tizzy, she and her cadre of biddies. You know they will sit in judgment of everything I have done here. I will be lucky to have any skin left on my back by the time they finish fileting me."

"Legendary, is she not?" Korah moved into her study and shut the door.

Alexa could not read him. His expression seemed fathomless, so she hedged, "She is one of a kind."

"Thank the Iron King for that. Don't worry. Simply install her in the Green Drawing Room. She and her biddies will be fine." He took her around the waist and whispered, "It is going to be fine. I am positive tonight will be a stunning success. Stop fretting."

Alexa draped her arms over his shoulders, not minding the horse smell that clung to him. The back of his hair was damp with perspiration. Her tone was playful, teasing. "That is easy for you to say, KbA. You have been out riding and playing with our son while I have been in here dealing with all the last-minute details. If this party falls flat, society will not talk about you." She pressed a kiss to his lips.

"Oh, they will talk about you." Korah smiled into her eyes. "They will say what an accomplished and sophisticated hostess you are. They will clamor to be by your side and insist we attend the Earl of Stuffy's next soiree, house party, or picnic."

"The Earl of Stuffy?" she asked, glowing under his praise, rarely given, precious. "I do not believe you have introduced me to that particular gentleman."

"I am relatively certain I have, white hair, bad breath, a paunch?" He kissed the side of her neck, and she made one of those sounds he liked.

"Oh, I do remember him," she said playfully. He had just described half their guest list. "I will install him in the Green Drawing Room with your mother."

"Wit and humor," he breathed in her ear. "I love you."

She inhaled sharply, closed her eyes, and froze.

"I brought you something." His soft words ruffled her hair. "Happy anniversary, Alexa."

She reached around and held his head, stopping time. She did not move. She did not speak. She did not breathe. For fifteen years, he never said a word, never acknowledged or gave any indication he realized another year had come and gone. Alexa knew when he announced the ball, however he failed to mention that it coincided with their anniversary, so she assumed it was a coincidence. They never celebrated the occasion, ever.

But she should have known. Korah possessed a legendary recall of dates.

"Korah," was all she could say, overwhelmed.

He pulled a small box out of his pocket. "For you."

Then he flashed that dimpled smile, and she was undone. She buried her face in his shirt, resting the flats of her palms on his chest. Silent tears pooled in her eyes.

"Hey," he said, surrounding her with his strength. "Don't cry."

She nodded convulsively and looked up at him. "Oh, how I love you."

"I do not know how, but I am thankful that you do." He kissed her forehead, a sardonic tilt to his mouth. "Now, open your gift. We are hosting an anniversary ball tonight, and you have a million things to do."

She laughed and leaned back in his arms. "You brat."

"That is my line, and I have been entirely remiss seeing that you stay one." He pressed the box into her trembling hands.

Alexa crinkled her nose at him, reveling in the playful banter. She opened the jewelry box, and her breath caught again. Nestled in the pale blue silk lay a pair of diamond teardrop earrings.

"For fifteen, the groom is supposed to give the bride crystal," he raised an eyebrow at her, "but what is the fun of that?"

"They are stunning." She traced a finger over the shimmering diamonds.

"I thought two teardrops were appropriate. They represent the first fifteen years, but diamonds are hard and can cut through just about anything. Next year, I will give you smiley faces. I believe I have a little more leeway for the sixteenth."

She closed her eyes and nodded. "Smiley faces are an excellent plan."

Alexa bounded up the steps to her chambers, two hours before the guests arrived, and an hour behind schedule. She threw open the door and almost screeched. "Gail, hurry with the bath. I am so late."

"It is drawn, my Esteemed. Come now, we have plenty of time, but we must be quick." Gail, her faithful lady's maid, stripped her day gown and shooed her into the bathing chamber.

"We will have to forgo the curled hairstyle we planned. A simple French chignon will suffice." Alexa hopped in the tub and submerged in a single movement.

"I can do better than a hairstyle you wear to breakfast, my Esteemed." Gail moved with an economy of motion, handing Alexa a soaped cloth. "Besides, you are to make your grand entrance after the guests have arrived. There is time."

"Oh, no!" Alexa protested. "I am to be down promptly at 9:00 pm to receive."

Gail shook her head. "That is not what Prince Korah told me. He gave instructions for you to take as much time as you needed. I am to send someone to tell him when you will appear at the top of the grand staircase."

Vigorously scrubbing her arms, Alexa did not spare Gail a glance. "You must be mistaken. The lady of the house always greets her guests. My mother-in-law will have an apoplexy if I break protocol."

Gail rinsed Alexa's back. "I am not mistaken. He told me himself before he went to dress."

Alexa paused and blew out a shaky breath, old fears gathering in her gut. This was the sort of thing he used to do… set her up for humiliation. Over the years, he played her a dozen times. "How did he seem when he said it?" she asked carefully.

"A bit more animated than normal," Gail replied, but a tiny smile hovered in the corner of her mouth.

"What is he up to?" Alexa asked, feeling her lighthearted mood evaporate.

"In this small thing, I believe you are going to have to trust him." Gail smiled and closed her eyes.

Alexa's insecurities rose out of the bath steam and swamped her. "Gail, I am afraid."

Gail opened a towel, "No, my Esteemed. You do not have to be afraid, not tonight. Come, let me show you what he brought when he issued those instructions."

Alexa allowed Gail to take her to her dressing room, instead of the three gowns she had altered and prepared for the night, a stunning cream-colored sheath hung on the dressing tree. Adorned with thousands of tiny crystal beads, it captured and refracted the fading sunlight. A small jewelry box, wrapped in matching blue paper to the one he had given her this morning, rested on her dressing table with a note.

"Give me a moment, please," Alexa said, overwhelmed.

When the door closed, she wandered over and touched the amazing dress. Clean lines with a simple cut, she knew without trying it on that it would fit her perfectly. It was a compromise between their two styles, an offering, and the first article of clothing he ever bought her.

She moved to the dressing table and opened the note.

I decided not to wait until next year.
KbA

Lifting the lid, she threw back her head and laughed, touched beyond measure, she lifted out a delicate diamond bracelet fashioned with three smiley faces.

That night, when she appeared at the top of the grand staircase, all eyes turned to the vision she was in shimmering crystal and cream. Korah called for silence and announced her himself, "Ladies and Gentlemen, noble guests, friends and family, I am honored to present Princess Alexa ben Seamus, my lovely bride."

Prince Eamonn turned away, tears stinging the back of his eyes. His brother, his broken and cynical brother, who lived a life of pain and quiet desperation had finally begun to live. It was the first time Eamonn ever saw Korah truly happy.

"What an absurd breach of protocol," Princess Mary said at Eamonn's elbow. He turned to glance at her and noted the lines around her mouth had softened, moisture hovered in the corner of her eye. "It is good," she whispered. Then without another word, and in a rustle of green silk, Mary retreated to her drawing room.

Sir Preston ben Worley came alongside her, offering his arm. "And it seems, my Esteemed Princess, that we were right. It has simply taken a few years for the truth to become evident."

Mary looked up at him with eyes that extinguished his satisfied smile. "But I wonder, Sir Preston ben Worley, how many years will it take for the truth about you to become evident?" She raised a finely arched eyebrow at him and left him where he stood.

Looking on from a secret observation spot at the top of the landing, Genevieve ben Willard shuttled a sleepy Peter off to bed.

"She look like an angel, didn't she, Auntie G.?" He held up his arms for her to pick him up. He snuggled in her warm embrace, sucking his thumb contentedly.

"She did indeed, Peter."

That night, Alexa scored the social triumph of the year. Ever after, their guests would remember that they bore witness to a truly beautiful, royal love story.

Part 8 - Private Inquires

April 15, 980 ME

Private Investigator - New York

At 10:05 am, Private Detective Thomas ben Hillary let himself into his dingy office in Midtown New York. The plaque by the door advertised their working hours as 9-5, but his secretary called in sick that morning, which was nothing unusual. She seemed to do that two days out of five, but she was a buddy's daughter, and Thomas owed her father several favors and quite a lot of cash, so he did not fire the girl.

Bending over with a groan, he picked up the mail the postman had shoved through the letterbox yesterday afternoon, which meant his secretary had left the office before two. He shook his head, dropped the dunning letters and junk mail on her desk, and put on the kettle to make an instant espresso.

Beneath the lumpy exterior of his ill-fitting suit, battered shoes, and persistent smoker's cough lay a brilliant investigator. However, he drank too much, spoke his mind too readily, and in general did not get along well with others. So, five years after becoming a detective in one of the roughest precincts in New York, he accepted early retirement and started his own firm. He might have made a go of it, but he found his clients more annoying than his superiors on the job, so word of mouth did not earn him a lot of work. He did, however, consult with his former precinct, and that kept the rent paid.

Just before noon, the bell rang, indicating he had a potential client. Thomas glanced at the cigar burning in the ashtray and decided whoever waited outside needed to learn to appreciate the aroma because he was not stubbing it out. Heaving his bulk out of the leaning chair, he hoped his bookie's leg-breakers had not come to check in. He was currently riding a streak of bad luck but still had a couple of days before they called in his debt, however sometimes the Guidos got anxious.

The woman standing in the hall hid her eyes behind dark glasses and used a beige scarf to cover her hair, but this was nothing unusual. Most of his clients concealed their identities and held on to their secrets, at least as far as they could. What they often failed to consider was that if they wanted an effective investigation, they needed to tell him everything. Withheld information wasted their money, which Thomas did not mind taking, but if they wanted answers, they needed to confess the truth. It would save them thousands in fees because he would just bill them until he uncovered what they were hiding. Most of them disliked that reality. People came to a private investigator for private matters. He understood their reticence, so he laid it out for them and let them make their own decisions.

"Good morning. I'm Thomas ben Hillary. Please come into my office."

The woman removed her dark glasses and took down the scarf. Long blonde hair fell around her shoulders. She extended an elegant hand and said, "*Guten morgen*, Mr. ben Hillary. I would like for you to help me find my daughter."

July 23, 980 ME

Kidnapper - New City

The kidnapper watched the young blonde leave her group of friends and set out on her own. His heart thumped as he followed her swinging ponytail at a discreet distance. She moved with a brazen confidence, not gawky or awkward as most girls were at that age. Instead, she strolled through the New City streets as if she owned them.

Gentle darkness settled over the city, and the kidnapper suspected she would walk straight home; she did not. He smiled as his quarry cut through Prince Eamonn Park. This was going to be too easy. But the park bustled with activity. Evening exercisers jogged, others played tennis, or shot hoops. Young couples unpacked takeout food on blankets, enjoyed a kiss, and a bite to eat under the brilliant sky. The balmy weather drew New City residents out of their houses to take advantage of the long summer night. He spotted a group of teens hanging out behind the baseball dugout, smoking cigarettes. The girls flirted, and the boys jostled one another, competing for their attention. He expected the girl to head toward them.

She surprised him by climbing up a sliding board and disappearing into the high turret of a toy castle, which was odd because if she was who he thought, she was fifteen, far too old to be playing on preschool equipment. Suspicious mothers eyed him because he had no business hanging out around this section of the park alone, so he aborted his surveillance and decided to bide his time. The girl was not going anywhere.

August 10, 980 ME

Lost Kitten - New City

The kidnapper followed his quarry for almost three weeks, and during that time, he became convinced she was the one. He found the inspiration for the trap in the park playground. She had not been playing in that castle, she had been visiting a stray cat with a litter of newborn kittens. The mother cat was one of a dozen strays she tended. The girl was an animal lover, a stray herself, an orphan, a throwaway kid. But the kidnapper knew her birth name. He knew who she was.

"Can you help me find my lost puppy?"

She never suspected a thing.

It was a double-cross. The person who hired him merely asked him to ascertain if she lived and to report her whereabouts. However, when Thomas ben Hillary dug into Sussanna ben Ross' case, he uncovered the truth, and he knew exactly who the girl was.

When he weighed his fee against the value of the information, he recognized if he played this right, he would be set for life. There were any number of power players who would not want her existence revealed, let alone having her identity made public. She was a dirty little secret.

He locked the door behind him, cutting off the girl's cursing shouts with a metallic thud. No one would hear her screaming down there. As he walked away, he smiled in evil anticipation, fingering the four carefully crafted ransom notes in his pocket. If any of them paid, he would be a millionaire many times over.

Six weeks after the Anniversary Ball at Gilead, anonymous couriers delivered four ransom notes, one to Princess Mary, one to Sir Preston, one to Prince Eamonn, and the last to Princess Alexa.

To a one, they paid.

To a one, they kept silent.

To a one, they hid the notes from Korah and each other.

No one told him there was a chance his daughter Hope was still alive, and no one told him she was in danger.

No one.

But Thomas ben Hillary never saw a shekel. He made the fatal mistake of turning his back on his hostage.

The girl never knew why that swine kidnapped her or what he hoped to gain, but Kayah ben Morte was created in that underground bunker.

Part 9 - Dun Dun Duhhhh

February 3, 1000 ME

Old News - New City - Himari and Genevieve

In the underground bunker The Resistance used to wage war against King Korah ben Adam's government, Himari Nakamura looked at Genevieve ben Willard, aghast. "You cannot just drop a bombshell like that then walk away, Auntie!" Himari insisted, following Genevieve into the living room. "What do you mean, if Kayah is who you think she is, she looks exactly like her mother?"

Genevieve collapsed into her favorite recliner Reuben had brought downstairs for her. Before all this began, she spent hours in it, knitting, watching cooking shows, and reading detective stories, but just now the familiar, soft cushion offered no comfort. Her bones felt brittle, her mind fragile in remembrance. When she looked at Himari, tears streamed down her cheeks. "It was horrible." She covered her mouth and stifled a cry. "I think it caused everything. The final straw, I think."

Himari knelt in front of Genevieve and took her hands. "What?"

"Do you have access to the old newspapers?"

Himari blinked and spoke slowly, "Is there a particular paper and date you are interested in?"

Genevieve inhaled a quivering breath. "New City Chronicle, February 3, 981 ME."

Himari grew still. "That was nineteen years ago, today."

Genevieve closed her eyes and nodded. "The events took place the day before, so the papers covered it the next day. That's a little serendipity going on for you, Himari."

"Somehow, I do not like the sound of this one."

Genevieve covered her mouth and said behind her fingers, "No, you should not. Go pull up the paper. I will sit here while you do."

Himari froze as an eerie feeling swept over her, akin to what she experienced the first time they entered Quadrant G. It was a forbidden place, somewhere they should not be. "Auntie, can't you just tell me?"

Genevieve shook her head. "No. I need you to find the article and the picture, then tell me I am just an old woman seeing ghosts."

"Okay," Himari whispered and rose on legs that turned to jelly. The bank of computers before her seemed like Pandora's Box. "And this article might be about Kayah's mother?"

Genevieve nodded.

Himari brought her folded hands to her lips, her mind calculating. She, Kayah, and Lavinia had been best friends since '77. Somehow, they always assumed Kayah's mother was dead, that she was truly an orphan. But if Genevieve was right, and Himari was looking for an article written in '81, that meant Kayah's mother had been alive when they were sixteen.

As she sat down at the computer, she decided she would do this for Genevieve, and herself, because she would never be able to leave it alone, but she might not tell Kayah. Despite her outward veneer, Kayah was not made of stone. She bled quietly from the wounds of life. And for the last few months, Himari watched as Reuben ben Judah patiently and lovingly dressed and bound those wounds. Kayah deserved a bit of happiness. Himari refused to deliver another blow. It would be cruel.

It took ten minutes to pull up the archives.

The headline read, 'Assassination Attempt on the Prince Thwarted.' A sick feeling washed over her as she zoomed in on the article. A sketch dominated the front page, a duplicate of the Angel of Kensington Park, a woman standing in the stirrups of a stallion aiming a weapon—at Prince Korah ben Adam.

Himari gasped.

February 15, 1000 ME

The Closest Thing to a Father - New Jersey - Kayah and Filippo

"You have lost your damn mind!" Kayah pointed an accusing finger at Filippo. "Sir Preston ben Worley is not a mobster. He is a knight of the realm, a gentleman."

"A gentleman who turned you into an assassin?" Filippo challenged.

"That does not make him a mobster. Do you know who he sent me against?" Kayah's nose flared. "Child molesters, rapists, and pornographers who got off on technicalities, that's who."

"Ah, are you sure?"

She looked out the window, watching the landscape fly by as they sped out of New York. "Yes."

Filippo made a skeptical sound and continued, "But then he baited you with Bologna. He knew you, Kayah. He knew what you would do." Filippo aimed a finger at her like a gun, making a shooting noise. "It was the first shot in the mafia war, and he used you as a weapon."

Kayah paled. "Son of a bitch, the prototype, the codes…"

Filippo cut her a sidelong glance. "I heard about the theft when I was undercover at Massimo's. It was a devastating loss to the Martinellis. They invested millions into the development of it. Then you stole it, and Himari wiped the research so they could not remake it. It set off a chain of events."

Kayah threw her head against the headrest and closed her eyes. "In more ways than one. Tell me what you know."

"There are two families, the Martinellis and the Giovannis." He braked and brought the car to a stop as traffic snarled again. Wearing an enigmatic expression, he offered his hand. "My name is Roberto ben Claudio, and I am a Giovanni." He had never truly seen Kayah shocked, but he succeeded in shocking her. She looked at him aghast and did not shake his hand.

"You are mafia?" she breathed.

He put his hand back on the wheel and kept driving. "By birth."

"What the hell is that supposed to mean?" Kayah looked like she was about to punch him.

"It means that my mother was born to a man who was the head of the Giovannis. My uncle is the current don." His voice held no pride, only resignation. "My mother… she never wanted me in the family business. She married my father and moved away. My father is a painter." His soulful brown eyes held decades of sadness. "I have not seen either of them since I left Italy thirteen years ago and became Filippo."

"So, you were a mobster?" Kayah studied him through fresh eyes.

He laughed without humor. "I wanted to be. I had a fight with my mother. I was a stupid hothead with a hard-on and could only see the money and the power, the women." He threw his hands up. "It was not a good decision. She was right. The Martinellis, they did not want a new Giovanni. I made a mistake, and they used that as an excuse to put a contract out on me. I might have stayed, but I would have had to swear the oath to my uncle for his protection. They would not have touched me then, but it would have bound me forever. After I saw the truth, what that life was like, the cost was too high. So… I fled."

"Docs Himari know this?" Kayah's voice was low, like a slow-burning fuse.

"A little. She knows I had to leave Italy because the mafia was trying to kill me, so I cannot go home, and she can never meet my family. She does not know the rest." Lines of fatigue showed along his jaw and under his dark eyes.

"Then why are you telling me, and what does any of this have to do with Sir Preston and Bologna and the price on my head?"

"I might not have been a mobster, but I am a male Giovanni, the grandson of the head of the family. They made sure I learned my history."

Then he told her the story of how the old Duke and his grandfather parlayed a deal that brought Giovanni power to Alanthia. "Of course, I was young, and they did not tell me who they used to broker the deal or any of the names of the men. It was enough for them to show me that our enterprise was far-reaching. They were proud and wanted me to know. The arrangement ceded the Martinellis power in Italy, but Giovanni power grew across the globe."

He gave her a pointed look. "Bologna upset the balance of power that had been in place for decades."

"How?" Kayah ground out.

"The Martinellis became greedy. They saw how the Giovannis prospered in Alanthia, how they became rich on the technology, while Italy stayed in the dark age. They sent Massimo abroad. Facetec was a front for his mission, but there was actual technology behind it. But the Giovannis do not want facial recognition software in Alanthia, eh?"

"I suppose they would not," Kayah said darkly.

Filippo pressed his lips together and shook his head. "It was a double-cross. The Martinellis planned to use Facetec to destroy the Giovanni empire in Alanthia so they could take over. They sent Massimo to the New City, away from New York where the Giovanni operation has always been located. Without the programming, they were like a dead fish in the water, but they go ahead with the plan and send Massimo to establish Martinelli on the west coast."

"Then Gus…" Kayah covered her face.

"Then Gus and his friends rebuilt Facetec, and the plan was back in motion," Filippo confirmed.

Kayah squeezed her eyes shut and pounded her thigh with her fist. "And the supposed jihadists?"

"Were sent by the Giovannis."

She snarled, "By your family?"

"Yes," Filippo answered in a strangled voice.

"And that is why you went undercover, to spy for your family after they killed Gus?"

"No! I went undercover because I thought *they* killed Gus. So did you. We all thought it was a setup for the insurance, eh? That Massimo was running a Ponzi scheme, a con. It is what we all thought." He looked hurt that she would believe the worst of him. "They are my enemies. They cost me my family, my name, my manhood. To leave and hide like a scared dog, you do not know what that was like."

Kayah turned away, staring at the wreckage on the side of the road. Quiet for a mile or so, she said, "I think I understand that."

"I suppose that you do." Filippo reached across the console and squeezed her hand.

Kayah squeezed back.

"Giovanni may have started in Alanthia with the consent of the royals, but that changed when Korah took the throne in '85. I came to Alanthia two years after, but I remember that it was a prominent topic of conversation in Italy. My uncle was very concerned that the Alanthian part of the family was in active opposition to Korah." He made a very Italian shrug. "But what does Filippo ben Vincente care about that, eh? He does not. So, for many years, I never even think about it."

He turned, pointing his finger, the light of discovery in his eye. "But the Martinelli do, eh? Marco ben Massimo, he is actively courting King Korah. He goes to the Palace, promising Facetec software will catch the girls, and it does. Korah, he pays the reward. Suddenly, the financial losses are restored, they have the big favor of the King, and working software. It is a terrible time for the Giovannis and a good time for the Martinellis."

"I still do not see how all of this goes back to Sir Preston," Kayah said and grabbed the sides of her head in frustration. "Or why they put a hit out on me?"

"Who has been around since Prince Adam's time? Who lives in New York? Who hates King Korah? Who sent you to Bologna? And out of whose office did I watch my uncle leave three weeks ago?" Filippo looked at her with pointed resolution. "I called Himari yesterday; she told me you were pardoned. Who would not want you talking about your past assignments, Kayah?"

She narrowed her eyes, glaring at him.

"The hit coincides with your pardon. You told him, didn't you?"

"He is my lawyer. Of course, I told him." But as she said the words, the truth crashed in on her.

He had lured her to his office with a promise to tell her who her parents were but had actually planned to kill her. She covered her face, hiding how much his betrayal hurt. Sir Preston ben Worley was the closest thing she ever had to a father.

She sobbed, three hard, heart-wrenching sobs.

Then she stopped.

She took a deep breath, rolled her neck, hearing it pop, and when she turned, Kayah ben Morte said, "I will annihilate him."

Filippo grinned. "This time, Kayah, you don't have to do it outside of the law. You got the Ruling Prince on your side, and we got a Director of the FBI that also needs to hear this story."

Kayah seemed to come back to the present. "Where are we going, by the way?"

"To find Thaddeus ben Todd."

Kayah screamed.

Filippo jerked the wheel, tires squealing, brakes locking up.

Cars ahead of them piled up and crashed. A truck jumped the median, and all hell broke loose on the road to Rephidim.

February 16, 1000 ME

The Second Family Album - Gilead - Peter and Astrid

"Look at this," Astrid exclaimed, cradling a large, leather-bound book in her lap.

Peter ambled over to the table, indulging his curious wife as she played scavenger hunter. "What is it?"

"Drawings and sketches of you as a little boy." She flipped through the book, fascinated. "Oh, my gosh, look how adorable you were."

"I have seen those. My mother had a book like that."

Astrid turned to the front and looked up at him with sad eyes. "This was your father's."

"No wonder it is still here," Peter replied drolly. "Though, I suppose the original is likely destroyed, so it is a good thing they had a copy here. I was entirely too cute not to have it recorded for posterity."

Astrid laughed and studied baby Peter's button eyes. "I like this dress you are wearing."

"That is a christening gown," he protested. "It is not a dress. It is probably somewhere around here, if the truth be known. There are trunks full of old clothes. That brown robe and gown you wore on our wedding night was a classic example. It was gorgeous, by the way. You were gorgeous."

Astrid smiled up at him through her black mascara. "Jarrod has excellent taste. Though, I think it was your mother's. He found it in her old chamber where I dressed and bathed. It seemed fitting after meeting her."

Peter sighed through his nose and pointed to a drawing. "Look how pretty she was." The sketch of Alexa and Peter showed him standing on her thighs, obviously not walking yet, as she puckered for a kiss.

Astrid turned the page and was taken aback. A likeness of adult Peter, dimple and all, sat on a playroom floor with dozens of horses scattered around, Korah and his son.

Peter's brows furrowed. "I have never seen that one," he said in an inscrutable voice.

Nor had he seen any of the other sketches contained in this book. They depicted a life he did not remember, a man he did not know, and a time before hatred. It was almost unbearable to behold. Astrid turned page after page of Korah and Peter together, the love between father and son documented in indigo and vellum.

Peter walked away, staring out the window onto the grounds of Gilead. "I thought I dreamed that," he said quietly and cleared his throat. "I thought I made it up because the reality was too terrible." He turned and pointed at the offending book and snarled, "What the bloody hell is that?"

"Peter?" Astrid's eyes grew enormous as she pulled out a folded note. She studied it with shaking hands, looked up at him and said, "This is a letter from your father, and it's addressed to you."

Damage Assessments - Golden City - Josiah and Simon

The aged Alanthian Ambassador to the Golden Kingdom, the Honorable Simon ben Joshua, hobbled into Prince Josiah's office at the Alanthian Embassy, bowed with stiff formality and said, "Please forgive my tardiness in attending you, my Esteemed."

Prince Josiah rose and returned the bow. "Ambassador Simon, welcome and do come in."

The old man shuffled across the office and collapsed with a groan into the chair Josiah indicated. "Thank you, my Esteemed. I fear I have been abed with an attack of the gout."

"Ah," Josiah empathized, "very painful."

"Bothersome," barked the ambassador. "But we are not here to discuss my ailments unless you have a couple of weeks to listen. I understand you are a doctor, so if you've got a pill that can make this blasted gout feel better, I would not be opposed. Otherwise, we will get down to it."

"I think we can arrange both, Ambassador." Josiah smiled.

"You are the spitting image of your father, aren't you?" Simon lifted thick glasses to his beaked nose and studied Josiah, then lowered them, and blinked.

"I have been the Alanthian Ambassador to the Golden Kingdom since your Grandfather Adam's time. He appointed me soon after he took the throne in '37." He pointed a gnarled finger at Josiah and continued, "In case you are trying to work out the math, that's sixty-three years. I will be a hundred next January, the Iron King willing."

His clear gray eyes sparkled with humor and intelligence. "Which basically means, I am an old fart, and you will be the fourth, and assuredly the last, Alanthian Ruling Prince I will serve under. Though, under Korah," he shook his head, "I was not official."

He smirked and waggled an eyebrow. "But as you know, we opened diplomatic relations January 1st of this year."

Josiah nodded, his brown eyes dancing with amusement. "I do indeed, Ambassador. I trust you played a role in the negotiations."

"You are darn right I did." Simon nodded decisively. "It took years, and I got no support from home. I have been an island for the last fifteen, using my personal estate to keep the Embassy open." Simon raised a brow. "I did that even after Korah seized our family funds in Alanthia and placed my poor son, Luke, under house arrest until he died. Only then did he release the estate."

"Thank you for your sacrifice and long years of dedicated service. Would you be referring to my father's friend, the Earl of Stockton, Luke ben Simon?" Josiah asked.

A shadow passed over the old man's face. "Aye, he inherited the title from my brother, who died without issue. Luke knew from a very young age he was to become the Earl, so he stayed in Alanthia after graduating from the RMA. But I think his early years in the Golden Kingdom impacted him greatly. He never faltered."

"I am sorry for your loss," Josiah said.

"Aye, thank you. It is a curse of the elderly, to have your children pass before you. I'd not seen him for eighteen years."

"Well, you have my humble thanks for your service and your family's sacrifices. The least I can do is see you are reimbursed for your expenditures in keeping the Embassy open, with interest, of course."

The aging ambassador grinned.

"Your Granddaughter, Lady Joanna, has offered to serve at court, to attend my wife and Prince Peter's wife, the Duchess. She will travel to the Golden City for the wedding and the coronation."

Simon's lips pursed, the deep crevices growing pronounced. He turned aside and murmured, "I did not think I would see her again before I passed on. That is very generous of you, on both counts."

"It is my pleasure, Ambassador," Josiah said with sincerity.

Simon was quiet for a moment. "That she would leave those kids, tells me something. It tells me something about you."

He turned to meet Josiah's eyes. "I do not have to remind you of the perilous situation we are in. Alanthia is a hair's breadth away from the Iron King smashing it to smithereens. I have been in court every day for fifteen years, begging and pleading for His mercy on our land. He has stayed His hand, but I fear His patience is exhausted. You have no leeway. Korah used it all up, all of it."

He pointed a bony finger and continued, "And it's not about technology. It never has been. You make a mistake if you think it is. It is about rebellion, about pursuing power outside the Iron King, about going elsewhere for your answers, and seeking your own way; and in the process, making yourself king, and not Him. 'Twas Korah's downfall."

"Korah's downfall was his insanity," Josiah countered.

"That is where you are wrong, and where your youth and inexperience will get you in trouble," he chastised and gave Josiah a cold, gray look, stormy with emotion. "I've known Korah ben Adam since he was a boy in short pants. History did not start yesterday, and if you are to become a wise ruler, you would do well to remember that. You must learn to look below the surface, even if your emotions get in the way."

Josiah was taken aback. "Sir, considering he murdered my mother and my father, nearly beat me to death, and tortured my wife, judging the man insane has nothing to do with emotion."

"He killed your mother?" Simon raised an eyebrow at Josiah. "That is news to me."

The muscles in Josiah's jaw worked, as he ground out, "He did. He confessed to my father's corpse."

Simon rubbed his chin, random gray whiskers making a dry, scratchy sound. He shook his head in profound sadness. "He killed them both over the same woman."

Josiah furrowed his brow. "What are you talking about?"

Simon dropped his hand to his lap and turned. "His wife. He was avenging her death."

"Both my parents died before Aunt Alexa," Josiah protested.

"You are not looking deep enough, and that will get you in trouble. The Ruling Prince of Alanthia does not have the luxury to make those kinds of snap judgments!"

Josiah jumped to his feet, furious. "Ambassador," he boomed, "recall to whom thou art addressing."

Simon did not back down. He was too old, this was too important, and he was having too much fun. "I appear to be addressing your Grandmother Mary, right there."

Josiah's mouth fell open, flabbergasted.

"Oh, you will remember her, now won't you?"

Josiah glanced away. "Yes, I remember her."

Simon cleared his throat, driving his point home. "So then, you will recall the kind of woman she was."

"I do." Josiah sat down; his temper abated. "Severe, I believe, is an appropriate adjective."

The corner of the ambassador's mouth lifted in a rueful smile. "You are being quite charitable."

Softening his tone, Simon plunged ahead. "My Esteemed, do you presume to know everything there was to know about a complicated man like Korah ben Adam?"

Josiah's nose flared. "I know enough."

The Ambassador shook his head. "You base this on your impressions of him when you were a little boy, or perhaps the madman he became? Listen to me now. There was more to him than met the eye. I tell you this, not to excuse the great sins of the man, but to teach you, and show you how you must approach complex situations and problems. Things might not always be as they appear on the surface."

Josiah recognized Ambassador Simon's wise counsel, and though the subject of his uncle was abhorrent, he nodded his assent and listened.

"Have you ever pondered why Prince Antiochus of Greece was punished so severely for his rebellion while Alanthia was not?"

Josiah's heart pounded hard in his chest as he confessed, "I assumed it was Greece's proximity to the Golden Kingdom."

"Bah!" Simon waved away the foolish notion. "You think distance means anything to the Iron King who exists beyond space and time?"

Josiah grabbed the back of his neck, gone stiff with tension. "No, I suppose not."

"Did you ever wonder why the Iron King did not strike Korah ben Adam dead after what he did to your father?"

"Often." Josiah's voice shook. "It has been the greatest question of my life."

"I expect it would be. But the Iron King knows the first from the last, and He had His reasons. I do not pretend to speak for Him, but I have been on this Earth, and served in His courts, for many years. Perhaps during that time, I learned how to look through His eyes, at least a bit. And I can tell you, Korah ben Adam was the saddest little boy I have ever seen, and he was a nice little boy."

The sentiment hung in the air. Simon let Josiah ponder that before he continued, "Neither his mother nor his father ever showed him a moment's kindness, love, or affection, at least that I ever saw, and I spent quite a bit of time at Gilead in those days.

"He ran away several times before he went off to the RMA. Think of it, he was a Prince of Alanthia, and he ran away from home. What kind of life must he have lived in that house to make him do that?"

Josiah pursed his lips but remained silent.

"Korah disappeared when he was ten years old, just took off at the Hewies. Adam thought he was with Mary, and Mary thought he was with Adam. He was gone for almost two weeks before anyone noticed. The Royal Guard found him two months later, hiding in a circus, caring for the horses and trick riding in the ring."

"Korah ran away with the circus?" Josiah asked incredulously.

"Indeed, and he ran away again when he was nineteen. But that time, he did not join the circus. He met and married a girl, and they had a daughter."

"What?" Josiah's eyes widened in shock. "I did not know that."

Simon shook his head. "There are very few who do. It was dirty business, how the family reacted. I was against it and left Alanthia shortly thereafter." His face became pinched, and he lost the spark that had animated him thus far. He seemed to grow ancient in the telling.

"Prince Adam and Sir Preston ben Worley found out where he was hiding, some tiny village in Pennsylvania. They kidnapped him and burned the town to the ground, killing his wife and his baby daughter. Afterward, they put him in a mental hospital and kept him there until he agreed to marry Lady Alexa. They marched him down the aisle ninety days after his wife and daughter burned to death."

Despite his abhorrence for his uncle, Josiah recoiled. He imagined what he would feel if his family did that to him and Davianna. They were expecting a baby, though they had told no one. But what would he become if someone burned them alive, then forced him to marry another woman? "That is abominable."

"It is what they did and more. They had commitment papers drawn up. If Korah ever tried to leave Alexa or did anything Adam or Mary deemed inappropriate, they had the power to put him back in a straight jacket and leave him there."

Josiah pressed his fingers into his left eye socket, feeling the pulse pounding beneath his fingertips as he realized this story was true. He remembered whispers, shouts, small bits of halted conversations, his uncle's black moods, and exchanged glances between the adults. He had not understood them when he was a child, but everything came into sudden, horrifying clarity. "What role did my father play in this?"

Simon steepled his hands and brought his index fingers to his mouth. "You were there. You saw what happened that day at the Hewies. We were both there."

Josiah turned to Simon, confusion written all over his face. He started blinking as pictures flashed across his mind, then he paled. "At the polo match? That's who that was?"

Simon nodded, closing his eyes.

"Oh, my Lord," Josiah breathed, "no wonder."

"So, you see, Prince Josiah, there is more to the story."

Lying quietly on the sofa in Josiah's office, unseen by either man, Davianna wept silently. She had fallen asleep reading a book and by the time she awoke, she was too embarrassed to reveal her presence. She knew what happened at that polo match.

February 2, 981 ME

The Pitch - New City - Korah

Saturday, the last day of competition of High Equestrian week in 981 ME, dawned clear and crisp. To Prince Korah ben Adam, the sky seemed bluer, the grass smelled sweeter, and he felt stronger and more alert than he ever had in his life. He closed his eyes and smiled, letting the sun warm his face, at peace standing on the pitch beside his pony. The Alanthian National Anthem played, his beloved wife and son were in the stands, and he was about to play the game he loved.

All was right with the world.

When the match began, there was magic in the air. It was one of those rare occasions when horse, rider, and mallet unified in perfect harmony. He heard nothing outside of his own breath, the pounding hooves on emerald grass, the satisfying smack of the ball as he drove toward the goal for the first score.

Out of the corner of his eye, he caught a commotion, a rider falling from his mount, but Korah drove onward, oblivious. He shot the ball unimpeded and turned his pony with a smile. The crowd behind him erupted in a cheer, and then he lost all sense of time.

He was transported back to that moment of discovery in Endor. His shock turned to elation. She was there, just as she had been that first day, standing in the stirrups, aiming a gun at him. Before he could react, before he could call out, before he processed what his mind refused to believe, Eamonn came alongside her on a thundering horse, lifted his mallet, and with the skill honed by a lifetime of practice, hit Sussanna ben Ross square in the temple.

Korah screamed.

He leapt from his horse and ran as she and the weapon fell to the ground. He reached her in seconds, cradling her head, crying. Sussanna blinked once, said his name in the precious and rare way she had, and died in his arms.

The scream of anguish that erupted from his heart imprinted itself on the brains of everyone present. It was a cry of unearthly pain, the sound of a desolate soul ripped asunder—destroyed.

They tried to separate him from her body, but he scrambled and grabbed the gun, holding them off. He protected her, tried to shield her, and begged her not to die, not to be dead. "Come back to me!"

Royal Guards surrounded them, blocking the spectacle. Officials forced an evacuation of the stands, and still Korah refused to give her over, refused to listen to reason, refused to see.

It took four hours before he relented, before he let his valet, McSwilley, usher him from the pitch. Prince Korah ben Adam left the field a completely broken man.

Part 10 - The Beast

February 16, 1000 ME

Dear Son - Gilead - Peter and Astrid

Peter backed away, recoiling like the letter Astrid held out to him had morphed into a venomous snake. "I do not care. I do not care what that says." He pointed a finger at her. "Burn it with him. Let it join him in Hell."

"The man who wrote this," her voice caught, "is the one you need to remember."

"Why? So I can grieve? So I can hurt more? So he can open another vein and inject more poison into me?" Peter held up a palm, his pinky jutting at an odd angle, a remnant of the torture he had endured. "No! I have paid with enough blood. I do not care what he had to say."

Astrid looked at him with compassion. He was flesh and blood, held together by cobwebs and tape in places. His father had inflicted most of the grievous wounds. "Do you want me to open it? I won't read it aloud, and if it contains anything that would hurt you, I will burn it; and we'll never speak of it again. It might be something, in time, that you will want, but we won't know unless one of us reads it. It can be me. He can't hurt me, and my job is to protect you."

"If you want to read it, read it. But keep it to yourself." He turned toward the door. "The trucks with the horses from the Palace should arrive soon. I am going to supervise. Then I am going to ride." He paused with his hand on the nob. "Damn your curiosity, Astrid."

"I'm sorry," she said, but the slamming door cut off her apology, and she knew he had not heard.

She turned the note over and found it sealed with old-fashioned wax, imprinted with the family crest, a castle and a dragon. She thought it appropriate for Korah and slipped her nail under the seal.

03 February 981 ME
Dear Peter,

I do not know when you will find this letter, if ever. If you do, you will have looked through the sketches and seen how much I loved you. I am sure it will be difficult for you to understand how I can write that, after what I have done, but it is the truth. This last year with you and your mother has been the most joyous of my life, which is astounding because I never thought I would find happiness again. But I promised your mother that I would try, and I did, truly I did.

You were the first step. 'Will you play horsey with me, Daddy?' Those sweet words cracked a wall I built around my empty heart, and you filled it completely. I adore you.

You will grow up to be a wonderful, strong, and wise man, of that, I have no doubt. Alas, the only way you will be able to do that is if I remove myself from your life. It devastates me to say goodbye to you, but after what happened yesterday, I cannot go on. I cannot put myself back together again. Please believe me; I am sorry.

But I fear what I will become. The darkness is already swallowing and reclaiming me, so I am writing as quickly as I can, while the daddy that loves you is still alive. I go now to murder the beast before it takes over, breaks loose, and kills everyone.

Take care of your mother. I love you, Son.

Korah ben Adam

Astrid shuddered, holding the suicide note. He had obviously not done it. The beast had broken free and done exactly what he feared it would do.

March 28, 981 ME

Lady in Red - California Coast - Korah and Angelica

"Chukka, what are you doing here?" Angelica ben Omri asked as she sashayed up to the cabana overlooking the Pacific.

Korah turned, his hazel eyes drooping and dead. "Go away, Angelica."

She scanned the grounds and said, "You royals do insane asylums rather well. This place is swanky, much nicer than the last place they put you."

"Go away," Korah repeated, closing his eyes and reclining on the cushioned chaise. "I am not allowed to have any visitors. I am dangerous."

She tsked. "They do not know how dangerous you are."

"Oh, I think they do." The three attendants he nearly killed certainly did.

"Did you honestly attempt to hang yourself?" she asked, inspecting him as if he had committed a fashion *faux pas*.

"Go away, Angelica. I am convalescing," he said in a monotone.

"Your valet deserves a commendation. Really, Korah, what a waste that would have been."

He turned his back on her. "I doubt it."

"What are they giving you? You sound like a zombie."

"You would know all about zombies, now wouldn't you? Or is that your little protégé Charlotte's forte?"

She chuckled and settled beside him in a lounge chair. "There you are. I was wondering if they drugged my Chukka completely out of existence."

Droll cynicism dripped from his tongue. "Perhaps an exorcism is in order. Chukka is not a very nice man."

She sighed with long-suffering resignation. "Who wants nice? Power is much sexier, and you, my dear, are on the cusp of it. If you would ever stop mewling around about your dead wife."

"Shut up, Angelica." He turned on her, his pupils going black. "Just shut the fuck up."

"No, I will not. I think I have been quiet long enough." Angelica delighted in the darkness lurking just below the surface of him. She called to it, offered it a treat, and coaxed it out of hiding.

Examining her long, red fingernail, she swirled it in the air, making green sparks fly from the tip.

"I could not understand it. For years, the Black Mansion was hidden from me, the Book of Power gone, all of it concealed since the fire." She touched his thigh, rather higher than was strictly friendly. "You know it is the anniversary today."

"I am well aware, which is why I am a zombie." He removed her hand decisively.

Nonplussed, Angelica continued, "The shroud in Endor made no sense until your little polo match; then it all became clear." Angelica gave him a bottom lip pout. "I am sorry, Chukka, but with the last of the Guardians gone, I acted on a hunch, and I was right. The Book of Power is released!" She smiled, self-satisfied and feline. "I came straight to your side. To offer my condolences, of course, but to offer my services."

He gave her a sidelong glance.

"Don't you want to make them pay, Chukka? Don't you want to take revenge for what they did in Endor, for what your brother did on the pitch that has brought you to this place?"

"Angelica, why do you think I am currently looking at the Pacific Ocean, anesthetized?" He rolled his shoulders, trying to get comfortable. "Because when I am not, it consumes me."

"Encouraging." She tapped her pouty lips and said, "That is what I wanted to hear. Did I ever tell you why I left law school in New York?"

He rolled his eyes, bored. "I believe at the time you mentioned you killed someone."

"Tragic accident, actually."

Korah laughed. "I am familiar with those, so was my sister-in-law."

"Oooo, do tell." Angelica squirmed, experiencing a rush of pleasure.

"You first," he said, though he did not particularly care to hear anything she had to say.

Angelica swept her long blonde hair over one shoulder, the coy flirtation wasted on him. "The girl joined my sorority, but afterward I discovered she was completely useless. She took exception to some of my, how shall I say it, extracurricular activities. So, I gave her a little concoction to relax her nerves." She batted her eyelashes, feigning innocence. "She overdosed and died. Oops." She tapped him on the shoulder. "Your turn."

Korah was drugged enough to tell her. He had never told a soul. If he was honest, he never thought about it. The incident was hazy, more of a dream than reality. "It was strange, really. I did not mean to do it, or more accurately, I did not do it with any premeditation. I was simply on my way to lunch. As I approached the steps, I saw Margaret, realized we were alone, and pushed her over the railing. I did not break stride, watch her fall, or even stop walking. I just stiff-armed her. I don't think I even looked at her when I did it." He shook his head, confused. "I continued down the hall, used the second set of steps, sat down to lunch, and ate. I remember being annoyed that I had to pretend to be upset because I was hungry."

His eyes were glassy, faraway and distant. "It happened not long after Endor. Eamonn was so happy. He had a baby and a wife. I…" He scrubbed his hands over his face. "It was so strange. I think these thoughts but never do them. Like you are sitting at dinner and think, 'I could throw this glass of wine in her face right now.' But you don't. It was like that. One of those strange random thoughts that pop into your mind." He shrugged. "I just did it."

Angelica threw back her head and laughed. "What a delightful tale. I love it." She kissed his cheek. "You are wasted trying to be a moral man. You are a consummate villain, Korah. Please embrace this about yourself. I implore you. Otherwise, you will continue to lounge in insane asylums up and down the coast. Why fight it?"

He turned to her, looking resigned, but he said nothing.

Now that she had his attention, she pressed her point home. "Besides, the Iron King let it happen. He stood aside and let it all happen."

His nose flared in distaste.

"I have discovered a way to release a power that will fight Him. The Prince who held the Earth and controlled it in the Last Age did not keep men bound to their plows nor living in darkness. He encouraged discovery, technology, and personal freedom. You have always desired that, since your early days. It burns in your heart. You could be the one to set it free, to set him free, and to set yourself free from this moral prison you lock yourself up in.

"I have the key, Chukka. I know how we can take over the world, just like I did in Endor, but on a grand scale." She pitched her voice low, seductive, tempting. "Don't you want to see them bleed for what they have done to you? Don't destroy yourself, destroy them."

An image of Peter flashed through Korah's mind, his perfect little boy. "Get the fuck away from me, or I will snap your neck."

Angelica cackled and rose from her chair. "Keep processing, Chukka. I will see you on the other side."

October 22, 981 ME

For Your Own Good - New City Palace - Korah and Alexa

Korah went back to being a shell. Except now, when the drugs wore off, he was not hollow. He was a swirling tempest of black muck. Vile, filthy thoughts bombarded his brain constantly, and every day he feared what he might do. Soon after returning home, he awoke from a violent dream and stumbled into Alexa's room. "You need to take Peter and go visit your father."

She turned over in bed and held her arms out to him. He saw clearly that she did not understand. She was still trying to love him.

"I think that is a marvelous idea. A change of scenery might be good for all of us." Her tone was solicitous, soothing. It set his teeth on edge.

"I am not going. There is much to be done here, most of which backed up in my," he tilted his head and feigned a smile, "absence."

She rose but halted before she got too close. Good, she was learning.

"Korah," she held his eyes, "I do not want to leave you. You just got home, and we missed you."

He knew she spoke the truth. She had missed him, but she missed a dead man. He refused to see anyone while he was in the asylum, could not let her see him like that. She had come six times. He sent her away six times. She had taken Eamonn's advice and moved into the New City Palace during his illness. They thought a change of scenery, a new house, without the specter of his mother and father, might make a difference. They were wrong.

He closed his eyes, clinging to reason, fighting. "Alexa," his voice strangled, his teeth gritted, "you need to get away from me. You need to take Peter and go."

Something in his expression must have warned her he was serious because she nodded. "All right, on one condition."

"What condition?"

"That while we are gone, you will try as you did before. Do you remember?"

"I do, which is why I am sending you both away." He turned and said over his shoulder. "I do not want to hurt you, Alexa. Don't come back."

She left for six months on a Goodwill Tour. She should have listened to him, should have stayed away. Because by the time she returned, the Beast was in total control. Korah ben Adam was no more.

December 5, 981 ME

A Difference of Opinion - New City Palace - Korah and Eamonn

Two months after the doctors discharged Korah from the hospital, Eamonn stormed into Korah's office and slapped a file on his desk. "What in the hell, or shall I rephrase that? What hell are you trying to release on my kingdom?"

"Good morning. Somebody woke up on the wrong side of the bed." Korah leaned back in his chair, striking an urbane, cool posture.

"This," Eamonn picked up the papers and shook them at Korah, "has nothing to do with what side of the bed I woke up on."

"You should not let papers get you so riled up. What are they?" Korah asked, though he had a pretty good idea.

Eamonn leaned his hands against Korah's desk, his face flushed with anger. "The transcript of your speech last evening to the Business Council."

Korah grimaced. "It was terrible. You did not miss a thing. Poached chicken. Why do they always serve poached chicken at those dinners?"

"Dammit, Korah!" Eamonn threw the papers on Korah's desk and stalked over to the window. "Your speech is in direct contradiction with the law, Alanthian policies, and undermines everything

I am trying to do to diffuse the situation. Alanthia is a powder keg about to explode, and you are the damn match. Stop it!"

Korah dropped his veneer of indifference and snapped, "That powder keg is going to explode whether I light the match or not. You can either get on board or be blown up."

"If I get on board, I will get us blown up!" Eamonn swung around and pointed a finger at his brother. "This is rebellion. You are fomenting rebellion and lawlessness."

"For a phone?" Korah reached into his desk drawer and pulled out a broken, ancient device. "One of these will spell the end of Alanthia? Or will it just enable us to call across the kingdom? If I had one, perhaps I could speak to my wife and son."

"It is not about that, and you know it," Eamonn ground out.

"Then what is it about? Is it about keeping people on their farms, strapped to their plows, while we," he stalked over to the wall and flicked the electric lights on and off, "live in luxury? You did not seem to have a problem with technology when we were renovating this place."

"It was already here." Eamonn drew himself up, but his voice lost some of its conviction. He knew he was on shaky ground.

"Ah, yes, it was, but you did not balk when they refurbished it. You had the new sections wired and equipped, just as the ancient sections were. The reconstruction of this place is part of the reason people are clamoring," Korah said, growing passionate. "The innovations we discovered here provided the spark, not me. Besides, this movement has been brewing for decades, at least since the early '60s."

"Yes, I know all about your little stint with the technology radicals back then, but where did it get you? How different would your life have been if you had just come home, Korah?" Eamonn glared.

Black rage erupted inside Korah. He wanted to take Eamonn's head and shove it through the plate-glass window. "Home to what, Brother?"

Eamon took a deep breath and exhaled slowly. "I am sorry. That was uncalled for." He gestured to the sitting area, intent on making peace and having a rational discussion.

"You are right, the people are clamoring for it, and it might come organically, whether I give a thousand speeches against it," he gave Korah a pointed look, "or you a thousand for it. The fact remains that the laws forbidding technological research and production go back centuries. They are not for me to flaunt or change without the consensus of the other Ruling Princes and the blessing from the King," Eamonn said, resolute on this point. "I am working through legal and proper channels, Korah, but I will not sanction lawlessness or rebellion. It never ends well for the rebels."

Korah shot Eamonn a long-suffering look but held his tongue.

Eamonn pressed his point home. "Consider what is happening in Greece. There is full-scale rebellion in parts of the kingdom. The jihadists have taken root there and are slaughtering anyone who does not subscribe to their fanatical beliefs. The Iron King allows it because Antiochus is dabbling in things he should not be."

Korah crossed his arms and said dismissively, "Antiochus is a reckless fool."

"And what of Egypt? They did not have rain for forty years, Korah, forty years!"

"Are you planning to suspend our Easter Passover celebration, Eamonn?" Korah asked sarcastically, referring to the ill-advised measures Ruling Prince Benu took in the final years of his reign.

"You are missing the point!" Eamonn threw his hands up in a helpless gesture. "The Iron King's judgments against Egypt and Greece were a direct result of the rebelliousness of the Ruling Prince! What sort of ruler would I be if I risked the lives of our citizens, the fertility of our fields, and the security of villages for a phone?"

"It is not about a phone, Eamonn. It is about power, about giving ordinary people the ability to improve their lives. It takes power from us and gives it to them."

"To then do what? Because you know what men did in the Last Age. They used technology to propagate sin, to organize against the Iron King. If we let it loose, it will take over. You cannot control what happens. It is the proverbial Pandora's Box. Lucifer will not be bound forever, and how much easier will it be for him to find the Earth once again wired and ready for rebellion? Billions died last time, Korah, billions."

"And mother always accused me of being the paranoid one."

"God rest her soul." Eamon shook his head, still grieving the loss of their mother. "And I am not being paranoid."

Korah vehemently disagreed with Eamonn on all points, but he kept his opinions to himself. Instead, he envisioned a free Alanthia, a technological wonderland of prosperity and enormous potential. Then he contemplated digging up his mother's corpse and setting it aflame.

August 1, 982 ME

Every Quarter - New City - Korah

There was a stranger who came to see Eamonn once a quarter. He was not an official, did not sign in, and was never announced. The butler showed him to Eamonn's study, where he stayed for a quarter-hour, then departed. Korah noticed the man when he first returned from the hospital, specifically because the stranger shied away from him. Korah dismissed the incident, reasoning the man may have been a spectator on the pitch. Many who were could not meet his eyes.

The second time he encountered the stranger, his skittish behavior grew even more pronounced. The third time, Korah followed him. He wanted to know who he was and find out what his business was with Eamonn.

Korah tailed him through the New City. Keeping a careful distance, he was unobserved by his quarry or anyone else. He learned long ago he could move among people easily if he dressed in plain clothing. An hour after leaving the Palace, the man entered a small office where the lettering over the door read, 'Taylor Private Inquiries'.

Korah hung back, wondering why a private investigator was coming to the Palace once a quarter. If their business was official, Eamonn would have engaged the Royal Guard or the FBI. Something about the entire situation smelled rotten. He could not say why, but he suspected whatever his brother was up to involved him, and he planned to find out exactly what that was.

He took up a bench in the small park across the street, biding his time, as dark anger began building in his gut. Morning and night, he swallowed the pills that kept the rage at bay, kept it caged, but it was always there. In the waiting, it broke free, so by the time he stepped through the door of Taylor's Private Inquiries, the Beast was in full control.

"Mr. Taylor, I require a word," Korah said, closing the inner office door and engaging the lock.

The man failed to hide his shock at seeing Prince Korah in his small office, but he also failed to disguise a flash of guilt. He wore it just as surely as he did his ill-fitting suit. Trying to recover, he plastered a smile of false solicitude and bowed. "Of course, my Esteemed, welcome. What can I do for you?"

Korah's pupils elongated. Taylor backed up by instinct. "I have seen you at the Palace several times. What business do you have with my brother?"

"I am sorry, my Esteemed, but I cannot divulge that information. It is privileged."

Korah stepped forward, coiled to strike. "How can it be privileged when I am the subject of the inquiry, am I not?"

"No, no, no. I fear there has been a misunderstanding. I apologize for any confusion, and I am sorry, but I really must go, my Esteemed." Taylor tried to move past him, and the death adder struck.

Holding the man by the throat, Korah hissed, "Not until you tell me."

Taylor choked and gagged, clutching at Korah's hands, but he read menace in those reptilian eyes; and knew he was either going to speak or die. "Okay," he choked.

Korah threw him against the wall.

Taylor gave a mighty whoosh and felt a trickle of blood run down the back of his neck. Icy terror gripped his bowels, and the detective prayed he would not soil himself.

"I am waiting, sir," Korah said, his soothing voice at complete odds with his menacing demeanor. He did not flush, he did not breathe heavily, he simply watched and waited.

"I was hired two years ago," Taylor's voice shook, "after Prince Eamonn received a letter, he wanted me to investigate."

Korah inched toward him. "And what were the contents of this letter that it warranted a private investigation?"

Taylor scanned his office, looking for an escape.

Korah struck again with a quick jab to the gut. When Taylor was bent over, gasping, he grabbed his hair and yanked him up, screaming in his ear, "What did it say?"

"It was a ransom note!"

"Go on," Korah coaxed, tightening his grip.

"Please," Taylor begged, his eyes watering, his nose running. "It turned out to be nothing."

"Tell me!" Korah snarled.

"The writer claimed to have your daughter, Hope," the man sobbed.

Korah's vision went black as he flung the man into a set of filing cabinets with a crash. "What?" he raged.

"I'm sorry, my Esteemed." Taylor fell to his knees. "The Ruling Prince paid the ransom, but no one ever collected the money. The girl was not at the appointed place, and there was never another note." Taylor looked up, imploring. "I have searched for two years. There is no trace of her. We concluded it was a hoax."

"Do you have the note?" Korah demanded.

Taylor crawled across the floor and pulled himself up to his desk. Unlocking the top drawer with shaking hands, he pulled out a hefty file, dropped it, and backed away. "It is all there. Take it."

Korah glanced between the file and the pale, trembling man, then he smiled, and Taylor realized he was looking into the hazel eyes of a madman. They were the last thing he ever saw.

Eamonn discovered the same thing three years later because Korah never took another dose of his medicine, and the Beast demanded revenge.

January 6, 983 ME

Birthday Party Bombshell - New City Palace - Eamonn and Alexa

With Peter's fifth birthday party in full swing on the Palace lawn, Alexa burst into Eamonn's study. "Who was that girl, Eamonn?"

Eamonn met her eyes and answered gravely, "I do not know."

"Where is she now?"

"I had her removed and am having her followed."

"What was she doing here?" Alexa shrieked.

"I cannot say, but I am looking into the situation."

"She was talking to Peter! I could not believe it when I saw her.

What was she saying to my son?"

Eamonn walked to the bar and poured a drink. "You will need to find out diplomatically, of course."

"Obviously," Alexa snarled. "Do you think it was her?"

"I don't know, but she stared at me like Korah does when he is ready to pick a fight. It was uncanny."

Alexa groaned. "She looked just like her, like that woman."

"I know," Eamonn said, downed his bourbon and poured another. "Her face is permanently imprinted on my brain."

Alexa gave him a hard look. "Mine, too."

"Well, we could be mistaken. She might just be some girl hired to serve at the birthday party. Let's not jump to any conclusions."

Alexa stamped her foot in frustration. "Why didn't they both just die?"

"Alexa!" Eamonn said, taken aback.

She covered her eyes and shook her head. "I'm sorry. I am just so upset by the prospect of this. He got over it. He finally got over it."

"I know."

"We were fine, no, we were perfect. Then *she* shows up and tries to kill him." Alexa shook her fists, beside herself. "You realize there is a possibility if *she* survived the fire, then so did the baby, and that girl looked exactly like her."

Eamonn passed Alexa a drink. "Well, I suppose it is a good thing Korah was not here today."

Alexa accepted the vodka and downed it in a single gulp. "He is with his mistress, the other Endorite whore. They are like a curse, a disease that never goes away. The legacy of that place eats him alive, Eamonn."

"I'll fix it." Eamonn drew his shoulders back and set his jaw. "I have been protecting my brother since the day he was born. I will not stop now."

"I know, but I don't think he sees it. He has seen nothing clearly since that day on the pitch."

Eamonn gave Alexa's shoulder a light squeeze of encouragement. "He came out of it once. He will do it again."

Alexa deflated. After two years, her hope was fading. "What are we going to do?"

"You will not do anything. I will handle this." He took her empty glass and guided her toward the door. "Go now. They will notice your absence at the party. Leave the details to me."

Alexa squeezed her temples, a throbbing headache pulsing behind her eyes. "If that girl is his daughter, and we hide she is alive," she paused, "Eamonn, if he ever finds out, he will kill us both."

Who's That Girl? - New City Palace - Eamonn and Stephen

It did not take Eamonn long to discover how the girl got onto the grounds. She had been hired as temporary help to serve at Peter's birthday party, but Eamonn was intrigued to learn her application had been shepherded through the system by Stephen ben McSwilley, the son of Korah's long-serving valet.

He planned to examine her background check the Royal Guard ran on all employees, but that would have to wait until his head of security returned from his surveillance of the girl. To ask for it himself would raise suspicion. He needed to handle this with the utmost discretion, but he could question the boy. When he learned the young man had served Korah his supper, a change in routine, he suspected the valet's son and that girl were in cahoots, and decided to find out exactly what was going on.

"My Esteemed," the young man said from the door to his study, his voice and knees visibly shaking. "You wished to see me?"

Eamonn nodded. "Sit down, Stephen."

"Yes, my Esteemed," Stephen squeaked.

"I understand you brought a girl into service today. Who was she?"

"Kayah?" Stephen asked, his voice cracking. "I am sorry about that, my Esteemed. She is one of my classmates. I was trying to help her earn a little extra money by serving during the party."

"And is she a friend of yours?"

"Yes, um, well, sort of, but not really." Stephen flushed crimson. "I have known her since the sixth grade. We started at Euler together."

"The math and science school?" Eamon asked, unsure what to make of that. The academic requirements to get into Euler were stringent. Less than two percent of applicants gained admission.

"Yes, my Esteemed. She is an excellent chemist and a gifted

analyst, one of the most popular kids at school. Everyone really likes her."

Eamonn raised an eyebrow, understanding why this gawky young man might seek to earn favor with one of the pretty girls at school, but that he served his brother dinner suggested there was more going on.

Unnerved by Eamonn's silence, Stephen kept speaking. "She tries to hide it, and most of the kids at school don't know, but she is an orphan, so she attends Euler on a scholarship. I suppose that has given her a few rough edges."

"Ahh," Eamonn said, his mind processing the information. "That explains her impudent behavior during the party."

"Yes, my Esteemed. I am sorry about that."

Eamonn adopted an admonishing tone, channeling his mother. "While your motivation to assist someone of lesser circumstances is admirable, she clearly lacked the proper decorum or temperament required for royal service. You were raised in this house, and your parents are valued members of the staff. I should not have to remind you of the high standards we set."

Stephen hung his head. "I apologize, my Esteemed. It will not happen again."

"Very well," Eamonn soothed, then hoping to take the young man off guard asked, "You served the Prince's dinner tonight, why?"

Stephen paled. "My father was tired. I offered to take the tray up."

Eamonn raised a dark eyebrow. The boy was lying. He suspected whatever the girl was up to, she was using Stephen to get to Korah. "Is that all?"

Stephen nodded, his prominent Adam's apple bobbing. "Yes, my Esteemed."

"Very well, Stephen. Goodnight."

The boy all but ran out of the study. Eamonn watched the door close, reviewing what he had learned. An orphan? Eamon calculated that Stephen would have known the girl at least five, perhaps six years. Sussanna died two years ago, which meant she probably was not living with her mother when she died.

A knock on the door interrupted Eamonn's thoughts.

"My Esteemed," Oliver ben Parson, his head of security, entered, "would you like a report?"

"By all means, Oliver."

"I followed the young lady as you requested. She left here and headed straight for one of the older sections of town. There is a derelict farm at the edge of Baker's Corners. She ducked under a broken section of fence and entered a rocky alcove. I observed from a distance, scouting the area. Twenty minutes later, I saw a young Asian girl leave, followed shortly thereafter by a big young man dressed in overalls. At dusk, the target reappeared, and I resumed the tail.

"I thought she may have detected my pursuit because her path seemed random, erratic. Then I realized she was feeding several stray animals. Finally, she entered the Home for New City Orphans and did not reemerge."

Oliver frowned. "I returned to investigate the deserted farm and discovered an ancient underground computer facility. They have a lab down there and are obviously doing illegal research."

Eamonn's nose flared, trying to fit the pieces together. "Keep the place under surveillance. I want to know who is going inside, specifically I want to know if Stephen ben McSwilley is involved."

"The valet's son?" Oliver asked.

"Indeed," Eamonn said gravely. "Report only to me and bring me the background check on that girl."

Two days later, soldiers raided the bunker, and Kayah ben Alanthia, aka Kayah ben Samuel, aka Hope ben Korah was arrested. The prosecutor in the case had strict orders to ensure the girl was imprisoned for as long as the law allowed.

To himself and to Alexa, Eamonn claimed he had done it for Korah, that his brother's sanity hung in the balance. But the real truth was that Prince Eamonn ben Adam was his mother's son, and Mary would never have tolerated some wild seed of his brother's youth, by a would-be assassin, polluting the royal bloodline. He certainly could not tolerate having the girl three heartbeats away from the throne. If anyone ever discovered her identity, time in prison would overshadow any play she might make to take power. While unpleasant, it was the cost of leadership. Sometimes sacrifices had to be made.

What Eamonn did not realize was that the instrument of his destruction had been delivered into his brother's hands, courtesy of the royal daughter Eamonn sent to prison.

September 2, 985 ME

Guest List - New City Palace - Korah and Marduk

"Hand it over, I want to review the names," Marduk, in the guise of Secretary Tristin, said, extending his hand.

The Palace steward cast a questioning eye to Prince Korah at the blatant flaunting of protocol, but the Prince demurred, and the steward passed the list.

"Leave us." Tristin dismissed him with a wave of his hand.

The steward again glanced toward Korah, who nodded.

The steward lifted a haughty chin and bowed. "I remain at your service, my Esteemed." He put particular emphasis on the latter half of the sentence.

Korah concealed a smile. His staff bristled under the imperious manner of the Dark Master, and it gave him a tiny measure of satisfaction that he kept at least that much control. He regretted he would now have to reassign the steward. The Dark Master did not abide insult. If he removed the man, he would live. If he did not, he would have a fatal accident.

"It meets with your approval, Tristin?" Korah asked.

By mutual agreement, when they spoke aloud, they maintained the charade that Marduk was human, the Ruling Prince's closest advisor. Marduk did not need to speak to communicate with Korah, he could, and often did, merely invade his mind, and take control. Sometimes Korah had a memory of it, sometimes not. He tried to convince himself that it was Marduk who did the cruel things he did, but that was not always the case. It was him, and he knew it.

Tristin studied the list, running his finger down the names. "I see you have invited Eamonn's closest allies, Stockton, Philadelphia, Sedgefield. Do you think that is wise?"

Korah shrugged. "I think it would appear suspicious if we excluded them, and I doubt Sedgefield and Philadelphia will make the trip."

"Shame we cannot merely kill them all," his guttural voice whispered into Korah's mind.

"Again, suspicious," Korah answered aloud. He did not like answering telepathically if he could avoid it, but he hid that fact. There were many things he hid from the Dark Master.

He learned quickly that Marduk exploited every weakness to the most terrifying degree. Anything Korah feared, Marduk perpetuated. Anything Korah loved, Marduk destroyed. However, the Dark Master failed to comprehend the cunning intelligence of Korah ben Adam. He was cocksure and arrogant, certain a mere human could not withstand a mind invasion by one such as he. Marduk never truly understood who he was dealing with. Korah spent a lifetime deceiving everyone, hiding the dark things that lurked in his mind. In his own right, Korah was a master.

In the first days of Marduk's release, Korah realized he needed to guard his every thought. The Dark Master was not his mother, who had been able to read his facial expressions and moods when he was a child. Hiding his emotions for her gave him the necessary training he needed while dealing with Marduk.

He imagined his mother's reaction to Secretary Tristin and laughed. Princess Mary would have been a formidable foe. She might have made a run at him before Marduk cut out her vicious tongue and fed it to her. That would have been fitting. But she had been in the grave since December of '80. She had not lived to see Korah's final fall. He was glad she was dead. They were all dead now, except Peter and Alexa.

As Marduk exerted more and more control, Korah found himself once again bargaining with the devil for the lives of his wife and his child, but this time, he did it on his own terms. He took the tender feelings he had for them, the love, the affection—delicate and precious things—and put them in a box, then locked it with a permanent key. He hid it, deep inside his mind, away from Marduk's probing and detection, safe from the Beast, inside and out. Korah did not allow himself access, did not even look at the box, because if he did, the Dark Master would kill them, of that Korah was certain. Outwardly, he treated his family with contempt, the softest emotion he allowed himself or them. It became easier as time went on, a habit, and with every cutting remark, every proverbial slap in the face, every cold rejection, another shovel of dirt buried the box.

Tristin threw the list on Korah's desk. "Add more maidens to the invitation list. I want my choice."

Korah raised an eyebrow in speculation. "Your choice?"

Tristin grinned, lascivious lust shimmering behind black eyes.

"It has been quite some time since I have laid between the thighs of a woman, Korah. I desire to do so again."

Korah rubbed his jaw in contemplative silence. "You tempt his wrath."

"He has ignored me. Perhaps he has grown old and is no longer as fearsome as I remember." Tristin's chest swelled with pride. "Perhaps, he does not see all in this age."

Korah glanced at a stack of missives from the Golden Kingdom. "The letters seem to suggest otherwise."

"Yet, he does nothing, to you or to me." He grabbed his crotch with enthusiasm. "I think a little pussy is worth the risk, don't you, Korah? I think you fuck that pretty little pussy you've got upstairs regularly. Why don't you let me fuck her? What do you say to that, Korah? How about I fuck your wife?"

Korah rolled his eyes. "You can if you want, but she is not that great. If I had to risk the Lake of Fire for some pussy, it would not be hers." He shuddered with true revulsion, "Trust me," he pointed to three names on the list, "much better pussy."

"Who is better, your mistress or your wife?" Tristin teased with an evil gleam in his eyes.

"Angelica is feistier. Alexa cries a lot."

Tristin oozed menace and said, "I made her cry. I gave her a brief glimpse of the real me while she was sleeping."

Korah pressed his temple. "Great, now she will crawl in my bed sobbing."

Tristin recoiled, "I hate a crying woman, screaming is okay, fighting is better. The sobbers, oh, I despise them."

Korah studied the guest list with intent. "Charlotte," he pointed to the name, "is promising, one of Angelica's proteges. She is a voodoo priestess, talented."

Thus, they began perusing the guest list, discussing the potential maidens with whom Marduk would mate.

Korah recalled the steward and said, "I approve this list, please send the invitations today."

"As you wish, my Esteemed." The steward bowed and walked backward out the door as protocol demanded. He nearly crashed into the young Prince who hung outside his father's study.

"Is that the guest list for the Coronation Ball?" Peter asked.

The steward smiled fondly. "It is indeed, my Esteemed. Would you care to review it?"

An odd expression passed over Peter's face. "No, that is unnecessary."

He gestured for the steward to walk with him. As they made their way down the hall, the steward observed that Prince Peter's confident strut would have marked him a royal even if he wore beggar's clothing.

"It is going to be a grand affair, is it not?" Peter said conversationally.

The steward stiffened. The house should still be in mourning, but he did not speak aloud what everyone thought. "I believe it will be an event to remember."

"I would like to add a name to the list. Please send an invitation to my friend, Persa ben Yereq, of Rivergate Farms in Redding California."

The steward grinned. "Your friend, a young lady your age? Is Prince d'Or already a ladies' man?"

Peter winked in exaggerated roguishness, comical on the face of an eight-year-old. "I am, and she is older. I think she is twenty, and she has a boyfriend, but we will not invite him, just her."

The steward resisted the urge to ruffle the little imp's blond hair. "Where did you meet a twenty-year-old woman, my Esteemed?"

"At the World Equestrian Games. I really liked her. You will put her name on the list?" The Prince's cocksure shell faltered and behind the sparkling emerald eyes, a very sad little boy looked up at him.

The steward's heart broke. For all Peter's bravado, he was lonely. The steward caught the way he looked at his father, longing for a simple smile, a kind word, or sign of affection, that never came.

"Please tell me her name again, my Esteemed. I will have her invitation delivered by a special messenger, just for you."

Prince Peter flashed him a smile, a genuine one, that lit up the room and made the steward glad that he could do this small thing for the little boy.

October 22, 985 ME

One of the Dark Days - New City Palace - Alexa

Instead of a proper coronation in the Golden Kingdom, Korah went his own way and planned the event in the New City. Claiming it signaled a new era, he solidified his rebellion against the Iron King, and if that was not bad enough, he chose one of his black days to do it.

Alexa was no fool. He did it on purpose. With Korah, nothing happened by coincidence. He was as calculated as an astrophysicist. Officially, he claimed the Coronation was a fitting end to the Feast of Tabernacles and invited pilgrims from across the kingdom to spend their traditional week in tents on the ample grounds of the New City parks.

For Alexa, she could garner no happiness, could not muster excitement that her husband was assuming the Alanthian throne today. He was a usurper, an imposter. The throne should never have been his. Eamonn had only been forty-five when he died.

The night of Eamonn's murder, Korah came to her bed, and for a brief instant, she saw him again, the real Korah. He made love to her like he had in the tender year. Not in the distracted, business-like way he had since the disaster on the pitch. But he had used her to establish his alibi, and she had fallen for it.

Then Peter showed up in her bedroom with Josiah in tow, bearing the news that Korah was plotting to kill his nephew. She realized then what he had done, and she knew Josiah was in grave danger. So, they staged a suicide. Josiah penned a note, and Alexa helped him escape with enough money to get to the Golden Kingdom.

For months they waited for word, biding their time, pretending they did not know the truth, but nothing happened. Josiah was a smart, resourceful young man, but he was just that, a young man. Alone and grieving, any number of calamities might have befallen him along the road. She knew there was a distinct probability Josiah was not coming back, and Alexa had to prepare for the future.

The future was Peter.

Keeping him alive and safe to assume the throne when Korah's crimes were uncovered became her number one priority. When that happened, he would need Alexa at his side. No one would have Peter's interest at heart more than she. So, she calculated and planned. She paid attention to the issues, observed his advisors, listened in on conversations, and absorbed it all.

In the end, Alexa saw too much.

Part 11- Sons & Daughters

The Visitors Arrive - Gilead - Astrid and Genevieve

"Thank you for coming, Genevieve." Jarrod ben Adriel said, moving to greet their new arrivals. "Mrs. Nakamura, welcome to Gilead."

Himari stepped through the massive oak doorway and entered a world where time had stopped. The immense Grand Foyer was decorated with a mixture of art and weaponry, huge shields and swords, sumptuous tapestries, and priceless paintings. The art took her breath away, and she thought with a pang that Filippo would love it. "Wow, I read about this place when I was in school, but I never took a tour."

Genevieve inhaled the potent scent of furniture polish and antiques and said, "I lived here for almost twenty years."

Himari cut her a quick glance, noting the difference between the Castle and Genevieve's tiny ranch house. "But your place has internet."

"We have more than the internet, don't we, Himari?"

"Mrs. Nakamura, I outfitted one of the salons with equipment. I fear it is not what we assembled at Genevieve's, but it may suit your needs." He nodded to the waiting footman. "Sedric will show you to the Yellow Salon." Himari's face registered her surprise, and Jarrod gave a non-committal shrug. "It was a precautionary measure."

"Jarrod is a wonder," Astrid said as she came into the foyer, wearing a slate blue sweater and gray trousers. "Welcome to Gilead, ladies."

Genevieve curtsied, "Your Grace, thank you." She straightened, seemed to decide something, and said, "I am going to hug you."

"Okay," Astrid said with a chuckle. "Thank you for everything you did while we were running." Then she turned to Himari. "You too, Sunflower."

Himari bowed with Japanese grace and said, "It was my honor."

They stood in the foyer, smiling at one another.

Genevieve looked up at the ceiling and turned to Jarrod. "What are all these weapons and shields? The Grand Foyer never looked like this. Who thought this was a good idea?"

"I believe it was for the tourists." The corner of Jarrod's mouth quivered with a suppressed smile. "I cannot say whose idea it was, but it brings to mind the keep of a Scottish laird, does it not?"

They both burst out laughing, sharing what was no doubt a private joke. Himari and Astrid exchanged bemused looks. The tense air hovering around the valet slackened for a moment. He had called the bunker this morning and asked them to come to Gilead. He had not said why but given the violence at the Palace two days ago, Himari suspected Peter might be reeling, which meant Auntie G. was being called into action.

"Forgive us," Jarrod apologized. "Mrs. Nakamura, Sedric will take you to the Yellow Salon. Please ring if you require anything."

As Himari walked away, Astrid cast her eyes about, uncertain what to do, but with enough manners and sense not to leave her visitor standing in the foyer. "Um, would you like to come in and have a seat?"

"Shall I have tea brought into the Green Drawing Room, your Grace?" Jarrod offered.

"I think that would be lovely, thank you." She smiled and wondered if she was supposed to lead the way or if he would show them into the room. It was daunting, all the things she did not know.

Jarrod picked up on her uncertainty and intoned. "If you ladies would follow me?"

"Oh my," Genevieve exclaimed, looking around. "I am so glad they did not change this room. It is exactly how I remember it. I half expect Princess Mary to come strolling in."

Astrid perched on the edge of a sofa and asked, "You knew her?"

"Indeed." Genevieve sat down, noting the young Duchess' troubled expression. "I came to Gilead with Princess Margaret as her companion."

Astrid folded her hands in her lap and nodded. "That is why I asked Jarrod to call you. He did not come into Peter's service until the early '90s. I wanted to speak with someone who was here before, specifically in 981 ME."

Genevieve stiffened. "Of course. How can I be of assistance?"

Astrid rose from her perch, retrieved the bound sketchbook, and placed it on the table in front of Genevieve. "I need you to tell me if these are real."

Genevieve eyed the book. "All right." As she flipped through the pages, she traced the lines of Peter's face. "He was such an adorable little boy." When she got to the picture of Korah and Peter on horseback, she covered her eyes. "So long ago, such a brief moment in time."

"They are real?" Astrid suspected but needed confirmation.

"Yes, they are. Did he see this?"

"He did, and it upset him. He's been out riding since."

"Like father, like son." She flipped through the drawings. "I had almost forgotten. He was such a troubled man, dark and sarcastic. But there was this one year." Genevieve tapped the book as her voice trailed off.

Astrid bit her thumbnail, then ventured ahead. "There was a letter from Korah in the book addressed to Peter. He would not read it, but I told him I would. Unfortunately, it created more questions than answers. What I want to know is what caused that man," she pointed at the book, "to become such a monster?"

Genevieve shook her head. "I suppose the time has come for me to tell the tale, but Peter needs to hear the whole truth because it did not start or end in '81. This house," she looked around, "suffered because of secrets, because of what happened."

"I do not know if he will listen. This has shaken him up. No matter how he tries to pretend otherwise." Astrid stared at the blown glass chandelier. "There is a small part of him that wants to grieve his father, and he does not understand why. I think that book holds the reasons, and if you can shed some light on it, that will help him get through it."

Peter rode like the Devil was after him. Tearing through the woods, bending low over the saddle, he pushed his horse and himself. The groundskeepers maintained the riding trails, keeping them clear of debris and fallen limbs. Peter and the stallion careened down the path in a headlong charge. He had left his phone behind, fearing if he brought it with him, he would call one of his dealers. He wanted to get high, he wanted to hit someone, so he rode.

At length, the working portion of the estate came into view. Modern and ancient blended, horses and wagons stood alongside tractors and balers. Mack would feel at home here. Peter did not. Nevertheless, a few of the workers spotted him, and he would be remiss to not speak a word. He walked his tired horse up to the barn and nodded with thanks to the groom, who offered to tend to the animal.

The man in charge looked unconcerned about Peter's unexpected arrival. He pocketed his work gloves and smiled. "Prince Peter ben Korah, good afternoon. I am Joshua."

The Worst of Filippo - Thyatira Woods - Kayah and Filippo

"I suppose there is one good thing to come out of you crashing the car. No mafia hitmen will find me out here," Kayah said as she reined her horse around a mud puddle.

"I did not crash the car. All the other cars, they crash into me." Filippo cursed in Italian as his mount stopped dead in front of the puddle, throwing him forward in the saddle. "What is a wrong with this horse? She is a scared of a puddle? Why you get me this one? She is a stubborn."

"You are the worst horseman I have ever seen." Kayah declared and trotted back to him. "Where did you learn to ride?"

"The worst hat, the worst driver, and now the worst horseman." Filippo threw a hand up in the air. "We did mostly walking. It was a small village I grew up in. We had wine and art. You do not need horses in the piazzas." Then he added in an irritated tone, "Where you learn to ride, Kayah? I cannot imagine they had horses in the orphanage. How you learn to ride like the pictures I saw of you in London?"

A ghost crossed her face, and she looked at the damp mud and leaf scattered ground. "It was part of my training. The Old Man insisted." She took the bridle on Filippo's stubborn horse and eased her around the puddle. Setting a slower pace, she elaborated, "I excelled at it, and I like animals."

Filippo's exasperation ebbed away with the smooth walk. Banged up with a pounding headache, the walk was easier on his bruised ribs. Kayah emerged from the wreck without a scratch. He, on the other hand, spent the night in the hospital with a concussion. Their car was totaled and with chaos ravaging the kingdom, they rode to Rephidim instead of trying to procure another vehicle. "Riding lessons, they saved your life, eh?"

"I supposed they did." She withdrew into herself, brooding.

"He did the training with you, huh? That is where you learned to do what you do?" Filippo asked.

Kayah glanced at him, anger bubbling just below the surface. "Horses, among other things. I knew how to defend myself." She had not spoken about Sir Preston since Filippo's bombshell revelation two days before. "He tried to teach me languages, but I am terrible at them. After the Civil War ended, he sent me to a farm in upstate New York. That is where I learned what I needed to know."

Filippo shook his head at the irony. "I went to art school. You went to assassin school."

"Not just that. It was a finishing school of sorts. We learned things like table manners, social etiquette, and ballroom dancing. I can name every Duchy, Earldom, and Barony, tell you who the current peer is, where their manor house sits, and what they call it. I learned to play poker, blackjack, whist, and bridge. You can drop me into a back-alley numbers game or the Duke of Renata's Red Salon. I will be equally at home. I don't sing, but I can play a passible piano.

"And yes, there was weaponry training and courses on civil engineering. We got to dabble in a bit of ordinance, so that was fun. Believe it or not, I have always been a decent chemist, so I can whip up something that will kill a man with a single drop. But unless I need to make something look like an accident, I skip the poison. A blade to the heart is so much more efficient."

Filippo cast her a sideways glance, remembering the man he killed the night they broke him out of Massimo's mansion.

Kayah continued, as if a damn had broken. "It was certainly better than prison, and I saw an opportunity to be more than I was. I was damn good at it," she paused, staring at the path ahead, "and it made the Old Man proud. He came up to the farm when I finished. I trained for a year and a half." She let a desperate note of hope escape her lips. "Filippo, are you sure?"

He nodded. "When I saw my uncle, I knew. He does not leave Italy, so I wondered why he was there. I did not go into the law office to get your key. I did not know who I would find. Maybe somebody would recognize me, maybe my entire family was inside and the minute I stepped inside, I am trapped."

His face clouded, and he resettled himself in the saddle to ease the stabbing pain in his ribs. "So, I checked into a hotel, and I thought about things for a few days. I did not know what I was going to do, and my mind, it was not right. I got to thinking if Sir Preston is a Giovanni, then maybe I have not been hiding all these years, maybe my Himari, she is in danger from me." He shrugged. "It was a bleak time."

"How did you hear about the hit?" Kayah asked.

"I am Italian," Filippo looked at her slyly. "And I am also a Giovanni. I keep my ears open, go to the right places… I heard about it the day before I found you. So, I called Himari, and she sent me your cell coordinates, so I picked you up."

"She has been very quiet since you left." Kayah gave him a pointed look.

"I got some black crow to eat, to make up for being a dickhead."

They rode in silence for a while, then Kayah asked, "Have you spoken to her?"

Filippo shook his head. "No, I called when we were leaving the hospital, but told her I would see her in Rephidim. We got to talk in person."

"Fix it, Filippo." Kayah trotted ahead and left him to contemplate the mess he had to clean up with his wife.

Through the Father's Eyes - Gilead - Peter

"You have been gone from Gilead for a long time." Joshua gestured to the stables. "I believe there is an old friend here who would like to see you."

Peter furrowed his brow, then smiled politely, and nodded.

The working barns lacked the ornate wood and shiny brass trimmings of the Prince's stables, but what it lacked in opulence, it made up for in the number of animals and earthy welcoming charm. Peter had no memory of this place, but his jaw dropped when he saw the occupant of the first stall. "Oh my, is that Mr. Buzzy?"

Joshua nodded. "It is. Go say hello."

Peter blinked and extended his hand. "Hey there, old fella."

The little pony tilted his head and seemed to study him, then nuzzled Peter's offered fingers, and blew out an excited whinny. He pawed at the ground and threw his head against Peter's hand in ecstatic recognition. Peter entered the stall, knelt, and hugged Mr. Buzzy's neck. The reunion of boy and beloved pony was poignant and powerful.

After a time, Peter realized he was not alone and turned to the groom, who stepped away to give them some privacy. "My father told me he had been sold. How long has he been here?"

Joshua smiled kindly and said, "He was never sold, Peter. Your father moved him here shortly after he became the Ruling Prince. He is a favorite with the school children who come to tour Gilead."

Peter smiled down at the horse and whispered, "You are a good pony. Do you give boys and girls rides?"

Joshua gestured for Peter to join him. "Would you like to see the rest of the facilities?"

Peter looked at his watch. "I fear I have been gone for quite some time. My bride might not appreciate being left to her own devices on the second day of our marriage."

Joshua nodded. "As you wish. I will drive you up."

Peter started to protest, then saw the groom tending to his exhausted horse and relented. While he waited, he visited his old friend. "I think you need your old stall back up near the house, or do you like it down here? We brought the horses from the Palace today, so you will not be alone."

He scratched the pony under the neck and said, "We spent a lot of happy times up there, did we not? I remember the day I got you." He sucked in his breath because he did.

"He is a fine mount," his father beamed as he handed Peter the reins, *"for a fine young prince."*

His memories of Mr. Buzzy were always just that, of Mr. Buzzy. They included no one other than himself and his pony. Standing in the stall with the little animal, he had several clear pictures of his father holding the lead line, adjusting the stirrups, and laughing.

He ran his fingers through his hair and shook off the memory, blaming that damn sketchbook. He gave the pony an absent pat and exited the stall, a bit shaken, and more than a little confused.

Joshua pulled up to the entrance of the stable, driving a wagon loaded with fresh hay. "I need to drive this up to the other stable. You don't mind, do you?"

Peter shook his head and hopped up on the seat beside the groom. "I do not."

Over the jingle of the harnesses, Joshua asked, "Did you know construction on Gilead, the Palace of the Alanthian Princes, was finished in 12 ME?"

Peter turned a curious eye. "No, I did not."

Joshua gestured over the tree line to the south tower. "It was an auspicious occasion, hosted by Prince Robert Malcolm. The Castle was intended to be a living symbol, a sign of the covenant between Alanthia and the Golden Kingdom. During the dedication cere- mony, they officially renamed the land and established your family as the ruling line of the kingdom. The word Alanthia means forever faithful and true."

Joshua guided the horses with an expert hand and continued. "This land has always been different. From its founding by pilgrims in the Last Age, it was set aside for the Son, settled by men and women who consecrated the land to Him. Yeshua personally dedi- cated the Castle as a renewal of that covenant."

"The Iron King stayed at Gilead?"

"Indeed, on the very first night," Joshua confirmed.

Peter watched as the east wing came into sight. The Castle was solid, and strangely he felt more at home here than he had ever felt in the New City Palace where he lived most of his life. "My wife mentioned she might like to settle here. There is something to be said about living in a house where the King has dwelt, to be rooted in the history of this place, the history of our kingdom."

"But Gilead also holds the history of your family, the men and women who preceded you." Joshua met Peter's eyes and held them.

Peter said nothing, transfixed by the infinite wisdom he read in that penetrating gaze.

"Peter, the sins of your Grandfather Adam brought curses upon his kingdom, his children, and his grandchildren. You must not continue to walk the same path as he." Joshua's countenance began to shine.

"Oh, my Lord," Peter breathed, his eyes widening as he scooted across the bench seat, as far away as possible.

"How quickly you have forgotten the words I spoke that night at your Penthouse, Peter. Only the power of the blood will break the curse that has been visited upon your father's line."

"I do not understand," Peter mumbled and looked away.

"I would have given you further instructions, but you did not come when I called you to the Golden City."

Peter sucked in a deep breath, unable to speak.

"What was it you said to Josiah? 'I have been ignoring royal summons my entire life.'"

Peter covered his face as shame swamped him.

"So, instead of seeking my counsel and heeding my call, you went your own way, taking vengeance and judgment into your hands. You sought the murder of your father and your own destruction."

Peter's chest heaved, and the wounds on his fists burned. He saw himself thrashing his father, who had not raised a hand to defend himself.

"Only my direct intervention stopped you, first, from killing yourself and then, your father. You have perpetuated a legacy of hatred, blood, and violence. Do you deny it?"

"No, Lord, I do not." He could not look up.

"Korah ben Adam ruled this land with my permission, and he did so until I deemed he should not!" Joshua's voice became thunderous.

Peter winced, recognizing the truth.

"Like Saul of old, I allowed him to rule while David wandered in the desert. When given the opportunity to slay the man who hunted and tormented him, David did not raise his hand against Saul because he was the anointed, chosen Prince of Israel."

Peter grimaced, realizing what a grievous sin he had committed in seeking his father's death, not only for the commandment it broke, but for a time, Korah ben Adam had indeed been the chosen Prince of Alanthia. "I do not have the heart of David, my

Lord. Please forgive me." Peter shook with violent tremors, afraid he would be struck down for the magnitude of his sin.

Joshua touched Peter's head. "Look at me, Son."

Convicted in the presence of the Lord's unblemished holiness, Peter could not hold Joshua's eyes.

Joshua traced a cross on Peter's forehead and the firestorm calmed. "I forgive you."

Peter blinked and beheld the wonder and majesty of The King.

"Your mother gave you to me as an infant, ensuring you were christened and sealed. Throughout your life, you have been adored and loved, surrounded by people who protected you and kept you from the path of destruction.

"Your father received no quarter from those who should have loved and protected him. Until now, you have seen the world through the eyes of a child, but true understanding will come when you see through the eyes of the Father. Read the book of Jonah, Peter, and understand my love."

In the next instant, the wagon was gone and so was the Lord.

Peter stood on the threshold of Gilead, alone.

A Matter of Degrees - The Golden City - Josiah and Davianna

Strolling on the upper terrace of the Alanthian Embassy in the Golden City, Josiah brushed a stray lock of hair out of Davianna's eye and said, "You are very subdued this evening, Minx."

She dropped her chin, looking away. "I fell asleep in your study today."

His hand stilled.

"I did not mean to eavesdrop, but I woke up, and you were talking to the ambassador." She bit her bottom lip. "I know I should have yawned or dropped my book or said something. I should not have listened, but I did, and I'm sorry."

"That is unacceptable, Davianna."

"I know. It was an accident, then I was embarrassed, and then…" She lost control of the tight grip she held all day and the words rushed out. "I knew most of the story the ambassador told you. Korah relayed bits and pieces the week I spent with him, but I wanted to hear the rest. I needed to know what made him like he was. I needed to understand."

Josiah's expression grew icy.

Davianna held up a hand, tears pooling in her eyes. "I knew you would not understand." She sprinted away.

Josiah looked up at the gleaming edifice of New Jerusalem, seeking strength and wisdom. The words of the old ambassador rang in his ears, 'Things might not always be as they appear on the surface.' He walked around the corner and found Davianna leaning against a railing, her breathing labored.

"I know you hate him," she whispered. "You have every reason to. He is the most terrifying person I ever met, wicked, horrible. But I don't hate him. I feel sorry for him, and I have been praying for him all day. I am glad he is not dead. I am glad he is not burning in Hell." She turned then, her face streaked with tears, her chin quivering, but raised.

"Korah made his choices. He could have turned from his wicked ways at any time. He did not," Josiah reminded her.

"Yes, he could have, but as long as he draws breath, he might still."

"How can you say that, after everything he has done?" Josiah threw his arms to the sky. "You forget what he did to us in that dungeon. He held a knife to your throat, then he beat me until you surrendered. I read the look in his eyes when he kissed you. He planned to take you to bed!"

She flinched but did not back down. She remembered the episode weeks ago, though she had not mentioned that to Josiah. "You are the most righteous man I have ever known, yet when we met Yeshua in the Valley of Ajalon, who were you more like, Yeshua or Korah?"

Furious, Josiah turned away and snapped, "I am nothing like Korah."

"It is a matter of degrees, Josiah! For all have sinned and fall short of the glory, all."

"I am not going to have this argument with you."

"I think you are," Davianna insisted, her nose flaring in anger. "Remember the angel's message to Peter the night they rescued us from Louisiana? 'It is the Lord's will that none should perish, but all should come to Him. Doubt no longer, finish thy journey well.' Our journey is not over, Josiah, and if Korah did not perish, then neither is his—or Peter's."

Josiah scowled at her, then turned and walked away.

"Where are you going?" she shouted, stomping her foot in anger.

"Out! Don't wait up."

Part 12 - Korah's Stand

When It's All Over but the Crying - New City Palace - Korah

Alone in the empty Palace, Korah watched the News 1 evening broadcast with a certain macabre detachment. Sondra ben Pierson rolled out decades of his misdeeds for the world to see, complete with photographs, video, and documents. He did not bother to watch to the end. He had lived it.

The crowd of protestors outside the gates grew daily, and after the report, they would surely increase. So, he called his Minister of Defense and quadrupled the security detail. The mob might just storm the Palace, looking for his head, and Korah was in no hurry to burn. He knew he was damned.

The second call he made was to his Attorney General, Nabal ben Caleb. Nabal answered on the first ring, freaking out over the broadcast, but Korah shut him down. "Just find out everything you can on this Angel of Kensington Park, and I will keep your name out of it."

He dropped the phone and picked up one of the morning newspapers strewn across his desk. The Angel was his daughter; he knew that without being told. One of the pictures captured her in the exact pose as her mother when he saw her the first time and the last, a beauty, an Endorite warrior, a Princess. He memorized the photos, marveling at her body. Her elegant lines reminded him of Sussanna, but she had inherited his lean strength. The picture of her hanging off the side of the horse aiming a weapon at some fat bastard on a motorcycle made him want to fly to London and kill everyone who tried to harm her. Pride exploded in his chest. She was magnificent, just like her mother.

The newspaper reported her name as Kayah ben Morte. He looked up the name Kayah. It meant a wise child, power, ability. He did not have to look up Morte. She adopted her mother's attributes in her first name and his in her second. He wondered if she knew her real name was Hope because that was what she had been to him and Sussanna, their hope.

He destroyed that hope, doomed them all the night he walked into Angelica's mansion and drank her vile potion. At the time, he thought it was just a spell, some kind of health charm. Out of his mind with worry, he did not truly understand the cost. In retrospect, Sussanna recognized the mortal danger he was in. She begged him to leave Endor, just as he had once told Alexa to leave him and not come back. He had not heeded the warning, neither had she.

And they had paid the price, his children and his wives. They suffered for his folly and his sin. His latest wife was on her death-bed, raving mad after being brutalized by Satan on their wedding night. He needed to stop getting married. It did not go well for his brides. Their life span was brief.

In that regard, Davianna ben David dodged a bullet. He thought about the brown-eyed girl often. She had drawn Korah out of the shadows, resurrected him from the dead. He did not know that man still existed, thought he murdered the last of his humanity with Eamonn; he certainly had with Alexa. Little Davianna, with her innocent smiles and unexpected kindness, quieted the beast. She sent it away for a while. It was an interesting week, to say the least. Bizarre, heady, and, for lack of a better word, it had been nice.

Korah looked at the newspaper photographs again and murmured, "Angel of Kensington Park, have you been in London all these years? Is the last Guardian of the Blood a Brit now?" Pacing his office, he wondered aloud, "Did your mother take you there? If she did, I'm glad. It kept you safe, far away from me and my family."

He stopped cold as a horrifying thought occurred to him. Angelica was barred from her book again. She gained access the first time when she killed the elder guardians with the plague. Sussanna and the other guardians were not yet of age, so destruction had not befallen Endor. When Sussanna died, Angelica regained access, but according to her, it was sealed again. Hope would not have been of age when Sussanna died, so that explained it. If Angelica saw this picture, would she put it together? He pinched his temples. Of course she would. She had known Sussanna longer than he, and these pictures were everywhere.

He closed his eyes, lamenting the fact that he no longer had the Dark Master at his side. But thinking of him seemed to summon his spirit and the stench of sulfur filled his study.

"Have you forgotten who you serve, Korah?" asked a voice booming out of the ether.

Korah looked around, suspicious. "I know who I serve. Where has he been, and who are you?"

"Someone who will take your kingdom from you."

"Get in line. I believe Lucifer is at the head, followed by my nephew, and then my son. Perhaps an argument could even be made for my most recent bride. So, who might you be?"

"I think you left someone out," the disembodied voice taunted.

Korah took a drink, half certain this was a hallucination. "Oh, who is that?"

"Your daughter."

Korah's blood chilled.

"My father sent me to deliver a message. He said you would remember. 'I get your babies, Korah. I get them all.'"

Korah dropped the glass. It shattered on the marble tile. "I did everything he ever asked me. I never made that deal."

"Oh, but you did. That was the bargain. You just did not read the fine print."

"I did it to save their lives!" Korah protested.

"They are still alive."

Korah covered his face, weary beyond imagination. "Who are you, and what do you want?"

"I am Rapha, and I'll be back soon." A malevolent laugh filled his study.

Korah felt the presence depart, but far from being frightened, he was furious.

He stalked out of his office, walked the empty corridors of the Palace, and started planning. It was time to figure out how to get out of that damned contract. This had gone on long enough.

February 14, 1000 ME

No Way Out - New City Palace - Korah

A terrible thing happened to Korah ben Adam in the days between the News 1 report and the Iron King's Proclamation; he saw himself. The man who reigned Alanthia for fifteen years looked in the mirror the day he lost his throne, and the only emotion he could muster was relief. It was over.

Free of the constant and malevolent presence of Marduk, he no longer had to guard his every thought, shield every desire or tender feeling. He blamed Davianna ben David for starting the process. Somehow, she had given him the Black Key, just not the one he sought. Davianna's key unlocked the door to his mind. The pictures of Hope kicked the door in.

His memories broke free in violent flash floods. They swamped him, carrying him down rapids of a black river. Overwhelmed by the experience, bitter memories choked him, and his evil deeds drowned him in shame. In times of rest, life giving, sweet water revived him, and he floated in gentle waves of soft memories. He swam in deep pools of old love, before being sucked under by whirlpools of despair. The memories, and the emotions they evoked, felt foreign, like a language he used to know but no longer spoke or understood.

He was sane enough to recognize he had gone completely insane.

During a lucid moment, he realized he was alone in the Palace. When the Iron King's order stripped him of his throne and threatened death to anyone who continued working for him, the staff stopped showing up. Even before that, he had taken a shot at a footman, which caused most of the servants to flee. In his defense, he was hearing voices at the time.

He saw ghosts and argued with apparitions. Wandering into empty rooms, he watched scenes and meetings from long ago, which played out in vivid detail, like movies on a screen. Sometimes, he sprinted down the corridors screaming curses at his son, his nephew, and the traitorous wives who deserted him. Other times, he sat catatonic, unable to move or speak. He found the kitchen and ate a little, but the only thing he knew how to cook was eggs and toast. When those ran out, he stopped eating.

The mob outside screamed for his blood, day and night. He thought about giving himself up, letting them have him. Imprisoned in his empty house, he watched them from the window. One evening, he walked outside, and they rushed the walls, but a grim-faced army captain ushered him back inside. He drank a bottle of brandy to fortify his courage to try again, but he was never a heavy drinker and passed out on the floor in the Blue Drawing room.

After that, he got quiet.

On New Year's Day, McSwilley left his medication with a note, "My Esteemed, please take this. Remember, it helped before. It can help again."

Korah ignored it, but he had not thrown it away. The night he saw Hope's picture, he started taking the prescription. And just as McSwilley said, it calmed the violent storm, quieting the Beast.

He often found himself in his study, looking at the pictures of Hope. Accessing his hazy recollections of Sussanna and Endor, he laid down in his bed and let the memories wash over his mind. In the pre-dawn hours of February 12th, he forgave Sussanna for trying to kill him. He stopped torturing himself over Hope and was glad she escaped life with him.

Humming a lullaby Sussanna had sung, he walked to the stables and tended his horses. The work did him good. It gave him the strength to continue.

He visited Alexa's room, sat on the edge of her bed, and wept until he thought he would die. The love he felt for her was buried so deep, he forgot it existed. He forgot the tender year; he forgot how much she loved him. Since her death, he coped by convincing himself that he had always hated her, and if she ever came to mind, he replayed the early years when he had indeed despised her. Remembering the later years would have destroyed him.

He opened her closet, but her clothes were gone, and the room no longer held her things. Yet her perfume sat on the dressing table. He inhaled the delicate scent all her own. She, more than anyone, stood by him. For twenty-one years, she tried to tame the Beast, to love him, and he killed her. He thought about hanging himself and wished he would have all those years ago. Eamonn and Alexa would still be alive, and Peter certainly would not have lived the hellish life Korah created for him.

On February 14th, he mustered his courage and went to the one place in the Palace he avoided thus far—Peter's room. Swamped with such guilt, he could barely cross the threshold. He realized in all the years they lived in the Palace, Korah had never once gone to his son's room. He had treated Peter worse than his own mother and father treated him.

He had his reasons, but they were cold comfort now.

Had Marduk discovered Korah loved Peter, he would have killed him, of that Korah was certain. Fearing Peter's death on such a visceral level, he did everything possible to prove to Marduk he felt nothing but contempt for the boy. But it backfired. Korah hid his love so deeply it died. And that twisted everything. He could not even look at Peter afterward, and if he did, he saw the ghost of the little boy he loved and the wife he had murdered.

When Peter returned to the Palace from the RMA, Korah tried to bring him into the New Way, to save him from the monster's wrath, but he also wanted to see if they might forge some sort of bond again. That also backfired. Peter wanted no part of it, and when he refused to marry Keyseelough, Korah tried to break him. In a life full of wicked deeds, that was perhaps the most calculated and depraved of them all.

He cried out in anguish, "Son, please forgive me. I was so wrong. I am so sorry."

But there was no answer. There was no redemption. There was no forgiveness. He made his choice long ago. He was damned. Lucifer promised to personally send Korah to Hell for aligning with Marduk. He knew after the wedding and the Iron King's proclamation, he did not have much time.

Silence had reigned in the Palace for weeks, so when the opening notes of a sinister song played over the speakers, Korah panicked. The reckoning had come. Dressed in a black robe, Lucifer chased him through the empty halls, laughing. Rounding a corner with the devil on his heels, Korah slipped and fell hard. His wrist snapped, but he kept running. He sought shelter in Alexa's room, the only place in the Palace he ever allowed himself to love and then only briefly, in secret. It had cost Alexa her life, and it seemed fitting to Korah that he should meet his end here. He huddled in the corner, broken, starved, and resigned to his fate.

However, his executioner was not Lucifer. It was Peter. When

Korah saw him, he cried out in pain and desperation. He deserved this, to be murdered by the only living person he loved. When the blows began, he did not defend himself, did not raise a hand to his son. He let Peter avenge a lifetime of abuse, neglect, and hatred on his body. He accepted his punishment, took it upon himself, and tried to take it from his son, to free Peter of his own Beast.

Blackness surrounded him. He drifted in and out of consciousness, but then he heard Alexa's voice, soothing and precious. He was thankful for the gift, moments before the flames swallowed him. Through a bloodied eye, he looked up at her and basked in her beautiful face, glowing like the sun. He heard her tell Peter to run and witnessed the love between them.

He spat the blood pooling in his mouth and croaked, "Alexa, I'm sorry. Forgive me."

"Korah," her face screwed up in despair.

"Don't let me die by his hand, please," he begged.

The sounds of the mob grew louder. Alexa reached down and grabbed the knife, raised it above her head. Peter and Astrid ducked through the passageway and disappeared.

Alexa stared down at Korah. "I cannot do this!"

Korah coughed blood. "Justice… what I did to you."

Alexa threw the knife aside, gathered his broken body, and dragged him toward the open passageway.

Korah writhed in agony.

She pulled the panel shut and cradled his head. "Oh, KbA," her voice broke, "my love, look what has become of you."

"So sorry, so sorry." Blood choked him, death rattled in his chest. He reached up with a quivering hand and touched her face. "Forgive me." Darkness pressed in on him, and he made a pitiful cry, his hand falling to his chest.

Alexa shook her head vigorously. Tears coursed down her cheeks. "No, not like this. I cannot kill you, but it is not His will that you die at the hands of our son."

With the last vestige of his strength, he reached up. "Lex, love you… all my heart, my… wife."

Her tears bathed his face. She pressed her lips to his and breathed life into his body. "In the name of the Father, the Son, and the Holy Ghost, I pray healing over you, Korah ben Adam."

Light flooded the passageway, and his body convulsed. He coughed and spasmed as his broken wrist, ribs, and fingers snapped into place. The internal hemorrhaging stopped.

Alexa was fading as he came back into himself.

"The rest is up to you, my darling," she called.

He was no longer dying, but he hurt all over. Blinking, he wiped the blood from his eyes, desperate to see. But she was gone.

He tried to sit up, but a malevolent force pushed him down.

"The rest is actually up to me!" cried an evil spirit.

Korah vomited. He thrashed and tore at his clothes, but he had no defense against the demon. Rapha took control and possessed him. When it was over, Korah lay on the cold cement floor, covered in blood and beaten beyond recognition.

The voice said, "Let's go, shall we?"

February 16, 1000 ME

Voices in Your Head - California - Korah

While the mob destroyed the Palace, Korah felt his way along a series of dark tunnels he never knew existed. At the end, he found a large cache of weapons and supplies. Surmising, he had just discovered how Peter escaped on New Year's Eve, he gained another measure of respect for the boy. Korah helped himself to the supplies, exited the tunnel, and headed for the stables.

"I cannot believe you do not know how to drive, Grandpa," the voice complained for what felt like the fiftieth time in two days.

"Shut up," Korah answered with profound irritation.

The voice launched into another tirade, lambasting him for his long list of failures, which culminated in his refusal to take a car in their escape.

Still terribly injured, concussed, and confused by the unfamiliar voice in his head, Korah did not grasp what was happening or where he was going. Like a small child, he simply did what he was told. When he managed to gain a few moments of lucidity and self-control, he realized he had lost all touch with reality. He had finally gone completely insane.

It was actually not a terrible place to be.

The ride was pleasant if the voice would just shut up. He had not taken a lone journey in decades. He did not have to make decisions. No one depended on him or asked him a thing. He was simply out for the ride.

It took a full day and night to clear the wreckage of the New City, which was devastated by the fighting. Korah was devastated by the fighting. Cuts and bruises covered every inch of his body, every organ, muscle, tendon, and bone ached. His eyes, lips, and cheeks were swollen, his left canine tooth broken and several more were loose. He bit his tongue during the beating and the inside of his mouth was so cut up it made speaking nearly impossible. The injuries and his garbled voice rendered him unrecognizable, which earned him sympathy and aid. He blended with those returning home after the rioting.

The voice in his head urged him to gallop, but Korah rode before he could walk, so he told the voice to shut up. He would not sacrifice the finest stallion in his stables by riding him for days at a breakneck speed.

"Kill the horse. Who gives a fuck?" the voice complained.

Korah jerked. Even insane he would not think that. He looked around, searching behind him. Who was actually talking to him?

"It sucks here. It sucks in here!" the voice screamed. "When was the last time you did a sit-up? Weak, you are so weak. I should have picked a better body. How are you King? King of what, the land of the lob cock, old motherfuckers?"

Korah stared down at his crotch with a frown. "Lob cock? Now that is uncalled for."

"I've been in your bedroom. You take a while to get it up, Grandpa. Though I can't say that I blame you, the Hag was not exactly stimulating. She's got saggy tits."

Korah remembered Angelica's tits when they were young. "They were not always saggy."

"It goes with your ball sack, which I swear hit the water when you sat on the toilet yesterday," the voice taunted.

"Can you please be quiet?" Korah felt every mile in his aching bones. He did not need reminding that he was no longer a young, viral man.

The strange jolt hit him again, and he went misty with detachment.

The voice whispered, "Get me to Pepperwood. I'll take over from there."

Part 13 - Alexa

February 16, 1000 ME

Digging Up Bones - Gilead - Peter and Astrid

Peter and Astrid stood arm-in-arm in Alexa's former bedchamber at Gilead. "That was quite a story Genevieve told," Astrid said, pulling Peter into a hug.

"It was," he said dully, his face impassive as he pulled away and walked to the picture window. The sun set over the crystalline lake, rays reflecting on the water like gold and yellow diamonds.

"I am not certain how I feel about Kayah ben Samuel being my half-sister. Though, I suppose I am grateful I did not sleep with her."

Astrid whirled on him. "What?"

"Relax, Red. I kissed her once several years ago. It was icky."

"Icky?" Astrid widened her eyes at him, a tremor of a laugh in her voice.

"I was a horny teenager. She was a hot babe. There was no chemistry. I thought it was because she had her hair dyed red at the time." He ran his fingers through his hair and looked up at the sky. "Thanks for that."

Astrid put her hands on her hips. "If you have not noticed, *I* am a redhead."

Peter turned, his eyes heavy-lidded with exhaustion. "And you are the only one I have ever wanted to kiss." He puckered in demonstration.

Astrid obliged. "Let's sit down." She pulled him onto the bed and settled beside him. "You will tell Kayah when we see her?"

"That I still do not want to kiss her, or that she is my sister?" Peter fell back on the bed in a whoosh of breath. "I suppose Auntie and I will. Not exactly the parents orphans dream of, are they? Two homicidal maniacs."

"But she has a brother." Astrid smoothed one of his eyebrows. "And you are an amazing gift." Then a horrified expression crossed her face. "Oh, hell."

"What?" Peter looked concerned.

"She outranks me. Am I going to have to curtsy to Kayah?"

The corner of Peter's mouth twitched. "You did not want the Princess title. That was one of your stipulations, not mine."

Astrid rolled her eyes. "I might have to rethink this. It was bad enough when it was Davianna, now Kayah. Geez, do you have any more family members coming out of the woodwork?"

"Yesterday, I would have answered with confidence no, but considering I had no idea that my mother was Korah's second wife…" A strange look passed over his face.

"What is it?" Astrid asked.

Peter shook himself. "Nothing, just this strange flash. It has been happening since we got here, between that sketchbook, Auntie's story, and my meeting in the stables." He exhaled deeply. "Speaking of that, I need to read Jonah. My mother always kept a Bible in her bedside table, see if there is one in that drawer, will you?"

Astrid scrambled off the bed. Ever curious, she did not mind. The drawer was largely empty. All that remained were neglected bits of paper, buttons, and a dusty sleeping mask. She pulled out an old book, surmising it was a Bible, but a quick perusal confirmed it was not. "This is an old diary."

Peter groaned, "I have dug up enough bones tonight. Please tell me it is not my mother's."

Astrid shook her head. "No, it is too old."

She set it aside, intending to investigate later, and pulled the Bible out. A miniature turned over and a little red-haired girl smiled up at her. Astrid grinned at the impish face and picked up the exquisite painting. "Look at this. Isn't she precious?"

April 8, 985 ME

World Equestrian Championships - Alexa

Princess Alexa ben Seamus stood in the receiving line at the World Equestrian Champion's Reception, feeling pensive. For the last three years, she did everything possible to shelter Korah. She smoothed over arguments, played the peacemaker between him and his brother, tried to ensure dinners included food he enjoyed, and generally tried to keep him calm. After the disaster on the pitch, the last place he needed to be was at an equestrian event. However, Alanthia was the host kingdom for this year's championship, and they had a duty to attend.

Contrary to the cool veneer of royal aloofness Korah typically displayed in public, tonight he morphed into the outgoing, sometimes outrageous, affable Prince Charming. She watched him with a calculated eye. All the warning signs were there. He had been almost giddy this week, and if he was amid a full-blown manic episode, an intense period of darkness would soon follow. Those she had grown to fear.

One brief year, one short moment in time, he had been hers, but he was lost again; and no matter how she tried to love him, she could not reach him. It felt like he had disappeared behind an impenetrable wall forever. If it was just her, she could cope. She could bide her time, gauge his moods, and survive. However, she was not alone.

Alexa's heart broke for Peter, who did not understand his father's illness, and as time wore on, he forgot. He forgot his father loved him. He forgot the magical year and began looking at his father the way Korah had looked at his mother. There was little distinction between the way Korah parented Peter over the way Mary had parented him.

They fought about it, and when, in a moment of unguarded anger, she said he was no better than his mother, he hit her. With that single blow, the fragile gossamer thread that held them together broke. He disappeared for several weeks afterward, and when he returned, he moved out of their room and never came back. He had hit her three more times, always when they fought about Peter, always when she could not stand the cruel treatment or the cutting remarks. She stopped pushing him to have a relationship with Peter, quit trying to draw him out, and stepped between them, protecting her son.

This February, she began crafting an escape.

As much as Korah seemed to despise them in private, he doted on them in public. He made a grand show of being the noble family man, the gracious, good-natured younger brother—the Prince. His glittering public devotion disoriented her because it was so converse to the life they lived in private. Sometimes at balls or functions, she allowed herself to forget it was a charade. It was the closest she ever got to her Korah, and she missed that man.

When Vanessa ben Hilton, the Baroness of Hendrix, came through the receiving line, Alexa smiled, happy to see her friend. As they exchanged a quick greeting and promised to catch up later, Alexa missed the trouble brewing between Korah and Peter. She caught the tail end when Peter deserted the line under the thunderous disapproval of his father and the slack-jawed astonishment of the girl's partner as her intrepid son stole the poor chap's date. A calming hand on Korah's elbow drew his attention away from Peter and back to the next person in line, averting a catastrophe, for now.

Dinner turned into an interesting affair. Often isolated from children his own age, Peter determined the little acrobat was as close as he was going to get to someone his size and escorted her to the head table. This amused Korah, who was not sorry to see one of his mother's old biddies moved to make room for Peter's new friend. Peter delighted the table with conversation, and even Korah laughed at some of his silly banter.

Alexa studied the girl as they ate. She looked familiar, but she could not place her. "Have we met before, Persa?" she asked as the waiters cleared their dishes.

Persa turned bright hazel eyes toward Alexa and said, "No, my Esteemed Princess, not formally. My fiancé, James ben Kole, and I have been competing for a decade, so we have seen you at the Hewies several times."

Korah lost his smile.

Peter did not. "I love the Hewies. It is my favorite week of the year."

"Mine, too." Persa leaned her head toward Peter, her face alight with mischief. "I eat fried apple dumplings for breakfast, lunch, and dinner while we are there."

Peter's eyes widened. "I love those, the ones with the powdered sugar and cinnamon?"

They both sighed with identical expressions of rapture.

Persa enthused, "The best ones are sold by that lady in the yellow and orange booth…"

"With a big gold tooth?" They finished in unison and died laughing.

"James said he could barely lift me in the finals this year after five straight days of apple dumplings."

Korah turned from his broody contemplation of the occupants of the ballroom and said, "I like them, too."

Alexa felt a jolt of electricity sizzle down her spine.

August 14, 986 ME

Richardson Avenue - New City - Alexa and Sir Preston

"My dear Goddaughter, what a pleasant surprise," Sir Preston ben Worley said as he rose from his desk. He moved a bit stiffly, but other than that, appeared in good health despite his advanced age.

Conversely, Alexa looked haggard. Her cheeks were gaunt and drawn, and no concealer could hide the dark circles under her eyes. "I hope I am not disturbing you," she said, extending her hands in greeting.

"No, of course not," he said graciously.

She looked over her shoulder at the closed door. "I left Peter with your man, so we might have a private word."

"Please come in. Shall I ring for tea?" Preston motioned to the sitting area.

"No, thank you." Alexa walked past the comfortable sofas and sat in one of the leather chairs in front of his desk, signaling that this was a legal meeting, not a social call.

He took his cue and settled behind the cluttered behemoth, prepared to conduct business.

Without preamble, she said, "The situation between Korah and me has become untenable. I wish to begin divorce proceedings."

Sir Preston again controlled his expression. "I see."

"Since ascending the throne, he has surrounded himself with characters of the most unsavory nature." Closing her eyes, she added in a rush, "I fear my life and Peter's life are in danger if we continue to dwell in the Palace."

"He lays hands on you?" Sir Preston lowered his prodigious eyebrows.

Alexa glanced away. "Occasionally."

"Can you avoid him, stay out of his way? Perhaps move to Gilead or one of the other royal estates?"

"He does not want us out of his control and flies into a rage if I suggest it. So Peter and I have become adept at living in the shadows," Alexa said, looking at her hands and setting her wedding ring to rights. She was so thin, it spun on her hand. "And Korah spends a lot of time with his mistress these days."

"Angelica ben Omri," Sir Preston snarled. "Were you aware that harridan caused my daughter's death?"

Alexa's eyes shot open. "No, I was not."

Preston gave her an ominous look. "It is one of the reasons we burned Endor to the ground, my dear. She polluted and perverted the population, waged war against the neighboring village, and created havoc. It was an evil place, Alexa. I know you never understood why we did what we did, but the Endorites were vile, a cancer on the kingdom. So, we cut it out and cauterized the wound."

Alexa hung her head. "All these years, I thought if I had told you I did not want him, you would have let him be."

"No, We would have pulled him out of there no matter what. Adam and Mary would never have allowed that marriage to stand. The judgment of Endor had nothing to do with you."

"I suppose it is ancient history, and it no longer matters, but I appreciate you telling me. I carried the weight of that for years."

"I should have relieved you of that burden." Preston reached across the desk for her hand. "I did not know."

Alexa took his big veiny hand and squeezed. "Sir Preston, I have to get out. Can you help me?"

Preston blew out a long, slow breath. "Korah will fight a divorce, Alexa. He has built a public persona as a family man, and the reforms he is pushing right now might be in jeopardy if his reputation takes a blow. You have been in royal life long enough to know how these things work." His massive eyebrows drew to a point over his nose. "The anti-technology religious zealots are up in arms. To them, divorce is a capital crime. I do not have to remind you how many assassination plots they have launched against him."

Alexa closed her eyes, reliving several terrifying episodes. From lone knife-wielding assassins to coordinated attacks on their convoys, they lived under constant threat.

Sir Preston's gray eyes held hers with calculating shrewdness. "If you leave him, they will brand you a fallen woman, which will put you in as much or more danger than if you remain in the Palace.

"You also must consider the number of supporters he has amassed for these reforms. If you do something that jeopardizes them, you make yourself a target for some disturbed kid, tinkering in his workshop, dreaming of tech glory and fortune."

He gestured to a stack of files on his desk. "Those are cases our firm has received from the AG's office. We are reviewing tech convictions right now in anticipation of the reformed laws. There are thousands of people behind bars who will be released when the reforms go into effect. A petition for divorce could derail everything, my dear, which will put you in grave danger from all sides."

Sir Preston tapped his desk with his knobby knuckles. "Take my advice, hold off starting proceedings until these measures go through and the dust settles. Alanthia is on the precipice of change. Those times are always volatile. I do not wish to see you get caught in the crossfire."

Seeing that his advice discouraged her, he gave her a solicitous smile and added, "I can start drawing up the papers. We will get to work on this, but you should bide your time before filing."

"Perhaps you are right." Alexa slumped in her chair and said to her lap, "I want you to amend my will, today, while I am here."

Preston straightened. "It is that dangerous?"

Alexa flushed. "Some days, but who knows what tomorrow holds? I need to make sure I provide for Peter, independent of what Korah can confiscate. I have written to my father; he and his solicitors are doing the same."

They spent the afternoon reviewing Alexa's estates, trusts, and accounts, then amended her will to ensure she provided for Peter in his minority as well as his majority. She came into her marriage with several trusts and accounts no one other than her father and Sir Preston were aware of. Those Korah would never be able to discover.

"Sir Preston, there are a few other items I need to share with you." She retrieved a letter from her bag. "This is for Peter. If anything happens to me, I want you to see he gets it, but only when he leaves his father. He must not have it until he breaks free."

"Alexa, if it is this bad, take a trip and go see your father. I am sure Seamus would be delighted to have you visit."

She held up her hand. "No, you were right. I can survive a few more months. I've made it twenty-one-years."

"All right," he said kindly. "Is there anything else I can do for you today?"

"Yes." She closed her eyes, sighing deeply, gathering her courage, then rose from her chair and opened the study door, making sure no one lingered outside. When she returned, she kept her voice just above a whisper.

"I require your absolute confidentiality regarding what I am about to tell you."

"Of course," he replied.

"Sir Preston, Prince Josiah did not commit suicide. We staged it. He escaped on the eve of Eamonn's funeral."

"Egads!" Preston's caterpillar eyebrows shot up in surprise. "Who knows of this?"

"Only me," she replied, keeping Genevieve and Peter's part secret, even from him. "He ought to be in the Golden City by now. I wait every day for the Iron King to proclaim he has arrived, but it has not happened. I fear a calamity may have befallen him, and if that is the case, then the presumed heir to the throne is Peter."

"Presumed?" Preston's quick mind leapt on the word.

"There is a remote chance that Korah's daughter, Hope, did not perish in the fires of Endor." Alexa pointed to the corner of his desk. "She is in prison on a tech conviction. She might even be in your files right there. I want you to take her case. Make sure she never knows who she is, because if it is not Josiah on the throne, it will be Peter, not her, not ever!"

"I am in full agreement with you, Alexa," Preston said gravely. "Korah ben Adam's daughter with an Endorite? That is a wicked combination."

They shared a look, silent understanding passing between them.

"I will take care of this," he assured her.

Alexa left Sir Preston's townhouse confident she had done as much as she could to secure the future. She put aside her nagging suspicions about the other one. The way things were going, that girl would not live out the year.

September 11, 986 ME

Triumph - New City - Korah and Alexa

Sometimes Alexa looked at Korah and could not contain how proud she was of him. The day they repealed the Alanthian technology laws he mounted the dais in front of the Capitol Building, triumphant. Throngs of supporters waved Alanthian flags and roared their approval as he stepped up to the podium to deliver his speech. He waved, flashing a rare dimpled smile, the genuine one, and joined in their celebration. Dressed in a superbly tailored charcoal suit and red tie, his blond hair caught the sun. The scene reminded Alexa of the day on the pitch at Eamonn and Margaret's wedding festivities. He was still so beautiful.

"When I was twenty, I took a tour of our great kingdom and lived as one of you. I shed my guards, left my privilege behind, and embarked on an adventure." Korah made eye contact with several people in the crowd, his glimmering with mischief and humor. "If the truth be known, I ran away."

The crowd laughed, bonding with him on a deeper level.

His voice rang with true nostalgia. "It was the most formative experience of my life, a time when I was first introduced to the vision of a new Alanthia. It opened my eyes to the freedom we might achieve through innovation and creativity. Those impassioned pioneers dreamed of a future we have made possible today."

The crowd erupted into ecstatic cheers.

"George ben Sandro is on the stage with me," Korah gestured to a middle-aged man wearing glasses and khaki pants a size too large. "George and his fellow crusaders have worked tirelessly to repeal the laws prohibiting technology research and development. I joined their cause in the early '60s, and I am happy to say," he turned his head and nodded seriously, "George, it took some time, but we finally did it."

George signaled with a thumbs up and a big smile.

Alexa clapped where appropriate, smiled when she should, gazed in loving, serious admiration when required, but for once, it was not an act. Korah delivered the speech of his life, rousing and heartfelt, worthy of the famous orator and great persuader he had become. For a decade, he pursued this goal, working almost around the clock since assuming the throne. It was the hardest fought political battle in modern Alanthia, and Korah came out on the winning side.

"No longer will Alanthians be held in bondage, chained to the darkness of the past. Together, we will illuminate the way for all mankind to retake what has been denied us too long. Technology, for all!"

His voice boomed across the lawn and the crowd echoed the cry back.

"Today marks the dawning of a New Age. Alanthia will be in the vanguard. As we speak, the engine of Alanthian manufacturing is already gearing up. The first automotive plant of the age is under construction. By spring, we will again travel by car."

The crowd shouted with approval.

In a dramatic moment, Korah raised a hand for silence, then turned and winked at Alexa. The crowd grew still, breathless with anticipation. They were enthralled, mesmerized by his charisma and charm. A small, tinny ring came from the podium. A born showman, Korah looked from his right to his left. Then a slow smile spread over his face as he reached into his suit pocket and pulled out a phone. "Hello?" he said dramatically.

The crowd went wild.

He held the phone aloft and proclaimed, "Soon, every Alanthian will have their own, thanks to the actions we have taken today."

A brass band played, confetti bombs exploded, as dignitaries and special guests surrounded Korah with hearty congratulations. Swept up in the throng of well-wishers and enthusiastic supporters, Alexa smiled, pretending to be a ditzy beauty with little understanding of the ramifications of her husband's actions today.

Contrary to her empty expression, she was perfectly aware that a fissure had cracked straight down the center of the kingdom, half on one side and half on the other. Those opposed to lifting the ban were not united by philosophy, ranging from those who objected for religious reasons to people who simply did not like change. But the opposition had one thing in common—Korah. He was the juggernaut, the face of the enemy.

Alexa understood how volatile the situation was, and despite the enhanced security she was keenly aware of the danger they were in, so she kept a close eye on Peter, who was milling around the stage by himself. When she spotted the little acrobat, Persa, she knew exactly where Peter would head. Anytime those two got near one another, they snapped together like magnets.

Alexa watched Persa with grudging admiration as she squared off with Tristin in a silent challenge that no one else ever dared. He loomed over her, glaring at her with those wicked eyes, but she did not back down, standing toe to toe with that evil bastard, telling him how it was going to be. The last time Alexa saw her, Persa's spirit was broken, but the set of her shoulders and the brilliant smile she flashed Peter gave evidence that a core of steel ran through the girl. Alexa realized she ought not to have written Persa ben Yereq off so quickly.

"Lieutenant ben Todd," Alexa said, pulling one of her favorite military guards aside, "will you please do me a favor and keep an eye on Prince Peter? He is running amuck in the Capitol Building with one of his friends, and I do not want him getting in trouble."

"Certainly, my Esteemed Princess, I am happy to oblige." Lieutenant Richard ben Todd flushed and added tenderly, "You must only ask."

Alexa looked up at him with coy tolerance, knowing he was smitten with her. "Thank you, Richard." Then glancing around, she asked, "Where is Lieutenant ben Robert?"

"Mack is down there with the protestors. They have him on crowd control."

Alexa followed the direction he indicated, noting the protest beyond the lawn had grown in size and volume. "Please ask Jo'zak to bring him up here. I would feel better if the two of you are with Peter today." She laid a hand on Richard ben Todd's arm. "Be alert. It might get rowdy before all is said and done."

Richard covered Alexa's hand with his own and gave it a squeeze, affection brimming in his soulful brown eyes. "We will make sure you are both safe, my Esteemed Princess."

"Thank you, Richard." Alexa graced him with a smile and returned to her duties.

Sir Preston came alongside her, murmuring, "That young swain looked like he was ready to kiss your feet. Is there something you would like to tell me?" He gave her a pointed look. "I hate nasty surprises."

Alexa furrowed her brow at him. "Lieutenant ben Todd is part of a unit assigned to the Palace on special occasions. He and his friend, Mack ben Robert, are nice young men. They are fond of Peter. If they are around, I ask them to keep an eye out for him."

Sir Preston studied the tall, lanky young man ambling away. "So, you are not lovers?"

Alexa gave him a double take. "No, we are not. I do not take lovers, Sir Preston." She gave him a fake smile, thoroughly irritated with him. "If you will excuse me. My friend, Lady Elizabeth ben George, and her daughter Joanna have just arrived. As you know, very few of Eamonn's allies are in attendance today. I must welcome them." She leaned in and hissed in his ear, "I have been at court long enough to know how things work. I never make foolish mistakes."

As Alexa left him, working her way through the crowd, Sir Preston thought that Korah ben Adam never truly understood why Princess Mary chose Alexa to be his bride. He gave credit to the old witch for knowing her business. No one would have made him a better wife.

Flashback - New City - Korah and Alexa

Korah elected to have the State Dinner at the Capitol Building's Great Hall instead of the Palace. Touted as a victory for the people, they celebrated in the people's building. Guests ran the social and political gamut, noblemen, legislators, dignitaries, entrepreneurs, and, of course, tech crusaders, some newly released from prison.

Korah's dynamic personality was on full display. He was magnanimous, charming, and the sound of his genuine laughter rang through the dining hall. As the catering staff began serving, he moved to the head table and relaxed into his chair, basking in the successful culmination of his life's work. He turned to Alexa. "Where is Peter?"

Alexa scanned the hall, then leaned to look past Korah, and saw the spot to Tristin's left empty. "He has taken up with Tristin's wife and has been roaming the corridors with her all day."

Korah shot a quick glance at his enigmatic advisor, who was looking thunderous, and remarked to Alexa with unusual candor, "That is dangerous."

The two parents shared a rare moment of unified concern for their son.

"I've set the Lieutenants, Richard and Mack, on his tail as guards. I am sure he is fine."

The dark look Korah sent her telegraphed he had not been referring to that; they both knew Tristan posed the danger. Before they could discuss it further, Peter and Persa rushed through the door, red-faced and a bit out of breath, but otherwise intact.

"He hates State Dinners." Alexa hid a smile behind her glass of wine.

"And receiving lines," Korah added with droll amusement.

Alexa nearly spit out her wine as a laugh broke free. Peter's abhorrence of receiving lines was legendary. She never realized Korah noticed.

The corner of his mouth lifted, and he raised a brow at her. "I do not miss much, Lex."

"No, you don't KbA," she said wistfully.

His eyes became hooded, and he looked at her with such longing she thought she might melt into a puddle in front of two hundred guests. Under the table, she reached for his hand. He let her touch him, let her squeeze his perfect, brutal hand, capable of delivering utter bliss and excruciating pain.

Turned to the side, hidden from Tristin's ever-present observation, he lifted her hand to his lips and kissed. His breath felt warm on her skin, a caress, a touch. Then he brought it to his heart, love in his eyes. He held her hand until dinner began.

They made speeches throughout the long day. Organizers set up booths inside the rotunda where tech enthusiasts mingled and exchanged ideas. Dinner was the last event in a stupendous day, a light-hearted, casual affair. Laughter and animated discussions filled the room. Entrepreneurs produced various small tech devices from their jacket pockets. Avid investors looked on with glee and imagined the fantastic profits they were going to make. For more than just Korah, this was a lifetime in the making. An air of optimism and excitement pulsed in the air.

Then a bomb exploded.

A waitress carrying a tray of fine crystal glasses stumbled and fell, drenching Korah in red wine. But when he looked down, he did not see wine; Korah saw blood. Plaster fell from the ceiling, filling the hall with white dust. Black smoke billowed just before a fireball roared through the room like the breath of a great dragon.

Korah snapped.

In his mind, they were not in the Capitol Building; he was in Endor covered in blood, surrounded by fire. The Royal Guards moved to evacuate him, but to Korah they became the men who seized him, who took him away, and murdered his wife and child.

He reacted in abject terror.

They would not take him, not this time. They were not going to kill his family. He would protect them to the last drop of blood in his body. Fighting off the guards with superhuman strength, he lifted Peter from his chair by the back of his coat, took Alexa around the waist, and bolted.

Another bomb detonated.

Korah did not falter, did not break stride, and he did not stop. Peter wrapped his arms and legs around him and held on. Korah barreled through the dark hallway. The guards cleared a path, but he did not see what they were doing. He was deep in Thyatira Woods, fighting, escaping.

They cleared the building, and he kept running. His guards shouted and motioned, trying to help him and the first family, but Korah turned on them like a wild animal, snarling. "Get away. Step back or I will kill you all."

A third bomb exploded.

Korah ran, carrying Peter, pulling Alexa by the arm.

Two soldiers materialized through the smoke, leading horses. "My Esteemed," one of them yelled, "mounts!"

Korah catapulted Peter into the saddle of one of the horses. "Follow me, Son." He pulled Alexa in the saddle with him, and together the royal family raced into the chaos of the New City.

Fire danced in ominous fingers, lighting the night sky. Citizens ran, screaming in terror. The ground shook as explosion after explosion rocked the New City. A fiery piece of rubble landed two yards from Peter's speeding mount. The horse shied and reared, but the young Prince kept his seat.

Korah yelled a whoop of encouragement, "That's my boy! Come on."

They cleared the concentrated attack, and Alexa looked around at the unfamiliar section of the city. "Where are we going? The Palace is that way."

"I have to get you both safe. They will expect us to go to the Palace." He turned. "Prince d'Or, is your mount sound?"

Peter's face was ashen, but he nodded once, emphatic. "Yes, Father."

"Then we ride. Can you keep up?" Korah held Alexa firmly around the waist, expertly controlling the horse with his free hand, focused on his son.

"I can ride like the wind," Peter declared with confidence.

"Of course you can. We are going to Gilead." Korah held his frightened son's eyes and ordered with paternal authority, "If anything happens to us, that is where you go. Do not go back to the Palace, understand?"

"Yes, Father." Peter cringed as another explosion rocked the city behind them.

"Good man," Korah said, setting off in a trot. The three of them rode through the night of fire and terror, to the sanctuary of Gilead, the Palace of the Princes.

Time and Again - Gilead – Korah and Alexa

They arrived near dawn, exhausted and filthy. When they stopped, Peter nearly fell out of his saddle, slumping over the mare's sweaty neck, his hands locked into fists around the reigns.

Korah lifted Alexa off the horse and held her swaying in his arms. "Are you all right?" he asked.

She blinked up at him, woozy. "Yes."

Korah moved to Peter's mount. "Son, are you okay?"

Peter nodded, tears streaming down his soot-covered cheeks. When Korah helped him down, he ran to Alexa and wrapped his arms around her waist in a desperate hug, burying his face in her singed dress. "I am fine," he managed to say, then began to cry. He had remained calm during their journey, but he was a little boy, and they were all shaken.

Alexa hugged him hard, breaking into tears herself.

Korah held them both, whispering words of encouragement and calm. At length, he nudged them toward the entryway. "Come on, you two. We're home."

News of the family's arrival roused the small contingent of staff, who hastily streamed into the entryway in various stages of dress.

Korah issued instructions. "See to the mounts. They served us well this long night." A footman scurried off. "Have the Master's Chamber and the Blue Bedroom readied and baths drawn for all of us." Several of the maids bobbed curtsies and left. "No one is to send word to the Palace that we are here, not until we are certain it is safe." His voice boomed through the corridors, emphasizing his point. "We will remain in residence, in secret, until I deem and not before."

He softened his voice and his features, resting a hand on his son's hair, matted with soot and ash. "Peter, do you require food before you rest?"

Peter looked up at him like a puppy who had been beaten but was suddenly treated kindly. "I am not hungry at the moment."

"You will be." Korah nodded to the butler. "Toast and eggs will suffice."

The sparse staff disbursed to carry out their tasks. The little family stood in the majestic entry hall, alone. Korah let out a shaky breath and wrapped his arms around them. "You are safe. I got you safe." He murmured into Alexa's hair, "I'm so sorry."

Alexa felt the trembling begin in his limbs; he had been strung taut as a piano string. "This was not your fault, KbA. You did not do this." She held his eyes, intent he hear her. "Come now. You are covered in wine and smell like your father."

Korah buried his head in her neck and laughed. "Heaven forbid."

Adopting a soothing tone, she said, "Let's show Peter where the Blue Bedroom is."

Korah nodded wordlessly, gathering himself and palming the moisture from his eyes.

Alexa guided them up the stairs. She almost suggested Korah go to the Master's Chamber ahead of her, but the energy pulsing off him stopped her. He was reluctant to let them out of his sight.

The efficiency of a royal household never failed to astound Alexa. No matter that they were not expected, nor had any family members lived here in four years, the small staff executed their duties with flawless industriousness. They laid clothing out for Peter, drew his bath, and left a small plate of food ready for him.

"I can bathe myself, Mother." At eight, Peter gave her a determined look.

Alexa nodded and leaned into Korah. "I know, Son. Get some rest, we will see you in the morning," she looked around in bleary observation at the dawn sky, "or after you awake." She waited until she was certain Peter was going to bathe, then left him.

Walking arm-in-arm, memories broke free as they strolled the old, familiar hallway. They lived together in this house for years, in pain and ecstasy.

"Do I tell you," Korah began as his voice cracked, "that you are an extraordinary mother? Do I ever tell you that?" His control broke, and he engulfed her, sobbing.

In the dim hallway of Gilead, with the sun beginning to crest the horizon, she held on as he wept. When the tumult subsided, he allowed her to lead him down the hall. His feet shuffled with fatigue, and his breath came in short gasps. Opening the door of the Master's Chambers released a flood of memories, sweeping them both away. She guided him to the bathing chamber and dismissed the servants with a wave of her hand. She stripped him of his stained white shirt, took away his red tie, let his dirty and singed coat and trousers fall into a heap. Then she joined him in the large tub.

Tenderly, she washed the filth from his face, stroked the long taut muscles of his arms, whispering comfort, and soothing the terrible storm raging behind his eyes. She floated into his embrace and let him hold her.

"You do not know how much I love you." Korah cupped her face, his voice raw, desperate sincerity shining in his hazel eyes. "I am afraid for you all the time. I am terrified that I will lose you, that you will be taken from me."

"Shh," she brought his hand to her mouth and kissed it. "I am here, we are safe."

"I thought they were going to kill you tonight, you and Peter." Great shivers wracked his body. "Like before."

"Korah," she called to him as the darkness crept in. "It is not before. It is now. Let me show you." She brought his hand to her breast. "I am alive, my love."

Korah stood, lifting her and pressing his body against hers. "Will you come to bed with me?"

Alexa pulled his head down for a kiss, then took a towel from the stand, wiping away the mixture of water and tears streaming down his face. They stepped from the tub. Puddles marked their footsteps toward the massive bed where they spent the magic year.

He sat on the edge and pulled her to him, suckling her breast and kneading the other in tender worship. She arched her back and gave herself over to his touch, longing for him, burning with an old, smoldering fire.

He pulled her down with him, touching with sure hands, his breath coming in deep gasps. "You," he trailed kisses down her belly, nuzzling golden-red curls at the apex of her soul. "I adore."

He nudged her legs apart, kissing the inside of her smooth pale thighs. She made one of those sounds he liked, and he feasted upon her like a starving man. When she was shattering under his tongue, he crawled between her thighs seeking entrance. "You are *my* wife, *my* wife, *my* wife."

He threw his head back in ecstasy as he entered her. A great spasm hit his body, and he cried out in joy to be with her, to truly be with her.

Alexa grabbed his buttocks holding him as tight and as deep as he could go, felt the electricity coursing through their bodies and shattered again, taking them both to heights they had never reached.

The baby they created in that red dawn would die with her mother, six weeks later, at the hands of the father who had so tenderly planted the seed.

November 8, 986 ME

Not Going Anywhere - New City Palace - Korah and Alexa

In the aftermath of the terror attacks, Korah went ballistic. Day and night, that evil bastard Tristin whispered in his ear, spewing vengeance, punishment. He pushed Korah to retaliate with a show of force so overwhelming that no jihadist would ever raise a hand against him and his family again.

The brutality Korah unleashed was barbaric.

Mass public executions, raids, and kangaroo courts delivered swift and decisive verdicts to those who lived past apprehension. The Kingdom splintered under the schism. But Korah was blind to the fallout, crazed that they attacked his family. Compounding his fear was the threat the mongrels behind the violence would gain a foothold in his Kingdom. They needed to be eradicated. There was no room in Korah's Alanthia for zealots. His vision, his sacrifice, his rule, would not be derailed.

Alexa and Peter became virtual prisoners in the Palace. Korah returned to Alexa's bedchamber full time, vacillating between icy indifference, and smothering possession. He was not her husband of old, this was an entirely new version of Korah, and he terrified her. The mania behind his eyes burned like a lit stick of dynamite. He was ready to blow. She knew she had to escape, to remove herself and Peter as fast as possible.

Two days of bliss at Gilead were not enough; they were simply not enough.

And just when she thought things could not get worse—they did. She was late. It sent her into a tailspin. Desperate for her monthly to come, she could not comprehend the cruel twist of fate. To have another child, at the height of this madness, was inconceivable. When she threw up her morning tea and her breasts grew hard and sore, she knew. She was pregnant, and if Korah found out, he would never let her go, but she had to try.

Over dinner, she said casually, "I am considering a trip to Capernaum until things settle down."

Peter cast her a quick glance. He was terrified.

Korah looked between them. "Are you two hatching some sort of plan?"

Alexa adopted a breezy tone. "Nothing like that. We have not been for several years, and since father's stroke, he has been lonely."

"No." Korah looked down at his half-eaten plate in broody silence.

"Korah, it might be safer for Peter and me to leave. Just for a while, until things settle down."

He slammed his hand on the table, making them all jump, rocking the dishes. "I said, no."

Alexa rose from her seat. "You are being unreasonable." She shot him a lethal glare and stormed out.

Korah pointed a finger at Peter. "Did you do this?"

Peter flinched. "No."

Korah pushed away from the table, his face an evil mask, and stormed after his wife. He flew into her bedchamber and slammed the door. "You are not to leave the Palace."

"I will not be held prisoner, Korah. Not in this house. Not with you the way you are right now. I cannot watch that wicked bastard, Tristin, pollute your mind every minute of the day. He is like a cancer, and you do not see it!"

Alexa stalked over to him. "I know he is the one who attacked Princess Philomela, I know it. The way he looks at me, the way he looks at Peter, he has the eyes of a devil!"

"Shut up, I will not have this argument with you again."

"I will not shut up! Not about him, not about what he is doing to you and to our kingdom. I would not be surprised if we discover he is the one behind these attacks! He is using them to weed out the opposition and crush everyone who tries to stand against you. Tristin sees how shaken you are and plays on your deepest fears. He is twisting your mind!"

Alexa shook her head, brimming with anger and righteous indignation. "Two days, we had two days without him in our lives, and it was wonderful, but the moment we returned…" She squeezed her temples in frustration. "I cannot live this way any longer. I cannot stay in this house with him or with you the way you are now. I am leaving."

"No!" Korah shouted, his mind fracturing. Alexa saw more than he thought. Daily, Marduk threatened to kill her and Peter, preying on Korah's fears, using his family as leverage. But it was not only him, the jihadists launched attacks against them every week.

Spewing vile rhetoric, their stated goal was his demise. If he died, Marduk would destroy Alexa. He would consume her and Peter. They could not fight him. She needed to shut up! He could feel Marduk listening, feel his presence in the room.

Alexa flushed red and spat furious defiance. "You cannot stop me."

He shook her, punctuating each word. "I am the Ruling Prince. You are my wife. I say when you can come, and when you can go."

She pushed him away. "It does not work that way, Korah. I am leaving, and I am taking Peter with me."

"No!" Korah's eyes turned black with panic. "You are not taking my son anywhere! You do not understand the danger we are in!" She had to stop. She had to shut up.

"The only person he is in danger from is YOU! You put him in danger. You abuse him! And I am done. I will no longer allow you to hurt my son. Do you hear me, Korah? Do you hear me?" she screamed in rage.

"I am keeping you safe!" Korah shouted back. "You are not going anywhere, neither is he."

"Stop lying to me! You are delusional." She shook her fist, her tone and expression mocking, reminiscent of his mother. "What do you care? All you want is the throne. Does it make you happy, Korah? I sure as hell hope it does because you killed your brother for it."

"Shut up!" Korah roared.

"Your brother, who loved you," Alexa snarled, "who did everything he could to keep you safe, to keep you sane."

"He lied to me," the Beast answered. "He found out my daughter might still be alive, and he kept that knowledge to himself."

"Because you could not handle it!" she shouted.

His eyes widened with shock and rage. "You knew?" Korah let the Beast loose and backhanded her.

Alexa stumbled backward with a cry, then flew at him like a wildcat, ready to tear him apart. "You went over the edge when you saw that woman again! Her! Her!"

"Eamonn killed her." He balled his fist and struck a blow to her gut.

Alexa doubled over in pain, whimpering, "The baby."

"The baby? The baby they let me believe burned to death? If Sussanna survived, then maybe so did Hope." He saw red, her treachery and absolute betrayal enraged him. "You knew!"

Alexa retreated to the corner but continued to fight, heedless of the danger. "She is better off without you. You do not care about your children. You sacrifice them on the altar of your own ambitions and give them over to that devil Tristin as playthings."

Commotion erupted in the hallway, sounds of shouting on the grounds, alarms blared. The Palace came under attack. Sliding over the walls, across the dark lawn, black clad jihadists waged war. Inside the Beast did too.

Korah flew at Alexa. "When did you know? When did you know my daughter might still be alive?"

She looked away, as real fear entered her heart for the first time. "Korah, I'm hurt, and I'm in pain."

"Pain? I'm going to show you pain!" He fell upon her, black wrath and rage that had no restraint. With his bare hands, Korah fulfilled the prophecy Alexa made in Eamonn's study all those years ago. He killed them both.

When he looked up, covered in his wife's blood, Tristin stood in the room. "She will make a convenient martyr." He grinned and spoke with a voice straight out of Hell. "I get your babies, Korah. I get them all."

Part 14 - Revelation

February 16, 1000 ME

The Message - Gilead - Peter and Astrid

Peter held the miniature from his mother's drawer, blinking at it in confusion. "Why did my mother have a painting of Persa?"

Astrid's jaw dropped. "That is not Persa. Look at the clothing." She scrambled beside him to get a better look. "This is old."

Peter's hand shook so hard, the miniature fell from his fingers.

Someone knocked. Astrid looked between the door and her stricken husband, then walked across the room, and decided to send whoever it was away.

Jarrod stood in the hall, his face pasty white, a shimmer of sweat on his forehead. "Your Grace, there is a messenger downstairs who requires a word with the Prince."

"He is indisposed at the moment," she said in her most imperious tone.

Jarrod swallowed hard. "Your Grace, it is important."

Knowing Peter had been through enough, she controlled her temper and said, "Shall I receive the messenger?"

Jarrod's ashen face twitched. Closing his eyes tight, he said unsteadily, "No, your Grace. He is here on Prince Josiah's orders."

Peter's strangled voice answered the summons. "Give me a moment."

Astrid shut the door and turned. Peter held the bible out to her. "Read it to me. I think I am going to need it."

She was familiar with the story of Jonah, but as she read, a new understanding bloomed. The verses opened in a way she never experienced before. She recognized Jonah the rebel, fleeing from the Lord, seeking his own path. She saw herself hiding in the hotel in Tel Aviv, locked away in the belly of the great fish. The significance of her deliverance and her obedience to go to the house of the enemy rang in her mind. Jonah mirrored her own reaction when the Iron King extended mercy to those she thought deserved punishment. As she finished the last chapter, her voice faltered as she read, "Is it right for you to be angry?"

Her words echoed in the silent chamber. She looked up. Peter's face turned ashen.

"Nineveh," was all he said. "Come on, we will hear the messenger together."

Lavender - Gilead - Peter and Astrid

"Thank you, Agent. Please keep us updated on the search for my father." Peter extended a hand to the messenger, then Jarrod escorted him out. Turning to Astrid, he said, "I thought it was over. I should have known Korah was too mean to die."

Astrid clutched the back of her neck. "Let's go to bed. It has been a long day."

"I am so confused," Peter sighed, raking his hands through his hair.

"It will be better in the morning." Astrid blinked up at him. "I'm sorry, Love, but I'm getting a headache."

He recognized the pain in her eyes and went to the sideboard to pour her a glass of water. "Drink this." He pressed it into her shaky hands.

She took a tentative sip.

"Do you have your tea?"

"It keeps me awake. Get me somewhere I can lie down." She closed her eyes against the flickering candles, awash with a sudden wave of dizziness and nausea. "Oh, no. It's going to be a bad one."

"Come with me." Peter took her around the waist.

"I'm sorry," she whispered, seeming to shrink as the pain hit her full force.

Peter eased her off the couch. "Hush."

Jarrod returned to the parlor, and Peter said, "The Duchess has a migraine. Please have ice packs sent to the Master Chamber and call for a doctor."

Astrid was nearly blind and whimpering by the time Peter got her to the Master's Chambers. Instead of putting her to bed, he guided her to the bathroom. "Go ahead. It always makes you feel better. I will hold your hair."

Astrid turned in Peter's arms with a pitiful cry and rested her cheek against his chest, feeling his heartbeat, strong and steady. The cotton of his shirt was smooth, his own personal scent just beneath the surface. She absorbed the strength of his body, feeling small and protected. "Peter, Korah won't come to Gilead, will he?"

"No, Love, he will not," Peter assured her, though her words sent a spike of adrenaline down his spine because he might.

Astrid let Peter attend to her as the migraine consumed her like a ravenous wolf. She lost her dinner, and he did indeed hold her hair. He washed her face, let her swish water to clear her mouth, helped her change into a nightgown, and got her into bed.

As Peter pulled the blankets over her, Jarrod wheeled a cart into the chamber, carrying an assortment of ice packs and warm water for tea. "My Esteemed, we have summoned the doctor. I brought lavender oil. It may bring her some relief."

Astrid opened one watery blue eye and whispered, "My mother made me a lavender pillow. I lost it when we were running. Thank you."

Jarrod bowed, "I shall procure a new one, your Grace."

After he departed, Astrid rubbed a drop of lavender oil on her temple and breathed, "He is amazing. I love Jarrod."

Peter nodded and eased an ice pack under her neck. "He has been a loyal and faithful servant for many years. We shall find someone to attend you. My mother had an excellent lady's maid. They became quite close. Auntie might know what happened to Gail, perhaps she is still in service."

Astrid smiled through the pain. "A lady's maid? Never in a thousand years did I ever expect to have a lady's maid."

Peter brushed a stray lock of hair hovering near her mouth and smiled. "Trust me, they become indispensable. 'Twas one of the hardest things for me when we were running. I am ashamed to admit."

"Even though he did not stock your cigarettes?" Astrid teased.

"Now that you mention it," Peter bent low, kissing her ear, and inhaling the warm lavender. "I must speak to him about that."

Astrid groaned, "Don't come back here smelling like cigarettes. You will make me vomit again."

"Korah cannot abide the smell, either. I think half the reason I took up the habit was to spite him."

"You would think he would like the smell of smoke, that bastard." Astrid pressed her fingers into her left eye, trying to relieve the pressure.

Peter winced, and a sudden thought occurred to him. "I think it scared him. He did not like fire," he amended with a scoff, "or he does not like fire."

For the space of a few heartbeats, he was quiet, looking around the room. "We came here the night they repealed the tech laws. We rode through the New City, through the bombs and fires to Gilead." He paused. "I forgot that."

"We were young when that happened," she whispered.

"Aye," he cleared his throat, "but this place holds more memories for me than I imagined."

"I like it here, but I understand if you do not want to stay."

Peter lifted her free hand and brought it to his lips. "We shall see. I admit, the riding is excellent."

"The horses arrived in good order?" she murmured, determined not to let the headache take her out of commission.

"Yes, though one was missing." He pressed her hand to his cheek. "I suspect he took it when he escaped. It was his, a beautiful animal that we both admired. Horses were the only subject we could discuss and not fight."

"Then there was at least that," she said just as the imaginary icepick hit her left temple. Despite her resolve, she gasped.

"I will inquire about the doctor. You rest, I will be back. Shall I send in a maid?"

"As long as she is not wearing perfume."

"Of course, no perfume." He laid her hand gently on the coverlet and left the room on silent feet.

Genevieve came to attend her. "You poor thing. What do you need?"

Astrid pulled the ice pack free and blindly handed it to Genevieve. "A warm cloth, it is cold in here."

Genevieve returned with a warm cloth and pressed it on Astrid's forehead. "Margaret suffered from migraines. Let me see your hand. There was a spot I could press that relieved the pain."

Astrid felt a wave of relief wash over her as Genevieve pressed between her thumb and forefinger. "Oh, that feels amazing."

Genevieve watched the color return to Astrid's face. "Good."

They sat in silence with only the crackling of the fire and the hum of the old house as background.

"Genevieve, how did he seem?" A tear escaped Astrid's closed eye. "I should be with him right now."

"Nonsense, you must rest. Himari is with Peter."

"I watched Princess Alexa raise the knife to kill Korah, but she obviously did not."

Genevieve bowed her head and murmured, "She loved him, your Grace. I realize that sounds strange, but she did."

"He was beautiful, like Peter, wasn't he?"

"He was, still is, I suppose, just older and a lot meaner," Genevieve said with a rueful laugh.

"I can see it," Astrid mumbled, feeling very vulnerable. "I think I have seen the worst of Peter, yet I still love him."

"Peter is not Korah, thank the Lord. But after looking through those sketches today, I remembered the way he was back then. He gave Alexa flashes of himself, enough to keep her holding on. He surrendered to the darkness when she died, but he grieved her. The house stayed in mourning for two years." She sniffed back a sudden unexpected tear. "I never saw him with anyone else. He dismissed his mistress and to my knowledge never took another. Despite being arguably the most eligible bachelor in the world, he never pursued another woman. I think he lived a very lonely life."

"What will they do to him when they find him?" Astrid asked, needing to know what they were facing.

Genevieve cleared her throat and gazed into the fire. "That will be up to Josiah."

Astrid groaned, "Poor Josiah, that puts him in a terrible position. I suspect he and Davianna might have trouble over it."

Genevieve took away the cooling cloth and asked, "Why do you say that?"

Astrid blinked. "Because there is a part of Davianna that loves Korah. She hides it, and I doubt she would ever admit it, but he got in her head. She mentions things, here and there, usually as it relates to the similarities between father and son."

"They are more alike than either of them ever cared to admit."

Astrid let out a long breath, relaxing as sleep crept over her. "Then I suppose my job is to make sure Peter never turns into Korah."

Yellow Salon - Gilead - Peter and Himari

"Do you like your new digs?" Peter asked from the doorway of the Yellow Salon.

Himari turned with a distracted air. "I am happy to be above ground, and I am ready to see my husband tomorrow."

"He is with Kayah? They arrived in Rephidim today?" Peter asked, looking grim.

"That was the plan, though there are no communications there. Mack rides out several times a week to catch a signal." Himari studied him with an odd expression. "How did we not recognize it? There is a strong family resemblance between you two."

Peter quirked an eyebrow at her, and Himari gasped. It was a quintessential Kayah expression.

"I suspect no one noticed because she always looks different," Peter said. "I think that threw us off. Besides, we were not expecting it."

"Why did Korah have her sent to prison?" Himari asked, wrinkling her forehead because that made no sense. "According to Auntie, he searched for decades, and she was right under his nose."

"I have no idea why he did half the things he did, but I am sure he never knew who she was."

Himari blinked rapidly, recalling an old memory. "Wait a minute, the day of your birthday party… maybe that's why they threw her out."

"What are you talking about? What birthday party?"

"It happened a few days before they raided the bunker and arrested us. Stephen got Kayah into the Palace, to serve during the party. They planned to get her in to see Prince Korah because we wanted his support for our research, but she never got a chance to speak with him. They threw her out, so we sent Stephen instead." Himari's eyes widened at the implication. "Your father was not at the party!"

"When was this?" Peter growled.

"January 983 ME," Himari said into the charged silence, "Wait, let me think. What did she say?" Himari's chest rose and fell as she closed her eyes, going back seventeen years. "She said they threw her out for being too pretty. She had a word with you, then Prince Eamonn took one look at her and had her thrown off the property."

"My uncle?" Peter scowled in confusion. "My uncle saw her and had her ejected?"

Himari nodded. "It was weird. I accused her of doing something." She cut him a knowing glance. "You know how she can be, but she swore she hadn't done anything."

Peter paused, thinking back. "Bloody hell, that is what she meant the night of the gala when she said she was glad not to be in a maid's uniform."

"The disguise she wore on New Year's Eve was stunning. I was video chatting with Filippo before he left. He turned the camera around so I could see her."

"I ran right into her and did not recognize her, not at first. I suppose that explains why Korah thought she was my grandmother." Peter covered his face and breathed into his hands.

"Oh, you are right! Auntie knew the second she saw those pictures of Kai in London who she was. You know she is rarely blonde. But she was when we were young, and she certainly was at that birthday party."

"That is why he killed my mother," Peter murmured to himself. Anguish and old fear flashed across his handsome face. "I never understood it. The last argument they had, he said, 'You knew, Eamonn knew, and you kept it from me.'"

"What?" Himari said, growing still. "Are you saying your mother and your uncle knew who Kayah was?"

Peter ran his hand through his hair and grabbed the back of his neck. "They might have…"

Himari shot out of her chair, furious. "They put Kayah in jail to get her out of the way! The entire thing was a fucking royal cover-up? They destroyed our lives!" She swept a hand at the computers. "I thought it was about the tech, but that was just an excuse."

Gripping the sides of her head, she raged, "She was an orphan with no one to help her! They let us all off, except her. They came after her with everything they could and set her up with some incompetent-ass attorney who could not even remember her name. He kept calling her Karen at the sentencing." Himari clenched her jaw, shaking with rage. "All these years, I thought they did it so Korah could steal our research."

Peter paled. "He did not know about any of it. I remember his valet was so grateful for his help keeping his son out of jail."

"Stephen's father was Korah's valet?"

"Yes, for years. They were close. McSwilley saved Korah's life." Peter cleared his throat. "Auntie G. told me the story today, how he discovered my father about to hang himself and talked him out of it. Korah pensioned him and his wife off early, before he took the throne."

Himari's mind worked and a horrible understanding dawned. "Korah paid for Stephen's college, made sure he got a job with the ministry when he graduated. I thought they cut a deal, that Stephen sold us out. Are you saying Korah did that as a favor to his valet?"

"Rather likely." Peter nodded.

Himari blinked back anguished tears and sat down heavily on the pale-yellow settee. "Stephen never talked about what his father did. We all knew he was in service, but Stephen always got this weird expression and said, 'One of the tenets of service is that we do not discuss the family nor the inner workings of the Palace.' We teased him mercilessly about it, but he never told us a thing."

"They swear an oath," Peter said, distracted and reeling from the revelation of his mother and uncle's treachery, and the real reason his father snapped the day he murdered his mother. Preoccupied, he added, "Royal life is difficult enough without reading about your bathroom habits on the front page. They know everything that goes on."

"Everything?" Himari clutched her stomach and looked sick. "So, it is conceivable Stephen knew your father had a long-lost daughter."

That got Peter's attention. "Likely he did."

Himari curled into herself, hugging her arms. "Stephen kept saying that nobody ever asked him what happened. At Gus' funeral, he looked at Kayah and said he did her a favor. Her life had not been all that bad, she had a bunch of houses. His last message was, 'Tell Kayah I was wrong.'" Himari hit her forehead with her palm. "He must have known, but he also understood what your life was like, living as Korah's son."

Peter closed his eyes, unable to stand the pitying expression on her face. "It was no secret above or below stairs."

"That is some bitter irony. His father stopped Korah from committing suicide, but Korah drove his son to it." Himari started to cry. "Peter, I saw the pictures. Stephen blew his head off, but not before he sent us all the codes, all the back doors. I think he compiled all that evidence they aired on the news that finally brought your father down."

"So, I suppose in the end, he broke free." Peter leveled a look at her. "That was all related to that Artificial Intelligence you were battling, which you kept secret from me."

Himari's eyes flew wide. "You had enough going on, and we took her down before you left the cabin. There was no way you guys were making it to the Golden City with Erica on the loose."

"The cabin?" An odd expression crossed Peter's face. "Are Bubba and Zanah still there?"

"Yes, I think so. We sent a food delivery up there right before the fighting broke out." Himari looked pained. "Have you met your new father-in-law?"

Peter reflected her sick expression. "No, but I suppose we will have to retrieve them."

Himari grimaced. "Filippo said they were quite a pair. I think Reuben had to restrain Kayah to keep her from throwing Zanah off the side of the mountain."

"Do me a favor. Do not send for them yet. Wait until our plane takes off. Of course, they will want to be at the wedding." Peter looked like he had just been served a gas station burrito for dinner. "If I was my father, I would just have them killed. My grandparents would have ordered the place burned to the ground, or perhaps we should take a page out of Uncle Eamonn's playbook and throw them in jail." Peter's voice dripped with droll irony. "When you consider it in that light, I suppose a con man and a mafia maven will fit right in with the royal family."

Himari smothered a laugh. "Do not forget, you've also added an assassin."

Peter got an odd look. "I have to make a phone call. Good-night, Himari."

Family Dinner - Pepperwood - Persa

"You look pretty tonight, Daughter, positively glowing," Yereq ben Grey said with a smile as he passed his empty dinner plate to Persa.

Persa returned his smile. "Thanks, Dad. I felt like dressing up a bit since I was not sick today."

He laughed and leaned back in his chair, rubbing his full belly. "Your mother was ill the entire time she was pregnant with you."

Persa stilled.

Old sadness crept into Yereq's eyes as he blinked up at her. "You are wearing her pearls."

Persa's hand flew to her chest, covering the delicate chain and pearl pendant, but said nothing.

"She would have liked that… to see you wearing them." Yereq held her gaze.

Persa turned away, going to the sink. "Then she should have stayed."

James glared at Yereq. The evening, up to this point, was pleasant. Persa's mother was always a sore subject, and he did not appreciate his father-in-law bringing it up. She was fragile, still reeling from their encounter with Rapha, in a delicate condition. The realization that Marduk could stalk Pepperwood scared Persa more than she admitted. He feared she might lock herself inside again, and if she did, she might never come out. They were dealing with enough without bringing Persa's mother into the mix. "I think we should be ending this discussion," he said tersely.

Yereq shook his head. "No, she needs to hear."

"I don't want to hear." Persa snapped her head around, her eyes flashing anger and old pain. "I do not want to hear how she had to go. Who has to leave their child?"

"She had her reasons, Persa."

Persa shouted, "You always say that. You always defend her, but you never tell me why she left."

"I cannot." Yereq sagged. "I promised. But she loved you, and she would have stayed, if she could."

"If you will not tell me the truth, then never speak of her to me again, ever!" She hurled a plate against the wall, shattering it into a dozen pieces. Her face flamed as she looked between them, then spun on her heel, and stormed out.

Yereq rose to follow, but James gripped his shoulder. "Leave her. You cannot talk to her when she is like this. She won't hear a thing you say. Let her calm down."

Flickers of concern danced over Yereq's face. "She needs to forgive her mother and put this behind her. With you two leaving for the Golden City tomorrow, I want you to take her to the temple, James. Make sure she deals with this. It might be the only place she can put it to rest. That's why I brought it up. It is not good for her or the baby to carry this anger around."

James had his own unresolved anger toward his mother and understood what a festering wound it could become. He sighed heavily. "I will try, Yereq, but she needs answers."

Yereq ran his hand through his thinning brown hair, slumping back into his chair. "When you return, if she has not done it," he paused, "then I suppose I will have to. They are all dead now, anyway."

"Who's dead?"

"Everyone who would have killed Persa, if they had known."

Persa fled the house, angry tears blinding her as she ran toward her sanctuary, to the horses. She did not bother with the overhead lights; she knew this place blindfolded. Her beloved mare whinnied a greeting. Persa stumbled into the stall and wrapped her arms around Lightning's neck, crying. "Why?" she said through an angry sob. "Why did she leave?"

Lightning grew agitated and stamped her feet, shifting in her stall. She blew muffled, warm breath into Persa's hair.

"I do not understand. I have never understood."

"I understand," Rapha growled out of the darkness.

Persa stumbled backward, terrified. "You are dead!" she choked.

"No, Mother, I am not that easy to kill, though you will be." His dark figure moved toward the stall, a black shadow of death. "I get my body back if you die."

"Stop!" Persa held out a hand. "You are not real."

"Keep believing that." The latch opened.

Lightning screamed and reared on her hind legs, striking the menacing figure in the chest. He flew backward with a grunt of pain.

Persa grabbed a hoof pick and made a break for it.

The monster caught her ankle, and she hit the ground with a gasp, losing her weapon in the fall. He was upon her in an instant, strangling her with inhuman strength. Looming above her, she saw his demon red eyes. An eerie wind blew, and a shaft of moonlight fell over both of them. Her eyes bulged as she realized who her attacker was.

His hands released, and he scrambled off her body. It was Korah who spoke out of the darkness, "Where did you get those pearls?"

Persa scooted backward, terrified.

Lightning head-butted Korah, and he cried, "Where did you get her horse?" He gasped in deep ragged pants but managed to croak, "*Fraulein Blitz?*"

Persa shrieked as Lightning began to glow silver, her mane and tail shining like white fire.

"Kill her, kill her," Rapha screamed, and Korah jerked.

"Shut up!" Korah rebuked. "*Bist du ein geliebtes Pferd?*" Is it you, beloved horse?

On the wind, a haunting voice answered, "Korah."

A hidden memory broke free, washing over Persa, as she recognized her mother's voice.

Rapha howled, "Get out of here! Get out!"

"No." Korah stumbled toward the glowing animal. "You get out!" He launched his body against Lightning and bowed backward in a guttural scream as Rapha's black spirit was ripped from his body.

Persa's eyes bulged as she watched it happen.

Korah collapsed in a heap, choking and coughing. Lightning nudged his prostrate form, blowing her breath in his face. His head lolled, and he opened his eyes. "*Fraulein Blitz, Danke schön.*"

Persa scrambled to her feet, grabbing the hoof pick, and staring at the scene in horrified fascination. She should have been terrified, screaming and running for help, but she just stood there. "What are you doing here? Peter said you were dead."

He turned his head, still on the stable floor. "I think I might be."

Persa clenched the hoof pick, trembling all over. "How do you know my mother's horse?"

"Your mother's horse?" Korah sat bolt upright. "This is my wife's horse. How do you have her pearls?"

Persa dropped the weapon as her hand flew to her collar bone, covering the necklace. "She left them for me."

"When were you born?" he cried and scrabbled up the stall, pulling himself to his feet. He took a swaying step toward her.

She backed up, horrified. "December 12, 965 ME."

Korah looked at her with huge hazel eyes, the mirror image of her own, and started counting the months on his fingers. "Nine! That was her surprise, the night of the fire. That is what she was going to tell me. I have wondered for decades, but I never imagined…" He covered his mouth, realization dawning. "Oh my God, Persa, you are my daughter."

Persa shook her head in vehement denial. "No, I cannot be. It is impossible."

"Your mother was Sussanna ben Ross, my wife!"

"And she never wanted you to know!" Yereq shouted as he stormed into the stable. "You wicked bastard. Get away from my daughter!"

Persa looked between them and shouted, "Tell me this is not true!"

Yereq flushed crimson as his face contorted. "She never wanted you to know, to keep you safe," he pointed an accusing finger at Korah, "from him and his kind! They tried to kill her, to burn her to death. She had to give away her baby to protect her from them, but they did not know about you! He never knew about you. The royals killed her, Persa, they killed your mother."

Persa stumbled backward, his words hitting her like a blow.

"Sussanna was not trying to kill you, you *fecking* evil son of a bitch!" Yereq charged Korah and threw him against the wall. "She overheard a plot. They were planning to kill you at the polo match. I tried to stop her, but she bolted—to save you!"

"A plot?" Korah choked, and his knees gave way.

Yereq was crying and turned to Persa. "She was at the Hewies watching you and James. She came to all your events, baby, every single one. But she could not speak to you! She sat in the stands, with tears streaming down her cheeks, and loved you from afar."

He snarled at Korah, "You have no idea what you did to her. The pain she endured, losing her children, hiding from your family, living like a fugitive in the shadows. She searched for your lost daughter until the day she died. She spent every shekel she earned hiring private investigators to find her. And she left me to keep Persa safe because she never wanted you to know! So keep away from my daughter. Get out!"

Korah's broken voice came out of the darkness. "She was not trying to kill me?"

"No! She was trying to save your miserable ass," Yereq yelled. "And it cost her her life."

Korah fell onto Lightning. His anguished cry carried to the heavens. "Sussanna!"

Lightning flashed a brilliant pulse of white energy.

The impact knocked Yereq to the ground and pushed Persa up against the wall.

Korah and the horse disappeared.

Blood Will Out - Rephidim - Kayah

Kayah and Filippo arrived in Rephidim at dusk. Kayah scanned the village in awe and said, "I have heard of places like this. I just did not believe they still existed." She dismounted and touched the velvet soft grass.

Filippo was not nearly as enchanted. "Is a little place. I hope they have espresso."

"You have a one-track mind, Filippo. Lavinia is here. I am sure she will make you an espresso."

"Would be good." Filippo groaned with the dismount, gingerly holding his bruised side.

Ernst ben Otto exited his small house beside the stables, greeting the recent arrivals. "*Guten Abend*, you need to stable your horses?"

Filippo looked at the elderly man as if he were the Savior himself. "Please, you take this stubborn horse. I wish to never see her again."

Kayah scoffed and turned.

Ernst froze mid-stride, his eyes growing as big as basketballs. "*Ich sehe einen Geist!*"

Filippo reached out to steady the man. "She is no ghost, are you okay?"

Ernst swallowed thickly and took a tentative step forward. "Sussanna?"

Kayah gave the old man a compassionate smile. "No, I am Kayah, Lavinia ben Anthony's friend. We have come to find her and Thaddeus ben Todd. Are they here?"

Ernst scrubbed his hands over his face and blinked, as if trying to clear his vision. "You look exactly like her. She was your mother?"

Kayah's face drained of color. "I never knew my mother."

"Sussanna ben Ross of Endor?" Ernst stepped closer, squinting.

Kayah's mouth fell open. "Who is that?"

He furrowed his brows, studying her intently. "Come, we will see." Taking her by the arm, he led her to the pasture fence and whistled.

"What are you talking about?" Filippo took Kayah's other arm and tried to pull her away, clearly disconcerted by the old man's odd behavior.

"Look." Ernst nodded off in the distance.

A huge black stallion emerged from the thick woods.

"Does he come to you?" Ernst pointed to the magnificent animal. "If he comes, then we will know."

"We will know what?" Kayah demanded, her voice climbing.

"If he does not, then it does not matter. I am then just an old man, seeing ghosts."

Kayah turned to Filippo, her expression full of pain and longing, tinged with genuine fear. "Filippo, go get Lavinia."

Ernst pointed and said, "Second row, four houses over, with a green door. She is there."

Filippo looked uncertain. "Kayah, you coming with me. We will go find Vinia. You do not have to do anything for this man." He tapped his temple, then cut his eyes at Ernst.

"Just go get her." Kayah turned her back on him, studying the horse at the edge of the forest.

"Mamma Mia!" Filippo threw up his hands in surrender and stalked off.

The smell of sweet grass and hay blew on the breeze, Kayah inhaled deeply, trying to calm her pounding heart. The stallion snorted and stamped a front hoof, tossing his head. His black mane was glorious, like the hair of a woman, fine and silky. "He is a Friesian," Kayah breathed in awe.

"He's more than a Friesian, *Fraulein*." Ernst concentrated on her, clenching his hands in anticipation.

Kayah squared her shoulders and tilted her chin up. Casting a quick glance over her shoulder at Ernst, she said, "Okay."

She took three steps into the open pasture and extended her hand. With a sharp command, she called, "Hei!"

The horse's ears turned forward, his head erect, alert.

"Come here," she called with authority.

The horse threw his head up and whinnied, calling back to her.

Kayah made a clicking sound with her tongue and chirped, "*Mir*." To me. With a hundred German lessons to her credit, she pulled it out of the ether, it seemed right.

Thundering hooves shook the ground as the horse burst into a gallop, obeying her command.

"*Mein Gott*," Ernst breathed.

Kayah spared him not a glance, focused on the majestic animal flying toward her. She stood her ground, not flinching. He came to a sudden halt, tossing his splendid mane and holding his silky tail high.

"Hello." She smiled at him. "You are beautiful. What is your name?"

"Do you know it?" Ernst whispered.

She blinked and took a step forward, moving in a dream. "I do." Placing her hands on either side of the horse's enormous cheeks, she stared into his brilliant brown eyes. "You are Heilig. Your sire was Ebenholz, and your dam was Schicksal. You are a mighty horse of Endor."

Ernst fell to one knee, bowing his head. "And you, Kayah, daughter of Sussanna, are a Guardian of the Blood."

"Kai?" Lavinia's husky whisper drifted in the air.

Kayah rested her cheek against the majestic horse's muzzle and turned, an ethereal expression on her beautiful face. "Vinia, this is Heilig."

"I see that, honey." Lavinia held her eyes. "Are you okay?"

Kayah nodded slowly. Then turned teary-eyed to Ernst. "You knew my mother?"

Family Ties - Pepperwood - Persa

James was on the phone with Peter when a flash of white light out of the stables abruptly ended their call. "I have to go. Something's happening." He hung up before Peter could say another word and hit the door running. He found Yereq on the ground, and Persa staring at him in shock. "What's going on?"

Persa ignored the question and shook her finger at Yereq. "You lied to me my whole life. You lied to me!"

Yereq got to his feet, reaching for her. "I did it to protect you. I promised your mother."

Persa shied away. The father she loved was not her father at all. He felt like a stranger; she felt like a stranger. Devastated, she asked, "Have you always known?"

"Yes." Yereq's shoulders slumped in shame. "I'm sorry."

"You are sorry?" Persa looked at James, wild-eyed. "He is sorry that he is not my father, though he pretended to be all these years."

"I am your father!" Yereq protested. "I held you seconds after you were born, and I loved you every second after."

"What the hell is going on?" James demanded.

Persa glared at Yereq. "My mother was pregnant with me when you met her?"

"Yes." Yereq bowed his head, the wind thoroughly knocked out of him. "I was trying to find Endor, to buy horses for Rivergate. I was a bachelor, and she was a beautiful woman in trouble, so I helped get her out of there and keep her safe. She agreed to come home with me."

"Nine months! He said nine months. So, I could be yours?" Persa was desperate for anything that would prove she was not Korah ben Adam's daughter.

"You are mine, in every way that matters." Yereq reached out again, and Persa retreated to the corner of the stable.

James stood gob smacked, watching the interplay.

"That does not answer my question!" Persa's voice rose to a high squeak.

"I loved your mother very much, but she was married." Yereq looked away. "We were not intimate."

"You were not even married?" Persa cried. "That was a lie, too?"

"We did not want you labeled a bastard. You were not. For your safety, we told everyone that you were our daughter." Yereq looked up at the ceiling. "She would have stayed, but a royal delegation came to Rivergate to buy a horse. Korah was not with them, but she hid from them. It spooked us both. She feared if they saw her or you, they would put it together. So, she left."

"Yereq," James snarled, "why would a royal delegation hurt Persa?"

Yereq set his jaw, angry the truth had come out like this. "Because Korah ben Adam was her sire."

James felt a jolt of electricity run up his spine. He snapped his head around and said to Persa, "You are Peter's sister?"

In the chaos, she had not processed that far. "Peter!" Covering her face, she whispered, "We have to tell him his father is still alive."

"He knows. He called just a minute ago to tell me, but there was something strange in his voice. I thought it was just the news." James blinked rapidly. "How do you know Korah is still alive?"

Persa let out a hysterical laugh, her eyes growing overly bright. "Oh, because that demon spawn Rapha is apparently not quite dead. He possessed Korah and brought him here to kill me." Her hand went to her throat. "I suppose I have my mother's pearls to thank for the fact I am not dead, and Rapha's body still is."

"What are you talking about?" Yereq looked very concerned.

Persa ignored the question, beginning to rave. "When Korah saw my pearls, he jumped off me. Then Lightning did that crazy, glowing thing she does sometimes, Korah hugged her neck, and a black spirit flew out of his mouth. We talked for a minute. He told me I was his daughter, and then Poof!" She clapped her hands. "He and Lightning disappeared."

She gripped the sides of her head, delirious. "I wonder if he knows that evil spirit was his grandson?" A crazed laugh erupted from her chest.

Then she whirled on Yereq, ready to fight. "That's why Tristin had me write you that letter, Dad." She mocked him with the last word and quoted the letter she just remembered. "'I know who I am now, and I have joined the royal court.' You did not question it, did you?"

"I forgot about that letter." Yereq paled, a horrified look came into his eyes. "Persa, you ran off with someone."

"No, I did not! I was kidnapped by a devil and held against my will for a year and a half, but you thought I was at court." She picked up a can of hoof shine and threw it at him. "Hell, I was at court. Ask Mack ben Robert, he saw me. He remembered. Look at the pictures of the State Dinner on 9/11, I am sitting at the head table four spots over from King Korah… my father! I spent the day roaming the halls with my brother."

She turned, blinking and dazed, and said to James, "I have a brother."

"You also have a sister." Yereq's words stopped Persa cold.

James swore under his breath and wrapped a protective arm around Persa. "Come now. I think we should be taking this inside. It's cold out here. Fey, you can lie down while your da tells us the tale."

Outwardly, James appeared as he always was, stable, calm, and caring—the quiet husband. Inside, he was raging. Korah… he hated Korah. In a flash, he was thankful to Yereq, thankful he kept Persa out of that monster's hands, but she had fallen into another's, and the ramifications for why the Lord allowed it began to dawn on him. The sins of the father visited upon his children. James put a protective hand over Persa's belly. "Is the baby okay?"

That jolted her, and she stopped, covering his hand with her own. Yereq came alongside them, fear written all over his face.

"Be still for a minute." Persa moved James' hand. "Right there, do you feel it?"

James closed his eyes, willing his baby to kick, then they shot open. "I did, like a little gas bubble."

"Yeah, fluttery, like butterfly wings." Then she turned to Yereq and swallowed, her eyes swimming. "Did you feel me kick?"

He sniffed and held her eyes. "I did, my darling girl, I did."

Persa went to him with a faint cry, ashamed she had spoken harshly. Surrounded by his strong arms, she smelled his familiar scent, saddle oil, and aftershave. Her stalwart, precious dad held her as she cried. He taught her to ride and trained her and James to a World Championship. He allowed James to move in with them when he was eleven years old. For all practical purposes, he raised them both, and he did it alone. He gave them the land where Pepperwood stood, plus the stock to begin. All these things he did, knowing his blood did not run in her veins. "I did not mean it. You are my dad."

"I know, honey." Yereq palmed away his wet eyes. "Let's get you inside. Jay is right. You need to lie down."

Persa settled on the comfortable, green sofa.

James draped a blanket over her, noting how dirty she was and how small she seemed. Bruises were already forming around her neck. "Are you sure you are okay?"

"I would not be opposed to a glass of water," she murmured, trying to put on a brave face.

James nodded and went to the kitchen. He checked all the doors and made sure they were locked before returning to the living room. Part of him wanted to call Peter ben Korah and tell the little shit to get his ass up here and explain what he knew, but Yereq's story was not over.

"So, I have a sister." Persa wiped her eyes, her voice gravelly and strangely disembodied.

Yereq blew out a shaky breath and nodded. "Jay, have you got anything stronger than water?"

"I believe I do, hang on." James walked to the kitchen and took down an old bottle of whiskey someone gave to him as a birthday present. Now he realized why they never opened it. He swam in whiskey the entire time Persa was gone. Tonight seemed an ideal time to dive back in. He filled both glasses and fell with a thud into the loveseat. Then he looked at Persa. "Do you want another half a glass of wine?"

"That won't do anything. A half a bottle might, but I don't think Junior would appreciate it."

James raised a toast to Yereq, who had already drained his glass and was filling a second. "How about you start from the beginning?"

Yereq nodded, beginning slowly. He told them how he had met Sussanna the day after the fire. "She was out of her mind with grief and sick from the early stages of pregnancy. I found her, slumped over Lightning's neck, delirious."

He flushed from the whiskey and remembrance. "She was the loveliest creature I ever beheld. She spoke with an accent, very soft Germanic. It was bonny. And her eyes? They were the color of the sea and changed from blue to green." Picturing her in his mind, he said dreamily, "Her blonde hair waved around her face, and she moved with a graceful elegance, so beautiful." He turned to James with a helpless shrug, man-to-man.

"She told me she was running from her husband's family. They were rich and powerful, and he married her outside of their wishes. So, they came to their village, abducted her husband, and burned the place to the ground. She said if they found her, they would kill her. So, I helped.

"Back then, it took months to make the journey. As time passed, she told me more. I assumed his family were nobles, perhaps a landed knight or a baron, but she blew that notion to smithereens when she told me who he was. That's when she confessed that she was pregnant. I traveled all the way across the kingdom in search of Endor, only to find it destroyed. But I got you, Persa, and you are worth more than a thousand Endorite horses."

They lapsed into an extended conversation about the horses of Endor.

"It is why I gave you Lightning and her foal." Yereq motioned with his head to their stables. "Bayard is an Endorite stallion."

"All these years," James raised his eyebrows at Persa, "we have had two legendary horses and did not even know it."

"Except on New Year's Eve when they started glowing," Persa remarked dryly.

"Oh, look at Peter ben Korah staring back at me, right there," James observed, laughing as he poured another drink. "How have I not ever noticed that?"

"I always have." Yereq drained his glass and let out a quiet belch. "I about lost my mind when he pulled you out of that receiving line, Persa. I thought for sure Korah would recognize you, but he didn't."

As he poured another glass, he added, "I think his wife did, though."

Persa sat up straight. "Princess Alexa? Why do you say that?"

"I watched you every second you were at that table. You and Peter were sitting there like two peas in a pod. You don't closely resemble each other, but your mannerisms are nearly identical, so's your humor, and your temperaments. His mother noticed. Korah did not." Yereq wiped his brow, the heat of the whiskey and adrenaline making him clammy.

"Then that damn invitation from the Palace arrived a few months later, and I was ready to jump out of my skin. But your mother," Yereq pointed at James, "was dead set on getting Persa into town for that ball." His hand shook slightly as he poured another full glass. "You cannot imagine how many times I had to bite my tongue when that old shrew dropped hints about Persa's inferior bloodline."

Persa brought her fist up to her mouth, trying to smother a giggle and not succeeding. "I cannot wait to stroll into her parlor and demand she curtsies to Princess Persa."

James threw back his head and laughed, then added darkly, "Oh, when I see her again, she is going to do more than curtsy."

"Yeah, she is! Get Peter on the phone and tell him to bring my crown tomorrow." Persa's eyes widened. "Wait a minute… if my mother married Korah, then we can add bigamy to his long list of crimes. Does that make Peter illegitimate?"

Yereq shook his head. "I doubt it. Sussanna and Korah's wedding was done in Endor. The records were surely burned, if not confiscated. Alexa's godfather is one of those high-powered, New York attorneys, he would have seen to the legal matters, especially after your mother showed up the day she died."

Persa yawned despite herself. "What happened? I remember that one year at the Hewies, there was a ruckus, and they ended a day early. You had Big Al and Tommy bring us home. They said you were going to stay to buy some horses, but I don't recall you coming home with any fresh stock."

Yereq covered his eyes and looked away. "No. I got ossified, crawled in a keg, and stayed drunk for a week or more. I don't exactly recall."

"But you remember what happened?" James prompted.

"I do." Yereq stared at the dark amber liquid in the glass, contemplating. "You two just finished your performance in the semi-finals. I spotted her. She was in the stands. She was always there." He held Persa's eyes, his swimming. "We would meet, she and I, after you finished, so we could talk about your routine. Many times she told me things to tell you both. Sussanna was an amazing horsewoman." He sucked in a deep breath, staring at the shiny cup on the mantel.

"That day, she signaled me to meet her outside the arena, but I got held up. I couldn't get straight to her. She was hiding because she knew the royal family would arrive for polo any moment. When I reached her, she was frantic."

February 2, 981 ME

Languages - New City - Sussanna and Yereq

Sussanna blended in with the crowd at the Hewies, watching Persa and James perform with pride glowing in her heart. "Yes, that is it. Hold it, one, two, three, four." She jumped to her feet, applauding the superbly executed lift and shouted, "Perfect!"

She tried to catch Yereq's eyes, but he was glued to the performance like the rest of the spectators. Three rows below her, she noticed a man not watching the ring. Turning back to Persa and James, she kept him in the corner of her eye. He kept checking his watch, then scanning the entrances, looking for someone. He had a furtive air about him, like he was up to something, and he had not once turned to the spectacular performance. The hair on the back of her neck rose in warning.

When she looked over at him again, he was gone. Sussanna relaxed, chalking the situation up to heightened nerves. Korah would be on the grounds soon if he was not already. Persa was not the only athlete she watched from the shadows.

As Persa and James took their bows and waited for their scores, she slipped out to wait for Yereq. Whispered voices, in a strange tongue, caught her attention. She knew without seeing him, it was the man from the stands. Ducking behind a wall of fresh straw, she listened. They were speaking Arabic, an uncommon language, but one she learned as a child. Sometimes an Arabian would find his way to Endor, seeking a horse, so she had heard it before.

"What is the news, do we go?" a man asked.

They were not whispering. Doubtless, they thought no one would understand them.

"Yes. We have confirmation. He is funding illegal research, a capital crime. The brotherhood is in agreement. Before this day is over, the vile infidel will breathe no more."

The other man made a satisfied grunt. "It is justice. Kill him on the polo field where the Princes have corrupted everything the Iron King meant the sport to be."

"And today, brother, we will be in paradise."

Sussanna's eyes widened. Prince Eamonn would never fund technological research, but Korah? Absolutely. When they lived together, he had been full of plans and dreams.

Yereq emerged from the arena, scanning the area, trying to find her. She shrunk back, desperate to remain hidden. The two speakers saw him and moved away. When they were out of sight, she flew at Yereq in a panic.

"Yereq, those two men, they were discussing a plot to assassinate Korah. They were speaking in Arabic, but I understood them." She looked around wildly. "You must help me. We must get to the polo grounds to stop them."

"Wait," Yereq called, but she bolted into the crowd, running.

In the distance, trumpets announced the royal family, and the brass band broke into the first notes of the Alanthian National Anthem. Yereq ran after her, but in her panic, she outmaneuvered and outpaced him.

The crowd was immense, as it always was when the Royal Team took to the pitch. Yereq jumped, trying to see above their heads, searching for Sussanna. He was less concerned for the Prince's safety than he was terrified for her. Five minutes into the first chukka, he spotted her. But, then again, so did everyone else.

She pulled a rider from his horse, leaped into the saddle with that amazing grace she always had and charged toward Korah. He was driving, a clear path to the goal, and did not see her. The pitch erupted into chaos as the other riders realized what she had done. Yereq followed her line of sight and spotted two men dressed in black robes.

They stood out in the crowd—martyrs.

Yereq had seen drawings of them. They would kill the Prince, then turn their weapons on themselves in the misbegotten belief it would earn them high glory with the Iron King.

He shouted. He knew he did. There was no force on Earth that could contain the terror beating in his heart. She rose out of the saddle, the horse thundering under her. She held that pose, unified perfection. He knew she carried a weapon since Endor. It was in her hand, sure and steady, aiming past Korah at the two men who drew back. He saw their surprise, a blonde avenging angel spoiling their plans.

He did not see Prince Eamonn. Yereq only had eyes for her. The next instant, she was falling. He had the absurd thought that Sussanna ben Ross had never fallen from a horse. He fought his way through the screaming crowd. They were pointing and shouting, watching the horror unfold.

Yereq saw Korah sprinting across the pitch. He fell on his knees at her side, cradling her head. Yereq echoed the cry that ripped out of Korah's soul, as they both watched the woman they loved die before their eyes.

February 16, 1000 ME

Whatever You Might Think - Pepperwood - Yereq, James, and Persa

Yereq's voice shook with the telling. "I did not understand, until that moment, how devoted they were to one another. I told myself she had not meant that much to him, that she was simply a fling. He had his rich wife and all the trappings of royalty. What could a simple horsewoman truly be to a man like that?"

Yereq bowed his head and sniffed. "I learned that day… I was mistaken. I deluded myself because I loved her and did not want to believe he could love her as much as I did."

Persa covered her mouth holding back a cry. She had held James in the same manner Yereq described. Reliving the devastation of seeing him dead, she asked, "What did Korah do?"

"He went mad. Right there on the pitch, in front of everyone, he lost his mind. It was as difficult to watch as her falling. You have heard the expression crazy with grief? Words cannot capture the genuine horror of seeing it happen to someone."

"What happened?" Persa asked, pulling the blanket up to her chin, fighting tears.

"He would let no one get close to her. When they tried, he held them off at gunpoint. For hours he just held her body in his lap, pleading with her not to leave him again, sobbing. It is a sound I never want to hear again." Yereq shivered and took another long pull of his whiskey.

"I could not bear it, and they ushered us all out. There was nothing I could do. If I claimed kinship, that would lead them to you." He screwed his face up in pain. "So, I left. I left my Sussanna on the pitch with the sound of Korah ben Adam still wailing in my ears.

"Never doubt, Persa. They loved each other. Do not make the mistake I made and think she was nothing to him. I think she was everything to him."

Persa sniffed back tears. She heard Korah cry out for her mother and recognized the truth. "You said I had a sister, what happened to her? Is she also Korah's daughter?"

"Yes, she is. And you've met her."

Persa sat up. "What? When?"

Yereq rubbed his head, tired and more than a little drunk. "You are going to be mad at me when I tell you this." He looked at Persa with his brown eyes, red-rimmed and weary. "At Mack and Lavinia's wedding, all three of you were sitting together. You and Peter and her, it was surreal."

"Kayah," James said, shaking his head. "That's who it is?"

Persa jerked her head around at him. "Kayah? Lavinia's friend?" She looked to Yereq for confirmation. "That gorgeous, scary woman is my sister?"

Yereq snorted a breathless laugh. "She is your mother to the life. Several of our older neighbors commented it was nice to see one of Sussanna's relatives in Redding. I thought for sure someone would say something. But like you said, she is kind of scary. I don't think they got up the nerve."

Persa templed her fingers and pressed them to her mouth, remembering that night. She dropped her hands in her lap and asked, "Does Peter know any of this?"

"No," James said. "I don't think so. He would have said. There is no way he knows," then added with a rueful laugh, "at least not on a conscious level."

"What do you mean?" Persa's head lolled to the side, exhausted.

"In his delirium, he kept calling you Kayah and saying he did not want to kiss you. I thought you were going to sock me in the stomach when I said that when we met her."

"Bloody hell. I stopped her from kissing someone." Persa turned bright red. "I had to go to the bathroom, and I walked in on her and Thaddeus ben Todd."

James laughed. "He went after her that night, shot out of his chair like a cannon when he spotted her."

"With good reason," Yereq slurred slightly, "he's an FBI Director, and she is a shady character. I did a little digging after the wedding, to see what I could find out about her." He swallowed thickly. "I thought I might put you two together, but I decided against it."

"Why?" Persa's voice cracked, and she took another drink of water.

"Well, she is a convicted criminal and spent a couple of years in prison. The lawyer who represented her on her appeal was familiar to me. I remembered him from Prince Adam's time, and Sussanna always claimed he was the one behind the fire. So, I left well enough alone." Yereq's head bobbed, and he gave her a drunken smile. "I thought she was probably more like Korah than Sussanna, and you are my good girl. You didn't need a bad big sister." His chin fell to his chest, nodding off in his chair.

The corner of James' mouth lifted, he had matched Yereq almost drink for drink. "Fey… I always knew you were a Princess." Then he too passed out.

Part 15 - Roman Road

Justice

For the third time in three days, Korah ben Adam thought he was dead. When he opened his eyes, he wished he was. Because he was in Hell, and he was very much alive. Blackness so thick it had presence pressed down on him. The screams of those in torment tore his brain apart. He could feel worms eating his flesh, sliding through his organs, feasting. Suffocating, his lungs could not draw breath, they burned like hellfire. The stench of sulfur smothered him, and he could only take in tiny sips of air. There was no oxygen down here. His tongue swelled in his mouth, and his teeth fell out. Supernaturally thirsty, there was not a drop of saliva in his mouth. His lips cracked but did not bleed.

Flames exploded around him. Fire covered his body. He could not move. He did not have the strength to even lift his hands but could feel his body. Korah could feel the pain. His bones were sticking through the flesh of his skin, but he was not dying. He could see nothing—blind agony, suffocating, burning, eaten alive but not consumed.

Over the anguish, he felt terror.

They were coming, evil spirits moving in to torture him. Wicked laughter rang through the darkness. "Korah," he heard Marduk's guttural voice, full of eternal hatred, a malevolent evil that took pleasure in his pain, "this is your reward. Welcome to Hell, faithful servant!"

He wanted to scream, but his lungs held no breath.

He was damned, in torment, for eternity, and he deserved it.

Justice had been served.

"Mercy, please God, have mercy! I am sorry, please forgive me!" Korah sobbed, "Yeshua!"

A brilliant light began as a pinpoint. He tried to reach for it, crying out in desperation. But a great chasm separated him from the light. It grew, illuminating him, torn asunder, aflame, consumed, alive.

"You call on me now?" the voice thundered.

"Forgive me, forgive me," Korah begged.

"Korah ben Adam, you have sinned against me in thought, word, and deed."

Korah began to weep.

"I am the Lord thy God. Thou shalt have no other gods before me."

On the chasm wall, a scene played before Korah, kissing Marduk's ring, calling him lord.

"I am guilty." Korah recoiled at himself.

"Thou shalt not make unto thee any graven images."

Another flash, Korah bowing in front of a statue erected to Marduk, foolish idol worship that got him nothing.

"I am guilty."

"Thou shalt not take the name of the Lord thy God in vain."

Korah's voice boomed a thousand blasphemies, idle words, vile language in his own tongue. He convicted himself. "I am guilty." His words were barely audible.

"Remember the Sabbath Day, to keep it Holy."

A hundred scenes played out on the screen. "I am guilty of this, too." Korah fell to his knees.

"Honor thy father and thy mother."

Korah screamed when that commandment was read, for he knew that he had not fulfilled the law. A thousand cutting remarks spoken and unspoken, his own thoughts were broadcast, his secrets on display. Hatred and disrespect were the order of his relationship with his parents. "I am truly guilty."

"Thou shalt not murder."

Korah sobbed. "No, please, no!" He did not want to watch, but his head was pushed up, forced to see his own hand lifted against his brother, Eamonn.

"Eamonn! I am sorry. Dear brother, please forgive me."

Then the scene changed. Margaret, falling to her death. He always imagined himself detached in that moment, but to his horror a flicker of a smile crossed his face as she fell.

"I am a vile and wicked man. She was an innocent, sweet woman. Forgive me."

A violent beating, the shouts and pleas of a man, the private investigator Taylor echoed in his ears. Korah watched himself kill the man without remorse or concern. He could not defend himself. "That was wrong, I should not have done that."

A dozen more murders flashed on the screen, not by Korah's hand but at his order.

As the screen changed, Korah began shaking his head back and forth, "Not Alexa, please no."

There was no mercy in Hell. He had shown no mercy to his wife. He sobbed, watching himself beat his beloved to death. Then, through the eyes of the Iron King, he saw another spirit and realized he had not only killed Alexa, but their unborn daughter.

He could not speak, he only wished it would stop.

"Guilty?" The Iron King demanded.

Korah nodded.

"Thou shalt not commit adultery."

Illicit interlude after interlude with Angelica ben Omri played out on the screen. Far from being titillated, his sin repulsed him. "Guilty."

"Thou shalt not steal."

"Guilty."

"Thou shalt not bear false witness against thy neighbor."

"Guilty."

"Thou shalt not covet thy neighbor's possessions."

"Guilty."

"By your own actions and the hardness of your heart," the Iron King said, rendering the verdict. "You condemn yourself. It is not I who condemn you, Korah ben Adam, but you have chosen this fate. Justice demands you be punished, eternally separated from me, in the flames that consume you now."

"You are a righteous judge, for I am guilty." Korah bowed, resigned to his fate—convicted.

Mercy

"However, you are not dead, Korah ben Adam. Not yet." The Iron King reached down into Hell and plucked Korah from the flames.

Korah sucked in a huge gasp of air as he cleared the suffocating sulfur. He felt the cool wind on his skin and swallowed a blessed drop of saliva. His bones shifted back into joint. "Mercy," he cried and fell in a heap, profoundly relieved of his suffering.

He blinked up and saw a small angel with him.

"Persa?"

"No, Korah ben Adam, I am Ilsidor. Come, I will show you why the Lord has given you mercy." She held out a hand to help him to his feet. Her touch revived him.

From above, he watched the moment of his birth.

"Take him away." His mother turned over in her childbirth bed. "Smother him for all I care."

"My Esteemed," the midwife coaxed, trying to hand her the child again, "thou art distraught. Simply look at him. He is a beautiful boy."

"I curse the very day I conceived him as I curse the day he was born." She pointed to her son and snarled, "I curse him. Call him Korah and may the Iron King swallow him in the desert, for he was born in rebellion, and in rebellion, he shall live."

The scene changed, Korah about six years old, walking through the woods carrying a small case, running away. A groom from Gilead called, "My Esteemed, where are you going?"

"On the pilgrimage. I heard them talking in the kitchen. Everyone is supposed to go to the Golden City. I am going. They do not want me here." His little lip started to tremble. "They said it would get me a blessing. So, I am going, and you cannot stop me."

"Prince Korah, you are too small to go on the pilgrimage." The groom looked down on the boy with kind eyes. "When you are older, you can go."

"They won't let me." Korah sulked. "They do not want me to have a blessing."

"That is not true," the groom admonished.

Korah balled up his fist and shook it at the groom. "It is true! We were in church, and the minister asked the little kids to come down to get a blessing. I wanted to go, but my mother made me sit. She would not let me go!" Big tears fell down his cheeks. "So, I am going on pilgrimage to get my blessing."

Six-year-old Korah started to cry when the groom picked him up and carried him back to the Castle.

The next scene featured a circus crowded with people. He was ten, wearing a trick rider's costume of bright red and black. No one in the circus knew who he was, they simply thought he joined their ranks at the Hewies. He was a talented rider for someone his age, and the crowds loved him, so they let him stay.

An evangelist outside the circus grounds was preaching. His voice carried above the crowd noise. Korah stopped to listen. In their sedate church at home, he never heard anyone talk about the Iron King this way.

"How many of you feel like nobody loves you, that you are going through life alone with no one who cares about you? You might even wish you had never been born or believe you are here by accident with no purpose. That is not true. That thought comes from our fallen nature. It comes from the sin that lives in man's heart. Your Father loves you! You are not an accident! You have a purpose! He is not here to condemn you, to catch you doing wrong so he can punish you. He is not looking for your faults."

That caught Korah's attention and he stopped, intent on the preacher's words.

"The Lord is compassionate and merciful, full of steadfast love for his children. He does not love as men love. He loves with an everlasting love. Don't you want to feel that love? Don't you need that love?"

Ten-year-old Korah's eyes welled with tears as he nodded emphatically.

"Your Father knows what you need before you even ask him. Think of that folks, he knows what you need. You need His love. You need His mercy. You need His grace."

Young Korah began to weep because his father cared nothing about what he needed.

"Your Father in the Golden City is not willing that any of His little ones be lost."

Korah hung his head. He was well and truly lost. He had run away a month ago and doubted anyone even realized he was gone. If they did, they did not care.

"The Scripture says, 'I will be a Father to you, and you will be my children.' Our earthly fathers will disappoint us, they will let us down, but the Iron King will never let you down."

Korah pushed through the small crowd. All his life, he never heard anyone say the Iron King loved him. He did not know the Iron King wanted him as his son. He only heard there were rules he had to follow, and he was afraid of the consequences if he did not. In his mind, the Iron King was a bigger, scarier version of his own father.

"How great is the love the Father has lavished on us that we should be called children of God." Sweat dripped down the evangelist's brow as he held up a big leather Bible. "Who wants to become a child of God and receive the Father's love tonight?"

There was a murmur in the crowd. This was preaching like they had never heard.

"Bow your head where you stand. I will come and pray with each of you so you can receive the love of God. Today, you can become His child."

With tears flowing down his face, Korah bowed his head. He desperately wanted to become a child of God, to receive the Father's love, to belong to someone. He waited in anticipation. The evangelist moved into the crowd. Korah waited, tears flowing from his eyes, "Please," he silently begged, "please pick me, please do not pass me by." With his head to the ground and tears falling in the dirt, the little gathering broke up.

No one touched Korah ben Adam.

Watching from above, forty-six years later, Korah saw the circus bosses hustle the evangelist off the property before he reached the desperate little boy. But as a child, he had not seen it.

He stood there, crying for himself because he knew that was the exact moment he determined that he would never be worthy of the Iron King's love. He believed the evangelist had seen his heart and read what his mother always told him, he was rotten, irredeemable, and damned.

"The Iron King did not reject me?" Korah's voice was very small, reminiscent of the little boy fading into the mist.

"No, Korah, it was men who failed you that night, not the Iron King."

"I never tried again." Korah hung his head. "I thought he hated me as my father did."

Ilsidor nodded. "He saw."

"Sussanna!" Korah reached out a hand at the next vision before him. Their wedding night, her dress draped over the rocking chair. He was asleep, and she was stroking his head.

"Bless him, protect him, Lord. He is lost and does not know that you love him. Help me to show him your love."

Then Korah saw Eamonn praying on his knees. "My brother Korah, please Lord, help him. He is hurt and so angry. Heal his heart, please?"

Korah turned away, ashamed.

"Korah," Alexa cried as he slammed the door to her bedchamber. She was naked, gasping for breath. He knew what he had done to her, had done it a hundred times when they were married. "Father, forgive him, he does not know what he does. Bring him to me, let me love him. Let me show him that I can be a good wife. Please, Lord, have mercy on us."

A cacophony of prayers rang in his ears, millions of them crying out before the Iron King.

"Guide him, Lord."

"Give him wisdom, Lord."

"Heal his heart as he grieves Princess Alexa."

"Heal our kingdom, Heavenly Father, and start with Prince Korah."

The volume and number of prayers prayed on his behalf astounded him as he closed his eyes and let them wash over him.

Then a very quiet young boy's voice broke through the cacophony. Korah's sobbed as he recognized his son. "I want my daddy back. Can you pwease help him in the hospital to get better? I miss him and our horsey time."

Korah covered his face sobbing. His beloved Peter had prayed for him.

"I heard them all, Korah."

Korah stilled at the voice, shamed again to the pit of his soul, afraid he was going back to the flames.

"It is why I had mercy on you, yesterday and today. Tomorrow will be up to you."

Grace

Korah opened his eyes in Endor, as it was. Looking around in wonder, instead of the idealistic village he remembered, he saw it through the Iron King's eyes.

"They are preparing to go to war, are they not?" Korah watched Angelica slinking among the ranks of mounted riders.

"Indeed, against the saints in Rephidim."

Korah turned and realized he was in the presence of the Savior. "Yeshua?"

"I AM." Yeshua gestured in the distance. "There you are."

Korah followed his direction. He and Sussanna were in the paddock behind their house, oblivious to the activities of the villagers.

"You were in it, not of it. I sheltered you from the evil of this place." Yeshua rested a hand on Korah's shoulder. A glimmering gold dome became visible to Korah. It covered their house, stables, and the pasture beyond.

"What is that, Lord?" Korah breathed in awe.

"It was a hedge of protection I placed around you whilst you were here." Yeshua gave Korah a rueful smile. "Jezebel was not pleased with it." He pointed to Angelica, who had sent her warriors off to do their worst. She strolled over to the paddock, glaring at him and Sussanna as they worked the horses.

Korah saw Angelica, not through human eyes, but with eyes that read the soul. Instead of a beautiful blonde in a flowing robe, he recognized a vile crone, with a black heart, staring at him with lustful covetousness.

"She desired you above all others," Yeshua confirmed what Korah could now see so clearly. At the time, he only had eyes for Sussanna and the wondrous horses of Endor, blind to the danger he was in.

"Sussanna knew, didn't she?" Korah's voice cracked as he watched lovely Sussanna, great with child.

"Sussanna was mine from birth, all the Guardians are. I seal them."

Korah hung his head, "I broke that, didn't I?"

"Indeed, you did but not in a vacuum. Behold."

Korah watched Angelica inside her study, brewing a potion, calling enchantments, studying a book that dripped with blood and gore. "What is she doing, Lord?"

"She is preparing your demise." Yeshua tilted his head, deep sadness in his hazel eyes. "If you would have called on me that night, I would have delivered Hope to you."

"I did not know, Lord. I did not know you would answer me. I thought you rejected me."

Korah watched himself call out to Angelica, watched himself read the words she gave him to speak. He wanted to stop his twenty-year-old self, to scream not to do it. But history was written. He recoiled at the knife, saw the cut, and watched himself drink the black potion of his destruction. "I did it to save them."

"Your blood did not save them, did it Korah?"

"No, Lord it did not." Korah realized his folly.

The scene shifted, Korah in his bedchamber in the Palace, crying out for Marduk's return. He crawled to the putrid enclave hidden in his bedchamber and removed a whip. He stripped off his clothes and bloodied his back, performing the ritual Tatbir, Marduk demanded.

"Those stripes did not heal you, did they Korah?"

"No, Lord they did not." Korah winced at the self-flagellation, brutal and fruitless.

The last and most painful, Eamonn's sacrifice, his brother's blood pouring out from the altar.

"That sacrifice did not save you, did it Korah?"

"No, Lord it did not." Korah fell to his knees.

"These stripes." Yeshua touched Korah's head and he saw the Savior being scourged.

Korah cried out at the sheer brutality of it. Each blow was one his sin brought upon the back of Yeshua.

"This blood."

Korah saw the crown of thorns pressed into the head of Yeshua, heard his anguished cry. The true king had worn a crown of torture.

"This sacrifice."

Korah was crying, heard the blow of the hammer on the spike, felt the tearing of tendons, and the excruciating agony of crucifixion.

This was the cost, the price the Iron King personally paid to keep him from Hell. And he had rejected it. He had scoffed at the notion, sought his own way, through his own power, through his own blood, and it brought him to ruin.

"What do I do?" Korah begged.

"Believe in me and the power of the cross, accept the gift of salvation. Turn from your own ways, repent of your sins, and follow me. Observe my commandments, ask me to change you. Ask me to deliver you."

Korah clutched the feet of the Savior. "Lord, I believe. You paid the price to save me from the fires of Hell. I never want to return to that place. Thank you, for I am not worthy. I have lived a life of sin and rebellion. I am sorry, and I repent of the evil I have done. I will study your word and try to live my life as a righteous man. Please change me, please deliver me. Please....save me!"

A brilliant light began to shine, Yeshua spoke over Korah. "By the power of the blood and the confession of your mouth, believe in me."

Korah convulsed with a huge gasp, gagging and choking. A repugnant black snake uncoiled from around his heart, released its tentacles rooted in his spine, pulled its wicked talons out of his brain, then slithered out of his mouth.

It coiled as if it would strike. Staring at the prostrate Korah with viperous eyes. It flicked a split tongue with a hiss. Pure evil.

Black original sin.

A single drop of blood from above turned it into a puff of smoke. It disappeared.

Redeemed

Yeshua picked up Korah and set him on his feet. His face shone with the light of eternal love. "Korah, my child."

A lifetime of pain melted away. The Creator claimed Korah as His own. He began to weep. Yeshua gathered him, a father comforting his son, an act of love, foreign and precious. "I do not understand," Korah whispered. "How can you accept one such as I?"

"The Iron King is a good and gracious Father who loves his children. He showed His great love by sending Me to die for you, while you were still a sinner."

The thought boggled Korah's mind, an inconceivable truth. They walked together in peace and light, Korah's heart calmed as his soul received the words of the Savior.

"Since you have been made right in God's sight by My blood, He saved you from condemnation. Man was created for fellowship with the Iron King, to walk together as we do now. Your fellowship with Him has been restored, while we were still enemies, you are saved through the death and resurrection of the Son."

Yeshua laid a hand on Korah's shoulder.

The Spirit of the living God rushed through his soul, binding the wounds and unlocking the bars that held him prisoner. Like a flower opening at dawn, love buried deep in his heart bloomed. Hope, Persa, and Peter… his children. He loved them, overflowing and bountiful. It was a supernatural restoration of what was lost, stolen, and destroyed. He stared in wide-eyed wonder at Yeshua and could not imagine sacrificing one of them for his enemies.

Yeshua smiled with deep understanding. "For the Father so loved the world, that He gave His only Son, that whoever believes in Him will not perish, but have everlasting life. Adam's sin brought condemnation to the world, but at the cross, I broke the curse of sin. Through my blood, I give you a new life and into a right relationship with God."

"A new life and a right relationship with the Iron King." Korah shook his head at the wonder of it all. "I suspect men will not be as forgiving as thee. I can expect no quarter from them or from Satan and his minions. They will surely kill me."

"Not so. As in the days of old, I protected Cain from the vengeance of man." Yeshua traced a cross on Korah's forehead, sealing him.

"What do I do now, Lord?" Korah whispered, awestruck.

"Read Psalm 84, Korah ben Adam, live Psalm 84."

Then the Savior was gone, and Korah ben Adam was alone, standing in the ruins of Endor.

Part 16 - What Was Broken

February 16, 1000 ME

Return of the Guardian - Thyatira Woods - Kayah

Ernst ben Otto turned out to be Sussanna's distant cousin, which made him Kayah's distant cousin and the first blood relative she ever met.

Heilig followed her into the stables and obediently entered a stall. Ernst looked between them both, flabbergasted. "No horse of Endor has dwelt in a stable in over thirty years. Those who escaped the night of the fire have lived wild in Thyatira Woods, to no man or woman would they come." Ernst nodded at Heilig. "He is the most friendly of those that remain, and we have developed a bit of a relationship in the years of our exile. Mostly, he comes around because I give him apples. He has a sweet tooth."

Kayah pressed her nose against Heilig's great muzzle. "He is a sweet baby."

Ernst laughed. "He is not a baby."

"Yes, he is." Kayah cooed.

"I suppose you are right, compared to the ancient ones." Ernst got a dreamy expression on his face. "Your mother had one of them, Blitz. She was beautiful, pure white and very powerful."

"What happened to her?" Kayah shut the stall door and scooped a large helping of feed into the trough. Her friends waited outside, wearing identical expressions of concern, but she ignored them, focused on Ernst.

"Sussanna or *Fraulein Blitz?*"

"Both, if you know it." Kayah inhaled a shallow breath.

"Sadly, I do not. I left Endor before the fire." He shook his head, looking down at his scuffed work boot. "I have never seen Blitz in the woods, though."

"Kayah, would you like to get settled in?" Lavinia asked, moving into the stables. "You have had an arduous journey, and I made supper, if you are hungry. Mack is taking Filippo to Grandma Eve's, but you can stay with us, okay?"

Kayah looked between Lavinia and Ernst, then raised a golden eyebrow. "I think I will visit with this kind gentleman for a bit." She paused as a sudden knot clogged her throat. "So, he can tell me about my mother."

Lavinia looked pained. "Mr. ben Otto, you told me you left your home on August 9, 963 ME. That was 399 days before Kayah was born and 13,341 days ago. I do not mean to be indelicate, but is it possible you are mistaken?"

In the two weeks since they arrived, Ernst spent enough time with the beautiful genius not to take offense, nor was he shocked at the interesting way her mind worked. "The horses of Endor do not lie. Besides, she is a mirror image of her mother, and I remember her well."

"*Sie ist verletzlich. Bist du sicher?*" She is vulnerable. Are you sure?

"*Das habe ich verstanden, Lavinia.*" Kayah even shocked herself with the words, I understand you, Lavinia.

"*Alle Wächter sprechen deutsch,*" Ernst said, giving Lavinia an 'I told you so' look.

Kayah's eyes grew enormous, and she paled. "*Les Gardiens parlent-ils aussi français? Qué pasa con el español?*" She looked around and in Italian asked, "*Dov'è Filippo?*" Where is Filippo? Her chest heaved, and she choked in Japanese. "*Himari ni denwa suru!*" Call Himari! Then she threw her arms up in the air and shouted in Hebrew, "Reuben, my love." Turning to Lavinia, her eyes shining. "Say something to me. Pick a language, any language."

Lavinia blinked in shock. "*Se poia glóssa miló?*"

"Greek! You are speaking Greek!" Kayah declared in absolute triumph.

Lavinia ben Anthony was fluent in twenty-seven languages and could read and converse in fifty-two more. On the night of February 16th, monolingual Kayah ben Samuel identified almost every one of them. Ernst ushered the pair to his small house while they laughed and quizzed each other. His heart warmed, basking in the restoration of something lost so very long ago.

Lavinia thanked Ernst for the cup of tea and asked, "I can attest that Kayah has always been abysmal at languages. How does she understand ones she has never even studied?"

Kayah propped her elbows on Ernst's rugged kitchen table and stared at him, refusing to entertain the thought that Sir Preston would be pleased with her.

"It was always the way with the Guardians." Ernst shrugged. "Languages were part of the role. Many travelers would come to Endor to buy the horses. It was not just anyone who could buy an Endorite horse. Even if they could find the village, there was no guarantee they would procure a horse. Most of the time, the Guardians would not sell."

This intrigued Lavinia, the businesswoman. "Why?"

Kayah shot Ernst a glance and answered, "Because it was not a business, it was a covenant. The Iron King entrusted them with the horses. Am I right?"

Ernst raised his sparse eyebrows at Kayah. "You will know when you meet them, just as you knew Heilig's bloodline from a touch. Those that remain, they will come to you."

A knock sounded at the door, and Ernst called for the visitor to enter.

"Am I interrupting?"

"Come in, Esmeralda, I want you to meet Kayah," Lavinia said in welcome.

Ernst grunted and rose from his chair. "I am having a meeting of the Ladies' Auxiliary." He nodded a greeting and asked, "You want tea?"

Esmeralda waved him away. "No, thank you, Ernst. Caffeine keeps me awake, and Claire does that well enough." She smiled in greeting. "Hello, Kayah. It is very nice to meet you."

Kayah returned her smile, intrigued by the woman's shock of curly white hair, incongruent on a face so young. "It is nice to meet you as well. You run the Center for Street Kids of Alanthia in New

York, right?" Kayah knew damn well she did. Her anonymous donation a year and a half ago funded the Center.

The smile Esmeralda gave Kayah reached her slate-blue eyes. "Part-time. I have a six-month-old, so I split the responsibility with another lady at the Center." Looking sheepish, she added, "Cami has been running it full time since we have been in hiding, but I suppose we will get back to normal soon."

"The new normal." Lavinia smiled ruefully. None of them quite knew what to expect in Josiah's Alanthia, but one thing was certain: her family would be in the New City for the foreseeable future.

"You're right," Esmeralda pressed her thumb to her chin, thinking. "But for the next few days, we get to live in the Rephidim Bubble."

"The Rephidim Bubble?" Kayah asked, sipping her fragrant tea.

Esmeralda caught Ernst's disapproving scowl and blew him a kiss. "Rephidim is a sanctuary. The machinations of the outside world rarely come here."

Ernst made a deep grunt. "We have a new road. It will bring it, trust me." He was still bristling about the emergency road they cut through the woods.

"You hid it well." Kayah shot Ernst a look. "Filippo and I could not find it."

Ernst reached across the table and took her hand, his smokey gray eyes shining in the bright lantern light. "You were meant to find us, Kayah ben Sussanna."

Kayah closed her eyes against the sudden flood of emotion at his words. "Thank you."

Esmeralda tilted her head, studying Kayah as a green aura, intense like fire, pulsed off her. With her thick blonde hair pulled high on her head in a ponytail, she reminded Esmeralda of someone, but she could not place who.

Lavinia focused on Esmeralda. "What color is she?"

Esmeralda blushed and looked at her friend with a hint of pique. "Lavinia…"

"Tell!" Lavinia urged. "Kai, Esmeralda sees auras. I want her to tell me what color yours is."

Kayah dropped Ernst's hands, and said in a voice dripping with sarcasm, "As long as it's not black, tell away."

Ernst pointed a finger at Esmeralda but did not comment. He

had known her since birth, knew she had certain abilities, but he never knew she saw auras.

"Bright green, like burning copper," Esmeralda answered with a shy flush. "It is unusual."

"Is not surprising. Kayah is a Guardian of the Blood of the Horses of Endor, and they are unusual," Ernst said, shining with pride.

Esmeralda jolted. "Endor?"

"Not all of us were wicked," Ernst admonished.

Lavinia rested a hand on Esmeralda's shoulder. "Kayah was an orphan and learned tonight that Ernst knew her mother. She was a horsewoman of Endor."

Esmeralda blinked rapidly at Kayah as her breath caught in her chest. "I think I have had a vision of your mother." She cleared her throat and reached across the table. "May I see your hand?"

March 28, 965 ME

Fire - Endor - Korah and Sussanna

"What is all this?" Korah exclaimed as he came in from the stables and found the kitchen table set with fine china and crystal.

Sussanna turned with a coy smile. "Do you like it, Prince?"

He shucked off his coat and hung it on the peg by the door. "I like the lady who prepared it." He swept her up in an extravagant kiss.

Baby Hope banged on her highchair in an enthusiastic greeting.

"Someone is jealous," Sussanna said between kisses.

Korah laughed, released his wife, and went to Hope. "Are you jealous?" He kissed the side of her neck, eliciting a high-pitched squeal of delight. "Daddy's girl is jealous of Mommy?" He lifted her up, heedless of the mess on her hands and face.

With the baby firmly settled in his arms, Korah sniffed the air. "Whatever you are cooking smells delicious. What is the occasion?"

Sussanna tilted her chin up, looking superior. "I will tell you when we put the baby to bed, but I have some good news."

Their eyes locked, as they shared an intense moment full of passion, adoration, and excitement. Sussanna moved toward him, pressing her body against his and whispered, "Korah—"

A deafening scream came from the stables, startling them both.

"Here, take Hope," Korah said, passing the baby.

He lifted his jacket off the hook and went to investigate. From the backdoor, he saw smoke and fire shoot out of the barn. Cursing, he hit the door with a crash. He had one foot outside when three men dressed in black seized him. A wet cloth with a vile-smelling chemical pressed over his nose and mouth. He fought against them as his vision faded to pinpoints. The last words he heard before darkness swallowed him were. "Bar the door, make sure they do not escape. Burn it to the ground."

Chaos erupted.

Men on horses, shooting weapons and throwing firebombs, invaded Endor. A massive force overran the village, a thousand men strong, intent on utter destruction. Sussanna flew to the window. As her neighbors and friends escaped their burning houses, the invaders cut them down with swords and bullets.

The streets of Endor ran with blood.

Hope began to wail. Fire raced up the east side of the house, and someone threw a firebomb through the window, shattering the glass and driving Sussanna backward. Holding the baby, she fled to her bedroom. Out the window, she saw the stables burning. A dozen men stood in the pasture, watching it burn, and making sure she did not escape.

She cried out, "Father in Heaven, help me." She ran to her closet and pulled out Korah's black cape. It covered her from head to toe, sheltering Hope from the smoke and heat.

"Sussanna, you follow me." A strange woman came out of the flames and extended a hand.

With her screaming daughter clutched to her chest, Sussanna grasped the saving hand. They ran through the conflagration engulfing the house. The woman hit the barred door, and it exploded off its hinges. Behind them, the house groaned like a beast coming out of the pit of Hell.

They ran toward the stables, supernaturally shielded, unseen by the men watching the house burn. All around, the fires of Endor leapt into the sky, turning the night into judgment day.

Inside the stable, the horses were panicking as flames engulfed the roof. Fire raced in jetties, igniting the bedding. The mysterious woman opened stall after stall, freeing the animals. Sussanna ran to Blitz, set Hope in a feed bucket, and saddled the horse. A minute after fleeing the burning house, Sussanna and Hope escaped the collapsing barn and fled into the sanctuary of Thyatira Woods.

With tears streaming down her cheeks and her baby wailing in her ears, Sussanna rode Lightning away from the destruction. Shouts of men and horses followed her. She heard what they said when they seized Korah and understood why they burned Endor. His family had come to take him, and they were intent on her and Hope's destruction.

She lived in dread of this day since the beginning.

For two hours, she rode without stopping, but Hope's plaintive cries demanded attention. She slowed the horse and dismounted to tend to her daughter. Hope's diaper was wet, and she was hungry. She removed the sodden nappy and wrapped her crying baby in her cardigan. Leaning up against a tree, she nursed Hope, whispering, "Is okay. Mommy is here. Mommy will protect you, little one."

"You cannot, Sussanna." The mysterious woman emerged out of the woods behind her. "They will find you and kill you both. They are tracking you with dogs, who hear her cries."

"No!" Sussanna covered Hope with her arms.

"I am sorry." The woman stooped in front of them and said, "If you keep her, she will die."

Sussanna hugged Hope, crying deep sobs. "Help us, as you did in the fire."

An otherworldly light began to shine around the woman, and Sussanna recognized her as a Gune. "That is why I am here, but there is a cost, Sussanna."

Sussanna looked up, confused and terrified. "The cost to save her life?"

The woman nodded. "She is a Guardian. I will take her to safety, and you will escape. No one will find her. No one will know who she is. She will be protected from those who seek to kill her for the blood that runs in her veins."

Sussanna thrashed in agony, kicking her heels in the dirt, clutching Hope to her chest. "Where will you take her?"

The woman glowed, bright as the sun. "I am Gune, sent by the Iron King to see that the child lives. She has a future, and He has a plan for her."

Sussanna felt like she was in a dream, the worst kind, too terrible to be real. "She will live, and He will watch over her. But if I keep her," her voice broke off in a sob, "she will die?"

A bloodhound howled in the distance, followed by the excited yelps of his fellows.

Sussanna snapped her head around at the sound. Hope began to whimper. "Don't cry, baby. Don't cry. This nice lady is going to take care of you." She pressed her lips hard against the precious blonde head. "Your mommy loves you. Your daddy loves you, too. I know you will not remember." Sussanna looked up, desperate. "Please, one day, please tell her. Please tell her how much she was loved."

Sussanna pressed Hope into Jelena's arms, mounted Lightning, and watched the Gune and her daughter disappear. Heartbroken beyond human imagination, she fled into the darkness.

February 17, 1000 ME

Morning Ride - Thyatira Woods - Kayah

Dawn light had just pierced the darkness when Kayah saddled Heilig. The tranquility of the stable surrounded her, and the warmth of the animals staved off the chill. She moved with a purpose, though not in a rush. She was peaceful for perhaps the first time in her life, at rest, not fighting an internal war with no name, always there, but now it was gone.

Sussanna ben Ross, a Guardian of the Blood, of the mighty horses of Endor, had been her mother. There was more to discover. However, she had a name, and she had a place.

Kayah rode out of Rephidim to find it.

Not an Ordinary Morning - Pepperwood - James, Persa, & Peter

James ben Kole felt like hot garbage. He woke up in his clothes, with a crick in his neck and a turd in his mouth, or at least it tasted like one. Persa lay asleep on the green sofa, and poor Yereq was curled up on the floor, drooling on a pillow that had fallen from the loveseat. A helicopter, with its blades whirling in the top pasture, woke him, and he groaned, "Fey, your brother is here."

"I don't have a brother," Persa mumbled, then her eyes shot open. "Jupiter's Moon, what time is it?"

Yereq made a sepulchral moan into the pillow.

James squinted at the clock. "Ugh, 6:45. What is he doing here so early? Going to kick his ass…"

Persa shuffled to the door and admitted a bright-eyed Prince Peter ben Korah.

He looked around, noted the empty bottle, and smelled the whiskey fumes from the glasses. "Have a party last night? Sorry I missed it."

Yereq pushed up on an elbow and whispered, "Not so loud, kid."

James rubbed his face vigorously and growled, "You're early."

"Only forty-five minutes, and since when are you still asleep at 6:45 am?"

James leveled bloodshot brown eyes at Peter, silently willing him to shut up.

Persa put an arm around Peter's waist and rested her head against his shoulder. "We had an interesting night. Come into the kitchen. I'll make coffee."

"Good, because I am dry." He tilted his mug back in demonstration.

Yereq smacked his lips. "He's not the only one."

James fell onto the sofa sideways, making a sickly moan. "This hurts worse than it used to."

They let out identical groans of misery, listening to Persa and Peter in the kitchen making coffee.

"I gotta get home." Yereq struggled to his feet and swayed. "Why did you let me drink so much?"

James cracked a crusty eye and glared at him.

"You've got a big day. I reckon you should go say hello to your new brother-in-law. I'm getting the hell out of here." Yereq staggered into the kitchen. "Have a wonderful trip, Daughter. I love you. See you when you get home." He kissed Persa on the cheek and made his escape, mumbling under his breath that Peter sure looked a hell of a lot like that son of a bitch.

Peter stared after him in bemusement. Normally, Yereq was quite personable. "What crawled in his whiskey glass?"

Persa pulled the cream out of the refrigerator, refusing to look at him. "We had a surprise visitor last night."

"I had one yesterday as well." Peter eyed her speculatively. "Mine introduced himself as Joshua… at first."

Persa startled, the words she was about to say dying on her tongue.

James shuffled into the kitchen. "Did you tell him?" he asked as he moved past them to the coffee pot.

"We were getting to it, Jay. Joshua paid Peter a visit yesterday."

James froze with the coffee cup halfway down from the cabinet. "Is that why you sounded so strange on the phone?"

"Part of the reason," Peter hedged.

Pregnant silence descended on the cozy kitchen. No one said a word. They all just looked at each other. A knock on the kitchen door made Persa jump. James motioned for their stable manager to come in.

"Morning," Johnson said, stepping inside, carrying the sweet scent of the barn. "Lightning is not in her stall or in the pastures."

James and Persa exchanged pained looks. On the fly, James spoke the truth. "She's with Persa's father. It's all right."

Johnson relaxed his shoulders. "That's good. I was worried for a minute." Then he recognized Peter and bowed. "My Esteemed."

"Johnson, it is a pleasure to see you again."

The taciturn man nodded and returned to his duties.

Peter waited until Johnson left. "Yereq did not have Lightning."

"Get your coffee and sit down." James poured his own cup, squeezing his temples, and looking slightly green.

Peter joined them at the small kitchen table. They spent many mornings like this, the three of them drinking coffee, eating breakfast in mismatched wooden chairs, each in their own spot. But this morning there was no breakfast cooking, and the dinner dishes were still in the sink, dirty pots on the stove. Persa's normally pristine kitchen revealed shards of broken glass glimmering in the morning sun.

"What happened last night?" Peter looked between them, growing impatient with their strained silence.

"It started when I got into an argument with my dad about my mother." Persa rubbed her collarbone, touching the pearl necklace.

Peter was not expecting that. Persa never spoke of her mother. His eyes widened as he noticed the bruising around her neck.

"Her name was Sussanna ben Ross. Does that mean anything to you?"

Peter gave her a double take and said, "Before yesterday, it did not."

Persa blew out a shaky breath. "But since?"

"She was Korah's first wife." Peter's heart pounded.

Persa reached across the table and took his hand. "And we learned last night that he is my biological father."

"Your father? Korah?" The impact of her words slammed into him, and he jerked back. "You are my sister?"

"I know it's a shock," she said, her voice breathless.

"No, it is just," he got up from the table, pacing. "I thought you were just some distant relative." With fumbling hands, he dug in his jacket pocket. "I found this yesterday, in my mother's old bedroom."

Persa stared at the miniature in open-mouthed astonishment. The hair was a shade darker, the clothes from a long-ago era, but otherwise, her face stared back from the burnished frame.

"Look at that," James breathed.

Peter cleared his throat, completely stunned. "Korah is your father? How do you know?"

Persa looked up from the miniature, an odd mix of emotions flickering across her face. "He told me."

"What? He was here? Is that what happened to your neck?"

Persa covered her mouth, her eyes swimming. "Peter, it is a very long story."

"Did he do that to you?" Peter demanded, his voice just below a shout.

James grimaced and clutched his temples.

"Yes and no." Persa looked away. "I think it was actually my evil spawn who tried to kill me. Korah stopped him."

Peter's head shook in extreme agitation. "What?"

"Rapha apparently did not die when we fought him three days ago. He possessed Korah and brought him here. He claimed if I died, he would get his body back." Persa slumped in her chair.

"You skimmed over that little detail last night." James scowled.

Persa gave James a big-eyed stare. "I was a little preoccupied with the question of my paternity."

Peter pressed his palms against the sides of his head. "I live the most insane life. If anyone ever says to me again that I am a spoiled, pampered playboy, I will beat them to death. I swear to you right now, I will kill them."

"Like father like son?" James said drolly.

Peter shot him a glare. "Shut up, James."

Persa covered a giggle with her hand, her chest shaking.

"This is not funny, Pers." Peter protested, but the corner of his mouth was twitching, catching her hilarity. "Are you okay?"

Persa nodded, her eyes dancing. He was her brother, and in that moment, she loved him deeper than she ever thought possible. She rose from her chair and took him around the waist. "Brother."

Peter picked her up, bringing them nose-to-nose. He closed his eyes and whispered, "Sister."

This Place Really is Hard to Find - Thyatira Woods - Kayah

Kayah was not lost, or at least that was what she told herself. She was simply exploring the enchanted woods. How big was this place, anyway? After riding for hours, every time she thought she pinpointed her location on Ernst's old map, she discovered she was nowhere near where she thought she was. She resisted the urge to ball the thing up and throw it away.

On the bright side, she collected several companions along the way. Seven magnificent horses joined her and Heilig as they meandered from indiscernible landmark to mismarked creek. In frustration, she looked up at the sky and said, "I could use some help down here, if you please?"

Several moments later, Heilig tossed his head and whinnied a greeting. A stunning golden horse appeared on a boulder above them and returned the greeting with a single stamp of her hoof. The herd called back and rushed forward in ecstatic welcome. This was clearly the matriarch. She held Kayah's eyes, ancient and intelligent, taking her measure, uncertain she approved.

"I'm new to this, your Majesty." Kayah tilted her chin up. "How about you show me where Endor was?"

The golden horse turned her head, as if considering Kayah's request, blew out a skeptical breath and stared.

"Please?" Kayah asked, her voice dripping with sarcasm.

The golden horse nickered, then with a toss of her glorious head, she trotted off, leading the way.

Kayah looked up at the sky and shrugged. 'Okay."

Saved - Endor - Korah

Korah stood in the square of the desolate ruins of Endor and shouted for joy. He fell to his knees, raised his arms to the sky, and smiled, a true dimple-flashing smile of freedom. "Thank you!"

The words seemed inadequate, but he kept repeating them, basking in the warm glow of love and deliverance. He was clean. He was forgiven. He was redeemed. Through clear eyes, he looked at his surroundings. Instead of seeing an overgrown field of destruction, he noticed the intense color of the leaves, smelled the clean scent of trees and grass. Winter crocus and lenten roses bloomed, wild and beautiful.

Scrambling to his feet, his eyes went to his home. Partially destroyed, the front porch stood intact. He walked dreamlike, stunned to see the rocking horse. Sitting beside it, he touched the faded paint, picked leaves from the mane and tail, and brushed a spider web from its belly. It was precious, a tangible reminder that life and love were real. He decided to take it with him when he left. His grandchildren should have it.

The front door sagged, but he pushed in. Gauging the ceiling, he made sure it would not collapse on top of him. 'You were in it, not of it.' Yeshua's words came to his mind.

Most of the living room was gone, grass and bushes reclaimed the space, but to his astonishment, the kitchen was still standing, the dinner table still set. He ran a finger over the ash-covered plates and wondered if there was enough soap in the world to bring the delicate ivory and yellow flower pattern back to life. Hope's highchair was in the corner, exactly where it had always been. He touched it in loving remembrance, but without tears or the agonizing pain he expected. In its place, peace.

Perhaps one day he would find Hope. She was alive.

Korah moved through the wreckage into the remnants of their bedroom. The massive dresser was still there, as well as the frame of their bed. "Forgive me, Pearle, for believing the worst of you. I thought you saw I was finally happy, and you set out to punish me." He lamented, "I should have known better, my darling."

His eyes rested on the old dresser. "I wonder." He opened the top drawer, which emitted a high-pitched squeak. Were they still there? Rodents and critters conveniently used the space, so he peered inside to be certain nothing was waiting to nip him. His watch was missing, no doubt pilfered by some scavenger over the years, so were his diamond cufflinks.

But he was not looking for those items. He set his mind on something more precious. His hand shook when he spotted it in the back corner of the drawer. Tentatively, he pulled the yellowed handkerchief with his initials embroidered in the corner. Carefully unfolding the fabric, he gasped. The two shekels he vowed to never spend, that had been given to him outside the New York Polo Club, were inside. He had written across one in blue ink, 'Freedom', the other, 'Adventure.' Standing in the wreckage of his marital bedroom, he remembered the boy who had written those words. Those two shekels represented a new life.

He truly had one now.

On an impulse, he stalked across the creaking floor and opened the closet. Their clothes were still hanging. He touched one of Sussanna's winter shirts with reverence, burying his face in the cloth, disappointed they no longer held her scent. He chuckled as he removed one of his old shirts, marveling at the size. He had been a lot trimmer at twenty than he was now. Glancing down, he realized he had dropped a considerable amount of weight since December.

Then he noticed the actual shape he was in.

He was filthy, covered in his own blood, his clothes were torn, and he stunk. Recalled to the natural, his stomach growled. It had been days since he ate. The old shirt did not seem like such an outlandish idea after all. He rifled through the closet and found a pair of trousers. Turning back to the dresser, he eyed it dubiously. Socks and underwear should be in the middle drawer. When he opened it, it gratified him to see, other than dust and a few odd rodent droppings, he had options.

"Old clothes for a new man," he said to himself. Putting the handkerchief in his pocket, he carried the bundle out of his house to see what else Endor still had to offer.

Even if the Black Mansion was still there, he would not have stepped foot in that vile place. Nothing in this world would ever compel him to go down that road again, nothing. Delivered from the fires of Hell, he knew the memory of that place would keep him on the path of the righteous for the rest of his natural life.

Even amid his insanity, he was a driven and focused man, pursuing his goals with zeal and a vigor matched by few. It served him well as a ruler. Despite his shortcomings and rebellion, Alanthia thrived during his reign. When Korah embraced something, he did not hold back, he was all in. He planned to pursue this new life with the same purpose. But first, he needed a bath and some food.

The Elsbeth's house was still intact. He wondered idly what happened to the family but surmised they died the night of the fire. A year afterward, he paid a private investigator, hoping his father lied to him and Sussanna and Hope were alive. The report was grim, no survivors. Several days after the massacre, the Rephidimites buried the victims in a mass grave. He heard the soldier's orders the moment before the world went black and remembered the force attacking Endor, so he never questioned the investigator's report.

The house was eerie, deserted, and dusty. He felt a strange compulsion to call a greeting. Rifling through the kitchen, he thought better of attempting the canned food. He was uncertain what the future held but did not fancy dying of botulism.

Unable to stand himself another minute, he decided to wash before finding food. Sussanna had given him quite an education on edible plants, and he surmised he might eat the bark off a tree at this point.

He discovered the bathroom in working order, though the pump took quite a bit of energy to get moving. The water was frigid, but he found a dusty bar of soap and managed to scrub off the blood and get the matted dirt and grime out of his hair. His tongue kept running over his broken tooth, but he was thankful the loose ones on the bottom had reset themselves. Shuddering, he remembered what it felt like in Hell when his teeth were rotting in his mouth.

"Thank you for saving me," he said to the ceiling.

Wrapped in a thin towel, he studied his reflection in the dirty mirror and thought he looked different. Using his ruined shirt, he wiped away the dust and stared at his face, looking for the seal but saw nothing visible.

He smoothed a few wild hairs on his eyebrow. They had grown unruly, and if he did not watch it, he would end up looking like that old bastard Preston ben Worley. The mirror revealed how beaten up he was. Bruises on his cheek and under his eyes turned a vivid shade of indigo. He sported a nasty gash over his left eye, and his right cheek looked like he stuffed it with cotton. But his eyes… He leaned in, fascinated. They were hazel again. He was not sure the last time he saw his eyes this color. In his mind, they had been black for a long time and because of that he rarely stared into a mirror.

He ran fingers through his wet hair. Thinner on top, hairline a bit higher, the blond was darker than it used to be and streaked with silver. Around his temples, it had turned completely white, so had his facial hair. He doubted he would find a razor, and even if he did, he liked this scruffy look. It was a marked contrast to the pol- ished, ultra-sophisticated facade he wore for decades. He scoffed, thinking it had been the face of a madman, a lunatic, a tortured soul. A stranger stared back at him, someone new, someone sane, someone different.

His sane stomach reminded him, he needed to eat.

He was pleasantly surprised to find his old clothes fit, though the waistband was snug. A noise in the house brought him up short. He stilled, feeling absurdly like Goldilocks.

As he stepped out of the bathroom, the heavenly smell of food assailed him. "Hello?" he called.

"Good. You are clean now. I am making for you food. You are hungry, no?" a woman answered.

Korah felt his heart fall into his stomach. He peeked around the corner and saw a statuesque woman of unimaginable beauty. His jaw dropped. Words left him.

"Come and sit down. She will be here shortly." When he did not move, she gestured impatiently to the chair. "Sit, sit."

"Who are you?" Korah moved, seemingly against his own will. The hair on the back of his arms stood on end.

"I am Jelena, and I am making you breakfast, Korah ben Adam."

"Who is the Lord?" Korah did not sit down. He was not eating a bite of food this woman offered him.

She flashed him a toothy smile. "Very good, Korah. You are testing the spirits. They have tricked you one too many times, huh?" A power pulsed around her, illuminating her perfect skin. "I am Gune. Yeshua is Lord and Savior."

Korah narrowed his eyes. "Is He your Lord, Gune?"

"Jesus Christ, the Son of Man, the Lamb of God, who takes away the sin of the world?" Her sapphire eyes shone with love and power. "He has delivered you from the pit of Hell this night, has He not?"

He raised an eyebrow at her. "I am not particularly keen to make a return trip, bacon and eggs notwithstanding." He moved to the door. "I think I saw some appetizing fiddlehead ferns outside. If you will excuse me, madam?"

"Oh, stubborn!" Jelena declared, taken aback.

Korah shot her a glare. "Not stupid and not taking any chances. I lived with that son of a bitch Marduk for fifteen years, and I am familiar with all the tricks, especially the angel of light routine. He played the jihadists and the New Agers for years with that one." He pointed an accusing finger at her. "I know Lucifer finally got a hold of the Black Key, and I know what it held in bondage. There is an army of elohim running loose now. I am intimately acquainted with their kind. So, sorry, sweetheart, I've been taken in by a pretty face before. It will not happen again. Enjoy your breakfast."

It was over a thousand years since any human shocked Jelena Zelenovich, but Korah ben Adam did it when he slammed the door and left her standing in the kitchen holding a spatula, speechless.

Breakfast - Thyatira Woods - Korah

Korah chuckled under his breath at the thunderstruck expression on the woman's face. She might be what she said, then again, she might not be. His stomach was not terribly pleased with his decision, but he remembered a story from his youth about Esau who gave away his birthright for a bowl of soup. Newly snatched from the fires of Hell, he was not gambling.

He tramped through the woods, recalling a wild cranberry behind their stables. He was gratified to find it was still there. The tart fruit exploded in his mouth. The juice stung a few lingering cuts, but it tasted delicious. He took a handful, dropped it in the small bucket he grabbed on his way out, and kept exploring, eating as he walked. He pulled a chickweed out of the ground and munched on the delicate leaves, reveling in the pleasant taste. Sussanna had loved it, and the horses did, too. He had not eaten chickweed in thirty-five years.

Korah saw a big patch of fiddlehead ferns, dozens of them. He gobbled down the last of his cranberries and got to work pinching the shoots. Nearby, a sodden log sported an equal bounty of morel mushrooms. He imagined Sussanna's delight if he had come home with those. He was going to eat like a king. The thought made him laugh.

He tramped back through the woods with his bounty and hoped the mysterious woman was gone. He needed privacy, and he was starving. After that, he had to figure out what he was going to do next. A Bible was on the top of his list, Psalm 84. He hoped it would help determine his next move.

She was not gone.

"I leave the throne room of the Most High to make you breakfast, and you insult me?" She bristled with indignation, as she tossed her long black hair over her shoulder.

"You wouldn't happen to have a Bible on you? If you do, I'll eat your breakfast." The idea took on a decided appeal. He could still smell bacon.

Jelena stuck her nose up in the air and said, "I can recite the entire Bible. I do not need to carry one."

"I seem to recall that Satan can do that too," Korah challenged.

"He would twist it and use it for his own wicked purposes. I do not. I am Gune." She paused and looked up, receiving a message from above. Sighing, she added begrudgingly, "There is a Bible in the top drawer of the nightstand in the house over there."

Korah followed her direction and started walking.

"You are looking for Psalm 84, but first I tell you Psalm 82."

He paused and turned around.

"It is the judgment of the elohim. None of them would utter the words that damn them to the Lake of Fire, would they Korah ben Adam?" She held his eyes, fierce and authoritative. "The detestable Marduk knows it is true."

Korah regarded her from behind a mask of bored cynicism. "Is that so?"

"You have not seen him." The corner of Jelena's mouth lifted, and she said, "He is wounded, and his injuries will not stop bleeding. He is dying, like a man."

Korah lifted a golden eyebrow at her, interested. "I thought he was immortal."

"We are all immortal, Korah. Our spirits and souls do not die. It is the flesh you refer to? That is dying on Marduk. He and all the other wicked elohim, they do not escape their fate. The Iron King judged them in the First Age."

Radiating glory and power, she took a step toward him. "He called them forth, to answer for their wickedness, the seventy who ruled over the Earth. In Psalm 82: 6-7, He rendered his verdict, 'You are elohim, sons of the Most High, all of you; nevertheless, like men you shall die, and fall like any prince.'" She raised a sarcastic black eyebrow at him. "You are familiar with the fall of princes, are you not?"

"Quite."

"They are dying as they become mortal." Jelena leveled a look at Korah.

"Even Satan?" Korah narrowed his eyes.

"Especially him."

Korah's stomach growled. "Well, Gune, I suppose we can talk more about this over breakfast." He picked up his bucket. "Do you know how to cook fiddlehead ferns and morels?"

Hope - Endor - Kayah

The sun shone high in the sky when Kayah and her herd arrived in Endor. As expected, the place was deserted. She hoped for a spark of memory, a glimmer of some long-buried shadow of recognition but nothing came. Out of the corner of her eye she detected movement and turned. A pure white horse appeared at the center of the village, and Kayah froze.

Nothing moved. The air grew still, the bird's songs ceased, the rustle of leaves in the trees arrested. Of all the magnificent horses in her company, the white horse was by far the most spectacular, standing twenty hands with a powerful chest and mighty shoulders. To Kayah's astonishment, the horses with her seemed to bow in reverent respect. Kayah dismounted Heilig and walked toward the majestic beast.

The animal held her ground, watching her through lovely blue eyes, a genetic rarity in a horse. Kayah knew before she touched her, who this was, an ancient one. "Blitz, come to me, for you were my mother's horse," Kayah called in German.

Lightning trotted forward and nuzzled Kayah's outstretched hand. Then, she lived up to her name as a jolt of electricity ran down Kayah's arm and burst in her brain.

Kayah saw!

She saw her mother as a child, climbing atop this magnificent horse and riding through the dense woods. She heard the melodic sound of laughter, smelled the crisp autumn air.

Then in a flash, her mother was no longer a child, but a beautiful young woman, flying over a clear brook. She burst through the thick hedge and came upon a man.

Peter!

However, when the man lifted his head, she knew it was not Peter.

She saw them working in the stables side by side. She heard them flirting, saw the interplay, then she saw them kissing. Kayah watched a beautiful love story unfold.

As her mother grew heavy with child, she saw the man caring for the horses while her mother sat on a bale of straw and laughed with him. She watched in wonder as the horses nuzzled newborn Kayah and felt their warm breath on her skin. Through her own baby hand, she reached out and touched their silky noses, then snuggled into her father's powerful arms. She felt his kiss and heard his murmured words, "Daughter, you shall be a superb horsewoman like your mother, a Guardian Princess. What a joy you are, beloved Hope."

Scene after scene played out—a happy family.

"Give her to me, Prince. You spoil her." Her mother's lovely voice drifted on the wind.

Her father danced away, teasing. "She is meant to be spoiled, Pearle. Look at her. How can I not spoil one such as she?" Then he blew blubbery kisses on Kayah's neck, and she squealed with laughter.

She lay between them, sleeping in their bed, safe and secure, with her daddy's arms sheltering them from the night. "Love you, little one," he whispered in her ear. She smiled in her sleep.

The scene grew dark. Heat hit her face. She heard her father shout and her mother cry; fire surrounded them followed by a desperate flight into the woods. She was scared and wet.

"No, no!" her mother cried, squeezing her too tight. "She will die if I keep her?"

Kayah sobbed, desperate to hold on, fighting panic.

"Your mommy loves you. Your daddy loves you, too. I know you will not remember. Please one day, please tell her. Please tell her how much she was loved."

The vision went dark.

Bereft, Kayah hugged the neck of the white horse, sobbing in the deserted village. Alone and desolate, she cried out for the mother who held her, for the father who loved her. Then, she felt a hand on her shoulder and turned.

Her mother stood before her, radiant in light, blonde and beautiful. "You are loved very much, my darling girl. Your mommy and daddy, neither of us wanted to leave you. Never think that."

Kayah, the indomitable, fierce, unassailable Kayah, shattered into a million pieces and fell into her mother's outstretched arms.

"It is all right, *der Liebling*. Daddy is here, too. He has looked for you your whole life. He never stopped looking for you. He never stopped loving you or missing you. Just as I did not, dear Hope. Beloved, do not cry. Mommy is here."

Kayah felt a second set of arms encircling her, strong and masculine, heard the ragged breath of a man. She was sandwiched between them—held.

"My loves, my loves," he whispered. "I have dreamed of this since the day we parted. Praise be to God."

At length, Sussanna pulled free and went to Korah alone. Kayah blinked at them in stunned wonder.

"Korah." Sussanna gave him the gift of his name and smiled, as lovely as the day they met. "I am so happy for you. It has grieved my heart to know the life you have lived. I did not want that for you. I never wanted that for you, Prince. But the Iron King, He has made it all new. He has restored what was broken."

Korah cupped her face, tears streaming down his. "I have loved you every moment since the day we met, Pearle. I never stopped. You have always held my heart. One day, we shall be together again, and no one will part us."

"I love you, Prince." She moved into his arms and kissed him.

He clung to her, the old familiar taste of her lips, the tender touch of her mouth, the precious feel of her in his arms. A gift.

She leaned back and smiled, her eyes hooded. Then she took Kayah's hand and put it in Korah's. "You love each other. Be good to each other." Sussanna tapped Kayah on the chin. "Be nice to your father."

Sussanna's face became wistful as she looked at Korah. "Yereq has told Persa the truth. She knows that she was loved, but you tell her for me, Prince. Tell her the story of our great love. And remember they are Guardians of the Blood, not just Princesses."

With those words, she was gone, leaving Korah standing in the square holding hands with Hope.

Kayah watched the apparition fade away, speechless. She stood stock-still, staring at the empty space where her mother had been. Korah's ragged exhale drew her attention. She looked at him dumbfounded. "You are my father?"

"Yes, I am." He sniffed and palmed a tear from his eye. "It is very nice to see you again, Hope."

"Hope?" Her voice sounded hollow.

Korah nodded. "It is your name. The one Sussanna and I gave you."

Kayah closed her eyes, as a thousand thoughts assailed her at once. "How did I end up in an orphanage?" She pulled her hand from his and turned away. "You… you put me in jail."

"He did not put you in jail." Jelena emerged from her place on the porch where she had been observing the little family reunion. Kayah's question was her cue to step in. "I can answer the other question, too."

Kayah whirled, her hand instinctively going to her belt. "Who are you?"

"Jelena. I am Gune, and before you argue, I have already established my credentials with your father, so we skip that." She waved a dismissive hand at them and said, "I placed you in the

New City Home for Children the night of the fires of Endor for your protection. One man knew Sussanna and Hope did not die in the massacre. He ordered the search of Thyatira Woods for you both, with orders to kill."

She held their eyes. "They were looking for a woman and a baby. Later, he searched the east coast orphanages for a blonde baby girl. But he never looked on the west coast, because by human means it was a six-month journey. So, you were safe from the men who sought to kill you and your mother."

"Why?" Kayah demanded.

"Your father can answer that question." She gestured with an extravagant flourish. "My work is done here."

Kayah blinked in shock as the second person disappeared before her eyes in less than five minutes.

Korah was a bit more circumspect, his keen mind processing what the Gune said.

"Why were they trying to kill me?" Kayah demanded. "Everyone is always trying to kill me. I'm sick of it!"

Korah gave her a knowing look that clearly conveyed he knew the feeling.

"Wait… are they still trying to kill me… because of who I am?"

Korah blew out a long breath. "I suspect that is so. You are my oldest child, the first of your generation in the royal line. Sussanna and I were legally married, thus you are legitimate. Margaret, Eamonn's wife, had three miscarriages before she carried Josiah to term." He looked at her with sad eyes and shook his head. "For five years, you were the heir to the throne."

Kayah's eyes widened.

Korah jerked as another thought occurred to him. "In the years that I reigned, when Josiah was presumed dead, under the Jerusalem Rule of Succession, you were the heir to the throne, not Peter."

Kayah's knees buckled, and she sat down in the dirt. "I spent my life in an orphanage, a throwaway kid."

"You were not a throwaway kid." Korah's voice broke as he kneeled in front of her. "I grieved you, I longed for you. I had no indication that there was even a possibility you were alive until," he paused trying to recall when he learned of the ransom notes, "the early '80's. There was a ransom note sent to my brother, but the money was never collected, and we could not find you."

"A ransom note?" Kayah hugged herself growing tiny.

Korah read the distress and softened his face, "Yes. Please tell me you were not kidnapped, that you were not in danger. Please?"

Kayah made a keening sound. "I was."

Korah pulled her into a tight hug. "I am so sorry. I did not know. He did not send me the note."

"I killed him," Kayah ground out, shaking in Korah's arms. "The next day, he came with food and turned his back on me. He did not know who he was dealing with."

Korah gave a rueful laugh, squeezing her shoulders. "My daughter."

"He was the first person I ever killed." Kayah sagged in his arms. "There have been many more since."

Korah laid a hand on Kayah's cheek, "You must repent of that and seek forgiveness from the Iron King. Trust me, Daughter, Hell is not a place you want to go."

Kayah scrambled up, leveling a fierce glare at him. "I killed a man who had a demon in him. Right before he died, the demon said, 'My father has been looking for you because your father sold you to him.'"

Korah hung his head, closing his eyes in shame. "That is not exactly true. The night you were born, your mother was in terrible distress. She labored for two days, and you were both dying." He looked toward the place where the Dark Mansion once stood. "Instead of calling on the Iron King, I sought the help of a witch. I did not really understand what I was doing, and I certainly did not fathom the cost. I was twenty, out of my mind with panic, but it was a great sin, and set us all on a path of destruction. Only the power of the Lamb redeemed what I did. I am sorry, Hope."

Kayah regarded him with eyes that turned green with emotion. "What happened to you? The last time I saw you, you were completely mad."

"An argument could be made I have been insane since I lost you." Korah laughed a bit shaky. "Wait, the last time? You have seen me?"

"Yes," she laughed, a bit unhinged, "you thought I was your mother."

Korah narrowed his eyes and stared at her. "My mother?"

Kayah raised a golden eyebrow at him and repeated the line she had spoken when she stepped out of the shadows outside of Alexa's bedroom on New Year's Eve. "What art thou doing down here? Attend thy guests!"

His mouth dropped, and he stared at her aghast. "That was you?"

Kayah controlled a hysterical bubble of laughter. "Yes."

Korah smacked his forehead. "You had salt and pepper hair that night, but I suppose there is a family resemblance. How did you know my mother always used court speech?"

"Sir Preston told me."

They shared a look of dawning understanding as Sir Preston's words echoed in Kayah's mind. 'Do everything in your power to ensure Prince Josiah assumes the Alanthian throne and I will tell you who your parents were.'

"That wicked, twisted, diabolical son of a bitch! He knows who I am!"

"He must have been the one who was searching for you and Sussanna. I always assumed it was my father's doing, that Sir Preston stayed behind, keeping his hands clean."

"He is the one who has put a hit out on me. It's not a mafia hit. It has nothing to do with crime." Kayah blinked back angry tears. "All my life, I thought he was the good guy, and you were the bad guy. I thought he was the father I never had, and you were the monster who put me in jail."

"Lord God, please help me not to kill that man," Korah prayed aloud.

They talked for a while, Korah showed Kayah the house where she was born, and the rocking horse that was her legacy from her mother's family. He told her about her mother. Beaming with the glow of the newly saved, he told her about his redemption. He asked her about her life, and they talked about London. She told him about her houses, and the money she made investing in technology. He puffed up with pride when she shared her success.

Kayah followed Korah into a deserted house, her mind processing the implications of her parentage, the treachery of her old mentor, and the royal blood flowing in her veins.

She was loved… It was all too much.

So, she simply focused on the man, her father. She studied the way he moved, watched the flex of lean muscle in his forearm, observed the regal carriage of his body. He was beautiful, even beat up and dressed in clothes from the sixties, he was a sight to behold. Before her arrest, she preferred him over Eamonn, but afterward she believed him a monster and no longer appreciated how charismatic he was. His magnetism drew her to him. It was an indescribable power that enabled him to persuade Alanthians to follow wherever he led. On a feminine level, she understood her mother's attraction and the reason Alexa stayed. She failed to comprehend that she exuded the same, magnetic energy that drew people to her.

"What are you searching for?" she asked.

"The Gune said I would find a Bible in one of these nightstands. There is a Psalm the Iron King told me to study when I asked Him what I should do next." Korah gingerly opened a drawer, careful of hidden surprises.

"He pulled you out of Hell? Why?"

Korah turned and took two steps to her, holding her eyes. "Kayah, listen to me now, I lived a wicked life, and I deserved that punishment. However, He saw as a young boy I sought Him, and He had mercy on me. I repented, accepted his sacrifice, and He redeemed me." He took her hands. "Have you done that?"

Kayah hung her head and nodded. "Yes, I did. Then, a few days later I encountered the demon, and I was not sure." She looked up at him, laughing in sudden remembrance. "Reuben told me that even if you presented yourself to the Iron King with a repentant heart and changed your ways, He would accept you."

Korah smiled.

She studied his face and observed they had the same ear lobes. "But after London, Reuben and I traveled to the Golden City, and I went to the temple. It changed me."

Korah closed his eyes and smiled. "That is good, Daughter." He took a deep breath and raised an eyebrow at her. "Who is Reuben?"

Kayah freed her left hand and showed him her pearl and diamond ring. "My fiancé, Reuben ben Judah. I met him in Italy last year."

"An Israeli?" Korah widened his eyes, surprised because mixed marriages between Jews and Gentiles were extremely rare.

She nodded. "He was Mossad but resigned to serve Prince Josiah. They are like brothers."

"I suspect Yehonathan was not pleased."

Kayah's forehead creased in thought. "He was not, but the Iron King permitted our relationship, perhaps now I understand why."

Korah raised her hand to his lips and pressed a kiss. "Because you are a Princess, but more than that, you are a Guardian of the Blood."

"I don't know what that means." Kayah strolled to the window and looked out at the square. Two dozen horses milled around the empty spaces. "Ernst ben Otto, a man I met last evening in Rephidim, explained some to me." She turned with imploring eyes. "My mother said you should explain what it meant."

Korah nodded. "It is not only you but your sister."

Kayah blinked in shock. "I have a sister?" Kayah had been so preoccupied with her parentage, the sight of her mother, and the revelation of her father, she failed to process Sussanna's message to Korah about Persa.

"Indeed, I did not know of her existence until last evening. The night of the fire, Sussanna planned to tell me she was pregnant but never got the opportunity." Korah's voice trailed off, there was another baby he did not know existed until last evening, but that child was dead, by his own hand.

"Who is she?" Kayah asked, then her eyes widened in realization. "Holy shit… Peter is my brother!"

"He is indeed." Korah took a deep breath, composing himself. "Your sister's name is Persa. She is a horse breeder in northern California with her husband, James. They have a successful ranch called Pepperwood."

"I have met her!" Kayah exclaimed, recalling the tiny woman.

Korah smiled, realizing the ranch's amazing success, Peter's love of that place, and that girl had all stemmed from the same source. He knew Peter fled to Pepperwood when he escaped, knew it was his refuge. Secretly, he rejoiced because Peter was protected there. Marduk raged he could not penetrate the hedge surrounding the ranch. Korah had pretended indifference. But he was no longer indifferent, and a horrified realization hit him. He recoiled, stumbling backward with an agonized cry. "Oh, Lord!" Falling to his knees, he gasped, "No!"

Kayah did not know what to do, she simply looked at him wide-eyed. "What?"

Korah buried his face in his hands, wracked with silent sobs, too terrible for noise. He had done everything in his power to protect Alexa from Marduk, though the wicked beast threatened to rape his wife regularly. But he had done something worse, he had taken Korah's daughter. Rapha… that was who Rapha was, and the wicked being took him to Pepperwood to murder his own daughter. That evil spawn kept calling him Grandpa and insisting he had a blood right to rule Alanthia. That thing, that beast, was a direct product of Korah's rebellion.

'You give them to Tristin as playthings!' Alexa's accusing words rang in his ears.

He writhed in agony.

"Korah," Kayah rested a hand on his back, "what is it?"

He blinked up at her, desolate. "He did not find you, did he? What that demon said to you, he was looking for you, but he never found you did he?"

Compassion welled inside her. He was utterly broken, looking at her in desperate fear. "Who?"

"Marduk," he spat the name.

Kayah drew back, and she said in a strangled voice, "No, but I played a role in his release. I delivered the device used to bring him forth."

A shockwave jolted Korah, and he jumped to his feet. "The hell you say?"

Kayah flushed. "I found it, in the place where the kidnapper held me, a computer lab from the Last Age. I tried to get into the Palace to see you, to sell it, or get your support for our research." She pulled at her hair thinking of that day and how her life would have been different if she had actually seen him. "They threw me out before I could get to your office, so I sent Stephen to do it."

Korah's eyes narrowed, dangerous and violent. "Who threw you out? Who saw you on that day?"

Kayah grew very still. "I was talking to Peter. He was just a little kid, but still charming." She smiled in remembrance. "I told him I had something magical, and if he got me in to see you, perhaps you would buy it as a birthday present for him. He pointed to his mother and said I would have better luck with her." Kayah cleared her throat, remembering the pale, distraught look on Princess Alexa's face when their eyes met.

"Then they blew the trumpets and Prince Eamonn and Prince Josiah came on the grounds. Everyone else was bowing and curt-sying. but I was curious because Prince Eamonn's picture hung in the orphanage. He was taller than I expected, so I looked at him. He did not like it." Her shoulders fell. "I thought they threw me out because I was pretty. That's what Peter said, that they did not let pretty girls serve at the Palace."

"That was my mother's policy. My father fornicated with the maids." Oddly, the rage that erupted in Korah's heart toward his wife and his brother died a supernatural death, quenched by the forgiveness he received. The standard and the bar were set high. "I am sorry that happened to you. I am sorry my family did that to you."

She leaned into him. "That is why they put me in prison." She cried, holding on to him. He would have stopped them; he would have protected her.

"No one will hurt you again, Daughter. I will not let them." Korah kissed the top of her head and held on.

At length, Korah found the Bible. They settled on a pair of dusty kitchen chairs, and he read Psalm 84 a dozen times.

He handed it to Kayah. She read the words and looked up. "I think it is clear what He is telling me to do."

Korah's face relaxed. "Did you note the author of the Psalm?"

"The sons of Korah?" she breathed in awe.

He shrugged, "They did not die in their father's rebellion and became Psalm writers."

At her startled expression, he looked away, unaccountably em-barrassed. "I looked it up, hoping to find redemption in the story. As a kid, it gave me bloody nightmares. Nobody wants to be swal-lowed up in the desert."

He smiled and tilted his head in irony. "Did you know the prophet Samuel was a son of Korah?"

Her hand flew to her mouth in shock. "No."

"You chose Samuel as your surname."

Their eyes held, sharing the moment of intense awareness and the complexities of the Iron King, the depth of his care, and the magnificent way He wove them back together.

Kayah looked down at the open Psalm and read verse five, "Blessed are those whose strength is in you, whose hearts are set on pilgrimage."

Korah gave her a sardonic smile and raised an eyebrow. "I wanted to do it as a little boy. It only took me fifty years to get around to it."

"How will you go? You are a wanted man and perhaps the most recognized face in the world," Kayah said, feeling genuine fear for him.

Korah shrugged a shoulder. "You say you have met Davianna ben David?"

Kayah drew back, surprised by his question. "I have. Josiah asked me to be her guard, but I suppose that assignment is now called into question." She winked at him.

"Indeed it is, Princess." Korah leaned his forehead towards her in affection. "You will have your own Royal Guard, and trust me, you will need it."

"I am no wilting flower."

She sounded like her mother, and he smiled. "Of course you are not."

"What does Davianna ben David have to do with your pilgrimage?" Kayah asked.

Korah gave a low rueful chuckle. "She is an extraordinary young woman. With no connections, no help, and no resources she evaded the pursuit of the entire world, natural and supernatural, for months. I suppose I will have to do the same."

Kayah shook her head. "She was captured. You captured her. I was there that night when they were arrested, and I helped her escape."

Korah looked away but pressed onward. "Only when the Iron King deemed she should be, and even then He had a purpose."

Kayah touched his shoulder and asked quietly, "What was the purpose?"

"I think there were many. Without Davianna, I would have never reached the point of repentance. I was too far gone, my fate sealed." Korah shifted, uncomfortable in the telling, unaccustomed to speaking openly to anyone. "When everything fell apart, I saw the newspaper photos of you in London and knew you were my daughter." He squeezed her hand. "I began to feel again, to love again, but it started with a brave pilgrim girl standing up to a mad king."

He smiled, the corners of his eyes crinkling, the dimple in his cheek flashing. "So I shall take a page out of her book and do this thing the Lord set before me."

Korah pushed to his feet and held his hands for Kayah to rise. "I will write to you along the way, to tell you how the journey progresses. I am certain it will be quite an adventure." His chest rose and fell as he took a deep breath. "I will write to Persa, too. I shall try with Peter, though he will likely burn my letters and not read them."

Kayah grimaced and suspected he was correct in his assessment. "Send them in care of Astrid, she will get him to read them."

Korah's forehead creased. "They are together? I heard she left him in Tel Aviv."

Kayah tilted her chin up at him, silently questioning how he knew that.

He shrugged. "I was the King until five days ago."

"Yes, I suppose you were." Kayah gently touched the gash over his eye. "I heard they are having a double wedding in the Golden City with Josiah and Davianna," she smiled with rueful sadness, "at Josiah's coronation."

Instead of causing him pain, a final weight of responsibility lifted from his shoulders, relieving a burden he was never meant to bear. "That is good."

He smiled, his hazel eyes soft. "Another example of how the Iron King used what I meant for evil for His purpose. The four of them… they are together because of what I did."

He looked away, his face flushed with embarrassment. "But I have to ask, are they happy? Is Astrid good for my son? Will she make him a good wife, or does she just look like his mother, and he is smitten by her pretty face?"

Kayah thought for a moment, then said, "I spent a few days with her in London. She is spunky and does not take crap off of anyone, including Josiah." The corner of Kayah's mouth twitched. "She laughs a lot, and she has a protective streak. She loves Peter. They are crazy about each other."

Korah covered his eyes and nodded. "With your Reuben is it the same? Is he a good man? Does he love you as you deserve?"

"More." Kayah's voice was barely a whisper. "He is everything to me."

Korah met her eyes. "Do not make him everything, Kayah. No human can fill that spot. It leaves you too vulnerable if something happens to them. I did that with your mother. She was my entire world, my heart, my soul, and when I lost her, I lost myself. There is only one who should be everything, but there is room to love everyone else. He does not demand that you only love Him. That is a hallmark of evil."

He touched her elbow, guiding her outside.

Kayah felt a sudden tightening in her chest. "I just found you and you are leaving."

"I wish it could be different," Korah looked off in the distance. "However, I have much to work out on this pilgrimage. It is said that the pilgrimage is for the man, not the King."

He turned back to her, soaking in her lovely face, her beautiful blonde hair. "You have the most extraordinary eyes. I was never," he paused, correcting himself, "we were not sure what color they were going to be. Some days they looked hazel like mine, and other days blue-green like your mother's. They still do, beloved Hope."

Kayah pressed her lips together, willing herself not to cry. Then Korah took her in his arms and hugged her tight. "Be safe, Father. Go with God and carry my love with you, always."

End of Book Notes

Korah ben Adam… his story haunted me for months. My beta readers looked at me with horror when I revealed M6 was going to be Korah's book. At one point, my husband actually got angry and said, "Why are you writing about the bad guy? I hate the bad guys." I knew then I was in for a monumental challenge, but I had to write this story.

In so many ways, Korah is just an extreme example of all of us. When Davianna confronts Josiah and asks, "When we met Yeshua, who were you more like, Korah or Him?" That hit home because she was right. It is a hard question, an impossible mystery, and the core of the gospel.

I love this book. I loved writing this book. It poured out of me like water. I was sick with the flu over the Christmas holiday and wrote sixteen hours a day. Being a bit obsessive and off kilter likely helped me connect with Korah.

Sussanna surprised me. She burst on the scene aiming a gun at Korah's head, and I thought, "Well, she is Kayah's mother." She turned out to be fierce, smart, and wonderful.

Alexa completely shocked me, I thought I knew her, but I had not even scratched the surface of Peter's amazing mother. She is arguably the heroine of this story. And as flawed as she is, I adore her. Her death was one of the most difficult passages I have ever written. The love and tragedy of Korah and Alexa broke my heart.

M1-The Black Key was unpublished when I finished writing M6-The Royals, so I was able to go back into M1 and make a few revisions. There is a scene at the beginning of M1 where Peter and Alexa take a walk in the garden. That was the last scene I wrote for her, and a loving farewell to a character who stole my heart.

Several themes run through M6, the first of which is the sins of the fathers are visited on their families. Adam's line pays a terrible price for his sins. Corruption and rebellion got a foothold in Alanthia during his reign. Mary, Korah, Kayah, Persa, and Peter all suffer and survive rape… that began with Adam.

I hoped you enjoyed exploring the parallels between Korah's life and Peter's. There are a couple nuggets that likely I am the only one who will ever see, but they are there. I wish I could take credit for showing that it was love that kept Peter from becoming Korah, but I was only the messenger.

Korah and Peter's relationship is more nuanced than I imagined when I began the series, and it will be interesting to see how it evolves. I once read that the sins we commit are like nails in a fence post. When the Lord forgives us, He pulls the nails out and throws them away, but for the people we hurt, there are still holes where the nails once were. Korah pounded more than a few nails into Peter. It will be up to the characters and the guidance from above to see where they go from here.

For Korah himself, he is a complex and intriguing man. I grew to love him, to feel his pain, and to understand what made him the way that he was. I also grew to respect and appreciate the visionary, driven man, who achieved some astounding things. I felt his pain and the depths of his fear and despair, but I also felt the love he was so afraid to show, the deep part of Korah.

I did a lot of praying before I wrote Hell.

It is real, and without Yeshua, our destiny.

I rejoiced when Korah was delivered. I hope you did, too.

There is very little black and white in M6, *every* character in the story has shades of gray. I suppose that is how life and people are, which is what I always try to bring to the page. I will let you be the judge whether or not I pulled it off.

I hope you liked it. I hope it shocked you, scared you, made you laugh, and made you cry. But most of all, I hope no one finishes M6 and feels they are beyond the power of redemption. If Jesus can save Korah ben Adam… He can save anybody.

In Christ,
Staci Morrison
January 19, 2019

P.S. – Could you do me a huge favor and drop a star rating or a review? Amazon has the most impact, but BookBub and Good Reads are fantastic, too!

Alanthia.com has some cool stuff for those of you who like the inside scoop, breaking news, newsletters, character pictures, and backgrounds.

From the bottom of my heart, thank you for going on this journey with me. If you've enjoyed the series, let me know. I would love to hear from you!